**Praise for #1 *New York Times* bestselling author
Lisa Jackson**

"Lisa Jackson takes my breath away."
—#1 *New York Times* bestselling author
Linda Lael Miller

"When it comes to providing gritty and sexy
stories, Ms. Jackson certainly knows how to
deliver."
—*RT Book Reviews* on *Unspoken*

"Provocative prose, an irresistible plot and finely
crafted characters make up Jackson's latest
contemporary sizzler."
—*Publishers Weekly* on *Wishes*

**Praise for *USA TODAY* bestselling author
Delores Fossen**

"Clear off space on your keeper shelf, Fossen has
arrived."
—*New York Times* bestselling author Lori Wilde

"Delores Fossen takes you on a wild Texas ride with
a hot cowboy."
—*New York Times* bestselling author B.J. Daniels

Lisa Jackson is a #1 *New York Times* bestselling author of more than eighty-five books, including romantic suspense, thrillers, and contemporary and historical romances. She is a recipient of the *RT Book Reviews* Reviewers' Choice Award and has also been honored with their Career Achievement Award for Romantic Suspense. Born in Oregon, she continues to make her home among family, friends and dogs in the Pacific Northwest. Visit her at lisajackson.com.

Delores Fossen, a *USA TODAY* bestselling author, has sold over seventy-five novels, with millions of copies of her books in print worldwide. She's received a Booksellers' Best Award and an RT Reviewers' Choice Best Book Award. She was also a finalist for a prestigious RITA® Award. You can contact the author through her website at www.deloresfossen.com.

#1 *New York Times* Bestselling Author

LISA JACKSON

DECEPTION LODGE

Previously published as *Sail Away*

**HARLEQUIN
BESTSELLING
AUTHOR
COLLECTION**

**HARLEQUIN®
BESTSELLING
AUTHOR
COLLECTION**

Recycling programs
for this product may
not exist in your area.

ISBN-13: 978-1-335-14687-8

Deception Lodge
First published as Sail Away in 1991. This edition published in 2020.
Copyright © 1991 by Lisa Jackson

Expecting Trouble
First published in 2009. This edition published in 2020.
Copyright © 2009 by Delores Fossen

This edition published by arrangement with Harlequin Books S.A.

For questions and comments about the quality of this book,
please contact us at CustomerService@Harlequin.com.

Harlequin Enterprises ULC
22 Adelaide St. West, 40th Floor
Toronto, Ontario M5H 4E3, Canada
www.Harlequin.com

Printed in U.S.A.

CONTENTS

Also by Lisa Jackson

Visit the Author Profile page
at Harlequin.com for more titles.

DECEPTION LODGE

Lisa Jackson

PROLOGUE

MARNIE MONTGOMERY TOSSED her briefcase onto the antique couch near the windows of her office. She marched straight to her desk, removed an earring and grabbed the phone. As she punched out her father's extension, she balanced a hip against the polished rosewood and waited, her fingers drumming impatiently, a headache threatening behind her eyes.

"Victor Montgomery's office," a sweet voice sang over the wires. Kate Delany. Efficient Kate. Victor's mistress and administrative assistant. She'd been with him for years, and hoped to become the next Mrs. Victor Montgomery.

"Is he in?" Marnie asked.

"Not yet. But I expect him any time." Poor Kate. So helplessly in love with Marnie's father. Loving Victor was easy, as Marnie could well attest. But sometimes that love became overpowering, and Marnie felt as if she'd lost a part of herself, hadn't been allowed to grow into the woman she wanted to be.

She heard Kate flip through the pages of what she assumed was Victor's appointment book. "Your dad called from the course about half an hour ago," Kate said thoughtfully. "He should be on his way back here, and it looks as if his schedule isn't too full this afternoon."

Marnie's lungs constricted. She cleared her throat. "Tell him I need to see him the minute he gets in."

"It's important?"

"Very," Marnie replied, replacing the receiver and suddenly feeling cold inside. Slipping her earring back in place, she noticed the expensive furnishings in her office, the thick mauve carpet, the panoramic view of Seattle's skyline from her corner office. Everything a girl could want.

Except Marnie didn't want any of it. She didn't want the forced smiles of the staff, she didn't want the knowing glances in the coffee room, and she especially didn't want the engraved brass nameplate that read: MARNIE MONTGOMERY, PUBLIC RELATIONS. It could just as well have read: VICTOR'S DAUGHTER. The people who worked "for her" in her department could function well without her. Victor had seen to that.

She tossed her pen into her empty In basket. Was it ever full? Were there ever papers and messages overflowing onto the desk? Did she ever have to put in extra hours? Did she even have to come back from lunch? No, no, no and no!

A nest of butterflies erupted into flight in her stomach at the thought of what she had to do. Rounding the desk she found a piece of letterhead, and rather than have her secretary type her letter of resignation she started writing it out in long hand.

How did one quit being a daughter? she wondered, her brow puckering as she chewed on the end of her pen.

How did she tell a loving father, who had tried all his life to do everything for her, that she felt suffocated?

How could she explain that she had to do something on her own, become her own person, live her own life?

Absurdly, she felt an urge to break down and cry tears of frustration, but because that was exactly what the weaker, dependent Marnie would have done, she gritted her teeth, refused to shed one lousy tear and started writing again in quick, sure strokes.

She couldn't quit being Victor's daughter, but she sure as hell could quit being dependent upon him.

CHAPTER ONE

ADAM DRAKE FELT the skeptical gaze of every man who sat around the polished table. They'd listened to him, scanned the thick sheaf of papers that was his proposal and leaned back in their chairs, without questions but exchanging knowing glances.

The three men in the room were potential investors from California, men who, so far, hadn't turned him down. Yet. However, Adam knew they each had doubts about his proposal—and concerns about Adam himself. He didn't blame them. His reputation was more than a little tarnished.

It was surprising that these investors had stuck around this long.

The lawyer, Brodie, reached into his pocket for a fresh pack of cigarettes. It seemed to take forever for the cellophane to drop onto the table. "I think I can speak for my associates," he said, looking to the other two men and receiving quick nods of approval. "We like the idea of expanding to Seattle, but we've got some reservations."

"This wouldn't be an expansion," Adam reminded the smooth man in the expensive suit. This was a point they'd haggled over before. "I'll own the majority of the hotel. Your capital will be returned, with interest in the amount specified in ten years." He flipped to page six of his proposal and slid it across the table.

Brodie lit up, scanned the neatly typed paragraphs, then flipped through the remaining pages of the contract. He shot a stream of smoke out of the corner of his mouth. "Right, right," he said thoughtfully. "But for the next ten years we would be part owners of *your* hotel."

"That's right," Adam replied, managing a tense smile. God, he hated this kind of politics. Depending upon other people, wealthy men, to finance his business operation. The thought of being tied to anyone bothered him. That was his problem. Bucking authority. Refusing to bend to the power of the almighty dollar.

So why was he here?

Because he had no choice. Victor Montgomery had seen to that.

At the thought of Montgomery and especially the lowlifes who worked for him, Adam's blood boiled for revenge. He forced his thoughts back to the present.

Brodie, eyeing him still, thumped on the contract with one manicured finger. "This looks good, Drake. Only a couple of clauses to reword, but what's really bothering me—" he blew more smoke to the ceiling and squinted at Adam, sizing him up for the thousandth time "—is what happened at Montgomery Inns last year..."

There it was. The noose again. The rope that would strangle him.

Adam felt the tension in the room. *Be cool,* he told himself, not showing a flicker of emotion though the sweat was running down his back and his nerves were strung tight as piano wire. "I was never charged with embezzling," he said evenly. His eyes moved from one man to the next.

"But Montgomery never hired you back," a tiny, apprehensive man sitting to Brodie's left, Bill Peterson, interjected. Behind glasses as thick as the bottom of a soda bottle, Peterson's nervous gaze shifted to each of the other men around the table.

"I didn't want to go back," Adam stated. That much was true. He'd never work for a snake like Montgomery again, though he itched to know who had set him up. The memory was still painful. Once, he'd respected Victor Montgomery and he'd thought the older man had felt the same for him. *Stupid,* he chided himself silently. Victor had shown his true colors and fired Adam swiftly, pressing charges against him, then, when there was no indictment, sending a severance check to him through his lawyer—*through his damned lawyer!* Victor hadn't even had the guts to face Adam himself. Only the lawyer had been witness to Adam's wrath and stared in uncomfortable silence as Adam had ripped up the check and tossed the confetti-like scraps into the air.

Brodie's voice brought him back to the present. "Look, Drake, before we go into direct competition with Victor Montgomery, I think we should clear this matter up. The way I hear it, there wasn't evidence enough to indict you, and yet the money that was skimmed off the Puget West project was never located."

The collar around Adam's neck felt tight, the blood thundered through his veins. The money had just vanished. No amount of going over the books had uncovered the missing cash. And in that respect, he was, as project coordinator, responsible.

"That's what we don't understand," Peterson said, while the third partner, a silent man with flat features, said nothing. "There should have been a trail. How could anyone have walked away with—what was it? Half a million dollars?"

Adam nodded tightly, though he hoped his expression was calm. "Five hundred sixty-three thousand and change."

The silent man whistled.

"That must have taken some doing," Brodie said, stuffing his copy of the proposal into his briefcase.

"I wouldn't know," Adam responded dryly.

Brodie's brows jerked up as he jabbed out his cigarette in the hotel ashtray. Apparently he didn't believe Adam. "You have to understand our position. We can't very well hand over several million dollars until we're absolutely certain that what happened over at Montgomery Inns won't happen to us." He offered Adam a regretful smile. "If you could ever clear up exactly what happened over there, then maybe we could talk business. In the meantime, I don't think we have a deal."

The other men nodded in silent agreement. Adam didn't blame them. If he were in their shoes he wouldn't trust a man who'd nearly been indicted for embezzling, a man still proclaimed a thief by one of the largest hotel chains on the west coast. Trouble was, Adam was sick of being a scapegoat.

Pushing himself upright, Adam pulled together a grim smile and shook each man's outstretched hand. He watched as Brodie shepherded the small group from the room. Only when the door slammed shut behind the Californians did he let out a series of invectives that would have made a sailor blush. He yanked off his tie and threw it over the back of a chair, then loosened the top buttons of his stiff white shirt. What had he expected? This meeting had been no different than the two others he'd put together.

Face it, Drake, he told himself, *you were convicted even though you were never tried.* With leashed fury, he knew that the black stain on his reputation wouldn't disappear with time. No, he had to find out who had set him up and why. Otherwise, he was finished.

He had his suspicions, of course. There were several people with whom he'd worked at Montgomery Inns who had been jealous of his rapid rise in the corporation, a few who were desperate, and still others who were just plain greedy. Any one of those people could have set him up to take the fall. And fall he had. Once one of Victor Montgomery's golden boys, he was now the black sheep. The Judas.

Until he could prove himself completely blameless, he would never be able to set himself up in business. As he saw it, he had no choice. He had to do some digging and find out just who had hated him enough to frame him for embezzling money he'd never seen. For the past year he'd tried to put the damned incident behind him, but it kept rising like a phoenix from the ashes of his career at Montgomery Inns, to torment and thwart him. Fortunately, he'd already started an investigation to prove his innocence once and for all.

"QUITTING?" VICTOR'S EYEBROWS shot up, and he stared at his only child in disbelief. He'd just walked into the office and found Marnie sitting, waiting, in one of the client chairs. Then she'd lowered the bomb. "Have you gone out of your mind?"

Marnie dropped her letter of resignation on his desk. This scene with her father was going to be worse than she'd imagined. Her father was shocked. Pain showed from his blue eyes, pain at the thought of her betrayal.

"Why for God's sake? And just what do you think you're going to do?" he demanded, slamming his golf bag into a corner closet, then ripping off his plaid cap and sailing it across the office in frustration.

Marnie opened her mouth to answer, but her father wasn't finished raving. "You can't quit! You're my daughter, for crying out loud!" He mopped the sweat from his brow and stuffed his handkerchief into the pocket of his golf slacks.

Marnie had been waiting for him for half the day. She wasn't about to back down now. She'd spent too many hours arguing with herself and gathering her courage to give in.

"I'm serious, Dad," she said quietly, her voice firm. "This is just something I need to do."

"Bull!" Her father crossed the thick expanse of putty-colored carpet and glanced at the calendar lying open on his huge mahogany desk. He flipped through the pages while Marnie surveyed his office with jaded eyes.

Opulent, befitting the reigning monarch of a hotel empire, the suite boasted inlaid cherrywood walls. Brass lamps, etchings, sculptures and buttery leather furniture added to the effect. Behind the office, a private bath with a Jacuzzi, a walk-in wardrobe and king-size bedroom, were available whenever Victor was too busy to drive home.

Grabbing the receiver in one hand, Victor punched a series of buttons on the phone. "Kate?" he barked, still flipping through his appointment book. "Cancel my two o'clock with Ferguson—no, on second thought—just stall him. Ask him to meet me at the site tomor-

row at—" he ran his finger down a page "—ten-thirty."
Scowling across the room at Marnie, he added, "Just
tell him that something important came up, something
to do with the opening of the Puget West hotel."

Marnie refused to meet the anger in his eyes and
stared instead through the bank of windows in his office. Glimpses of the rolling gray waters of Puget Sound
were barely visible through the tall spires of Seattle's
skyline. Thick pewter-colored clouds blocked the sun
and threatened rain. A jet, headed north, was nearly in-
visible through the low-hanging clouds.

She heard her father slam down the phone. "Okay,
let's get out of here," he said, and dropped the letter
of resignation she'd worked so hard to write into his
wastebasket.

"Can't we talk here?"

Grabbing his keys, Victor shook his head. "Not a
good idea."

Then she understood. Shoving her arms through the
sleeves of her coat, she asked, "Do you still really think
you've got some spies in the company?"

"Don't know."

"I thought all that was taken care of when you fired
Adam Drake."

Her father jammed a hat onto his head. "And I
thought you were convinced he was innocent."

"He was," she said flatly. "He got off, remember?"

"He just had a damned good attorney," Victor grumbled, snagging his jacket from the back of his chair.
"But that's over and done with."

"Then why're you still paranoid?"

"I'm *not* paranoid," he snapped. "Just careful. Come
on, I've got to check things out at the marina, see that

the repairs on the *Vanessa* are up to snuff. We can talk on the way."

"Okay," she muttered, barely holding on to her temper. "But you can't just toss my resignation into the trash and expect me to forget all about it. I'm serious, Dad."

"You don't know what you want."

"That's where you're wrong," she said quietly.

The firmness in her tone must have caught his attention. His head snapped up and for the first time since he'd entered the office, he seemed to see her as she really was. His lips pursed tightly and beneath his tan his skin took on a paler hue. "Let's go," he said, his voice much lower.

He didn't even bother changing from his casual pants and sports coat.

In tense silence they strode abreast through the corridors to the elevator. Marnie barely kept herself from quaking at his anger. He was a handsome man, a man who accepted authority easily. His features were oversized, his hair thick and white with only a few remaining dark strands, his eyes intense blue, his nose aristocratic. For a man pushing sixty he was in good shape, with only the trace of a paunch near his waistline. And right now he was beginning to seethe.

"I don't know what's gotten into you," he said when the elevator doors had whispered shut and with a lurch the car sped down sixteen floors only to jerk to a stop at the subterranean parking lot.

"I just think it's time I stood on my own."

"All of a sudden?"

She slid a glance in his direction. "It's been coming on a long time."

"Ever since that business with Drake," he surmised with disgust.

"Before that," she insisted, though it was true that nothing had been the same since Adam Drake had been fired. There had been a change in attitude in the offices of Montgomery Inns. Nothing tangible. Just a loss of company spirit and confidence. Everyone felt it— including Victor, though, of course, he was loathe to admit it.

"And then you decided to break up with Kent," her father went on, shaking his head as he searched the pocket of his jacket for his pipe. "And now you want to leave the corporation, just walk away from a fortune. When I was your age, I was—"

"—working ten-hour days and still going to night school, I know," Marnie cut in. Her heels clicked loudly against the concrete. Low-hanging pipes overhead dripped condensation, and she had to duck to escape the steady drops as she hurried to keep up with her father's swift strides.

She stopped at the fender of Victor's Jaguar. He unlocked the doors and they both slid into the cushy interior.

"You should be grateful…"

Marnie closed her eyes. How could she explain the feeling that she was trapped? That she needed a life of her own? That she had to prove herself by standing on her own two feet? "I *am* grateful, Dad. Really." Turning to face him, she forced a wan smile. "This is just something I have to do—"

"Right now? Can't it wait?" he asked, as if sensing her beginning to weaken.

"No."

"But the new hotel is opening next week. I need you there. You're in charge of public relations, for God's sake."

"And I have a capable assistant. You remember Todd Byers—blond, wears glasses—"

Victor waved off her explanation.

"Well, if he's not good enough I have a whole department to cover for me." That was what bothered her most. She didn't feel needed. If she walked away from Montgomery Inns, no one, save Victor, would notice. Even Kent would get by without her.

Her father fired up the engine and shoved the Jag into reverse. "I don't understand you anymore." With a flip of the steering wheel, he headed for the exit. "What is it you really want?"

"A life of my own."

"You have one. A life most women would envy."

"I know," she admitted, her spine stiffening a bit. How could she reach a man who had worked all his life creating an empire? A man who had raised her alone, a man who loved her as much as he possibly could? "This is just something I have to do."

He waved to the lot's attendant, then nosed the Jag into the busy streets of downtown Seattle. "A few weeks ago you were planning to marry Kent," he pointed out as he joined the traffic easing toward the waterfront. Marnie felt a familiar stab of pain. "But now, all of a sudden, Kent's not good enough. It doesn't matter that he's practically my right-hand man—"

"No, it doesn't," she said swiftly. Surprisingly, her voice was still steady.

"Why don't you tell me what happened between you

two?" he suggested. "It's all tied up with this whole new independence kick, isn't it?"

Marnie didn't answer. She didn't want to think about Kent, nor the fact that she'd found him with Dolores Tate, his secretary. Rather than dwell on Kent's betrayal, Marnie stared at the car ahead of them. Two fluffy Persian cats slept on the back window ledge and a bright red bumper sticker near the back plates asked, Have You Hugged Your Cat Today?

Funny, she thought sarcastically, she hadn't hugged anyone in a long, long while. And no one had hugged her. At that thought a lump settled in her throat, and she wrapped her arms around herself, determined not to cry. Not today. Not on this, the very first step toward her new life.

Victor switched lanes, jockeying for position as traffic clogged. "While we're on the subject of Kent—"

"We're not."

"He loves you."

Marnie knew better. "Let's just leave Kent out of this, okay?"

For once, her father didn't argue. Rubbing the back of his neck he shook his head, as if he could release some of the tension tightening his shoulder blades. He slid her a sidelong glance as they turned into the marina. Fishing boats, sloops, yachts and cabin cruisers were tied to the piers. Whitecaps dotted the surface of the restless sound, and only a few sailing vessels braved the overcast day. Lumbering tankers moved slowly inland, while ferries churned frothy wakes, cutting through the dark water as they crossed the water.

Her father parked the Jag near the pier and cut the engine. "I can see I'm not going to change your mind," he said, slanting her a glance that took in the thrust of her jaw and the determination in her gaze. As if finally accepting the fact that she was serious, he snorted, "God knows I don't understand it, but if you think you've got to leave the company for a while, I'll try to muddle through without you."

"For a while?" she countered. "I resigned, remember?"

He held up his hands, as if in surrender. "One step at a time, okay? Let's just call this…sabbatical…of yours, a leave of absence."

She wanted to argue, but didn't. Maybe he needed time to adjust. Her leaving, after all, was as hard on him as it was on her.

Her expression softened, and she touched his arm. "You and Montgomery Inns will survive."

"Lord, I hope so," he murmured. "But I'm not accepting anything official like a resignation. And I want you to wait just a couple of weeks, until Puget West opens. That's not too much to ask, is it?" he queried, pocketing his keys as they both climbed out of the car.

Together, hands shoved in the pockets of their coats, they walked quickly along the time-weathered planks of the waterfront. Marnie breathed in the scents of the marina. She'd grown up around boats, and the odors of salt and seaweed, brine and diesel brought back happy childhood memories of when her father had taken as much interest in her as he had in his company. Things had changed, of course. She'd gone to college, hadn't needed him so much, and Montgomery Inns had developed into a large corporation with hotels stretched as far away as L.A. and Houston.

A stiff breeze snapped the flags on the moored vessels. High overhead sea gulls wheeled, their desolate cries barely audible over the sounds of throbbing engines. *Free,* she thought, smiling at the birds, *they're free. And lonely.*

Her father grumbled, "Next thing I know you'll be trading in your Beemer for a '69 Volkswagen."

She smothered a sad smile. He didn't know that she'd sold the BMW just last week, though she wasn't in the market for a VW bug—well, at least not yet.

"So it's settled, right?" he said, as if grateful to have finished a drawn-out negotiation. "When you get back, we'll talk."

"And if I still want to quit?"

"Then we'll talk some more." He fiddled in his pocket for his tobacco, stuffed a wad into the bowl of his pipe, and clamping the pipe between his teeth, searched in his pockets for a match. Trying to light the pipe, he walked quickly down the pier where his yacht, the *Vanessa,* was docked. "Maybe by the time you think things over, you'll come to your senses about Kent."

"I already have," she said, controlling the fury that still burned deep inside her. Kent had played her for a fool; he wouldn't get a second chance.

"Okay, okay, just promise me you'll stick around until the new hotel is open."

"It's a promise," she said, catching up to him. "But you're not talking me out of this. As soon as Puget West opens its doors, I'm history."

"For a while." He puffed on the pipe, sending up tiny clouds of smoke.

"Maybe," she said, unwilling to concede too much. Her father wasn't a bad man, just determined, especially when it came to her and his hotel chain. But she could be just as stubborn as he. She climbed aboard his favorite plaything as the wind off the sound whipped her hair in front of her face. Someday, whether he wanted to or not, Victor Montgomery would be proud of her for her independence; he just didn't know it yet. She'd prove to him, and everyone else who thought she was just another pampered rich girl, that she could make it on her own.

ACCORDING TO THE *Seattle Observer,* the grand opening of Puget West Montgomery Inn was to be the social event of the year. Invitations had been sent to the rich and the beautiful, from New York to L.A., though most of the guests were from the Pacific Northwest.

The mayor of Seattle as well as Senator Mann, the State of Washington's reigning Republican, were to attend. Local celebrities, the press and a few Hollywood types were rumored to be on hand to sip champagne and congratulate Victor Montgomery on the latest and most glittery link in the ever-expanding chain of Montgomery Inns.

Adam Drake wasn't invited.

In fact, he was probably the last person good old Victor wanted to see walk through the glass doors of the main lobby. But Victor was in for the surprise of his life, Adam thought with a grim smile. Because Adam wouldn't have missed the grand opening of Puget West for the world!

As the prow of his small boat sliced through the night-blackened waters of Puget Sound, he guided the craft toward his destination, the hotel itself. Lit like the proverbial Christmas tree, twenty-seven stories of Puget West rose against a stygian sky.

Wind ripped over the water, blasting his bare face and hands, but Adam barely felt the cold. He was too immersed in his own dark thoughts. Anger tightened a knot in his gut. He'd helped design this building; hell, he'd even outbid a Japanese investor for the land, all for the sake of Montgomery Inns and Victor Montgomery!

And he'd been kicked in the face for his efforts—framed for a crime he'd never committed. Well, he'd just spent the past three weeks of his life dredging up all the evidence again, talking with even the most obscure employees who had once worked for the company, and he'd started to unravel the web of lies, one string at a time. He didn't have all the answers, just vague suspicions, but he was hell-bent to prove them true. Only then would he be able to get on with his own life.

And never again would he depend upon a man like Victor Montgomery for his livelihood. From this point on, Adam intended to be his own boss.

Close to the docks, Adam cut the boat's engine and slung ropes around the moorings. Before he could second-guess himself, he hopped onto the new deck and walked briskly beneath the Japanese lanterns glowing red, green and orange. Tiny crystal lights, twinkling as if it were the holiday season instead of the end of May, winked in the shrubbery.

His jaw tightened, and a cruel smile tugged at the corners of his mouth as he considered his reasons for showing up uninvited. Adrenaline surged through his veins. What was the phrase—revenge was always best when it was served up cold?

He'd soon find out.

Nearly a year had passed since he'd been hung by

his heels in public, humiliated and stripped bare, and tonight he'd seek his own form of justice.

Thunder cracked over the angry waters, and Adam cast one final look at the inky sound. He found poetic justice in the fact that a spring storm was brewing on the night Victor Montgomery was opening his latest resort.

He didn't waste any time. The pant legs of his tuxedo brushed against the wet leaves of blossoming rhododendrons and azaleas as he walked briskly, moving instinctively toward the side entrance and the French doors he knew would be unlocked and, with any luck, unguarded.

Music and laughter floated through the night as he stepped onto the terrace. Through the open doors, he saw that the party was in full swing, bejeweled guests talking, dancing, laughing and drinking from monogrammed fluted glasses.

Adam tugged on his tight black tie, plowed his fingers through his wind-tossed hair, then slipped into the opulent foyer. No one seemed to notice. As a liveried waiter passed, Adam snagged a glass of champagne from a silver tray and scoped out the milling guests.

A piano player sat at a shiny baby grand, and the nostalgic notes of "As Time Goes By" drifted through the crowd. Silver and red balloons, tied together with long white ribbons, floated dreamily to the windowed ceiling four stories above the foyer. Near the back wall a glass elevator carried guests to the balconies surrounding the lobby, and on the opposite wall an elegant staircase curved upward to the second story. In the center of the room, the trademark Montgomery fountain, complete with marble base, spouted water eight feet high.

Oh, yes, this hotel was just as grand as Victor Montgomery had envisioned it, the opening party already a success. Adam tamped down any trace of bitterness as he wandered through the crowd. It took a cool mind to get even.

In one corner of the lobby near a restaurant, a ten-foot ice sculpture of King Neptune, trident aloft, sea monsters curling in the waves near his feet, stood guard.

Just like good old Victor, Adam thought to himself as he spied Kate Delany, Victor's administrative assistant and, as rumor had it, lover. Dressed in shimmering white, her dark hair piled high on her head, Kate acted as hostess. Her smile was practiced but friendly, and her eyes sparkled enough to invite conversation as she drifted from one knot of guests to the next.

Scanning the crowd, Adam decided Victor hadn't made his grand entrance yet. Nor had his daughter. He looked again, hoping for a glimpse of Marnie. Spoiled, rich, beautiful Marnie Montgomery was the one pos-session Victor valued more than his damned hotels. An only child, she'd been pampered, sent to the best schools and given the post of "public-relations admin-istrator" upon graduation from some Ivy League school back east.

Despite his bitterness toward anything loosely asso-ciated with Montgomery Inns, Adam had found Marnie appealing. Regardless of her lap-of-leisure upbringing, there had been something—a spark of laughter in her eyes, a trace of wistfulness in her smile, an intelligence in her wit and a mystique to her silences—which had half convinced him that she was more than just another rich brat coddled by an overindulgent father and raised by nannies. Tall and slender, with pale blond hair and eyes a clear crystal blue, Marnie was as hauntingly beautiful as she was wealthy. And as he understood it, she'd become engaged to Kent Simms, one of Victor's "yes" men.

Bad choice, Marnie, Adam thought as he took a long swallow of champagne. Maybe he'd been kidding himself all along. Marnie Montgomery was probably cut from the same expensive weave of cloth as was her father.

Kent Simms fit into the picture neatly. Too ambitious for his own good, Kent was more interested in the fast lane and big bucks than in loving a wife. Even if she happened to be the boss's daughter. The marriage wouldn't last.

But Kent Simms was Marnie's problem. Adam had his own.

He heard a gasp behind him. From the corner of his eye he caught the quickly averted look of a wasp-thin woman with dark eyes and a black velvet dress.

So she recognizes me, he thought in satisfaction, and lifted his champagne glass in silent salute to her. Her name was Rose Trullinger, and she was an interior decorator for the corporation.

Rose's cheeks flooded with color, and she turned quickly away before casting a sharp glance over her shoulder and heading toward a group of eight or nine people lingering around the bar.

Adam watched as she whispered something to a woman draped in blue silk and dripping with diamonds. The woman in blue turned, lifted a finely arched brow and sent Adam a curious look. There was more than mild amusement in her eyes. Adam noticed an invitation. Some women were attracted to men who were considered forbidden or dangerous. The woman in blue was obviously one of those.

She whispered something to Rose.

Perfect, Adam thought with a grim twist of his lips. It wouldn't be long before Victor knew he was here.

CHAPTER TWO

MARNIE JABBED A GLITTERY comb into her hair, then glowered at her reflection as the comb slid slowly down. Shaking her head, she yanked out the comb and tossed it onto the vanity. *So much for glamour.* She brushed her shoulder-length curls with a vengeance and eyed the string of diamonds and sapphires surrounding her throat. The necklace and matching earrings had been her mother's; Victor had pleaded with her to wear them and she had, on this, the last night of her employment at Montgomery Inns. Just being in the new hotel made her feel like a hypocrite, but she only had a few more hours and, then, freedom!

"Marnie?" Her father tapped softly on the door connecting her smaller bedroom to the rest of his suite. "It's about time."

"I'll be right out," she replied, dreading the party. On the bed, a single suitcase lay open. She tossed her comb, brush and makeup bag into the soft-sided case and snapped it shut.

Sliding into a pair of silver heels, she opened the door to find her father, a drink in one hand, pacing near the door. He glanced up as she entered the room, and the smile that creased his face was filled with genuine admiration. He swallowed and blinked. "I really hadn't realized how much you look like Vanessa," he said quietly.

Marnie felt an inner glow. He was complimenting her. Her father had never gotten over his wife and he'd vowed on her grave that he'd never remarry. And he hadn't. Even though Kate Delany had been in love with him for years, he wouldn't marry her. Marnie knew it as well as she knew she herself would never marry Kent Simms.

He reached for the door but paused. "Kent's already here."

"I know."

"He's been asking to see you."

She knew that, too. But she was through talking to Kent about anything other than business. "I don't have anything to say to him."

Victor tugged on his lower lip as if weighing his next words. Marnie braced herself. She knew what was coming. "Kent loves you, and he's been with the company for ten years. That man is loyal."

"To Montgomery Inns."

"Well, that's something. The years he's worked for me—"

"If longevity with Montgomery Inns has anything to do with my future husband, then I should marry Fred Ainger."

"Don't be ridiculous," her father scoffed, leaving his glass on a table near the door, but Marnie could tell her comment had hit its mark. Fred Ainger, a tiny bespectacled accountant in bookkeeping, was about to retire at age sixty-five. He'd been with Montgomery Inns since Victor had purchased his first hotel.

"Okay, okay. We both know that Kent's time with the company doesn't really matter when you're choosing a husband," her father reluctantly agreed, smoothing his hair with the flat of his hand. He looked out the window to the city of Port Stanton flanking the banks of the sound. Smaller than Seattle, Tacoma or Olympia, Port Stanton, as gateway to the sound, was growing by leaps and bounds, and Montgomery Inns was ready and waiting with the Puget West as the city required more hotels for businessmen and travelers. "But Kent is loyal to the company."

Bully for Kent, she thought, but held her tongue on that point. "I'd rather have a husband who's committed to me."

"For what it's worth, I believe Kent is committed to you, honey."

Marnie knew differently. She also realized that she was going to have to tell her father why she was so adamant about rejecting Kent, or her father would badger her forever. In Victor's eyes, Kent was the perfect son-in-law. "I didn't love him, Dad." That much wasn't a lie, though she'd convinced herself during the duration of their engagement that she had. "Kent wasn't the man for me. He was your choice, not mine."

For a few seconds Victor didn't speak, and Marnie could almost hear the gears whirling in his mind. Her father didn't back down quickly.

He made a big show of glancing at his watch and pursing his lips. "Come on," he said, his keen eyes glinting. "Let's go downstairs. We can talk about Kent later."

Marnie shook her head. "*You* can talk about him later. I'm done."

Victor held up a hand to forestall any further arguments. "Whatever you say. It's your life."

Marnie wasn't fooled, and cast him a glance that told him so.

Victor held open the door for her, and Marnie stepped onto the balcony. The sounds of the party drifted up the four flights from the lobby. Even from this distance she recognized a few employees of the hotel chain, dancing or laughing with guests who had been sent special invitations, the chosen few who mattered in the Northwest—the mayor of Seattle and Senator Mann, several city council members as well as reporters for local television and newspapers. There were only a few faces Marnie didn't recognize.

All of Seattle's social elite had come to Puget West, drinking and laughing and showing off their most expensive gowns and jewelry, hoping that their names and pictures might find a way into the society columns of the *Seattle Observer* and the *Port Stanton Herald.*

Forcing a smile she didn't feel, Marnie stepped into the glass elevator, her father at her side. As the car descended, she stared through the windows, noticing the lights in the trees in the lobby, the ice sculpture of King Neptune and the three-tiered fountain of champagne wedged between tables laden with hors d'oeuvres. A pianist was playing from a polished ebony piano where a man listened, a handsome man, she guessed from the back of him. She noticed the wide breadth of his shoulders, the narrowing of his hips, the way his wavy black hair gleamed under a thousand winking lights.

There was something familiar about him, something about his stance, that brought back hazy memories. He turned to reach for a glass of champagne from a passing waiter, and as the elevator doors opened, Marnie found herself staring across the room. A pair of mocking, gold-brown eyes met hers, and she nearly missed a step.

Adam Drake!

What in God's name was he doing here? Didn't the man have a sense of decency, or at the very least, an ounce of self-preservation? Her father would love to have a chance to throw him out of the hotel! Even though he'd been proved innocent of the charges Victor had leveled against him, Adam Drake was definitely on her father's ten-least-wanted list.

Adam didn't seem concerned. A slow, self-mocking smile stretched across his jaw as his gaze collided with hers. He winked lazily at her, then took a long swallow from his champagne.

Marnie almost grinned. She'd forgotten about his irreverence, his lack of concern for playing by society's unwritten laws. Well, he'd really done himself in this time. Though she'd never really believed that he was a thief, there was a side to him that suggested danger, and she wondered just how much he knew about the half million dollars skimmed from the funds to build this very hotel. The guy had nerve, she'd grant him that!

Amused, she turned to see if her father had noticed their uninvited guest, but a crowd of well-wishers suddenly engulfed them. Victor tugged on Marnie's arm, pulling her along as he wended his way to the circular fountain and stepped onto the marble base, hauling her up with him. Newspaper reporters followed, elbowing and jostling to thrust microphones into Victor's face. Cameras flashed before her eyes as photographers clicked off dozens of pictures.

Victor laughed and answered each question crisply. Her father was always at his best in front of a crowd, but Marnie was uncomfortable in the spotlight. She tried to slip away unnoticed. However, Senator Mann, always hungry for press, fought his way through the throng to stand at her father's side, blocking Marnie's exit. Even Kent appeared. Predictably, he wended quickly through the tightening group to take his place next to her. She was trapped!

Gazing up at Kent's even, practiced smile, Marnie decided this wasn't the time to bring up the fact that Adam Drake had somehow turned up uninvited.

"Hi," Kent whispered, flashing a thousand-watt grin at her, though Marnie suspected the smile was for the press. He tried to slide his arm around her waist.

Marnie sidestepped him and somehow managed to keep her balance. "Don't," she warned.

"Come on, Marnie," he cajoled. "Just try to be reasonable—at least for appearances' sake."

"I can't—"

"Kent! Congratulations!" Mayor Winthrop's voice boomed as he approached and stretched out his hand. He was short and round, his straight gray hair painstakingly combed to cover a bald spot. "Beautiful hotel, Marnie, just beautiful!" he gushed, before turning all his attention on Victor and Kent.

Marnie managed a thin smile for the man, then, before Kent realized what she was doing, excused herself quickly and stepped into the sea of guests.

Enough with the spectacle, she thought, moving quickly away from the fountain. She had promised her father she'd show up at his party, but she wasn't going to pretend to care about Kent. How could she have ever made the mistake of thinking she loved him? Or that he had loved her? She must've been desperate.

Unconsciously, she glanced back to the piano, but Adam had disappeared and the pianist, taking his cue from Victor, had stopped playing so that the mayor and other city dignitaries could publicly congratulate Victor Montgomery on another glamorous project well done.

Marnie felt little of the pride she'd experienced at the completion of other hotels. Puget West had been different from the beginning. There had been problems and delays with acquisition, zoning, planning, architecture and then, of course, the scandal. At first Adam Drake, Victor's personal choice to supervise the project, had smoothed out the bumps, but later, when Kate Delany had discovered the errors in the books, all hell had broken loose and her father had blamed Adam for the mismanaged money.

The money had never been located. Over five hundred thousand dollars had seemed to vanish into thin air. Marnie had never believed Adam to be a thief, but no one had been able to explain what had happened to the missing funds.

Adam had never been indicted, but the public humiliation had been tremendous, the scandal reported daily in the business section of the *Seattle Observer*. And now he was here? Why?

Scanning the waves of people, she found Adam again. With one shoulder propped against a marble pillar, the jacket of his tux open, his tie loosened, his black hair wind-tossed, he looked rakish and self-satisfied. A small smile played on his thin, sensual lips. His eyes, dark above chiseled cheekbones, were trained on the fountain where Victor stood.

It was strange that he'd decided to come, but fitting, in a way. Adam Drake, before his downfall, had been invaluable to the company, one of the few in Victor's small circle of advisers. Adam had been the man who had found this very piece of land on the western shore of the sound and had negotiated a very good deal for Montgomery Inns. Without Adam Drake, Puget West never would have been built.

Marnie wondered why he had risked having his reputation blackened again. The man must be certifiable.

With difficulty, she forced her gaze away from him. Unfortunately she discovered Dolores Tate, Kent's secretary, lingering near the open bar, her wide brown eyes focused lovingly on Kent.

Marnie thought she might be sick.

Dolores didn't notice her; she was too involved with the scene at the fountain and her own appearance. Unconsciously, she lifted a hand to the springy brown curls that framed her Kewpie-doll face. Draped in a dress of gold sequins and chiffon, Dolores moved gracefully among the people near the fountain, smiling and stopping to talk with this group and that, seeming more a part of this party than Marnie felt herself.

Dolores probably was more at home here, Marnie thought as she tore her gaze away from the woman Kent had chosen as his mistress. Surprisingly, she didn't feel any surge of jealousy, just an annoying embarrassment that she could have been duped by Kent.

Rather than dwell on Kent, Marnie half listened to her father's prepared speech. Victor, public smile in place, was heartily thanking the community leaders for the privilege of building this "…dream-come-true on the banks of the sound for our fair community…"

On and on he went, interrupted occasionally by bursts of clapping or laughter as he related some funny anecdotes about the construction of the hotel. Marnie had heard similar speeches dozens of times before. For her father's sake, she hoped she appeared interested, though she couldn't keep her gaze from wandering across the expansive foyer to the pillar against which Adam leaned.

Marnie could almost feel Adam's hostility sizzling across the room. But Victor went blithely on, unaware that the man he was sure had tried to cheat him was present.

Kate Delany, too, didn't seem to notice Adam as she found Marnie and joined her. "Your father's pleased," Kate whispered into Marnie's ear.

"He should be," Marnie answered automatically.

"Mmm." Kate nodded. Her auburn hair was piled in loose curls atop her head, her silk dress shimmered as it draped over one shoulder. Emerald earrings, shaped like teardrops, matched the bracelet encircling one slim wrist—gifts from Marnie's father. The small white lines of disappointment near her lips were barely visible.

Marnie felt a pang of pity for Kate. She obviously still clung to the hope that she would someday become Mrs. Victor Montgomery.

As Victor finished, Kate slipped through the crowd toward the fountain. The guests erupted with enthusiastic applause and good wishes while photographers shot rolls of film of her father with the mayor, or senator, or with a dour-faced city councilwoman wearing a simple linen suit and an outrageous magenta hat.

Marnie slid another glance in Adam's direction and decided it was time she found out what he was doing here. They were compatriots, in a perverse way, she thought. Neither one of them belonged here. Only Adam had shown up despite the fact that he wasn't wanted; she, on the other hand, was wanted and would do anything to leave.

She accepted a glass of champagne from a waiter and then slipped through the guests toward the one man who had the guts to defy her father.

Adam saw her coming. He'd watched as she had disentangled herself from Kent and mingled among the clusters of people. She had been smiling at her father's jokes but not really listening. It was almost as if she were playing a part, putting in her time, and she'd cast more than one curious glance in his direction. Good.

She was beautiful, he had to admit that. Her wavy hair was pale blond, almost silver, her eyes were an intense shade of blue and even though she was often serious, Adam remembered that she laughed easily.

But she wasn't laughing tonight. No, Miss Montgomery appeared uncomfortable with all the hoopla, though she was dressed for the occasion in a silky dress that must have cost a fortune and in diamonds that sparkled around her wrist and neck. No one would doubt that she was Victor Montgomery's spoiled daughter.

He found it interesting that when she'd first spotted him she hadn't run to Daddy to tell him that a traitor was in their midst. Instead, she'd appeared mildly curious and now she was walking toward him.

The ghost of a smile crossed her full lips and her eyes twinkled for just a second. "Mr. Drake," she said, stopping just short of him.

"It's Adam, remember?"

"Impossible to forget," she replied, showing off a dimple. "Your name will probably be whispered in the corridors of Montgomery Inns for years. You're a legend, you know."

"As part of the poor and infamous?"

She plucked a shrimp canapé from a tray. "What're

you doing here? Don't you know you'll be drawn and quartered before the night is out? That's what they do to party crashers." She plopped the canape into her mouth and washed it down with a sip of champagne.

He couldn't believe that she was actually baiting him. Adam's mouth slashed at a sardonic angle. "And here I thought my invitation had just gotten lost in the mail."

"Right," Marnie replied dryly, her ice blue dress glimmering seductively under the lights. "If I were you, this is the last place I would've shown up."

"Never was one to miss a party."

"You must be a glutton for punishment. My father will flip when he finds out you're here—and he will, you know. It won't take long."

"I'm counting on it."

"Why?" For the first time, the teasing glint disappeared from her eyes. She lifted her glass to her lips and appraised him solemnly over the rim.

"He and I need to talk, and he's been dodging my calls." Adam glanced back to the fountain-cum-podium where Victor was introducing Kent Simms and congratulating him on his promotion to executive vice president. Adam finished his drink in one gulp, as Simms accepted Victor's hearty congratulations, shook hands with the mayor and rained a brilliant pretty-boy smile on the crowd.

"You've *called* Dad?" Marnie asked, apparently stunned.

Adam swung his gaze back to her. "Several times. Never got past Kate. Victor didn't bother to call me back."

"But—"

"I even stopped in at the offices. Kate ran interference. Wouldn't let me in to see him."

Marnie couldn't believe it. Her father hadn't said a word about Adam trying to contact him, and she would have thought, given Victor's feelings about Adam Drake, he would have ranted and raved for days at the younger man's impertinence. "What did you want to talk to him about?"

"Believe me, I have a lot to discuss with your father—or if I can't talk to him, Simms'll do." He cocked his head toward the fountain. "By the way, your fiancé seems to be enjoying himself. Shouldn't you be up there, basking in some of the glory?"

"It got a little crowded," she said, her lips tightening.

"I noticed."

"Adam Drake?" Kate's voice was low and cold. When he turned, her large eyes were suspicious, the color in her cheeks high. "What do you think you're doing here?" she whispered, then before he could answer, asked, "How did you get past security?"

"I helped design this building, remember—including the security system."

"You bastard," she shot back, ignoring Marnie. "You want to ruin it for him, don't you? This is Victor's night, and you're going to make sure that it blows up in his face!"

"I just want to talk to him."

"Well, you can't. Not tonight," she said, her features hardening. "If the press gets wind that you're here, it'll ruin everything! You've got to leave! Now!" Her voice had taken on a frantic tone that seemed to surprise Marnie as she watched the exchange in stunned silence.

"I'm not taking off just yet."

"But why would you want to stay? It'll just cause problems." Kate glanced nervously toward Victor.

Marnie laid a hand on her arm. "Relax, Kate," Marnie said, as if she, too, were trying to avoid a scene, but Kate raged on.

"Please, Adam, just go quietly, before you do something that can't be undone and everything's dredged up again. This is Victor's night. Please don't spoil it!"

"I need to talk to him."

"But not here—"

"I tried the office," he replied, fighting to control his anger. "You wouldn't let me see him."

"My mistake. Come back next week, I'll get you an appointment," she promised, pinning a winning smile on her face and slipping her arm through his, obviously intending to escort him to the door.

"I'll wait, just the same."

Frustrated, Kate stormed away in a cloud of exasperation.

"I don't think that's the way to win friends and influence people," Marnie said dryly.

"I'm not very popular around here, am I?"

She grinned. "I'm afraid you're persona non grata at Montgomery Inns. But my father still keeps your picture in his office—taped over his dart board."

He laughed, surprised that she would joke with him. The pianist began playing again, filling the lobby with a vaguely familiar big-band hit of the forties.

"Do you want me to tell my father you're here?" she asked, and he shook his head.

"I think it would be better if you stay out of it."

"Why?"

"It could get bloody."

"Then I'd better be there," she decided. "Someone— maybe you—might need a bandage."

"And soon," he said, spying Kent Simms, face flushed, plunging through the crowd and heading straight for Marnie. The glare in Kent's eyes was unmistakable—the territorial pride of the spurned male.

"What the hell are you doing here?" Kent demanded in a voice so low it was hard to hear over the crowd.

Adam finished his drink. "I was hoping to talk to Victor, but I guess you'll have to do."

"Forget it. Come on, Marnie, let's go," Kent ordered, grabbing her arm and propelling her toward a banquet room near the back of the lobby.

"Let go of me," she whispered furiously, half running to keep up with his longer strides. She considered making a scene, but thought better of it. No reason to call undue attention to Adam—he'd do enough of that for himself.

In the banquet room, she whirled around and yanked her arm free of Kent's possessive grasp. "What is it you want?"

His expression changed from anger to sadness. "You already know what I want," he said quietly. "I just want you, Marnie."

She couldn't believe her ears. What did it take to make the man understand? "I already told you it's over! I don't need to be manhandled or made a spectacle of! Where do you get off, hauling me in here like some caveman claiming his woman?"

"Caveman?" he repeated. "Weren't you just talking to Drake? Now there's someone who's primitive." He shook his head, as if sorry that she was so dense. "You know, Marnie, sometimes you can be impossible."

"Good!"

"You enjoy being perverse?"

"I just want you to leave me alone. I thought you understood that. If you don't, let me make myself clear," she said, drawing up to her full height and sending him an icy glare. "I'm sorry I ever got involved with you and I never want to see you again."

He glanced to one of the chandeliers high overhead. "I made a mistake with Dolores."

She didn't respond. She'd learned that his affair with Dolores had been going on for over six months. All the time that she and Kent had been picking out china, planning a wedding, looking for a house, sailing in the boat Victor had bought them as an engagement present, Kent had been sleeping with his secretary.

"You know I still love you," he said, and his expression was so sincere, she almost believed him. But she wasn't a fool. Not any more. "Give me another chance," he pleaded. "It'll never happen again. I swear it."

Marnie shook her head. "You can do what you damn well please, Kent. It doesn't matter anymore."

"I really did a number on you, didn't I?"

"I prefer to think that you did me a favor."

A light of challenge sparked in his hazel eyes. He leaned down as if to kiss her, and she ducked away. "Stop it!" she commanded, her tone frigid.

He ignored her and grabbed her quickly, yanking her hard against him. "Don't tell me 'no,'" he whispered, his face so close that his breath, smelling of liquor, fanned her face.

"Don't pull this macho stuff on me!"

"You love it." His grip tightened, and his eyes glittered in a way that frightened and sickened her. He *enjoyed* this fight.

Squirming, unable to wrench away, she stomped on his foot in frustration. The heel of her shoe snapped with the force. "Let go!"

Kent let out a yowl and backed up a step. "What the hell's gotten into you?" he cried, reaching down to rub the top of his shoe, as if he could massage his wounded foot. Wincing, he turned furious eyes on her. "I thought we could work things out, you know? I thought tonight would be the perfect time. Did you see me with your father and Senator Mann? The man knew my name! God, what a rush! And I come back to share it with you—the woman I love—and what do I get?"

"Maybe you're getting what you deserve," Adam drawled, coming up behind Kent.

A wave of heat washed up Marnie's neck. Oh, Lord! How much of their argument had he overheard?

Kent straightened, resting his foot gingerly on the floor as he eyed Adam. Adam was slightly taller, with harsher features, his hair a little longer, his whole demeanor laid-back and secure. Kent, on the other hand, looked military spit-and-polished, his tuxedo crisp, his hair clipped, his spine ramrod-stiff.

"I thought you were leaving," Kent said, glowering at Adam.

"Not yet."

Kent straightened his tie and smoothed his hair. "Does Victor know you're here?"

Adam lifted a shoulder nonchalantly, but his features were set in stone. "I hope so."

Instinctively, Marnie stepped closer to Adam, and Kent shot her an irritated glance, his eyes slitting. "Just what is it you want, Drake?" he demanded, stuffing his hands into the back pockets of his pants and angling his face upward to meet Adam's hard glare. "Why don't you just leave?"

"Not until I ask Victor if he knows who Gerald Henderson is?"

"Henderson?" Kent repeated, his expression so bland it had to be false. "Didn't he work for us?"

"In accounting," Adam clarified.

"I remember him," Marnie interjected, refusing to be left out of the conversation. "He left because he had health problems—asthma, I think. He had to leave the damp Northwest. And he got a better job with a hotel in San Diego."

"Still lives in Seattle," Adam replied. "Spends a lot of time fishing. If I'm not wrong, I think he's drawing some sort of disability or retirement."

Marnie glanced from one stern face to the other. "Didn't the job in California work out?"

"Who cares?" Kent replied. "Henderson's history."

"Maybe," Adam said, and the undercurrents in his voice jarred her. She was missing something in this conversation, something important.

Kent swallowed. "I don't think Victor would be interested," he said, but his voice lacked conviction.

"Not even if Gerald had an idea about the missing funds?"

"What?" Marnie demanded, shocked.

"It's nothing," Kent snapped. "Henderson couldn't possibly know—"

"Adam Drake?" Judith Marx, a reporter for the *Seattle Observer* who had obviously seen some of the hubbub, walked briskly into the banquet room. "I'm surprised to see you here," she said, her eyes taking in the scene in one quick glance.

The understatement of the year, Marnie thought.

"I wouldn't have missed this for the world," Adam drawled.

"Can I quote you?" she asked.

"No!" Kent cut in, his face flushed, a vein throbbing near his temple. "Mr. Drake is an uninvited guest, and if you print that I'll march over to the *Observer* and talk to John Forrester myself!"

"Mr. Forrester would never suppress news," the woman replied smartly.

Kent whirled on Adam, his voice low. "Whatever it is you want, Drake, it can wait until later."

By now, more than a few guests had drifted into the room. Kent was beginning to squirm. Whispers began to float around them, like tiny wisps of fog that lingered for a second, then drifted by.

"Mr. Drake?" Judith Marx obviously smelled a story. She wasn't about to give up. "I thought you vowed vengeance against this company."

"What I said was that I'd prove my innocence."

From the corner of his eye, Adam saw Kent motioning with a finger to a beefy security guard in the doorway.

"Wasn't that all taken care of?" Judith asked Adam, and he turned his attention back to the reporter. "You weren't even indicted." She reached into her bag for her pocket recorder. Kent glanced across the room, nodding to the two guards making their way inside.

Adam was ready for the two sets of hands that collared him and firmly guided him through a back door connecting the banquet room to the kitchen. He didn't struggle. There was no point. Obviously Victor hadn't seen him, or had decided to leave his dirty work to Kent. Either way, Adam wasn't finished. Not by a long shot. But his next move would be more subtle.

Hauling him through the service entrance, the security guards deposited him roughly on the wet asphalt near a delivery truck.

One of the two guards, a big bear of a man with sandy hair and a flat face, muttered under his breath. "Still gettin' yourself into trouble, ain't'cha?" Sam Dillinger had worked with Adam for years before the scandal.

"Looks that way, Sam." Adam brushed himself off as he stood. He managed a grim smile.

"I'm sorry, Mr. Drake. You know, I never believed you were involved in any of that thievin'."

"Thanks, Sam."

The other guard, a thickset man with short salt-and-pepper hair, snorted. He fingered the pistol strapped to his belt. "Don't show up here again," he warned. "Just haul your butt out of here and don't come back!"

"Be sure to tell Mr. Simms he hasn't seen the last of me," Adam said to Jim before sketching a wave to Sam. "See ya around, Sam."

"You bet, Mr. Drake. Good luck to you."

But Adam wasn't counting on luck as he left the two guards arguing about his guilt. He ducked his head against the rain that slanted from the pitch-black sky.

The dock was slick, the wind raw and cold as he strode purposefully back to his boat. Now that he'd come face-to-face with Kent Simms again, he realized that nothing had changed. And since he didn't have any proof other than Gerald Henderson's side of the story, he couldn't very well make accusations that could end up as slander. But from his reaction tonight, Adam was sure Simms knew more than he was telling. Adam had suspected Kent might be involved in the embezzling, of course, but he'd suspected a lot of people within the company.

Now, he decided, he'd start with Simms. He didn't like the way the guy was manhandling Marnie, and the thought of giving Kent a little of his own back caused Adam to smile.

So, his next step would be to have a little chat with Kent before he tackled Victor. The more information he could lay at Montgomery's feet, the better. And somehow, he sensed, Kent could tell him a lot.

Fortunately meeting Kent Simms face-to-face would be a simple matter. The *Marnie Lee,* a gleaming white cabin cruiser, and Simms's personal vessel, was moored on the second dock.

Adam wasted no time. He looked over his shoulder to make sure the two guards were still watching as he stepped into his small boat. Unleashing the moorings, he settled behind the wheel and gunned the engine. The boat took off, churning a white wake as the engine roared loudly and he headed toward Seattle.

Twenty minutes later, when he was sure the guards were satisfied that he'd left the shores of Port Stanton and had returned to their posts in the hotel lobby, Adam circled back toward the Puget West and the docks where gleaming vessels rolled with the tide.

He wasn't finished. Not by a long shot. Adam intended to board the *Marnie Lee* and wait in the cabin to have it out with Simms once and for all. As he spotted the showy white vessel he thought of her namesake, the lady herself, Marnie Lee Montgomery. How could a woman as bright as Marnie obviously was link up with a loser like Simms?

It was a mystery, he thought, then he remembered the tail end of their fight and decided that all was not bliss in the relationship between Victor Montgomery's strong-willed daughter and the man she'd chosen for a husband.

Adam felt a twinge of conscience as he lashed his boat to the dock, then climbed stealthily aboard Simms's expensive cabin cruiser. He didn't want to hurt Marnie; she'd always played fair with him. Though she'd been raised in the lap of luxury and been given anything she'd ever wanted, she seemed sincere.

Don't forget she's engaged to Simms. Even if they did have a lovers' quarrel, they were, as far as he knew, still planning to marry. That thought left a sour taste in the back of his throat, but he ignored it. Marnie's fate was just too damned bad. Any woman who gave her heart to a jerk like Simms deserved what she got.

MARNIE COULDN'T BELIEVE her ears! The minute Adam was escorted out of the hotel, Kent turned the interview with the reporter around and now, with his arm wrapped securely around Marnie's waist, he was confiding in the woman that Marnie and he were making plans to marry in mid-September.

"Congratulations!" Judith said, snapping her small tape recorder on. "What day is that, the sixteenth—seventeenth?"

"No!" Marnie cried, aghast. What had gotten into Kent? In all the years she'd known him he'd never been so bullheaded or downright stupid.

Kent's fingers tightened around her. "What she means is that we're not completely certain on the date. We've still got to accommodate everyone in the family—"

"What I mean is that there isn't going to be a wedding!" Marnie declared firmly, plucking Kent's fingers off her and stepping away from him. "Kent and I aren't getting married, not in September. Not ever."

"But—" Judith looked from one to the other.

Kent lifted his hands and shrugged, as if Marnie's announcement came as a complete surprise to him. He acted as if she were just some fickle female who couldn't decide what she wanted, for God's sake!

"You explain this!" Marnie commanded, her voice as cold as a winter day. Shaking with rage, she turned on the reporter. "I'd better not read about any wedding in your paper. Not one word!" Spine stiff, she marched straight through the banquet-room doors and to the elevator in the lobby.

Pounding on the button for the fourth floor, she bit her tongue so that the invectives forming in her throat would be kept inside. The elevator doors shut softly, cutting off the sounds of the party, and the car ascended. Furious, her insides shaking with anger, Marnie leaned her forehead against the cool glass. "Calm down," she ordered to herself. "Don't let that bastard get to you!"

The elevator stopped and she stepped through the opening doors, storming into her father's suite. What was Kent trying to do? He'd been acting strangely all night! How had she ever been foolish enough to think she wanted to marry him?

She stalked into the smaller bedroom. Her suitcase, packed and waiting, was where she'd left it near the foot of the bed. Good. She peeled off her gown, threw her jewelry into a case and stuffed the velvet box back into her father's safe.

By the time Victor knocked softly on the door to her room, she had changed into faded jeans, a sweatshirt and a down-lined jacket. "Marnie? You in here?"

"For the moment."

He opened the door and shook his head at the sight of her. "And where do you think you're going?"

She sent him a chilling glance. "I'm leaving. Remember?"

"Of course I remember," he said, holding out his palms as if to forestall an argument, "but I thought you might change your mind and wait a bit. Kent just told me he had Adam Drake thrown out of the party while I was wrapped up with Senator Mann. God only knows what's going to be in the papers tomorrow! I need you to talk to the press—"

"I just did." Marnie wasn't about to be sidetracked by her father's ploy. "*That* was a dirty trick, Dad," she said, yanking her suitcase onto the bed and snapping it open to double-check the contents.

"What?"

Satisfied that she'd packed everything she needed, she clicked the case shut. "You told Kent to give the press a wedding date, didn't you?"

"Of course not—"

"He never would have done it without getting the okay from you," she insisted. "He wouldn't do anything that might threaten his precious career with Montgomery Inns."

"I didn't—"

"Don't lie to me, Dad! It's belittling to both of us."

Her father seemed about to protest, then let out a long, weary sigh. "Okay, I suggested that Kent—"

"Oh, Dad, how *could* you!"

"We needed a distraction. I saw Adam Drake and knew he was here to stir up trouble and then that reporter woman, Judith Marx…" He shuddered. "She can be a barracuda."

"Then why didn't you confront Drake?" she asked, astounded.

Her father shook his head. "Only cause a worse scene. Anyway, I saw Drake and started to follow him into the banquet room when Senator Mann came up to me. Then the reporter started snooping around and I put two and two together. Instead of a big spread about opening this hotel, tomorrow's edition of the *Observer* would probably just bring up Adam Drake and all the problems we had getting this damned hotel built! Believe me, Marnie, we don't need any more bad press."

"Great. So *I* became the distraction," she whispered, exasperated beyond words.

"When Kent talked to me earlier I wasn't for it, but then I saw Drake and the reporter and I gave him the high-sign to go ahead and announce your wedding plans."

"You're incredible," she whispered in exasperation. "Absolutely incredible!" Hooking a thumb to her chest, she added, "We're talking about *my* life, Dad. Mine!"

"Marnie, you have to understand—"

"Oh, I do, Dad," she said, feeling sad as she realized that the company meant more to him than her happiness. "You can give Kent a message for me. Tell him that I'm taking the *Marnie Lee*. If he throws a fit, remind him that half of it is mine. So I'm taking my half—too bad his half is attached."

"Wait a minute—at least tell me where you're going."

"I don't know," she admitted.

"You don't know?" he repeated. "You can't just leave without a plan."

"That's exactly what I'm going to do. The next few days I'm going to figure out just what I want to do with my life. Take some time to think about it, then, when I get back, I'll let you know. Goodbye, Dad." More determined than ever, she headed out of the suite and down a short hall to a private elevator, which took her to the underground parking lot. From there it was only a few steps to the back of the building.

Outside, the wind ripped through the trees and the black water of the sound moved in restless waves. Marnie followed the path beneath the line of dancing Japanese lanterns.

Reaching the dock, she spotted the *Marnie Lee* and smiled faintly. Wouldn't Kent be tied in knots when he learned she'd taken the boat he'd come to think of as his? Kent had used the boat for the past six months. He'd be shocked to his toes when he found out she had taken command of the sleek vessel Victor had given them as an engagement present. Let him stew in his own juices—September wedding indeed!

Tossing her suitcase on board, she felt better than she had all night. She unleashed the moorings holding the *Marnie Lee* fast then climbed to the helm. The engine started on the first try, the dark waters of the sound churning white. Biting her lip, Marnie maneuvered the craft around the other vessels and toward the open waters of Puget Sound.

She decided to head to Orcas Island.

There was an old resort on the island, a resort her father planned to refurbish, and the old hotel would be the perfect place to camp out the first night. From there she would decide what she was going to do with the rest of her life. She couldn't be Victor Montgomery's baby forever. Nor did she want to be Kent Simms's wife. That left Marnie Montgomery, a single woman who had dutifully done everything her father had requested, from college to her career at Montgomery Inns.

Marnie let out the throttle and the boat sped forward, the prow knifing through the choppy dark water, the wind tearing at her hair. She let out a whoop of pure joy!

For the first time in her twenty-four years, she felt completely free. She closed her eyes and felt the soft caress of the wind on her face.

The next few weeks were going to change the course of her life forever!

CHAPTER THREE

ADAM TRIED TO MOVE his cramped muscles. He'd been hiding in a storage closet in the hold for forty-five minutes, according to the luminous face of his watch, and for the last fifteen the boat had been moving, cutting through the water at a pretty good clip. The *Marnie Lee* pitched and rolled as they traveled, and Adam guessed that the storm was stronger than the weather service had predicted. The force of the gale didn't seem to deter Simms though; he never turned about.

Good. The farther they were from Port Stanton, the better. Adam couldn't wait to see the look on Simms's face when he appeared on deck.

Adam gave Kent another fifteen minutes, then eased himself from the tight quarters. He'd stashed an overnight bag in the galley because he'd learned over the past year to be prepared for anything. He didn't know how long he'd be stuck with Kent—he hadn't worked that out yet. A lot depended upon Simms's attitude and what kind of deal they could cut, because Adam was sure that Kent Simms was up to his eyeballs in the embezzling mess. There was a chance that Simms hadn't been involved, but the probability was slim. From his overreaction at the sight of Adam, to his insistence that security be called, Simms looked guilty as hell. Yep,

Simms was hiding something. Adam just had to find out what it was and how it was tied to the embezzling.

He glanced up the stairs, felt the lash of rain and wind and decided to give Kent a couple more minutes while he changed. Tossing his bag into an empty cabin, he stripped out of his tux and slid into jeans, flannel shirt, sweater and high-tops. Finally he flung a black poncho over his head.

Using sea legs he'd acquired in the navy, he climbed up two flights to the bridge and twisted his lips into a grim smile at the thought of scaring the living hell out of Simms. If nothing else, Simms's reaction would be worth the rocky ride.

Flinging open the door of the bridge, he stopped stock-still. A blast of wind caught the door, ripping the door latch from his hands. Papers rustled and caught in the icy breeze. Marnie Montgomery, planted at the helm, nearly jumped out of her skin. With a scream that died in her throat, she whipped around and fumbled in the pocket of her jacket, presumably for a weapon. The helm spun crazily and the boat shuddered.

"Drake? What the hell are you doing here?" she cried, her face ashen, her hair blowing in the wind as she scrabbled to regain control of the spinning wheel. "You nearly gave me a heart attack!"

He was as stunned as she. Marnie? Here? At the wheel in the middle of a gale-force storm? The wind was fierce, the waters of the sound rolling and unpredictable.

"I asked you a question," she said, her blue eyes dark as the angry ocean. "And close the door, for crying out loud!"

Damn his rotten luck! Adam caught hold of the latch

and pulled the door shut behind him. The door slammed tight, shutting out the wind and rain.

Papers stopped blowing, and Marnie's blond hair fell back to her shoulders. "Well?"

His entire plan—spontaneous as it had been—depended upon getting Simms alone. Now he had to deal with Simms's angry lover. Terrific! Just damned terrific. "I'm looking for Kent Simms."

"Here?" she said, laughing bitterly. The disgusted look she sent him accused him of being out of his mind. "You expected him on board?"

"Isn't he?"

"Not if he has a brain," she muttered. Scowling, she added, "I think Kent's back at the hotel, living the good life, kissing up to my father." She turned her concentration back to the sea.

So she was still furious. Good. Her anger might work to his advantage, Adam thought. Now that he was on this pitching boat in the middle of a storm, he had to improvise his hasty plan, and though he wasn't quite sure how, he knew instinctively that any rift between Simms and Victor Montgomery's daughter was a good sign.

"What do you want with him?" she asked, never taking her eyes off the boat's prow.

"We need to talk."

"About what?" Her voice was casual, but he noticed a glint of suspicion in her gaze as she hazarded a quick glance in his direction. "No, don't tell me. Let me guess. This has something to do with the reason you crashed the party, doesn't it?"

When he didn't immediately respond, she plunged ahead. "And since I don't think you're interested in filling out a job application for Montgomery Inns, you must want to talk about the money that's missing from the Puget West project. Right?"

It galled him the way she talked about the embezzlement so flippantly. He'd gone through hell in the past twelve months, and she acted as though it didn't really matter, just a little inconvenience.

She wasn't finished. "If you want my advice—"

"I didn't come here for—"

"You should just get on with your life."

"I'm not here for advice."

"Then you shouldn't have stowed away on my boat."

Her boat? "The *Marnie Lee* belongs to Simms."

She smiled at that, and her face softened a little. Even under the harsh lights of the bridge, with her hair still wet and her face without a trace of makeup, she was a beautiful woman. "*Half* of the *Marnie Lee* belongs to Kent. Unfortunately for him, his half is nailed to my half and I decided to leave the party early."

"Why?"

She sent him another hard look, a line forming between her brows. "It was time," she replied, without giving him a clue to her motives.

"Does it have anything to do with your fight with Simms?"

Marnie started to answer, then held her tongue. *She* should be the person asking questions, not the other way around! What the devil was Drake doing on her boat? She felt nervous and hot, though the bridge was barely 50° F. Adam had always put her on edge; his angled features, thick hair and intense eyes fairly screamed "sexy," but she'd ignored his rakish good looks when she'd worked with him. She knew a lot of attractive men, but Adam was different. He was more than just simply handsome. There was a restlessness about him, an earthiness coupled with repressed anger that caused her to react to him on a primal level. Kent had called Adam primitive and for once he'd been right: there was a certain primal sexuality to the man.

So here he was, in the tiny bridge, a storm thundering outside, the boat lurching and tilting, and all she could think about was keeping distance between herself and him.

"You made a mistake," she said flatly.

"Just one?" One side of his mouth lifted.

Marnie gripped the helm and felt her palms dampen with sweat. All she wanted was to escape her past and sort out her identity. But now she had to deal with Adam Drake. Even though he had come to her rescue at the party, she didn't want him fouling up her first real bid for freedom. "Look, you've got to get off the boat."

"Why?"

"You're not part of my plan."

He snorted and tossed back the hood of his poncho. "We've got more in common than I thought. You weren't part of mine."

"Let's get one thing straight—we've got nothing in common."

He glanced at her sharply. "So you're a believer in the great lie, too. You really think I skimmed off money from the Puget West project."

"There's been no other explanation," she said, hedging.

"I was cleared, damn it!" In two swift strides he was so close to her that she noticed the gold flecks in his brown eyes. His nostrils flared in outrage.

"You weren't cleared," she said evenly, "there just wasn't enough evidence to indict you."

He drew in his breath sharply; the air whistled through his teeth. "Well, Miss Montgomery, I guess I was wrong about you. I thought you might be the one person in the entire Montgomery Inns empire that realized I'd been set up. But you're just like the rest, aren't you?"

"No, I'm different. I ended up with you as a stowaway. I didn't ask you to come on board, did I? As far as I'm concerned, you should get off my boat." She considered telling him that she'd stood up to her father and the board, declaring him innocent, but decided the truth, right now, was pointless.

Adam's gaze raked down her. "What do you want me to do? Walk the plank?"

"If only I had one." He could joke at a time like this? The man was incorrigible! There was a slight chance that he was a thief, and now he'd stowed away on the boat, proving that he obviously had no scruples whatsoever. And yet there had been a time when Marnie had relied upon his judgment, had trusted his interpretation of the facts. She had sat through many meetings with Adam in attendance. He always spoke his mind, arguing with her father when necessary. Unlike Kent, who worked diligently to have no mind of his own and think exactly like her father. The proverbial yes-man. She shivered at the thought that she'd once believed she loved him. She'd been a blind fool, a rich girl caught up in the fantasy of love.

The *Marnie Lee* groaned against the weight of a wave, and a tremor passed through the hull. The wheel slid through Marnie's fingers, and Adam grabbed hold of the helm, his arms imprisoning her as he strained against the wheel. "Only an idiot would sail in a storm like this," he muttered.

An idiot or someone hell-bent to have a life of her own, she thought angrily, surrounded by the smell of him. The scent of after-shave was nearly obscured by the fresh odor of water and ocean that clung to his skin. His hair gleamed under the fluorescent bulbs in the ceiling and his features were set into a hard mask as unforgiving as the sea.

"Do I have to remind you that you've shown up uninvited twice in one night? That must be some kind of record, don't you think?"

"I don't know what to think right now," he admitted, his eyebrows thrust together and deep lines of concentration etching his forehead, "but I sure as hell can come up with a hundred places I'd rather be."

"That makes two of us," she snapped, as his arms relaxed and he stepped back, giving her control of the vessel again. "We'll put into port at Chinook Harbor."

"That's where you're going?"

"It's a little out of the way." *But worth it, to get rid of you,* she thought unkindly. She didn't need any complications on this trip, and any way she looked at it, Adam Drake was a complication. He stepped away from her, and she commanded the boat again, glad for the feel of the polished wheel in her hands. A hundred questions plagued her. What did he want with Kent? Why had he stowed away? How involved in the embezzling was he? And why, oh Lord, why did she find him the least bit attractive? The man was trouble—pure and simple.

The storm didn't slow down for a minute. Harsh winds screamed across the deck and waves curled high to batter the hull repeatedly. Marnie's stomach spent most of the trip in her throat, and she didn't have time to consider Adam again. He made himself useful, helping read the charts and maps as they headed into the cluster of San Juan Islands.

Her plan was to drop him off in Chinook Harbor, spend the night on the boat, then, as soon as the storm passed, sail around the tip of the island to Deception Lodge, an antiquated resort her father wanted to restore. Making camp in a potential Montgomery Inn bothered her a little; the lodge still belonged to her father and as long as she was seeking shelter on Montgomery soil, she wasn't truly free.

"But soon," she muttered as she spied a few lights winking in the distance, lights that had to be on Orcas Island.

"But soon—what?"

She shot him a look that told him it was none of his business, and was about to turn inland when she spotted the buoy bobbing crazily ahead.

"Watch out," Adam commanded, but the sea swelled under the boat like a creature climbing from the depths. "Marnie, you're too close!"

Panicked, she checked the gauges. "Too close to what!"

CRACK! The *Marnie Lee* trembled violently, and for a second Marnie thought the boat was about to split apart.

"Damn it, woman, get out of the way." Adam shoved her aside and threw open the door.

"You can't go out…" Her voice was carried away by the cry of the wind.

"Just steer the boat, for God's sake!"

Horrified, still trying to set the *Marnie Lee* back on course, she watched as Adam tied a rope around his waist, then worked his way around the bow, rain beating on his head, his hands moving one over the other on the rail. He paused at the starboard side, leaned over, then braced himself as another swell rolled over the deck, engulfing him. Marnie's heart leaped to her throat. She saw the lifeline stretch taut. Her stomach lurched as the wave retreated and Adam, drenched, still braced against the force of the wave, appeared again.

"Thank God," she whispered, her throat raw, "Now, Drake, damn your stubborn hide, get below deck and dry out."

Another torrent of water washed over the deck and once again Adam vanished for a few terror-filled seconds. This time, when the water receded, he moved along the rail again before disappearing on the stairs.

She guided the ship by instinct; she'd learned sailing from her father years before. But all the while her nerves were strung tight, her ears cocked to the door.

Nearly ten minutes later, Adam returned to the bridge, dripping and coughing saltwater and glaring at her as if she were responsible for the storm. "There's a crack in the hull—a small one on the starboard side, on line with the galley," he said. "Not a big gash, but it's not going away. You're taking on water—slowly. I used some sealer I found downstairs, but it won't hold, at least not forever." His eyes were dark and serious. "You've got to turn inland."

"But there's no port for miles."

"You don't have a choice. The island's close enough. Just head for land. We'll worry about a harbor when we get closer." He picked up the microphone for the radio and started to call the Coast Guard, but Marnie flipped the switch, turning off his cry for help.

"We'll make it ourselves," she said, refusing, in her first few hours of freedom, to give up any small bit of her independence. "Besides, I think the storm's about over, the rain's stopping."

"Did you hear me, Marnie?" he demanded, ignoring her assessment of the situation. "Rain or no rain, sooner or later, this boat is going to sink like a stone. And we're going to sink with her."

"But not for a while. Right?"

"Unless we hit something else."

"How long do we have?"

"How the hell should I know?"

"Ten minutes? Twenty? Two hours?"

"Hell, I don't know, but you can't take a chance like this!"

"Why not?" she demanded, cranking hard on the wheel and checking the maps of the area again. They weren't far from her destination, the point where Deception Lodge was sprawled on high cliffs over the ocean. If she could beach the *Marnie Lee* soon, she wouldn't have to call for help and suffer the indignities of having Victor running to save her only to remind her that she wasn't yet ready to fly on her own wings. Well, damn it, he was wrong. And so was Adam Drake. "Don't tell me you're worried about your neck, Mr. Drake."

"No more than I am about yours." Sarcasm tainted his voice.

"Then help me get this boat to shore."

He eyed her for a minute. "And for that, I get what?"

"A bargain? Now, you want to bargain with me?"

she asked incredulously. She couldn't believe her ears. "Isn't staying alive enough?"

His lips curved crookedly. "Give me a little more incentive. My life this past year hasn't been that great."

Unbelievable! While the boat rocked beneath them, he wanted to barter. Marnie didn't have time. "Okay, okay already. So I'll owe you one," she said, furious until she saw the glint of satisfaction in his dark eyes.

"All right, Marnie. You steer. I'll keep the gash from getting any worse." He started for the door but stopped, glancing back over his shoulder, his hair falling over his eyes. "What is this, anyway—some sort of quest? What're you trying to prove?"

When she didn't answer, he strode out the door. Marnie wasn't about to confide in him; he could bloody well think what he wanted. After all, he hadn't been invited along. She owed him nothing. Not even an explanation. Besides, if anyone had an explanation coming, it was she. What the devil was he doing looking for Kent on this boat?

She struggled with the helm until her muscles began to ache. Then, as she turned east, the storm abated. Waves still washed over the deck, but the wrath of the storm was spent, the wind no longer keening over the black water. The clouds, which had so jealously covered the moon, thinned to become a gauzy filter for weak moonlight.

Squinting, Marnie saw the island, a huge black shape rising from the frothy swell of the ocean like a sea monster. They couldn't be far from Deception Point, she thought wildly, but in the darkness she couldn't see well enough to make out the rocky cliffs. No lights glowed in the dark, guiding her to a port, but she wasn't about to complain.

She slowed the engines, creeping in with the waves. In too close and she'd scrape bottom; too far out and they'd have a helluva fight in the life raft to get to shore.

Below decks, Adam heard, rather than felt, the change in speed. So they were going to dock. Finally. Victor's daughter had more guts than he would've given her credit for—maybe more guts than brains, considering the situation. He sealed the cut in the hull again with the sealer he'd found in a storage closet, and decided the craft wouldn't sink as long as she was stable. The gash was above the waterline and had only leaked when the boat had listed badly. Unless the sea rolled the *Marnie Lee* onto her starboard side again, the boat wouldn't settle to the bottom of the ocean. Or at least he hoped not.

So why hadn't she let him radio for help? What kind of game was she playing? Was she the kind of rich woman who needed thrills?

She'd always seemed so down-to-earth. Beautiful but never too flashy. Elegant but not extreme. So why the sudden boat trip in the middle of a storm? And why not call the Coast Guard?

Could Marnie Montgomery be a woman running from her past?

That particular thought intrigued him. He climbed the slippery steps to the bridge. Marnie barely glanced his way. "You'd better drop anchor," he said, checking the charts again. "Any closer and you're asking for trouble." His gaze slid to hers, and for an insane moment he thought he read more than anger in her stare. But that was crazy. As far as he knew, she hated him, thought he was a traitor to Daddy's precious company. She looked away, but not before he recognized female interest for what it was.

"Okay, let's do it." She released the anchor, and the boat settled, rolling with the tide but no longer listing.

Adam, still wondering about her reaction, worked on the inflatable life raft and loaded it with supplies.

"Get your things," he ordered when the raft was pumped up.

While she climbed to the lower cabin, he hurried back to the bridge and made a quick call to the Coast Guard. She'd be furious with him, but so be it, he thought, as he loaded his pockets with matches, flares and a first-aid kit he found in a cupboard beneath the radio.

Within minutes they were both in the life raft. Leaning his back into the oars, Adam rowed for shore. Marnie reached for the second set of oars, but he shook his head. The air was still cold, the wind still gusting, and he felt an unlikely sense of chivalry. "I can handle this. Relax."

"No reason," she said, her back stiffening as she threw her weight into the task.

Adam didn't argue with her. If she thought she was helping, fine. He wasn't up to another argument. Rowing backward, he watched her arms strain, the muscles of her back move fluidly. She wasn't a wimp by any stretch of the imagination, and he grudgingly admired her gameness. The *Marnie Lee,* lights blazing, was stark against the dark sky. They rowed without speaking; only the sound of the waves and the occasional burst of wind disturbed the silence as they approached the beach.

Adam dropped his oars, climbed over the side and

slid into the chest-deep icy water. Towing the raft inland, he said, "I radioed the Coast Guard."

She snapped her head around. "You did *what?*"

"I didn't think you'd want your father to worry, and the Guard needs to know about the *Marnie Lee.*"

"You had no right!" she cried, outraged.

"Probably not. And it's not that I care a lick about your dad. I just thought, from the looks of things, you wouldn't want him sending the cavalry after you. Hey—stop—you don't have to—"

But Marnie slid into the frigid sea and together they pulled the raft onto the beach.

"Anyone ever call you stubborn?"

She laughed a little, even though she was shivering.

Adam sized her up and realized he'd never really known her in the few years they'd worked together. "What is it with you, anyway, Montgomery? You've got a helluva chip on your shoulder."

"Isn't that a little like the pot calling the kettle black?" she threw back, her teeth chattering, as the two of them dragged the raft high onto the sand, away from the tide.

"Yeah, but I didn't grow up in the lap of luxury."

"Well, I did!" she replied, tossing her wet hair out of her eyes and reaching for her bags. "And that's the problem. Look, I'm not going to argue with you anymore. There's a lodge where I'm going to camp out for the night, and if you want to come along, fine. If not, I don't really care. It's about a two- or three-hour hike into town. That way—" She pointed the beam of her flashlight south. "Your choice." With that she grabbed the bags and started, with the aid of a flashlight, north along the beach.

Adam didn't ask any more questions. He didn't really give a damn. He was only interested in Marnie to further his cause. Period. Whether Miss Montgomery knew it or not, she was going to help him find out what happened to the missing half million dollars.

CHAPTER FOUR

SWEARING UNDER HIS BREATH, Victor Montgomery slammed down the phone in his suite. Damn Marnie and her stupid independence! His hands were shaking so badly, he stuffed them into his pockets. What was wrong with that girl? Downstairs in the lobby, two hundred of the most important people in the Northwest were milling through the hotel, sipping his champagne, toasting Montgomery Inns while Marnie could have lost her fool life! If she were here now, he'd wring her neck! Instead, he had to act as if nothing were wrong. As if his wayward daughter hadn't walked out of his life. As if he weren't worried sick about her.

"Problems?" Kate asked, smoothing his lapel with her long fingers and offering him an encouraging smile. Kate was a good woman, he thought, trying to get a handle on his emotions. At least *she* had enough sense to do what she was told!

"Marnie."

Kate raised an interested eyebrow and sighed. "She's almost twenty-five."

"And therefore can do anything she damned well pleases, is that it?"

"She's not a baby, Vic. You can't tie her down forever."

"I can try, damn it!" He shoved a hand through his

hair and wondered when he'd lost Marnie. And why? Hadn't he given her everything money could buy? Hadn't he put her through the best schools, hired the best nannies, spent as much time with her as he possibly could have? If only Vanessa were still alive. Maybe then...

"Senator Mann's waiting for you," Kate reminded him gently. She refilled his glass and handed him the fresh drink.

"I know, I know, probably hoping for a campaign contribution," Victor grumbled.

Kate chuckled deep in her throat. "Probably."

Still worried about Marnie, Victor took a swallow of the whiskey and waited for the fiery warmth to settle in his stomach. Maybe then he'd calm down. He thought about confiding in Kate but didn't. He'd never confided in a woman except his wife. Even Marnie hadn't heard his worries or dreams, not really. God, he missed Vanessa. She'd been gone so long...

Pulling himself back to the present, he touched Kate affectionately on the shoulder. "Tell the senator I'll be down in a minute and send in Kent, will you?"

"Of course." With another smile, she swept out of the room in a billow of familiar perfume and white silk. A beautiful woman, he thought. A gracious woman. A woman he could live with. If it weren't for the memory of Vanessa.

Adjusting his cuffs, he glanced in the mirror and frowned at his reflection. He was getting old. Not that fifty-seven was near the end of the line, but more than a few crow's-feet were carved near his eyes and his hair was thinner and whiter than it once had been. His weight was starting to become a problem, and sometimes, damn it, he just felt tired.

As he grew older, he wanted more from life than a string of hotels, not that the business wasn't important. It was. But he wanted, *needed,* a daughter who worked with him, a daughter who was happily married, a daughter who would become the mother of the grandchildren he intended to spoil rotten.

A quick rap on the door and Kent, not one hair out of place, strode into the suite. Shutting the door behind him, he turned back to Victor. "Kate said you wanted to see me." He flashed his easygoing smile.

Victor liked Kent. The boy was so eager. He reminded Victor of himself twenty-five years before. Waving the younger man into a chair, he said, "It's about Marnie."

The all-American smile faded as Kent sat down. "I thought she left."

"She did. And apparently she took the *Marnie Lee* with her."

"What!" Kent blanched and leaped back to his feet. Then he sank back into his chair. "But she couldn't have," he said, one hand rubbing the opposite forearm.

"I just got a call from the Coast Guard—"

"Oh, my God, there's been an accident!"

"Marnie's fine," Victor assured the younger man, though Kent didn't seem relieved. In fact he appeared more agitated than ever. Well, he'd just had a helluva shock. Hadn't they all? Victor poured Kent a stiff shot and handed him the glass. The drink shook in the boy's hands.

"What happened?" Kent asked, tossing back most of the bourbon.

"As I said, Marnie took off in the *Marnie Lee*. She thinks she owns half of it, you know. And really she does. I did give it to the both of you as an engagement present."

"So that gives her the right to take off and leave me stranded?" Kent asked, dumbfounded. "God, what's gotten into her?"

"She wants to be independent."

"But it's like a damned hurricane out there." Kent strode to the windows and stared out at the gloomy night.

"Well, it's not quite that bad," Victor said, though he halfheartedly agreed with the man he'd hoped would become his son-in-law. "But Marnie has this…thing—ambition, if you will…to be her own woman. She tried to resign, but I talked her into taking a leave of absence instead, and she's off to, quote, 'find herself.' Whatever the devil that means."

"In the *Marnie Lee*." Kent yanked hard on his tie, and his face became a mask.

"The boat's in a little trouble," Victor admitted. "At least that's what the man said."

"Trouble?" Kent said, alarm flashing in his eyes.

Victor was touched. Despite anything Marnie said to the contrary, Kent Simms loved her. "Nothing serious, but it could have been."

"Wait a minute," Kent said, his eyes narrowing. "What man are you talking about—someone from the Coast Guard?"

Victor sighed. "Well, no. I heard it from the Guard, of course, a Captain Spencer, but he was radioed by some man, a passenger Marnie had on board."

"*Passenger?* This just gets better and better, doesn't

it? So now she's with some man! Good God, Victor, what's going on?" Kent finished his drink and wiped the back of his hand over his lips.

"I don't know." Victor tugged thoughtfully on his lower lip. Kent's worries infected him again. He'd half calmed himself down, but now he felt a rush of concern as Kent poured himself another drink and paced from the windows to the door.

"I don't like this, Victor. I don't like it at all." He tossed back his second bourbon in two swallows.

"Neither do I."

"She's been acting crazy lately." Kent jammed his hand through his hair in frustration. "I wonder who the devil is with her."

"I wish I knew." Swirling his own drink, Victor asked, "Maybe this new independent streak has something to do with why you two broke up."

Kent shook his head. "It's been coming for a long time," he said, effectively closing the subject. "Do you have any idea where she put into port?"

"That's a problem. The boat is anchored off Orcas Island, the westerly side. My guess is that she plans to spend the night camping on the beach or…"

"Or what?" Then Kent appeared to understand. "You think she may be holed up in Deception Lodge."

"Quite possibly."

"Then let's go get her." Kent strode to the door, eager to charge off and retrieve his lost maiden.

Victor admired the boy's spunk, but he motioned him back into the room. "It's just not that easy. I promised Marnie I wouldn't interfere."

Kent's mouth went slack with disbelief. "So you're

letting her—and this *man*—hang out alone in the lodge?"

"Yes." Victor drained his glass as he remembered the determination in his daughter's fine chin. And the *man,* whoever he was, had had the decency to call the Coast Guard. His curiosity was burning as to the man's identity. Victor nevertheless decided that this time he had to trust Marnie. Though she hadn't spoken of a male passenger on the boat, she was entitled to live her own life.

"You can't just let Marnie and some guy shack up in Deception Lodge!"

"I don't think I've got any other choice."

"But you're her father," Kent protested, his face flushed, his lips thin and hard.

"That's the problem."

THE LODGE OCCUPIED a long stretch of the headlands, three rambling stories of sloping roofs and shingled gables. Most of the windows were still intact, Marnie noted, as she swung the beam of her flashlight over the weathered siding and covered porch. Only a few glass panes had been boarded over. The old structure had once been grand, a unique out-of-the-way retreat for those who spent their summers in the San Juan Islands.

Now the lodge's grandeur was little more than a memory. One creaky shutter banged against the wall, and the porch sagged a bit at the northerly end. Dry leaves rustled as they blew against the door.

"Needs a little work," Adam remarked, eyeing the rustic old building as he set his bags on the creaky floorboards of the porch.

"Nothing the Montgomery touch can't fix." She fit a key from her ring into the heavy lock chained across the double doors and twisted. The lock held firm for a second before springing open. Marnie let the chain fall to the porch and shoved open the doors.

Inside, she swung the beam of her flashlight over the lobby. Yellowed pine paneling dominated the room. There was a massive rock fireplace and all around the room, scattered like leaves in the wind, were tables with upside-down chairs stacked atop them. Furniture, draped in sheets, had been shoved into one corner of the cavernous lobby.

"You planned on staying here?" Adam asked, scanning the dusty interior with a grimace.

"Just for a few days." The beam of light dancing ahead of her, she walked to the wall behind the desk and found a bank of light switches. She flipped each switch in turn, but nothing happened. The room was still dark except for the pale lights from their flashlights.

"You're staying until…"

"Until I figure out my next destination."

"Another Montgomery Inn?"

She threw him a dubious smile over her shoulder. "No."

Adam rubbed the crick from his neck, and Marnie could feel his eyes following her. She couldn't quite figure him out. Sometimes she felt as if there were a hidden side to him, as if he were, as her father claimed, evil. Victor had told her often enough in the past year that Adam Drake was a predator, always on the move, ready to stalk his next prey.

She wasn't anxious to believe her father's opinion that Adam was such a lowlife. From her own dealings with him, she'd found Adam Drake to be honest and hardworking. He'd been tough, but Adam's toughness, mixed with pure cunning, had worked many deals in her father's favor. In those days Victor had praised Adam Drake for his ruthlessness, for his sense of knowing "when to make the kill."

So was he really a wolf in sheep's clothing? Or a man who'd been turned into a scapegoat? Marnie wondered if she'd ever know the answer. Not that it mattered. Adam was an inconvenience for one night. Nothing more.

"So this is Victor's next project," he mused, running the beam of his flashlight over the staircase and upper balcony. Cobwebs caught in the light, and dust swirled in the illumination.

"One of many." Spying a short hallway that separated the bar from the kitchen, Marnie headed toward the back of the lodge. She remembered seeing blueprints of this place in her father's office and had listened with interest as Victor had expounded on the "renovation and rejuvenation" of the old lodge where he'd spent many happy summers as a boy.

Following the bobbing trail of the flashlight, she walked briskly down the hallway and found the door she was looking for, a door, according to the aged drawings of Deception Lodge, where a narrow flight of steps led to the wine cellar. She pulled on the knob, but the door wouldn't budge. "Great," she muttered, setting her flashlight down and grabbing the old knob in both hands. The door wasn't locked, she thought, just swollen in its frame. She tugged hard, throwing her weight backward. Finally the old wood gave and she nearly fell as the door popped open. The dank smell of water seeping through cement permeated the air, but she found what she was looking for: an electrical panel.

Crossing her fingers, she threw the switch and immediately the old lodge was awash with light. "Bingo," she whispered, before trying to find a thermostat for the furnace. Certainly there was one somewhere. She walked through the back halls until she discovered not one thermostat, but three, one for each floor of the old building. She flipped the switch, and heard a clang and rumble as the furnace for the first floor kicked on. "Two for two," she told herself, smiling with satisfaction as she dusted her hands on her jeans. Now, if only her father didn't rush out here in a panic when he received a call from the Coast Guard. Facing Victor again tonight wasn't in her plan.

Nor was Adam Drake, for that matter. What in the world was she going to do with him? He didn't seem inclined to leave her, and she experienced ambivalent feelings about his being here. Sure, she could use the company and he'd helped her save the *Marnie Lee,* she thought guiltily, but he cramped her style as far as her independence was concerned. She could hardly claim to be a self-reliant woman when a man had linked up with her.

"But only for one night," she reminded herself again. "Tomorrow he's history." If the *Marnie Lee* could limp into harbor, she'd take Mr. Drake back to civilization, put the boat up for repairs, then wait until the *Marnie Lee* and the weather cooperated.

And where will you go? she asked herself for what seemed to be the ten thousandth time. Alaska? Hawaii? L.A.? Mexico? "Wherever I want to," she muttered as she made her way back to the lobby.

Adam hadn't been idle. He'd stacked yellowed newspapers in the grate, and with the help of a few dry leaves and a chunk of fir, attempted to light a fire. He struck a match and held it to the tinder-dry fuel. The leaves and paper caught instantly, and flames crackled over the dry logs.

Marnie caught him leaning back on his heels, surveying his work and warming his palms against the small heat. His poncho had been discarded, hung on a peg by the front door, and his wet shirt clung to him like a second skin. His hair was beginning to dry, but still shined beneath the light shed from the wagon-wheel chandeliers suspended overhead.

He glanced her way when she entered, and rose to his feet. "Success," he said, motioning toward the sconces mounted against the walls.

"Some. At least we'll have light and heat, though I don't know about the furnace. There might not be much oil in the tank. But so far," she said, crossing her fingers, "it's humming along."

"All the comforts of home." His eyes met hers, and his expression turned jaded. "Well, at least all the comforts of *my* home. I can't speak for yours."

"Are you going to badger me for the night? If so, you may as well start walking. There's a town a few miles down the road."

"Believe me, *you* weren't part of my plan."

"Then we've got something in common."

"I doubt it."

Boy, did he know how to get under her skin. "For your information, not that it matters, until today I lived with my father."

"And now?"

She lifted a shoulder. "I guess I don't have a home."

"Unless you count the waterfront condominium in Seattle?"

"My father signed the lease."

"But you lived there."

"It wasn't mine."

"What about the Tudor on Lake Washington?"

"My father's."

"So you *are* on some kind of independence kick, aren't you?" His eyes narrowed dangerously before he turned and using a long stick, prodded the fire. "The poor little rich girl. Had to leave all Daddy's money, but had no other means of transportation than her yacht. Sorry, Marnie, it just doesn't wash."

"Then what do you think I'm doing?"

"Having a temper tantrum—an adult temper tantrum, but a tantrum nonetheless."

"And you," she said, shoving her hands in her pockets and crossing the room to show him that she wasn't the least bit frightened of him, though in truth, he did scare her. "What're you doing?"

"Just lookin' for the truth."

"From me?"

"You'll have to do," he said, beginning to unbutton his shirt. "I'd really hoped that I could deal with Simms tonight." She watched his fingers as the buttons slid through their holes, and the back of her throat turned desert-dry. What was he doing? Stripping? Right in front of her?

He didn't seem the least self-conscious as he said, "I have to admit, getting the truth from Simms isn't likely to happen. But you... I don't know." His shirt was halfway unbuttoned, revealing a hard chest with curling black hair and tanned skin stretched taut over corded muscles.

"What do you want to know?" she asked, forcing her eyes back to his face and flushing when she caught just the trace of amusement in his eyes.

"Everything."

Oh, God, he was pulling his shirttails from his jeans and slipping his arms from the sleeves! His torso was rock-hard and solid, the muscles moving fluidly as he tossed the shirt over the fireplace screen and positioned the screen in front of the grate.

Marnie let out the breath she hadn't even realized she'd been holding. He was only drying out his clothes. Of course. And in the back of her mind she'd half expected him to try to seduce her. What an idiot she was! He wasn't interested in her sexually.

And she wasn't interested in him. Yet her gaze kept wandering to his chest and the sinewy strength of his arms.

"What do you think Kent could tell you?"

"How he embezzled the money."

"Kent?" She turned her gaze back to his face to see if he was joking, but his features were stone-sober. "Embezzle?"

"Why not?"

"And jeopardize his future with the company? No way." Marnie shook her head. She'd seen Kent Simms in a new light these past few weeks, and she knew that nothing was more important to Kent than his position at Montgomery Inns. Tonight had proved it.

Snakes! They were both snakes! Victor and Kent. "Five hundred thousand dollars isn't enough for Kent to risk everything." She rubbed her chin thoughtfully, inadvertently smudging her jaw with dirt. "In fact, I wouldn't think he'd do it for a million."

"A half million is a lot of money."

"Not to Kent's way of thinking," she said bitterly.

Adam sat on the hearth and took off his shoes. Water dripped onto the floor. "You're not very kind to your fiancé."

"Ex-fiancé," she said swiftly.

"Lovers' spat?"

"Something like that." She didn't see any reason to confide in Adam. She hadn't even told her father about Kent's infidelity and might never. Kent's betrayal was too humiliating. To keep looking busy, she found a mossy log propped against the hearth and tossed it onto the fire. The moss ignited in a spit of flames. She barely glanced at Adam again, afraid she'd already said too much, afraid her eyes would wander over his broad expanse of naked skin. "So are you going to get dressed?" she asked, unable to keep the irritation from her voice.

"Do I bother you?"

"Yes!" She spun on her heel and felt her cheeks go warm as she saw the firelight play against his skin.

His gaze touched hers for a heartbeat, then he walked, barefoot, leaving wet footprints in the dust, to the door, where his bag was lying open, and withdrew a shirt—the same white shirt he'd worn to the party. Rumpled silk and muddy denim—a new fashion statement.

"So why do I bother you, Marnie? You think I'm a thief?"

"I don't know what to think," she admitted. "All I want to do is get through this night."

"If I took the money, why would I show up at Victor's party, hmm?" He finished tucking his shirt into his Levi's and looked up at her, his dark eyes intense and probing.

"Maybe you want to clear your name so that you can dupe someone else into hiring you."

"No way. I'm through working for someone else." He smiled coldly. "I guess I'm on an independence kick, too. You know, Marnie, we're more alike than I'd ever guessed." Laughing bitterly at his own joke, he reached for her bag and tossed it to her. "You should change, too. Wouldn't want Victor's daughter to catch her death."

"I didn't say I was on an independence kick."

"Aren't you?" He regarded her so intensely that she was uncomfortable.

"I'm just taking a vacation."

"Sure. In the middle of a tempest."

Rather than get caught in this argument, she grudgingly took his advice and decided to change. Her shoes squished and her jeans and sweatshirt were soaked in seawater. Shooting him an angry glare, she carried her bag to the restroom behind the lobby desk.

The sinks were dirty and stained. She twisted on a knob, but no water flowed from the spigot. "Give me strength," she prayed, stripping out of her wet clothes and tossing on a dry pair of jeans and a sweater.

When she finally returned to the lobby, she found Adam had moved a couple of old couches close to the fire. "I figured we needed something to sleep on," he explained.

Sleep. She doubted she'd even close her eyes tonight. She ran her fingers over the back of an old, dusty couch. Sleep would be impossible while lying this close to a man who had nearly been indicted for embezzling from her father, a man who had the nerve to stow away on her boat, a man who was too damned virile for his own good.

THIS WAS GETTING him nowhere, Adam thought darkly. He hazarded a glance at Marnie asleep on the other couch, her hair falling in a lustrous blond wave against her cheek, her breathing deep and even. She'd told him nothing. Nothing!

Disgusted, he rolled over, biting back an epithet at the broken spring that was poking into his back. Somehow he had to convince Marnie that he wasn't the enemy, that she could trust him, that she should open up to him. But how? She was angry with Simms and her father right now; maybe he could play upon that. If he could just keep her with him, there was even a chance that he could pretend interest in her. Most women couldn't resist male attention, but Marnie Montgomery wasn't most women.

And she, though she claimed otherwise, could still be involved with Simms. A slow smile spread across his chin at the thought of making love to her, at claiming Simms's woman for his own. But as soon as the thought came, he shoved it aside. Though making love to Marnie held a certain appeal, he wasn't into primal male urges. Seducing her to get back at Simms was beneath even him.

He'd done his share of womanizing years before, and nothing good had come of it. He'd grown up on the wrong side of the tracks in Chicago, been raised by an elderly aunt whom he'd easily duped and had gotten into more trouble with the law than he should have. Along the way there had been girls and women, and not one face he could remember.

The minor scrapes with the law had convinced his aunt that Adam needed more direction, and he'd been forced to sign a hitch in the navy, where he'd spent four years finding out how tough life could really be.

From the navy he'd gone on to college, where he'd met more women—coeds. By this time, he'd figured out that most women were more trouble than they were worth, always after something.

After graduation, he'd landed a job with a hotel in Cleveland and been transferred to San Francisco, where he'd caught the eye of Victor Montgomery.

The rest was history. From the time he'd been hired on with Montgomery Inns, Adam had thought his life was right on course. Victor had taken to him, and Adam's quick rise up the corporate ladder had surpassed all of his contemporaries, including Kent Simms.

Kent, who had been with the company longer than Adam and had graduated at the top of his class at Stanford, had never liked Adam Drake. Simms had let Adam know more than once that he didn't approve of Adam's less-than-conventional methods of business.

Adam had never cared much for Simms, either, though he hadn't given the man much thought. And he'd never considered Simms capable of anything more devious than greed. Raised in an upper-middle-class family, Kent had always been seduced by money—he'd had a taste of it growing up in California, but he'd always hungered for real wealth.

However, Adam doubted Kent had the guts to sabotage Adam's career just to gain more favor with Victor. The plan could too easily have backfired.

No, subterfuge wasn't Kent's style. However, wooing Victor's daughter was right in character. Adam didn't think Kent was capable of love—and in that respect they were twin spirits. Adam thought love was over-rated and probably nonexistent. However, he imag-ined Kent's supposed love of Marnie was tied up in the golden ribbon of Montgomery wealth.

Snorting in disgust, he rolled over again. This time he faced her, saw the firelight play upon the slope of her cheek. He noticed the sweep of her lashes and the regular rise and fall of her chest, as if she hadn't a care in the world.

Poor little rich girl, he thought again, the unhappy princess. With a soft sigh, she flung one arm out, and the old bedding they'd scrounged from an upper hall was tossed aside. Though fully dressed, her sweater was untucked, exposing a slice of abdominal flesh that, even in repose, appeared taut and nubile.

Stop it! He squeezed his eyes shut. *Enough!* He had to quit thinking of her as a woman—she was Victor Montgomery's daughter. Nothing more.

All he had to do was get through tonight and use her tomorrow. Find out what she knew about the embez-zling scam and get the hell out!

CHAPTER FIVE

OPENING ONE EYE, Marnie noticed an old coffeepot nestled in the warm coals of the fire. On the hearth, a half-full jar of instant coffee, two spoons and a few ceramic cups had been set out.

A gift from Adam? she wondered, stretching and rubbing the sleep from her eyes. She glanced at his couch, found it empty, and blinked herself awake. Her mouth tasted rotten, and she felt dirty and grimy. A cup of coffee would help.

As she twisted off the cap of the jar, she thought about Adam. He must've found the utensils in the kitchen, though the coffee and the water to make it with had obviously come from the galley of the *Marnie Lee*.

So why the uncharacteristic act of kindness? He needn't have troubled himself. Stretching her cramped shoulders and neck, she looked around the room, half expecting to see him, though she could tell by the atmosphere in the lodge—the silence and the cold, stagnant air—that he wasn't around. But he'd be back. His bags were still by the front door, and his clothes, stiff and dirty, were strung across a fireplace screen. Only his poncho and beat-up running shoes were missing. He might just be outside searching for more firewood, or walking to the nearest town to phone for help.

Or maybe not. He hadn't exactly made a beeline to

get off the boat when he'd found her at the wheel. Sure, there'd been a storm, and he couldn't have done anything but stay on board, and yet once he'd gotten over the shock of discovering her on board, he hadn't been in a hurry to abandon her.

Not that she cared, she told herself as she poked at the smoldering logs. Right now, Adam Drake was just extra baggage.

She grabbed the handle of the metal pot and sucked in her breath as she burned her fingers. Dropping the kettle, she stuck her fingers in her mouth. Some of the water spilled onto the coals, hissing loudly. "Son of a... gun!" she muttered, shaking her hand to cool her reddened skin. "Smooth move, Marnie. Real smart. Now you know why you should have been a Boy Scout!"

One step backward for independence, she thought wryly as she glanced over her shoulder, half expecting Adam to appear on the balcony and laugh at her. But there wasn't so much as the scrape of leather on the dusty floorboards, not the flicker of a shadow. He'd obviously taken off early this morning while she'd slept. Lord, she must've been dead to the world. Hard to believe. Marnie Montgomery, the world's greatest insomniac, sleeping as if drugged, while a strange man—perhaps a thief—was stretched out only a few feet away. She hadn't even surfaced when he'd rattled around with the coffeepot.

Slowly the pain in her hand retreated to a dull ache. She wondered about Adam and his cockamamy story. Why unearth all that scandal about the embezzling again? Was he really so innocent that it mattered? The fire popped, and she kicked at a spark that spewed onto the hearth. Adam Drake, the eternal mystery and bane of Montgomery Inns.

What would her father say? She could picture Victor now, his face suffused in red, his lower lip trembling in rage when she told him she'd spent the night with Adam Drake. It would be better if Victor never knew. After all, this whole trip was about her bid for freedom, wasn't it?

Wrapping her hand in an old towel, she picked up the coffeepot more carefully this time and poured a stream of hot water into the chipped cup. Steam rolled from the hot water as she stirred in a spoonful of the dark crystals. The smell of coffee mingled with the scent of burning wood, and surprisingly, she relaxed, sipping from her cup.

Despite a night on a lumpy, dusty couch, no food for hours, the feel of grit against her skin and her disturbing companion, Marnie Montgomery felt better than she had in a long, long time. She was on her way to being her own woman, she could feel it in her bones. Tucking her knees to her chin, she cradled her cup and let the steam caress her face.

For years she had craved adventure. And now, feeling the hot coffee burn down her throat, she'd gotten the adventure of a lifetime. With some twists she hadn't expected. Between last night's storm and Adam Drake, all her plans had been shot to shreds. And the surprising part was, she wasn't even worried.

She, who had fussed that every press release, every meeting, every party be perfect down to the very tiniest detail. She, who had spent hours color-coordinating napkins and linen, balloons and flower arrangements, seeking out opinions from Rose Trullinger, her father's interior decorator. She'd labored over brochures, and if one line wasn't to her liking, she'd insisted it be fixed. At the news conferences she'd been poised, every hair in place, wearing expensive suits, her speeches prepared to the letter.

And why wouldn't she be a perfectionist? After her mother's death she'd been raised by several nannies, all of whom had assured her that to win her father's approval she should be the new "lady" of Montgomery Manor, the little girl who acted like an adult. Miss Ellison, her favorite nanny, the one who had marched into her father's palatial home a week after her mother had died, had taught eleven-year-old Marnie how to fold her napkin on her lap, which utensil to eat with, and how to write proper thank-you notes on her engraved stationery. Never was she to wear anything wrinkled or soiled, and no dress could be worn twice to a Montgomery Inn function.

Her education had been planned since her birth, and though at college she'd rebelled a little and worn her jeans one whole week without washing them, all her lessons were so deeply ingrained that she was still the epitome of social decorum.

If it hadn't been for those summer vacations with her father, when he taught her how to fish and swim and steer a boat, she might have turned into the perfect little angel Miss Ellison had tried to mold.

No wonder a man like Kent had been attracted to her…and repulsed. The Ice Maiden, as she'd heard herself called on more than one occasion.

Spontaneity hadn't been a part of her vocabulary. Until she'd written her letter of resignation to her father. Well, she'd certainly changed. Almost overnight. She swallowed a smile when she thought of feisty, birdlike Miss Ellison. In her own way, Marnie had loved the pert Englishwoman with her smooth, implacable expression and warm eyes that were always partially hidden behind rimless glasses. Miss Ellison had been kind and warm to Marnie, though unbending in her perception of who Victor Montgomery's daughter should be. Miss Ellison's interpretation was that Marnie was to become the princess of Montgomery Inns and heir to the throne—that worn boardroom chair now occupied by Marnie's father. Of course, Miss Ellison had anticipated that Marnie would marry well, and her husband, the new prince of the Montgomery empire, would be handsome and intelligent and kind and ride up on his white charger to swoop Marnie away.

With a short laugh, Marnie glanced down at her hands and noticed the small wedges of dirt beneath her nails. If only Miss Ellison could see her now. How appalled the tiny Englishwoman would be. Miss Ellison had never approved of Victor teaching Marnie how to tie a half hitch, use a jackknife or site a gun. In fact, Miss Ellison would have been absolutely apoplectic if she could have witnessed Marnie last night as she'd attempted to steer her boat through the driving rain and howling wind.

As for Adam Drake, surely Miss Ellison would cluck her tongue and find him "…entirely unsuitable! Too earthy, darling, too dangerous. Mark my words, he's the type of man who uses women to get what he wants. And we all know that he was involved in that nasty business with your father. Stole from him, he did. No matter what the court decided. You can see it in his eyes. He's no good. No *breeding,* you know. I don't trust him. Not at all…"

Marnie rotated her cup in her hands and pondered her situation. Standing, she stretched her spine and heard the bones in her back pop. The first order of business, she realized with a frown, was to get rid of Adam Drake. She didn't want him and he didn't want her. He had been shocked to his socks to find her behind the helm last night. At the thought of his stricken, rain-washed face, she smiled. He'd been ready to tear Kent limb from limb, and he'd ended up facing Victor Montgomery's daughter.

She finished her coffee, poured another cup and wondered what Adam hoped to learn by talking to Kent. Kent knew nothing of the embezzlement; he'd even admitted feeling foolish having not discovered the discrepancies in the books himself. Fortunately, Kate Delany, Victor's ever-vigilant assistant, had noticed that certain receipts hadn't balanced with actual checks and that the computer entries had been tampered with.

Kent had been flabbergasted. He'd never been fond of Adam, that much was true. They were both too competitive, and Adam had always outshined Kent.

Marnie thought back to those days when she'd been in business meetings with Adam. He'd been the apple of her father's eye. Always on the lookout for a new hotel site, first with the figures on the competition. He had a way of explaining a future project so that everyone in the room understood him.

Adam had been popular with the employees, especially the women, who found his hard edge and competitive spirit a challenge. Even Marnie had considered him attractive, though she hadn't let him know it. No, until Kent had started wooing her so relentlessly, she'd made it a personal policy not to date anyone remotely connected with the company. If only she had stuck with her own unwritten law and never gone out with Kent.

Refusing to dwell on the humiliation that being engaged to Kent Simms had caused, she walked onto the front porch, half expecting to find Adam, but he was nowhere to be seen. She strolled across the wet beach grass of the headland and stared down sheer cliffs to the restless sea churning wildly over fifty feet below. Angry blue gray waves pounded the rocky shoreline, sending up a salty spray that smelled of brine and kelp. Sea gulls floated on the gusts high overhead, and far in the horizon, blending eerily into the fog, fishing boats trolled the waters.

Knowing the fishermen were out there comforted her a little. She and Adam weren't entirely alone in this deserted stretch of the islands. But she was free. Looking south, she spotted the *Marnie Lee,* not listing, thank God, but rocking gently on the swells. The boat's white hull gleamed in the morning's gray light. She thought she spied the inflatable raft riding the waves near the yacht and realized Adam had gone back to the boat, probably to check the damage to the craft. For a heart-stopping second, she wondered if he intended to take off and leave her stranded. Panic seized her, but she forced herself to calm down. If Adam's intention had been to abandon her and steal the boat, he could have left at any time last night. And he probably wouldn't have taken the time to leave hot water and coffee for her. Relaxing, she realized that whether she liked it or not, she had no choice but to trust him.

Her brows drew together. Trust a man her father considered a traitor of the worst order? "This could get messy," she thought aloud.

She considered Adam again. There was certainly something dangerous about him, a hidden side to him that was as dark as it was ruthless. A fascinating side.

So THIS WAS WHERE Simms spent his hours away from the office, Adam thought harshly as he eyed the largest cabin on the *Marnie Lee*. He scowled at the brass fittings, oiled teak furniture, all bolted down, of course, and the silk bedspread and sheets. Yep, Simms really knew how to live in style.

With Marnie.

How many hours had Marnie spent lying in this very bed, making love to Simms? Adam's stomach clenched, and a sour taste inched up his throat. She claimed she was through with Simms, and Adam was inclined to believe her. And yet, she'd once been Kent Simms's lover, had once intended to become his wife. "No accounting for bad taste," he muttered, leaving the room and ignoring the pounding in his head at the thought of Marnie and Simms making love. It wasn't any of his business. Period. She was Victor's daughter and Simms's ex-fiancée. Nothing more.

She might have information that would help him get to the bottom of the embezzling scam, but then again, she might know nothing of the vanished half million. He'd have to find out one way or another because he was running out of time. Brodie, Peterson and the rest of that particular investment group had slipped through his fingers. And the next group would, too, unless he proved himself innocent.

He made his way to the galley. Checking his handiwork on the hull, he noted the *Marnie Lee* seemed watertight. She wasn't in any immediate danger of sinking, which was good, because the plan that was forming in his mind wouldn't work unless the boat remained afloat.

He grabbed some more provisions, clean towels and a couple of sleeping bags. Up in the bridge he radioed the Coast Guard again, this time identifying himself at the captain's insistence and explaining that he and Marnie would be taking the boat in for repairs as soon as possible. He asked for the weather report and was told that there wasn't another storm front coming in for at least three days.

"It's supposed to be overcast, a little rain, but nothing serious for a while," Captain Spencer assured him. "You sure you don't need any assistance?"

"I'll call if there's trouble. We'll put up at Chinook Harbor within a couple of days," Adam replied, his mind spinning the lies that were part of his scheme.

"Anything else?"

Adam thought for a second and smiled slowly, gripping the microphone until his hands ached. "Just one more thing," he said slowly. "Pass the word along to Victor Montgomery at the Puget West in Port Stanton. If you can't reach him there, he's probably at corporate headquarters in Seattle. Tell him that I'm with Marnie and we're both fine. We'll spend a couple of days up at Deception Lodge while the boat is being repaired. I wouldn't want him to worry about his daughter."

"Will do, Mr. Drake. I'll let him know you radioed."

"Thanks," Adam said, wondering if Victor would show up in the company helicopter to personally throw Adam out of the lodge and make sure that Marnie's virtue remained intact. After all, in Victor's opinion, Marnie was keeping company with a thief and traitor—the very devil himself. That thought warmed the cockles of Adam's vengeful heart. There was a chance that Victor would confide in Simms, and Simms, outraged that his lady fair was in the hands of a criminal, would come charging up to the island as well. That would be even better.

Adam would be waiting. But he had to convince Marnie to spend another couple of days in the lodge. That shouldn't be too hard; he'd just have to lie a little, and lying was becoming easier all the time. As he saw the situation, he was battling for his reputation, for his ability to make a living. He thought of the California investors who'd dismissed him so summarily. Brodie had said it all. "We can't very well hand over several million dollars until we're absolutely certain that what happened over at Montgomery Inns won't happen to us."

So Adam had to clear his name, and the only man who had been able to help him at all had been Gerald Henderson. But even Henderson's information had been sketchy. Gerald had been a CPA and worked in accounting with Fred Ainger. He was convinced that Adam was innocent, but Adam hadn't been able to pry any more information out of him. Either Gerald didn't know who the guilty parties were or he was afraid of retribution.

Adam's back was to the wall. And if he had to lie to Marnie to get what he wanted, so be it. It only followed that if he had to use Marnie as bait to get to her father, that's what he would do. After all, it wasn't as if he were putting her in any danger. But once she discovered that he'd deceived her, all hell was sure to break loose.

He only hoped it happened after he got his audience with Simms or Victor Montgomery.

MARNIE COMBED HER wet hair. Shampooing had been difficult without hot water. She'd had to heat water on the fire, then she'd sponged all the dirt from her skin. She was drying her hair near the flames when she heard

Adam's tread on the porch. The door burst open and he strode in, as grungy as she was clean, and deposited a huge bag on the floor.

"You brought more supplies?" she asked, eyeing the bag.

"Everything I could carry."

"But why? We're leaving…" Her voice faded as she understood. "Something's not wrong with the *Marnie Lee,* is it?"

"She'll be fine," Adam said easily. "But there's another storm brewing—might be worse than the last. The Coast Guard advised us to stay put."

She dropped her comb, her hair forgotten as she glanced at the window and the overcast day beyond. "Another storm?" she said, her heart sinking at the thought of being cooped up with Adam any longer. His restless energy made her nervous, and the way he stared at her, as if trying to read her mind, bothered her. "You called the Guard again?"

"Mmm." He was unpacking the bags, laying out more food and supplies on the hearth. "I thought I should explain our position. And I wanted an updated weather report."

"It would be better if you hadn't," she said, walking to the window where she balanced a knee against the sill and rubbed her arms. The horizon was bleak. The waters seemed lonely. Where once she'd spied three fishing boats, now only one trolled the steely depths.

As a young girl she'd spent a lot of time on the ocean. Her father had taught her to read the weather's slightest signals. A fragile breeze stirred the branches of fir trees near the lodge, but the sky was far from dark.

"When's this storm supposed to hit?" she asked, trying to keep the suspicion from her voice.

"Early afternoon. Maybe sooner. No way to tell." He tossed a piece of mossy oak onto the fire and kicked it into place. The flames crackled and hissed. Adam rubbed his hands on his jeans. "The weather can turn quickly up here."

"I know, but I think we could limp into port," she said, testing him, though she really doubted that he would lie to her. What would be the point? No doubt he was as anxious to be rid of her as she was to lose him.

Adam shrugged. "It's your call, Marnie, but it wouldn't hurt to wait it out. The boat's holding water now, but one more shot against that hull and it might split wide open."

"It wouldn't take long to make it to Chinook Harbor or even Deer Harbor." She bit on her lower lip thoughtfully, resting her hands on the windowpane. She wasn't used to making these kinds of decisions alone, and Adam wasn't much help. Not that she wanted his help, she told herself. This was, after all, her bid for independence.

"You're right," he said suddenly, before she could change her mind. "We can probably make it. Okay, let's go." He grabbed his bag and the two sleeping bags and shouldered open the door. "Kill the fire."

"It couldn't be any worse than last night," she pointed out as he walked outside. She ignored the fire and followed him onto the porch. The wind blew harder than she'd expected, and she watched as the first thin drops of rain began to drizzle from the leaden sky.

"Last night was bad enough," he said, squinting as he stared at the horizon. "But this storm, bad as it's supposed to be, should blow over soon and why take a chance?" He was across the porch now, starting for the path. "However, if you're sure you want to try it, just pack what you need. We can leave the supplies here." Head bent against the rain, he started along the sandy path that led through the rocky forest, to the beach.

Indecision tore through Marnie. What if he were right? What if she, in her foolish anxiety to leave this place, put the *Marnie Lee* in jeopardy? Then all her quick words about standing on her own would come back to haunt her. Her father and Kent would never let her forget her aborted attempt at freedom. "Adam! Wait!" She ran the length of the porch and watched as he turned on his heel, his back rigid, his face, as he spun to glare at her, a mask of impatience.

His jaw was dark with the start of a beard, his lips thin and compressed, his brown eyes reflecting anger. "Make up your mind, Marnie. What's it gonna be?"

She checked the sky again. It suddenly seemed more ominous. The clouds were burgeoning. The timeworn phrase, better safe than sorry, flitted through her mind. "We can wait. A few more hours won't hurt, I suppose."

Tossing her a look that silently called her a wishy-washy female, he hauled the bag onto his shoulder, brushed past her and headed back inside.

"Women," he muttered, making the word an insult.

Marnie bit back a hot retort and waited a few seconds before she followed him back into the lodge. The man really got under her skin. Who was he to sneer at her? It wasn't as if he'd been invited on her ill-fated cruise. He'd stowed away, like the thief he probably was. She stormed inside where Adam was once again opening up his packs. To look busy, she stoked the fire and prod-ded the logs, causing flames to shoot to the back of the blackened fireplace. Adam's eyes never left her back-side. She could feel his gaze boring into her. Well, he could look all he wanted. She'd put up with him for a little longer, but if the storm didn't break by mid-afternoon, or if she didn't see any evidence of a serious squall on the horizon, she'd pack everything up herself, if she had to, and sail to Chinook Harbor. Adam Drake could do whatever he damn well pleased.

"DRAKE? SHE'S WITH Adam Drake?" Kent sputtered, his eyes rounding incredulously as he stood in the middle of Victor's Seattle office. "What the hell's she doing with him?"

"I wish I knew." Victor reached into the inner pocket of his jacket, withdrew his pipe and opened the humidor on his desk. "I would've known earlier, but the captain of the Coast Guard ship that took the message called Port Stanton before he reached me here."

"We've got to go get her! That man's crazy. You saw how he barged in on your party, and I don't have to re-mind you what he did to our publicity!" Kent snapped the local section of the paper onto Victor's desk. The headlines, bold and black, announced:

Disgruntled Employee Returns To Opening Of Puget West

Adam Drake, whose employment with Montgom-ery Inns was terminated last year when half a million dollars disappeared...

"I know what it says," Victor grumbled, clicking his lighter to the bowl of his pipe and inhaling. He let out thick puffs of smoke. "I just don't know what to do about it."

"Well, the first thing I'd do is impound that damned boat of his—the one he left at Port Stanton. The security guards saw him take off in a boat, so he must have doubled back and left it at the hotel."

"Maybe—"

"Then, I'd go up to Deception Lodge and haul Marnie back here! For God's sake, Victor, no one can even guess what Drake's got up his sleeve!"

"You think he'll hurt Marnie?" Victor asked, eyeing Simms as he paced nervously in front of the desk.

"He's desperate. After that fiasco last night, I did some checking through a P.I. who owes me a favor. I'd already had him looking into Drake because of the problems last year. Anyway, according to the P.I., Drake's planning to get back into the business. But there's a catch. Anyone he approaches for financing turns him away. He's talked to groups from L.A., Houston and Tokyo. No one will touch him."

Victor drummed his fingers on his desk as he considered his nemesis. Once he had trusted Drake with his fortune, and had anyone asked him about the most ambitious vice president he'd ever promoted, Victor would've replied that he would trust Drake with his very life—or the life of his daughter. He'd had that much faith in the bastard. But, of course, his opinion had plummeted when he'd realized that Drake had slowly but surely embezzled him out of a sizable chunk of his wealth.

The money hadn't really been an issue, but the lack of loyalty had. Victor required absolute loyalty from his employees. In return, he treated them well. But not, apparently, well enough for a scoundrel like Drake. He glanced up at Kent, edgy as he paced from the windows to the bar and back. It took all of Victor's willpower to remain calm. "Look, I don't like this any more than you do, but there's nothing I can do."

"*Nothing you can do?* Marnie's your daughter, for crying out loud!"

"Precisely." Victor's fist connected with the top of his desk, jarring his arm. "And if I interfere in her life, she'll never forgive me!"

"She might not get the chance," Kent said, his face flushed. "Drake's backed into a corner. And we all know how a cornered wolf reacts. You could press charges against him for kidnapping—or trying to steal the *Marnie Lee!*"

"We don't know what the hell happened to put Drake on the *Marnie Lee,* so I can't start making wild accusations. Besides, I don't give a damn about that boat."

"Well, I do!" Kent said, his face reddening. "Remember, half of it's mine. *I* should press charges."

Victor waved off that argument. "Forget it. At least for now. According to the Coast Guard, Drake plans to put up for repairs in Chinook Harbor."

"*He* plans. What about Marnie?"

Victor clamped his teeth onto the stem of his pipe. As far as he was concerned, Marnie had gotten herself into this mess, she could damn well get herself out.

"Well, what're we going to do?" Kent demanded, coming over to stand in front of Victor's desk and leaning over the cluttered surface.

At that moment Kate tapped lightly on the office door and poked her head in. "Ty Van Buren on line two."

"Thanks, I'll take it," Victor said, then noticed the nervous twitch of Kent's mouth. The poor kid was worried sick about Marnie. "There's nothing we can do right now." He reached for the phone. "Except wait. It's Drake's move."

CHAPTER SIX

THE AFTERNOON WORE ON, the weather growing slightly worse, but the storm that had been predicted never developed into anything more serious than a slight squall. As the hours dragged by, Marnie was on edge, overly aware of Adam in the lodge, his maleness seeming to fill the cavernous rooms. She felt the weight of his gaze, smelled his musky scent, heard his tread as he moved from room to room, pacing the lodge like a lion. Some of the time he'd spent chopping wood, as if he expected to be here longer than a few hours, or to focus some of his energy, she didn't know which. He'd also scouted and explored the lodge stem to stern and top to bottom. Marnie hadn't accompanied him. The less she was forced into contact with him, she figured, the better for both of them.

They hadn't said more than a dozen words to each other. Marnie had done some exploring herself, kept the fire burning, and sorted out the supplies Adam had brought from the boat, all the while keeping one eye on the weather. If only they had a radio, she thought in frustration as the night loomed ahead, then she'd hear the weather updates and know what to expect.

As it was, she was facing another night alone with Adam, and the hours marched steadily onward. The shadows in the rooms lengthened, and Marnie silently kicked herself for not following her instincts and taking the boat to port. She should never have trusted Adam. He'd probably invented the whole story. But why? No, his lying to her didn't make any sense. She wasn't about to kid herself into believing that he *wanted* to stay here with her.

Her stomach grumbled, and she eyed the sorry prospects for a meal. She heard Adam walk into the room, and without looking over her shoulder, she snagged two pieces of bread and a jar of peanut butter. "So what happened to your storm?" she asked, spreading a thin layer of peanut butter on one slice of bread. Not exactly hearty fare, but the sandwich would have to do.

She took a bite and twisted on the hearth so that she faced him. Adam, who had been in the basement, brushed the cobwebs from his hair but didn't answer immediately.

"The storm," she repeated. "Remember? The one that kept us trapped here all day? The one with the gale-force winds that the Coast Guard was so worried about?"

He shoved up his sleeves. "Maybe it'll hit tonight."

"Maybe," she replied, studying him as she took another bite. Would he lie to her? But why? It just didn't make sense.

She watched as he moved to the window and scanned the sky, as if he were looking for something, expecting something to appear in the gloomy heavens. Perhaps he had been telling the truth. Maybe he did expect a storm of hurricane proportions. Still, she wasn't convinced. She decided to call his bluff. "Maybe you didn't even call the Guard."

Tossing a glance over his shoulder, he rained a sarcastic smile in her direction. "Why would I lie?"

"You tell me."

He snorted and faced her again, his hands resting lightly on his hips. She tried to keep her gaze on his face, but couldn't help noticing the way his fingers spread over the pockets of his jeans where the faded denim stretched taut across his lower abdomen. She quickly averted her eyes, focusing on the window instead.

"You disappoint me, Marnie."

"*I* disappoint you?" she repeated, startled. Why, all of a sudden, was she so aware of him? Was it the storm gathering outside, the charge of the forces of nature, or the warm atmosphere in the lodge that made her realize just how intimate the situation had become? Her stomach clenched, and she pushed the remains of her sandwich aside. A few seconds before she'd been ravenous, now she couldn't swallow another bite.

"I thought you were different." He turned back to the window and propped his foot on the sill as he stared toward the sea.

Knowing she shouldn't ask, but unable to stop herself, she said, "Different from what?"

"The rest."

When he didn't elaborate, she waited, her senses all keyed on her reluctant companion. The back of his neck was tanned bronze, and his hair curled behind his ears. His buttocks, beneath his jeans, shifted as he threw one hip out to balance himself.

Marnie's throat was suddenly as dry as a desert wind, and she realized that she'd been holding her breath, waiting. But for what?

Adam was the sexiest man she'd met in a long, long while and, damn it, she was responding like a boy-crazy teenager. Perhaps it was just the surroundings and the fact that she was imprisoned here with him, but she was more attuned to his lazy sensuality than she'd thought possible.

His voice caused her to jump. "Everyone at the company thought I ripped off your old man. But you—" he pressed his palms against the damp panes "—well, I guess I expected too much."

She felt an immediate need to explain herself, as if she should be ashamed for her actions, though she hadn't done anything wrong. What did she care what Adam Drake thought of her? He could be the sexiest man alive and there was still a chance that he was a thief. Maybe that was the cause of her fascination with him, she thought darkly. The fact that he was truly forbidden fruit.

"You said you knew Gerald Henderson?" he asked, before her thoughts took her too far from the conversation.

"Mmm." She slammed back to reality and hoped the heat in her cheeks was from the fire and not from her ridiculous fantasies.

"What kind of a man would you say he is?"

She lifted a shoulder. "I only knew him as an employee," she admitted. "He worked in the accounting department with Fred Ainger and Linda Kirk. I met him at meetings and company parties and occasionally in the halls or cafeteria, but I never got to know him personally." She was glad for a turn in the conversation, though she sensed that Adam was leading her into dangerous waters. Nonetheless, talking about Montgomery

Inns was better than the emotion-charged silence and her own imagination.

"Would you say Gerald was dishonest?" Adam asked, rubbing his index finger over his thumb.

"Absolutely not." Henderson had worked for Victor Montgomery for twelve years before his sudden retirement last spring. There had never been a word of impropriety linked to him.

"He wasn't even close to sixty-five. Why do you think he retired?" Adam lifted his head, his hard gaze locked with Marnie's, and Marnie's breath caught in her throat. For a heart-stopping second she thought she saw more than just a single question in Adam's eyes, as if he were just as aware of her as a woman as she was of him as a man. She swallowed with difficulty, and his gaze, golden brown and unwavering, held hers.

"I told you earlier that I thought Gerald was having health problems," she finally responded when she captured control of her tongue again. Oh, God, if only he'd quit staring at her! "Stress-related, or allergies, I think. Anyway, he didn't come back to work for the hotel and was supposed to go on to another job."

"You ever see the medical bills?"

"No, but I wouldn't. It's not my department…"

His razor-thin lips curled into a smile that was a blatant sneer at her naïveté, and her temper started to rise.

"He reported to Fred," she said quickly, wondering why, all of a sudden, his opinion of her mattered in the least.

"And Fred reported to…?"

"Personnel on matters like this, otherwise to… Kent."

"Who, in turn, reported to your father," he said, filling in the obvious blanks.

"Yes." Suddenly defensive, she felt as if she owed it to her father to straighten Adam out. "I don't know what you're trying to say, Drake, but my father didn't steal money from himself. That's ridiculous."

One side of his mouth lifted in a crooked likeness of a smile. But his eyes were cold and serious. "Henderson seems to think that someone close to Victor is cheating him. And despite the general low opinion of my reputation at the company, Henderson believes I was framed."

"By whom?"

"That's the half-million-dollar question, isn't it?" he drawled, his eyes still trained on her face as if he expected some sort of reaction from her.

"How were you 'framed'?" she asked, unable to keep a hint of sarcasm from her words.

"I don't know," Adam admitted, and for the first time since she'd discovered him aboard the *Marnie Lee,* she was convinced of his sincerity. He let out his breath in frustration and shoved both hands through his hair.

"Henderson couldn't tell you?"

"Couldn't or wouldn't. He's afraid, I think. I couldn't get any more information from him." Adam eyed a scuff mark on the floor and rubbed it with the toe of his worn running shoe. The room was beginning to grow dark, only pale light filtered through the glass to illuminate the rough angles of his face. For a second Marnie wondered about him, about his private life. As far as she knew, he'd never married, but she wished she knew why. He was handsome, his features sensual, his body firm and hard. He was intelligent; he'd displayed his sharp business acumen on more than one occasion. Until last year, when all hell had broken loose, he'd been a successful corporate executive. At that point he'd had good looks, money and a future that could only be described as stellar.

Until he'd been accused of theft, Adam Drake had been considered a real catch—one of the most eligible bachelors in Seattle.

If one were looking.

Marnie wasn't. Or at least she told herself she wasn't.

Even so, her gaze was drawn to the vee of his shirt front and the dark hairs that curled against his tanned skin. Afraid he might catch her staring, she focused on the wall behind him and ignored the irregular beat of her heart. It was natural to be uncomfortable around him. She was a woman, after all, and she obviously wasn't immune to his rugged maleness. A pity. If only she could look past that raw sexuality that seemed to emanate from his deep-set eyes.

"So you think Kent set you up?" she finally asked, though her throat was uncomfortably tight.

Adam looked pained. "I never would have guessed he'd have the brains or the guts to do it."

"Henderson could be wrong."

"He could be. But he isn't."

"Well, even if he's right—and I'm not saying I go along with this—he could be talking about someone else in the company, someone other than Kent."

"Still trying to defend that bastard, are you, Marnie?" Adam shook his head and muttered something indistinguishable under his breath before adding, "Some women never learn."

The words cut like the bite of a whip. She, alone, had stood up for him to her father, pointing out that a man was innocent until proven guilty. Though she wasn't completely convinced of his innocence, she couldn't believe he was actually a thief. Oh, she'd been back and forth on the subject, never really knowing, but she'd argued Adam's case bitterly to her father. Not that it had made any difference. In Victor's book, Adam had done the unthinkable: he'd betrayed a trust.

Of course, Adam had no way of knowing about her feelings or the fact that she and her father had been at odds over his dismissal. Though she wanted to rub it in Adam's face right now, she didn't. He wouldn't believe her anyway. His last cutting remark had been testimony to that.

"Believe me, Drake, I *do* learn from my mistakes. And the mistake I made was in believing you and letting you stay here with me. If you ask me, *you're* the bastard," she said coolly, though her blood was beginning to boil. "Ever since we got on this island, you've insulted me and made innuendos about my father." Involuntarily, her fingers curled into tight fists. "If you don't like the present company, I suggest you hike to the nearest town. There's a map in the *Marnie Lee.*"

A ghost of a smile played on his lips. He reached into his back pocket and whipped out a folded piece of paper. "Got it," he said. "But if I leave, what will you do?"

"Muddle through somehow," she replied. "I really can take care of myself."

He cocked an insolent eyebrow. "That remains to be seen."

"Watch me!"

"Oh, I will," he said, and his voice was suddenly silky smooth. To Marnie's consternation, he sauntered across the room to the archway leading to the old dining room.

She couldn't help herself. Knowing that she was flirting with danger, she shoved herself from the hearth and walked quickly across the dusty plank floors, through the arched entrance to the dining area and down two creaking steps to the bar where Adam, behind the counter, was wiping a glass with the tail of his shirt. On the bar, thick with dust and cobwebs, was a bottle of whiskey. The label was yellowed and blurred with grime.

"You're not really going to drink that, are you?" she asked, appalled.

Mocking her, he poured a stiff shot into the glass and threw her own words her way. "Watch me." He tossed back the drink and didn't so much as flinch as the liquor hit his throat. He held up a glass to her.

"I'll probably have to get you to a hospital to pump your stomach," she said. "Who knows what was in that..." She walked closer and motioned to the bottle.

"Who cares?"

"I do," she said crisply. "I didn't want you on this trip in the first place and I certainly don't want to clean up after you...or play nursemaid."

"No?" His gaze strayed from her eyes to her neck and lower still. "Playing nursemaid could be fun."

Goose bumps appeared on her flesh. "What it would be is a disaster," she countered, and wished her voice didn't sound quite so breathless.

As if he caught the subtle change in her attitude, he motioned to the bottle. "Join me?"

"I don't think liquor's the answer. Especially not that—" she wrinkled her nose "—bottle."

His eyes gleamed. "Liquor's not the answer to what

question?" he asked, and his voice sounded fuller from the whiskey.

"I think we should keep our wits about us."

"Speak for yourself." He poured himself another drink, then propped one arm on the bar and vaulted over the counter to land lithely beside her.

She felt smaller then, with him so close. His scent, earthy maleness blended with the faint muskiness of old Scotch, wafted across her face.

"Anyone ever told you you're too uptight?"

"Thousands," she retorted.

"Well, they're right." One side of his mouth lifted, exposing teeth so white they gleamed in the shadowy room. He touched her arm and she drew away, stepped back from fingers that felt warm and inviting.

He didn't back down. "Afraid, Marnie?"

"Of what? You?" She shook her head, lying a little. She was petrified of him, but not for her life. Physical violence wasn't his style; however, he could be devastating in other ways.

She quivered as he touched her again and saw his gaze flicker to her mouth. Without conscious thought, she licked her lips and heard him respond with a low groan.

Marnie knew she was in trouble.

"Why the hell do you have to be so damned beautiful?" he growled as he lowered his head and molded his mouth to hers. She knew she should stop him, that kissing him was madness, but the feel of his lips, warm and supple, caused a response so deep she actually shook.

Don't let me fall for a man like this, she thought, and willed herself to remain impassive. Though the blood in her veins heated and pulsed, she didn't move, but trembled slightly when he drew her close. His lips moved urgently against her mouth; his tongue, prodding, sought entrance.

Every instinct told her to let go, fall against him, give in once. What would it hurt? But in the back of her mind, she heard a warning, and with all the will-power she could muster she pressed her palms against his chest and shoved. "Let me go," she said, her voice a breathless whisper. "What do you think you're doing?"

He yanked his head back, but still his strong arms held her firm. "So all those stories about you are true?" he asked, cocking an insolent brow over his laughing brown eyes.

"What stories?"

"The stories of the ice maiden," he said, and she wanted to die. Her face washed with color, but she set her jaw and forced a cool smile.

"You thought you'd be different?"

A muscle bunched in his jaw, but was quickly tamed. "No, but I thought a woman whose standards were so low that she'd bed a snake like Simms, might have hotter blood than rumor had it."

She slapped him. Without thinking, she raised her hand and smacked the palm against his cheek and he, damn his black heart, had the nerve to laugh.

"So the lady does have some passion after all."

"Get out, Drake," she insisted, quivering with rage. "Remember when you said you were disappointed in me, well the same goes for me! I had faith in you. I even told my father that you couldn't possibly have stolen anything from him. I argued with the board of directors. And I was wrong, wasn't I? You're just as bad as everyone said."

His dark eyes sparked, and before she could react, he grabbed her. Whirling her off her feet, he maneuvered her against the bar, cutting off her escape. This time his mouth crashed down on hers with a punishing force that ripped through her body. His hands clamped her close, and she could barely breathe as his tongue pressed hard against her teeth.

She tried to fight him. This was no way to start any kind of relationship, but she couldn't help but yield to emotions that were tearing through her. Love or hate, she couldn't tell, but her breathing was labored, her heart hammering in her chest, the rational side of her mind losing a battle with her war-torn emotions.

His kiss was as impatient and demanding as the man himself. His arms surrounded her waist, pressing against her spine and forcing her breasts and abdomen to flatten against the solid length of his body. Through her clothes, she felt male muscles straining, a hard, lean frame moving against hers. Her back was pressed against the bar, and he leaned over, forcing her backward, his heaving chest nearly crushing her as she half lay on the dusty counter.

"Dear, God," she whispered, her voice rough when he pulled his mouth from hers and stared down into her eyes. "What—what are you doing?"

"Making a point." His hand moved slowly upward, past her ribs to her breast, which was rising and falling with each of her shallow breaths.

"Don't—"

His fingers caressed the sweet mound as his lips found hers again, and this time the kiss was more gentle, his mouth wet and hot, his tongue quietly prodding.

She sighed, and in that split second he shifted, his

legs moving between hers, his tongue gaining entrance to her mouth. A warm whirlpool of desire swept her in its loving current, and all her skin tingled in anticipation. The smell of him invaded her nostrils and she tasted the tangy salt of his skin.

This is sheer madness, she thought, but couldn't stop the current of passion that carried her without protest as he lifted her sweater over her head and she felt the chill of the old lodge brush against her skin.

"Marnie, sweet Marnie," he moaned, gathering her close, his face pressed into the hollow of her breasts, the air from his lungs torrid. His tongue was rough and erotic as he licked her skin, skimming the sculpted lace of her bra. Her breast grew heavy and anxious, her nipple tightening into a hard bud of anticipation.

He didn't disappoint her. His lips surrounded her nipple, and his teeth and tongue parried and teased, causing her body to silently beg for more of this sublime torture.

He was all too willing to comply. She felt the heat of his body, the hard thrust of his hips against hers, the exquisite torment of his mouth as he moved lower, unsnapping her jeans, his tongue licking a path of liquid fire around her navel to delve even lower.

Marnie sucked in her breath as he eased the rough fabric of her jeans over her hips, past her thighs, to her knees. Only when his fingers slid upward past the elastic of her panties to caress her buttocks, did reason invade the dreamlike fog of her mind.

Self-respect grappled with passion, and she dug her fingernails into his shoulder. "Please," she whispered, "I can't... I just can't do this..."

Still he perused her, his hands shifting to the warmth between her legs.

"Adam, please, no!" she cried.

His body stiffened for a second before he drew away, his face contorted as he struggled to rein in his galloping desire. "Sweet heaven," he whispered, his hands shaking as he tried to steady himself. "So you're not an ice maiden after all," he muttered, his eyes still smoldering. "You're a tease."

"No, I—"

"You wanted me, damn it!" he thundered, before jamming his hands deep into the pockets of his jeans.

"No—I..." His expression accused her of the lie as she struggled back into her clothes. Ridiculously she felt close to tears, but she wouldn't let him see that her emotions were frayed, her nerves strung tight. Her fingers trembled as she zipped her jeans. She could feel his gaze on her, and from the corner of her eye she saw him move to the wall, and crossing his arms over his chest, continue to stare at her. At least he was several feet from her, she thought, finally lifting her head.

"I just want the truth."

"I don't understand—"

"You wanted me," he repeated, eyes blazing.

For several heartbeats she didn't answer, couldn't. The truth was more than she could bear. How could she want this man—the very man who had probably cheated her father? And even if he hadn't stolen the money, he'd hidden in her boat and practically forced himself on her. And the lies. She knew that the storm that had been predicted had been fabricated, but why? So he could seduce her?

A tingle of delight skittered along her arms, and

she ignored it. She was *not* the kind who enjoyed the thought of men lusting after her...

"Yes," she finally allowed, her fingers trembling as she snapped her jeans and straightened her sweater. "I wanted you."

"But you stopped. Why?"

"Things are too complicated between us," she said, her voice wavering. "You're the last man in the world I should..." She motioned with her hand frantically.

"The last man in the world you should bed?"

She sucked in her breath. "Yes. The *last* man."

"That's probably why you want me."

"I don't think—"

"Well, it's certainly not love, is it?"

"No, but..."

He advanced slowly on her, and it took all her willpower to stand her ground. "You know what I think?" he asked, his eyes deepening to the color of dark chocolate.

"I'm not sure I want to."

"I think you'd like to let loose, I mean really let loose. That's what your journey into the storm was, wasn't it? So why not take it all the way?" He touched her hair, his fingers groping beneath the pale strands to capture her neck and draw her face next to his.

She swallowed and stared into his eyes, her heart racing, her pulse throbbing all over again.

"Come on, Marnie," he whispered, "take a chance." He kissed her then, and this time she wound her arms around his neck. Nothing that felt this wonderful could be wrong, she told herself, kissing him back and drinking in the smell and feel of him.

His weight pushed them both to the floor, and this

time there was no holding back. As he stripped off her clothes, she worked on the buttons of his shirt and shoved it off his shoulders. Her fingers explored the sinewy strength of his arms and chest, flexing in the springy hair that covered his sleek muscles. Groaning, he kicked off his jeans and rolled over her, his tense male body gleaming and naked in the growing shadows.

"That's better," he whispered as she twined her hands in the thick strands of his hair, kissing him with all the passion that ripped away her pretenses. He moved, slowly at first, letting her feel the length of him against her sensitive skin.

Instinctively, she dragged him closer, and he kissed first her lips, then her closed eyes and then her breasts. Her nipples ached until he suckled, and a molten heat swirled deep in her core, causing an ache to burn between her legs.

A final protest deep in a dark corner of her mind told her that she was dancing with the devil, that only heartache would come of this, but she was past the point of caring, teetering on the brink of sensual fulfillment. His knees wedged her legs apart. She moaned low in her throat, waiting, wanting and feeling every inch of him as, with one swift thrust, he entered her and a blinding light flashed behind her eyes.

"Adam," she cried, her voice as raw as the sea.

"I'm right here," he whispered against her ear.

She moved with him, feeling each glorious stroke as he claimed her for his own with ever-increasing tempo. Her body fused with his, his skin sliding against hers, as the explosion rocked them both, sending her over the edge of desire and into the sweet oblivion of afterglow.

"Marnie," he whispered over and over again, as his

breath slowed and the beating of his heart echoed her own. "Oh, Marnie." Strong arms surrounded her, and again she felt tears prick her eyelids, but she fought them back. She'd have no regrets, she told herself, not ever. This one moment of passion, be it forever or fleeting, she would treasure. Nothing could destroy it.

CHAPTER SEVEN

ADAM SPENT A GOOD PART of the night making love to Marnie. In the hours between their passionate bouts of lovemaking, he lay on his back, listening to her breathing, and wondered if he was losing his mind. Though physically he wanted her as he'd never wanted another woman, he knew that loving her so intensely was a mistake. But he couldn't stop himself. Her luscious body called out to his baser instincts, and her soft blue eyes touched his intellect.

He'd known more than his share of women in the past. Hell, he was no saint. But no woman had confused him so.

Marnie was different. Sometimes utterly naive, other times fiercely self-sufficient, she was a sensual enigma that, had he more time, he might be inclined to unravel.

But she's Montgomery's daughter, he kept reminding himself as he stared down at her. Sunlight was streaming through the windows of the lodge, and Marnie, curled next to him, looked almost angelic.

A very sexy angel. After her initial reluctance, Marnie had turned out to be a willing and responsive lover, as insatiable as he was.

He rubbed his chin impatiently. What the hell was he going to do with Victor's willful daughter? Make love to her until he was satisfied and had his fill of her? Or lie to her and use her in his quest for absolving himself of all blame in the embezzlement? Or let himself get involved with her and see just how far it would go?

Seeing her sleeping peacefully, her pale hair falling over her cheek, her dark blond lashes lying against her creamy white skin, his gut reaction was to stretch out beside her and start kissing every inch of that perfect, delicious body. Let the future bring what it would. Right now, all that mattered was Marnie.

"God help me," he muttered, knowing that she was bound to get hurt, as he overcame the urge to slowly drag the sheet from her shoulders and see the morning light against the perfect skin of her breasts. Just thinking about her rosy nipples, hidden coyly by the sheet, caused a hardening in his loins all over again.

You're the bastard, she'd accused him yesterday, and damn it, she'd been right. He couldn't get enough of her, and yet that's exactly what he would have to do, get his fill of her before he dropped the bomb: he was only using her to get back at Victor. Inside he winced at his own cruel calculations, but he overcame his squeamishness where Marnie was concerned. After all, using her had been part of his plan—hadn't it? And maybe some small part of him had thought that by bedding Montgomery's daughter, he would gain some sort of convoluted revenge against Victor, a man who had scorned his loyalty.

Adam had been the fool, of course. The military had instilled in him a sense of loyalty, and he, upon joining Montgomery Inns, had transferred that loyalty to Victor Montgomery. Talk about misplaced faith!

So he'd planned to use Marnie, and maybe even had started his sexual advances with thoughts of revenge.

His strategy had backfired, of course. Now he didn't want to hurt Marnie, and yet he saw no other alternative. She was in the way. Again he glanced at her, and it was all he could do not to touch her hair and smooth her cheek with his palm.

When she'd challenged him yesterday, he'd planned to prove to her that she was no better than other women, that she, too, had emotions and feelings and passion, that just because she was Victor Montgomery's daughter didn't make her any different.

And he'd proved his point—very well. Too well.

He felt like the proverbial heel, but there was nothing he could do to rectify things. What would the next step be? Offer to marry her out of some misguided sense of duty? No, that was too Victorian. Besides, Victor would only claim that he was a fortune hunter, bent on ruining everything he cared about. And truth to tell, Victor would be right. Because he didn't love Marnie. He couldn't. And she didn't love him. Oh, sure, they cared about each other…at least a little. But what had transpired between them was pure animal lust.

They were trapped, forced into intimacy, and they found each other darkly alluring. All that sexual tension had exploded into unbridled passion, and there was nothing more to it—no complicated emotions, no need to make promises for a future that didn't exist.

He buttoned up his shirt and stared down at Marnie—the princess. What he was planning to do to her was brutal, but he had no choice.

Swearing under his breath, he finished dressing and walked outside. Victor hadn't taken the bait yesterday, so Adam would have to make sure that this time Marnie's old man had no options.

VICTOR MONTGOMERY didn't like being manipulated. Not by anyone and especially not by Adam Drake. Nonetheless, that's exactly what had happened, he thought angrily. So here he was, feeling totally helpless, about to jeopardize his daughter's trust by playing into Adam Drake's hands. He strapped himself into his seat in the company's helicopter and noticed his companion, Kent Simms, doing the same. The pilot was already checking gauges and flicking switches, and the chopper's huge rotating blades picked up speed.

"I told you we shouldn't have just sat on our butts," Kent complained over the noise of whirring blades as the chopper lifted off.

The pilot steered the craft upward before heading north, flying over tall skyscrapers and the vast waters of the sound. "The minute I heard Drake was involved, I knew there would be trouble," Kent continued, fiddling with his seat strap and trying to get comfortable."

"I only did what Marnie wanted." Even to his own ears, the excuse sounded lame.

"The only way to deal with a man like Drake is to take the offensive. Once he's got the upper hand, it's all over."

"Marnie doesn't want my interference."

"You don't know that. We haven't heard from her, have we?" When Victor shook his head, Kent rubbed his chin nervously. "Yeah, right. For all we know, she's being held hostage by Drake—"

"He wouldn't go that far," Victor intervened. "There are laws—"

"He got off scot-free once before, didn't he? A viper like Drake always slithers out of the trap. As for Marnie, she's a woman. And I don't have to tell you that sometimes she doesn't make the right decision."

"Amen," Victor said under his breath. He didn't want Kent to know how upset he was, so he held his tongue. But when he'd spoken to Drake, he could barely talk. Claiming that the phones on the *Marnie Lee* were inoperable, Drake had mustered the gall to have the Coast Guard patch a call through to Victor. The conversation had been short but to the point. The *Marnie Lee* was still anchored near the beach at Deception Lodge, but Drake didn't know when they'd put up for repairs. It had been all Victor could do to respond civilly to Drake, but he'd had no choice. Marnie was with the bastard.

That situation had to change. Especially given Marnie's emotional state right now. The breakup with Kent, this ludicrous bid for independence, and her own ambivalent feelings for Drake all added up to trouble— deep trouble.

Victor sighed. When Kate had told him of the embezzlement, Victor had informed the board members. It had been Marnie, alone, who had tried to convince Victor and the rest of the board that Adam Drake had been innocent. At the time Victor had assumed that she was just being her normal, trusting-the-underdog self. Now he wasn't so sure. Was it possible that his straitlaced daughter could fall for the sensual much-touted charms of Adam Drake?

Disaster! That's what it was. Pure, unadulterated disaster! Victor should never have let her leave the other night! He should have put his foot down.

From the corner of his eye, he saw Kent squirm. Kent's tanned face was unnaturally pale, his usual smile missing. He was agitated and tense and had tried to

talk Victor out of flying north with him. "I'll take care
of this," he'd said, when Victor had explained about
Drake's phone call. "Marnie's my responsibility."

"She doesn't think so," Victor had pointed out, as
he'd grabbed his jacket and punched the intercom button to have Kate request a pilot for the chopper. Kate,
too, had voiced her concerns, but that was because she'd
felt a little like Marnie's mother. Well, she wasn't. And
Victor was still president of the corporation, and no one,
including Kent Simms, Kate Delany or Adam Drake,
for that matter, was going to tell him how to handle
his corporation or his daughter. He watched Kent nervously scratch his arm. The boy was sweating bullets
over Marnie.

"I just hope she's okay," Kent said, wiping an un-
steady hand across his lips.

"She will be." Victor's gaze moved to the bubblelike
windshield and beyond to the restless green-gray water.
"It won't be long."

"I can't get there fast enough," Kent said, nervously
biting his lip.

Victor silently agreed, but they would just have to
hang on for a couple of hours. A quick copter ride to
Deer Harbor and a rental car to Deception Lodge. He
and Kent would see Marnie by nightfall. And then, by
God, she was going to listen to reason!

As for Adam Drake, if he'd so much as laid one finger on Marnie, Victor would personally skin him alive!

MARNIE WAS GETTING used to Adam's long absences.
In the few days they'd been on the island, he'd been
out as much as he'd been in the lodge. Both mornings,
she'd awoken to find him gone. But their relationship

had altered since yesterday, and she didn't know if the changes were for the better or the worse.

For all of her twenty-four years she'd lived her life on a single track, a track carefully laid by her father. And now, in the span of forty-eight hours, she'd jumped rail and headed off in new directions that were both frightening and exhilarating.

She changed clothes and folded the sleeping bags, still smelling of sex, and her mind was filled with blistering memories of passion she'd never known existed, passion hidden deep within her. Blushing at the vivid thoughts, she poured herself a cup of coffee and headed outside, where she balanced one hip on the porch rail, sipped from her cracked cup and waited for Adam to return. The morning was brilliant and warm. A vibrant sun climbed steadily in a clear blue sky, and a breath of sea wind stirred the fir branches and fluttered the new leaves in the oak trees. Birds skimmed the surface of the calm sea. Either Adam had lied about the storm or the weather service had been badly mistaken. All trace of clouds had disappeared, and the sunshine was warm against her face.

She tucked her chin on her hand. Adam Drake was a complication she hadn't anticipated, a wrinkle in her life she wasn't prepared to deal with. They'd become lovers, but she could hardly call them friends. Their lovemaking had been so explosive, so fierce and savage, that she felt drained afterward, as if she'd been in an emotional battle in which both sides were victorious.

"Silly girl," she chided herself, and brushed a pebble off the rail and onto the damp earth surrounding the porch. She'd never been a romantic and she wasn't about to start having idle fantasies now. She couldn't stay up here with Adam forever, and yet, as anxious as she'd been to leave Montgomery Inns behind, she now felt ready to settle in for a while, let this love affair run its natural course… But that was impossible. They hadn't talked much, though he had asked her questions about the company, questions she wouldn't answer. He'd brought up the embezzlement, but she wouldn't speculate about what had happened, not with the man her father presumed to be the thief.

She heard the sound of footsteps and trained her eyes on the stone-strewn path, which cut through the thick stands of trees and lush ferns. Within seconds Adam appeared and her stupid heart did a quick little flip at the sight of him. This wasn't supposed to happen, this lust, but she couldn't seem to control her emotions.

"Did you go back to the *Marnie Lee?*" she asked, dusting off the seat of her jeans as he stepped onto the porch and shifted the bag he'd slung over his back from one shoulder to the other.

He sent a quasi-smile her direction. "Yep."

"And?"

"And she's still above water," he answered. For a millisecond a hint of reluctance glimmered in his eyes.

"But everything was okay?" Marnie pursued, sensing he was holding back on her, that he was hiding something from her, protecting her from bad news.

"Everything's fine," was his gruff reply. Shoving open the door, he hauled his bag of supplies into the lobby and dropped the heavy bundle on the floor. Without another word, he walked into the dining room, and Marnie had the odd sensation that something was terribly wrong. Suddenly Adam had grown sullen and distant.

Because of last night? she wondered. Did he think

she'd expect some sort of commitment from him now? Nothing could be further from the truth. She was her own woman, able to make decisions regarding her body on her own.

But still his glum mood bothered her. And he was now in the dining room, where their first explosive encounter had occurred. Marnie struggled to keep her breathing even.

Knowing that he was avoiding her, but unable to leave well enough alone, she followed him and found him seated on an old bar stool near the window, the opened bottle of liquor in one hand, a half-full glass in the other.

"Something happened," she stated, boldly pulling up a stool next to his and straddling it.

He flicked a glance her way, then drained his glass. "What?"

"Nothing," he muttered, and she noticed that his expression was as hard-edged as ever, any sign of tenderness wiped away.

"For God's sake, Adam, *something's* going on."

He stared at her a long while, his eyes going over every contour of her face, as if he were memorizing each tiny detail. "I just think it's time to celebrate," he said, his jaw sliding to the side.

"Celebrate?" she repeated, a kernel of fear settling in her heart. "Celebrate what?"

"The cavalry."

He was making no sense whatsoever, and yet there was something in the way he considered his words that indicated he wasn't telling her everything—that indeed he did have a secret he hadn't shared with her. "What cavalry?"

His lips quirked. "Oh, you know. Those mighty fighting men from Montgomery Inns."

Marnie's stomach contracted as he poured a second glass. She shivered from the sudden coolness in the room, as if they'd never shared a second of passion, a drop of love, as if they were, again, mortal enemies. "Someone's coming here? Someone from the company?" she whispered.

"Good old Victor, unless I miss my guess."

She was suddenly stone-cold. He had to be kidding. "My father's in Seattle."

"Correction. He *was* in Seattle."

"He wouldn't come up here."

"I invited him."

"You *what?*" she cried, her voice as rough as the whiskey he'd poured into his glass. "But how?"

"Through the Coast Guard."

"But why?" She thought about their passionate lovemaking. It had all been an act, a way to bend her will to his so that she would trust him, and the minute she let down her guard he had the nerve to contact her father! "You used me!"

For a flickering moment she thought she caught a glimpse of regret in his face, but it was gone so quickly she wondered if she'd imagined a shred of remorse in his hard features. "What have you done, Drake? What did you say to him?"

"Only enough to get him here."

"You told him about *us?*" she nearly screamed, denying the overpowering urge to lunge at him. "You had no right—"

"I just said I didn't think we'd be back for a while. That's all."

"But you intimated that there was something going on between us!" she guessed, livid. Who was this...this beast she'd slept with? Warm and loving one minute, treacherous and deceitful the next! "How could you?"

"I didn't say anything about last night," he shot back.

"But you said enough to get him up here!"

"I might be wrong," he replied, his gaze cutting. "Maybe Kent will come to the rescue on his white steed. That would be better yet." He studied his liquor for a second, then took a long swallow. "Nah," he said finally, "Simms doesn't have the nerve. Not unless he shows up *with* Victor."

Marnie's entire world tilted. "Oh, God," she groaned, her future suddenly bleak. Her father would be furious. He'd label her a traitor, brand her as disloyal for openly consorting with the enemy. "You're out of your mind," she whispered, trying to think straight.

"I think you could use a drink," he said, and his voice was kinder. He touched her hand, but she drew quickly away.

"Don't!" she snapped. "Don't touch me!"

He started to hand her his drink, but she swatted the glass to the floor, and liquor spattered his jeans and splashed against the window to drizzle down rough pine walls. She wanted to cry but wouldn't let herself, wouldn't give him the satisfaction of seeing her fall apart. Slowly inching up her chin to meet his gaze, she demanded, "Why do you hate me? What have I done to you?"

"I don't hate you, Marnie," he said quietly, and a fleeting sliver of conscience showed in his expression. "But you're Victor's daughter."

"And for that you're trying to ruin my life?" Agony

mingled with remorse in his expression, before his face turned hard again. He started to pour yet another drink, then, cursing, screwed the cap back onto the bottle. "You *slept* with me, damn it," she charged, outraged and wounded.

"And you slept with me!"

She opened her mouth, then let it snap closed. She'd been a fool to let him get close enough to hurt her. "Yes, I did. As if that makes what you did all right. Don't turn this argument around!"

In frustration, he pinched the bridge of his nose between his index finger and thumb. His eyes squeezed closed. "I didn't mean to hurt you," he said. "I had no intention of—"

"Seducing me?" she cut in, remembering the first time he'd kissed her. "Or forcing me?"

His eyes flew open, and purple color suffused his neck. "I didn't *force* you to do anything you didn't want to!"

That was true enough, she supposed, but she was aching inside from the wounds he'd inflicted. "You didn't hurt me," she lied, managing to keep her voice steady.

"I hope not, Marnie." The way he said her name was like a balm. He stared into his glass. "I've done a lot of things I'm not very proud of, some of them happened in the last couple of days, but I've never stolen from your father and I've never forced any woman to sleep with me."

"So why don't you leave?" she said, hoping to pull together a little of her shredded dignity.

"I thought you could help me find some answers,

and if you couldn't, then I knew Victor or Kent could supply them."

"So you did use me," she said, her voice tight and weak.

"Yes, damn it!" he exploded, leaping from his bar stool and striding back to the bar where he slammed the bottle on the counter next to the mirror. "I only want my life back, my self-respect!"

"So do I," she threw back at him. "And I'd like to think that what we shared last night was more than a cheap trick to lure me into a compromising position with my father. What is it you want from me, Drake?" she finally asked, her voice shaking as she climbed off her stool and marched up to him. She stopped when she was mere inches away, the toes of her shoes close to his battered sneakers.

"I don't want anything from you," he said slowly. "I'm after Simms or whoever the hell set me up. I just thought you could give me some information."

"About what?" she demanded.

"About who in the corporation would be a suspect."

"I thought you'd decided Kent was your scapegoat."

He sent her a look that was absolutely chilling. "I suppose I deserved that," he admitted with a cold smile. "And I'd put money on Simms being the culprit, but I don't understand his motive. Unless he had debts I don't know about, I don't know why he'd jeopardize having it all—by marrying you—for half a million."

"*I'm* not marrying anyone."

"That's encouraging," he said, and his mouth shifted into his first honest smile of the day.

"I can't tell you anything about Kent that you don't already know. I thought I loved him and that he loved me, but I was mistaken and I thank my lucky stars that I wasn't foolish enough to marry him. But I don't think he stole from my father. He's not that stupid…and it would take a lot more money for him to betray Dad."

"But he would do it?"

"Loyalty isn't Kent's strongest quality," she said grimly, thinking of Kent's affair with Dolores.

"So what about Fred Ainger? He's about to retire and he lives the good life. I don't think Social Security and his pension at Montgomery Inns will cover his wife's extravagances."

"Fred's too honest."

"Is he?" Obviously Adam wasn't convinced. His eyes narrowed thoughtfully, as if he were squinting to read extremely small print. "How well do you know Rose Trullinger?"

"Well enough. You can't possibly imagine *she* would embezzle. She's in interior design. How could she possibly juggle the books?"

"Doesn't she have access to a computer terminal?"

"Yes, but—"

"And isn't it linked to the entire Montgomery Inns chain?"

"By secret access codes." This was too farfetched. Adam was really reaching.

"Rose has an ailing husband who can't hold a job, and three daughters in college."

"Just because people need money, doesn't mean they'd steal!" she said in exasperation. This conversation was getting them nowhere, and they were avoiding the issue that was on both their minds. Marnie could think of nothing but their lovemaking, and though

Adam had changed the topic, she wasn't finished having it out with him.

"I have a question for you," she finally admitted.

"Shoot."

His golden brown gaze held hers. "What about sleeping with me?" she demanded, bracing herself for the pain of his rejection. "Didn't it mean anything?"

He hesitated just a second before answering coldly. "Last night was sex."

"And that's all?"

His eyes bored into hers, and the air between them fairly sizzled with electricity. He swirled his drink, tossed it back and slammed the empty glass on the bar. "That's all it could ever be."

She wanted to hit him. To slap him so hard he would take back the ugly words, but she couldn't. Because he was speaking the truth. They had no future together, no love, just sex.

"They're right about you," she finally said, her jaw wobbling ever so slightly and hot tears building behind her eyes. "You're just as bad as Dad and Kent think."

"Probably," he agreed as she spun and stumbled blindly up the steps and through the lobby. She had to get away from him, had to pull herself together. She shoved open the door with her shoulder as tears started to stream down her face. She couldn't break down in front of him, wouldn't let him see her cry.

"Marnie!"

Oh, God, he was following her!

She ran, around the corner to the back of the lodge. His footsteps crunched in the gravel behind her, and he caught up with her at the weed-strewn parking lot, near a spreading maple tree with branches that provided a green canopy. "Marnie—wait. Just listen to me." He grabbed hold of her arm, and though she tried to pull away from him, he was much stronger than she, and she was wrenched back against the solid wall of his chest.

His arms surrounded her. "Marnie, Marnie, Marnie," he whispered against her hair. "Don't hate me."

"I do!" she lied, wishing she could pull away. "All you are is trouble. My father was right!"

"Your father's wrong about a lot of things, and so are you." He stared down into her shimmering eyes, and she wanted to collapse against him, to beg him to take back the cruel words, but of course he wouldn't.

"Just leave me alone!"

But he didn't. Instead his lips crashed down on hers, possessive and hard, demanding and comforting, and she struggled hard to pull away. But his arms were powerful, his mouth hot and wet, his will as strong as her own.

Her body reacted, sagging against his hard male contours, her arms slackening until she fought no longer and was aware of only Adam. The smell of the sea wafted over the musky scent of him, and deep in the distance she heard birds startled at the sound of a car's engine. Closing out all sounds, she clung to him and molded her body tight against his.

Groaning, he moved so that her back was pressed hard against the rough bark of the maple, but she didn't care, and when his hands moved upward along her arms, she shuddered with want. Her mouth opened easily to his practiced tongue.

Vaguely she was aware that something was wrong, that the sounds of the day had changed, but she didn't know or care why. She was lost in a savage storm of emotion, and as his hand surrounded her breast, gently massaging her flesh through her sweater while his tongue tickled the inside of her mouth, she gave in to all the wanton pulses firing her blood.

Until he stopped. As quickly as he'd pulled her to him, he released her. "Someone's coming," he said as the whine of a car's engine split the air and the nose of a white sedan rounded the final curve in the gravel lane.

Quickly Marnie straightened the hem of her sweater and swiped at the tears still standing in her eyes, but not before she met the furious gaze of the driver of the sedan. Her heart plummeted. Right now, she wasn't ready to face her father.

Victor's polished leather shoes landed on the gravel as the car rolled to a stop. "What the hell's going on here?" he said in a voice so low and menacing Marnie could barely hear it over the dull pounding of the surf. His gaze landed in contemptuous force on Adam. "Well, Drake, you got what you wanted. I'm here. Now what?"

"I just want to talk to you."

Marnie hadn't even noticed Kent in the passenger seat of the car, but there he was, climbing out of the sedan, his shoulders stiff, his mouth a white, uncompromising line. His whole attitude reeked of disdain, as if he could barely stomach the scene unfolding before him. However, Marnie knew him better than most and she saw something more than he'd like to show, something he was trying to hide, something akin to fear that touched his features.

The wind picked up, shoving Marnie's hair in front of her eyes, as her father reached her side. "Are you all right?" Victor asked, grabbing her in a huge bear hug.

His face was filled with fatherly concern, and Marnie realized she'd wounded him bitterly by leaving with Adam.

"I'm okay."

"You're sure?" He held her at arm's length, as if he could see the scars on her soul, scars inflicted by Adam Drake.

"Dad, believe me. I never felt better." From the corner of her eye she saw Adam stiffen.

"And what about him?" He motioned to Adam, and Marnie recognized a spark of rebellion in Adam's eyes. "He treat you right?"

"No one 'treated' anyone," she said evenly. "And you're here now. Why not talk to him yourself?"

A muscle flexed in Victor's cheek, and the wind blew his tie over his shoulder. He hesitated just a second, but finally said, "All right, Drake. Let's get this over with. What's on your mind?"

Adam told him. Right there in the old parking lot with the first few storm clouds rolling in from the west. Rain began to fall from the dark sky as Adam explained his theory of being set up and he didn't stop, not even when Kent scoffed at him.

Victor listened, though Marnie guessed he wasn't buying any of Adam's theories.

"All I want is another chance to prove that I'm innocent," Adam finally said, "and a public apology from you, absolving me of all guilt when that proof is uncovered."

"You're out of your mind," Kent said. "You've got no proof of a conspiracy against you or whatever you think happened. You're grasping at straws, man."

"Maybe your straw," Adam said with a slow, cold smile, challenging Kent without so much as lifting a finger. Kent rose to the bait, his jaw set and his handsome face flushed dark. He was ready to fling himself at Adam, but he must have thought better of his actions, for he straightened his tie instead and backed down. For the moment.

Victor remained unswayed. "All right, Drake, you've had your say. And I've listened. And I only have one thing to say to you—keep the hell away from my daughter. As for your cockamamy theories, keep them to yourself. You screwed me over, Drake, and I have a long memory. So don't try to drag innocent people's names through the mud, because it won't work with me." He'd slowly built himself into a rage. "Come on, Marnie—" He reached for her arm.

"I'm not leaving."

"What?" Her father stared at her as if she'd lost her mind. "Of course you're coming with me, now get your things and—"

"Listen, Dad. Nothing's changed," she said, wincing at the lie. "I'm not coming back to the company. The paper I gave you was a resignation, not a request for a leave of absence. And I haven't forgotten what you did on the night of the party." From the corner of her eye, she saw Kent go white.

"But you're coming back to Seattle," Kent said.

"Not yet."

"For God's sake, what's gotten into you?" he sputtered. "Has Drake brainwashed you?" Flinging one hand in the air, he turned to Victor and as if Marnie hadn't a mind of her own said, "You talk some sense into her and take her back with the car. I'll sail the *Marnie Lee* into port and have her repaired."

"Over my dead body," Marnie cried. "*I'm* responsible for the boat, and I'll take care of her."

"And what about him?" Kent hooked an insolent thumb in Adam's direction.

"He's his own person. He got what he wanted from me, didn't he?" she said, coloring a little. "He got you both up here. He can do whatever he pleases."

"For God's sake, Marnie, listen to reason," her father begged, but she turned swiftly on her heel and headed back to the lodge. She was tired of men—all men—manipulating her, using her, thinking about her from their own selfish perspectives. Well, the whole lot of them could rot in hell. Victor for smothering her, Kent for betraying her and lying to the press about marrying her, and Adam for seducing her and playing with her heart.

If only she could run to a nunnery, she thought sarcastically, but stopped dead in her tracks. She wasn't running *away* from her problems, she was running *to* a new self-sufficient life. She'd start her own publicity firm, just as soon as the *Marnie Lee* was repaired.

She threw things in her bag and listened, hoping for the sound of a car's engine as it left, but instead she heard the door of the lodge open and slam shut. "You're leaving." Adam's voice startled her. She'd expected her father.

"That's right."

"Where're you going?"

"Don't know."

"Marnie, I—"

She shouldered her bag and brushed past him. "Don't bother apologizing, Adam. It's not your style." With one last glance that she hoped appeared scathing, she pressed forever into her memory how he looked just then, with three days' worth of stubble on his chin, his hair uncombed, his clothes unclean. Her father was right. She was better off without him. So why, then, did her heart ache so?

She left Adam in the lobby. Her father would see that Adam was duly thrown out and that Deception Lodge was secured. Oh, she'd bungled this first attempt at independence, she thought miserably as she hiked down the trail leading to the beach where the rubber raft awaited, but her mangled attempt was because of Adam. She should never have let him get so close to her.

Rain peppered the ground, puddling in the sandy path and giving the forest a fresh, earthy cleanliness that reminded her of Adam.

"You'll get over him," she predicted, but wondered just how long it would take.

CHAPTER EIGHT

HE'D BLOWN IT. With Marnie. With Victor. With Montgomery Inns.

Adam threw his few new belongings into a nylon bag and slung it over his shoulder before heading to the office of the fleabag of a motel he'd called home for the past week. He'd stayed in Chinook Harbor, knowing Marnie had checked into a hotel on the other side of town. Several times he'd tried to contact her. So far, she hadn't responded.

He didn't really blame her.

Ever since the confrontation with Victor in the parking lot of the lodge, Adam had relived the scene over and over again in his mind. He should have anticipated the outcome. Marnie, furious with all of them, had left without so much as a glance over her stiff shoulder, and Adam had felt the unlikely urge to run after her. And what? Apologize? Ridiculous! He couldn't start letting a woman foul up his plans—especially when that woman was Victor Montgomery's only child, his princess.

As for Victor, the old man had looked as if he wanted to kill Adam right on the front porch of Deception Lodge. Somehow, Victor had managed to control his thirst for blood and had, instead, made a big show of kicking Adam off Montgomery property. Vic-

tor had been white with rage, shaking as he'd chained
the front door and slammed the padlock shut, swearing
and threatening to call the police.

"This is it, Drake," he'd growled, his voice so hushed
Adam had barely heard it over the sound of the surf.
"You've pushed me too far this time. The inns were one
thing. Money, I can always make. But my daughter..."
By this time Victor's lips were bloodless, his blue eyes
colder than ice. "I'll never forget how you used and humiliated her to get to me. If you breathe one word of this
to anyone, I swear I'll call the authorities and then I'll
personally wring your worthless neck!" With that, he'd
stalked to his car, and Adam, every muscle aching with
restraint, hadn't lunged at the man, nor begged forgiveness. He'd just stood there and when Victor had opened
the door of the Mercedes and stared at him, Adam had
met Victor's unwavering hate-filled gaze with his own
steady scrutiny.

Victor's reaction had been predictable. As had Marnie's. The odd man out had been Simms. Everyone else
had acted right in character. Victor had been the indignant, furious father; Marnie a proud woman who'd discovered that her lover hadn't cared for her. But Simms
had been strangely quiet and subdued for a jilted fiancé.

Thinking of Marnie, Adam winced. She had been
an innocent in all this. Sure, she'd been in love with
Simms, but she'd never done anything directly against
Adam. In fact, if she were telling him the truth, she'd
protested his innocence to the board of directors of
Montgomery Inns and she'd trusted him not to hurt her.

He closed his eyes, willing the image of Marnie's
beautiful face from his mind and concentrating in-

stead on Simms—the man she was supposed to marry. Simms's reaction to the scene at the lodge had been odd, to say the least. Instead of being pleased with Adam's dressing down by Victor, instead of reveling in Adam's verbal lashing, Simms had seemed more interested in Marnie and their damned boat. It had been all Victor could do to restrain Simms from chasing down the path after Marnie. No smug smile cast in Adam's direction, no supercilious look down Simms's nose. No, in fact, once over the initial shock of seeing Adam, Simms had only been interested in Marnie, the yacht and the well-being of both.

Maybe the bastard really did care for her, Adam thought with a grimace, as he checked out of the motel. He handed the cashier his credit card, hastily scribbled his name and stuffed the receipt in the pocket of his stiff new jeans.

Outside, the weather was warm, sunlight spangling the waters of the marina several blocks downhill. Boats of all sizes and shapes were tethered to the docks. The shipmasts looked like telephone poles spaced too closely together. Hulls gleamed in the sunlight, and sails flapped noisily before catching the breeze that blew steadily across the harbor. The air was thick with the smells of fish and seaweed, the cloudless sky littered with gulls and terns.

He spotted the *Marnie Lee* as he walked toward the waterfront. Chinook Harbor was a sleepy little village where people knew everything about each other and loved to gossip. Adam, from nights spent at a local watering hole and from days lingering over coffee at a popular diner, had learned from a few discreet inquiries that Marnie had placed her yacht in the care of Ryan Barns, a sailor with a reputation of caring more for boats than for his wife and small daughter.

He'd also learned that the repairs would take several weeks.

Marnie would either have to stay on the island and wait, or return to Seattle, or continue on her flight for freedom by some other means of transportation. Though she'd never fully confessed that she'd left Montgomery Inns to start a life of her own, Adam had guessed as much. Her argument with Victor at the lodge had confirmed his suspicions. Her bid for independence won his grudging approval. Few women, or men for that matter, would give up the good life just to prove themselves.

Yep. Marnie was one helluva woman.

Marnie, Marnie, Marnie. It would be best if he stayed away from her. But right now, he couldn't. Not yet. Despite all the pain he'd already caused her, he had to convince her to help him again.

Fat chance, he thought, irritated with how he'd bungled their relationship. *What relationship?* he thought irritably, and sighed in self-disgust. He'd destroyed any chance of her trusting him again.

A few tourists and townspeople wandered along the streets of Chinook Harbor. The air was clean and clear, the only evidence of the storm of the past week the streaks of mud lining the sidewalks and clogging the gutters.

Adam trekked the two blocks to the pier, hoping to spy Marnie, but was disappointed. The woman behind the desk of Barns's Charters and Repairs, Renada, if the smudged nameplate on her desk could be believed, cast him the same patient smile she always gave him, but she wouldn't let him near the *Marnie Lee.*

"Sorry, Mr. Drake, no can do," Renada said, as she had each time he'd visited. "You know the rules. Now, if you'd like to talk to Mr. Barns, I'll just call him…" She reached for the phone on the corner of her desk, but Adam shook his head. He'd already talked to Barns and gotten nowhere.

He turned to leave just as Ryan Barns himself swung through a back door. The man was short, wiry, with several tattoos decorating his beefy forearms. Sweat stains darkened the faded blue material of a T-shirt that matched the color of his eyes.

"Mr. Drake, back again, I see," Barns drawled, snapping a grimy cloth from the hip pocket of sagging jeans and wiping black oil from his hands on the rag. He smelled of diesel and tobacco. "Don't tell me. Ya come wantin' to get on board the *Marnie Lee* again."

"I'm looking for Miss Montgomery."

Barns sniffed and stuffed the oily rag back into his pocket. "She ain't here, but I told her you came snooping around here the other day and she was fit to be tied. Told me in no uncertain terms that you weren't allowed on her boat, that you and some guy named Simms were strictly off-limits."

"Is that so?"

Barns nodded and let out a whistle between slightly gapped front teeth. "I don't know what you did to that little lady, but she's madder'n hell at you."

"Just tell her I'd like to talk to her."

"Already did," Barns replied amiably. "And she told me to tell you to—" he glanced at his secretary who was just lighting a cigarette "—how'd she put it, Rennie? Something about buying a one-way ticket to hell—no, no, that wasn't it."

Renada let the smoke roll out her nostrils. "I think it was more like, 'Tell Mr. Drake he can stow away on the next steamer bound for hell, but he's not to set foot on the *Marnie Lee.*'"

"That was it!" Barns grinned and snapped his fingers. "I thought she was jokin', but she never once cracked a smile."

"Just tell her I was here again," Adam said as he left Renada and Barns chuckling at his expense.

In the motel's parking lot, Adam tossed his bag into the trunk of his rental car, then climbed behind the wheel. He knew where Marnie was staying, he'd just wanted to give her time to cool down before he showed up on her doorstep. But she'd refused to return his phone calls, and the one time he'd stopped by her hotel, she'd refused to meet him for a drink.

Adam couldn't wait any longer. He had to talk to her. Whether she wanted to see him or not.

So what're you going to do? Shanghai her? That particular thought brought a lift to the corners of his mouth and a warm feeling deep in his gut. Though he'd tried, he couldn't forget making love to her—hot and wild, savage and yet laced with tenderness, their lovemaking had burned bright in his mind. Especially at night.

He'd thought about finding himself another woman; there were lots of bored women in this town who had cast interested glances in his direction, but he'd never so much as tried to catch their eyes. No, right now, all of his sexual fantasies were tied up with Victor Montgomery's daughter.

Forbidden fruit.

Nonetheless, no other woman would do. Not until this mess with Montgomery Inns was resolved and Marnie was out of his blood forever. He flicked on the Ford's engine and edged into the slow flow of traffic.

One way or another, he had to convince Marnie to see things his way.

THE NOON SUN BEAT down with the intensity of July rather than late May, though no one had jumped into the pool, which sparkled invitingly near Marnie's table. Beneath a striped umbrella, Marnie sipped her tea and finished the crumbs of her croissant. She scanned the headlines of a Seattle paper she'd purchased in the lobby, unable to keep from looking for any information on Montgomery Inns.

The last time she'd seen her father, he'd been as angry as she'd ever seen him.

And Adam. She couldn't think of him without hurting inside.

"Moron," she muttered at herself as she sipped her tea. For the first time in days she'd felt like eating. So she'd ordered lunch on the veranda and settled in at this table flanked by planters overflowing with pink-and-white tulips and pale yellow daffodils. Only a few feet away, the aquamarine water in the pool shimmered invitingly.

Maybe she was finally getting over Adam, she thought, still scanning the paper.

Right. And maybe horses have learned to fly. Idly, she stirred her tea.

Somehow, she had to get on with her life. Without Adam Drake messing it up. She thought about how he'd planned her seduction, how he'd played with her emotions and how gullible she'd been. Believing him. Trusting him. She'd even fantasized that she'd been falling in love with him.

Silly, spoiled little girl. Used to getting your way. Well, when it comes to men and love, you just don't seem to learn. First Kent. Now Adam. What a pathetic list of men to fall in love with!

"I'm not, never have been and never will be in love with Adam Drake." She shoved her plate aside, licked her fingers and flipped through the classified section of the paper. Maybe having the *Marnie Lee* put up for repairs was a turn of good luck. She couldn't just climb on the boat and sail away from her problems. She had to face her future. A future without Kent, without Montgomery Inns and definitely without Adam.

She could move anywhere she chose. She had enough money to start her own public-relations firm, and if she were frugal, she could manage for nearly a year before she'd have to get a job to supplement her income.

She couldn't just take off on the boat and put off her decision about where she was going to live forever. She ran her fingers down the classified section of "business opportunities." Maybe there was a firm she could buy—on a contract, of course—and in time...

"Marnie?"

The sound of Adam's voice was like a jolt of electricity. She visibly jumped and snapped her head around to find him standing just outside the shade of the umbrella. *Oh, please, God, no!* Her heart thumped crazily at the sight of him, but she set her jaw and eyed him coolly. "I thought I made it clear—I don't want to speak to you."

"I got the message." He grabbed a chair from a nearby table, twisted it around and straddled it, his eyes squinting against the sun as he looked at her.

"I don't think you did. I never want to see you again."

"Never's a long time."

"Not long enough." She scooted her chair back, intending to leave, but he reacted too quickly, reaching out with the speed of a striking snake, his fingers closing tightly over her wrist.

"Just hear me out, okay?"

"Why?"

"Because it's important."

"Believe me, Mr. Drake, we don't have anything to discuss."

"I don't blame you for being angry."

"I'm *way* past angry, Adam. In fact, I'm beyond furious and enraged. Even livid doesn't quite describe—"

"Just listen to me."

"No—"

"Please," he said softly, and her heart turned to mush.

She had to remind herself what a black-souled bastard he really was. "There's no point, Adam," she said, pulling hard on her hand, but he didn't budge. "Let me go."

"No."

"I'll call security."

"And cause a scene?"

"Yes! You don't have an exclusive on creating a scandal, you know," she gambled. She'd been brought up believing in decorum and doing the right thing, but Adam blew all her beliefs right out of the water.

"Don't I?" His mouth stretched into a crooked, dangerous smile, and his golden brown eyes seemed to catch the rays of the sun. "We'll see about that," he drawled, standing, the pads of his fingers moving slightly against the inside of her arm. Marnie's pulse trembled and he felt it; she knew he did, by the spark of recognition in his gaze.

"What're you doing?" she whispered, conscious of more than a few pairs of eyes turned in their direction.

"Convincing you to listen to me."

"How?" she asked, her heart fluttering tremulously though she was still trying to draw away as she realized he intended to kiss her! "Oh, no—"

"See that man in the corner—about forty, round glasses?"

She couldn't help casting a glance to the edge of the veranda where the man, wearing a plaid sport jacket and brown slacks, was watching them intently. She froze.

"He's a photographer for the local paper."

"Sure," she said, hoping to sound sarcastic.

"He is."

"I don't have to listen to this," she said quickly, though she spied a camera on the table next to the man in question. She tried to yank away again and Adam, standing, drew her from her chair, wrenching her close so that her body slammed into his. His arms surrounded her, and he lowered his head as if he were going to kiss her. "Adam, don't—"

"Struggle if you want to. Make a scene. But think about it," he whispered against her ear. "Because if that man takes your picture and it somehow finds its way to the front page of the *Seattle Observer,* your father will probably see it."

"You're bluffing," she accused, but her heart nearly stopped when the man in the corner, as if looking for a cue from Adam, picked up his camera. Adam nodded imperceptibly and Marnie gulped. "You hired him, didn't you?" she whispered, horrified at the realization. "You hired him to do this so that—"

"Now listen, Marnie," Adam cut in, all humor leaving his face. "He's not going to do anything unless I give him the high sign."

"You wouldn't!" she whispered. How devious was Adam? To what lengths would he go?

"Watch me." His lips brushed over hers and even though a part of her was mortified, her body, at least, was thrilled. Her skin tingled where he touched her.

"Let go of me," she commanded. But if anything his grip tightened, and when he kissed her again, her breath was lost somewhere between her lungs and her throat, her mind caught between now and forever.

"Just listen to me," he said softly, when he raised his head from hers and she was conscious only of the rush of blood in her ears, the dizzy sensation in her mind.

"You're crazy! If you think I'm going to—"

"Come on, Marnie, what've you got to lose?" he asked, and when his gaze found hers, her throat squeezed at the tenderness in his eyes. *It's all an act! He's using you again! Don't let him! Marnie, use your head!*

"Just hear me out. I promise I'll be good."

"I don't think that's possible," she said, her voice

sounding odd when she finally found it again. "Just remember I don't *owe* you this, you know."

"Of course not. You're doing it out of the goodness of your heart," he quipped, but when she looked for a spark of levity in his expression, she found none.

She tried to remember why she should be furious with him, and though the reasons flitted through her mind, she refused to listen to them. And her temper, usually quick to flare, wouldn't ignite. Not with everyone on the verandah staring at them. "Let's get out of here."

"Now you're talking." He slid his fingers to the crook of her elbow and propelled her forward on a straight path between the tables to the foyer of the hotel. She scrabbled for her purse, but didn't put up any further argument. In her peripheral vision she noticed the blur of red-and-white flowers, early petunias, she guessed, and heard the clink of glasses as diners turned their attention back to their lunches, but everything else, save Adam's strong presence, faded into the background.

This is nuts, Marnie kept telling herself as he guided her past the front desk and into the elevator.

"What floor are you on?"

"Four."

He slapped the button, and the elevator doors closed before he finally trusted her not to bolt and released her. Her head started to clear. She realized they were headed for her hotel room and trouble. Big trouble. She couldn't be confined in a small room with a bed with Adam Drake! She couldn't trust him and she certainly couldn't trust herself!

The elevator stopped with a thump. The doors parted,

and Adam stepped onto the floral carpet of the corridor. Marnie didn't move. Before the doors closed again, Adam reached inside, grabbed her and hauled her out of the elevator car.

"Don't!"

"Come on, we don't have all day."

"For what?" she replied, her old fire returning as she jerked her arm back.

"For me to convince you to help me."

"W-what?" she sputtered, then laughed. "You're not serious, are you? You think *I,* after the way you treated me, would help *you.* Oh, come on, Drake! Never."

"Don't you want to know the truth?"

"I think I do. You were involved. Period. I don't know how deeply. I'm not sure if you were the brains behind the operation or just plain duped by someone else. Whatever the explanation is, I don't care."

"I don't believe you."

She turned a corner and stopped at 431, her room. But she didn't unlock the door. "Thanks for the escort. Not that I needed one. And as for that dirty trick—the one with the photographer—it was your last!"

He grinned at that. "Don't count on it."

His smile touched a corner of her heart, but she refused to be drawn into his web of lies again. "As far as I'm concerned, you're out of my life."

"Remember, you owe me one."

"I—what? As I said, I don't owe you anything—"

He leaned closer, and his thumb touched the slope of her jaw. "I remember distinctly you telling me that you owed me. Remember the deal we made? In the storm? You wanted me to help you get the boat to shore…"

His breath swept across her ear, and she licked her lips as she remembered that first fateful night of the storm and the pitching deck of the *Marnie Lee* when Adam had told her of the crack in the hull. "All deals are off," she said firmly.

"I never thought you'd be the kind to welsh, Ms. Montgomery."

"And I never thought you'd sleep with me just to get back at my father!"

He sucked in his breath. "Marnie, I—"

"I think you should leave."

He didn't move so much as an inch. "Then you don't want a partner?"

She was reaching into her bag, searching for the room key. "Partner? What kind of partner. Never mind—" she held out her palm and shook her head "—I don't want to know."

"A business partner."

Her heart dropped to the floor in disappointment. "Now I *know* you're joking," she said, finding her key and trying to sound cool and sophisticated. She couldn't let him know that she cared for him—even a little.

"I'm dead serious. I need you and you need me."

"I don't *need* anyone," she said, "especially not you." She shoved her key into the lock. Glancing over her shoulder, she said simply, "You're too much trouble, Mr. Drake, and right now I don't want or *need* any more trouble than I already have."

She took one step across the threshold before his hands grabbed her hard on the shoulders and spun her around, pushing her against the door frame. She barely caught her breath before his mouth crashed down on hers with a kiss as strong and demanding as the waves pounding the shore. His lips moved expertly along the contours of her mouth, gliding easily, molding to her skin until slowly her stiff resistance yielded and she kissed him back. Her mouth opened slightly, and his tongue darted between her parted lips, flicking and teasing as he pressed her body hard against the door-jamb, the wood cutting into her back as his hips pushed forward to pin her abdomen tight against him. "You're a liar," he breathed into her hair, and a familiar warm ache began to throb deep inside her. "You do need me."

"No." Oh, God, why did she sound so weak?

"And I get the feeling you like trouble. You need some spark in your life—a little shot of danger to spice up that dreary existence of the spoiled little rich girl."

"You bastard," she hissed, struggling again. "You don't know anything about me! How dare you—ooh!" Cupping her nape, he drew her head to his and kissed her so hungrily her knees threatened to buckle. She tried to resist, to fight him, but her arms and legs wouldn't respond and all her defiance slipped away.

She sagged against him, suddenly anxious to feel the sinewy muscles of his body straining through his clothes. When he at last dragged his mouth from hers, her breathing came in short gulps and her mind was reeling out of control, stumbling into risky territory, a region where she might just let herself trust Adam again. Her hands trembled as she pushed him away. "I...hate you."

"I know." He kissed her again, and she couldn't breathe.

"You... I...we can't do this."

"Sure we can," he drawled.

"*I* can't. This madness has got to stop."

"Not yet, Marnie. Not until I convince you that it's not madness. I need your help."

"We tried this once before. It didn't work! It'll never work!"

A lock clicked two doors down the hall.

What now?

An elderly man, wearing a fedora and carrying a wooden cane and newspaper tucked under his arm, stepped into the hallway from his room. Locking his door, he sent a cursory glance in Adam and Marnie's direction. A soft smile bowed beneath his snowy moustache as he passed, and Marnie blushed to the roots of her hair as she guessed his thoughts. He probably concluded that she and Adam were involved in a lovers' spat.

Ridiculous! But close enough to the truth to bother her. "I don't have anything else to say to you," she insisted, as, over the top of Adam's shoulder, she observed the elderly gentleman pushing the elevator call button before leaning on his cane.

"Just hear me out."

The elevator doors opened and a family of four exited, two boys clamoring down the hall while their parents struggled with shopping bags.

This was outlandish! She hated the scene they were making, inwardly wincing at the knowing glance the twelve-year-old boy sent her as he raced past.

"Okay—but you've got five minutes," she said, already deciding that listening to him was a mistake. She shoved open her door and they stepped inside. Adam locked the door behind him, and Marnie felt an overwhelming sense of desperation. She crossed to the bureau and rested her hips against the polished edge, refusing to even acknowledge the queen-size bed dominating the small suite.

"What I've got is a simple business proposition for you," Adam said.

"I'm all ears." She couldn't help the sarcasm.

"Oh, no, Marnie, there's more to your body than that," he drawled, sitting on a corner of the bed and staring at her with those golden brown eyes.

"Just get to the point." She walked to the window and fiddled nervously with the blinds. She felt his gaze on her backside, and her skin prickled.

"Okay," he said, smiling at her obvious discomfort. "I know you want to start your own business and that you haven't quite figured out where to land yet."

"How do you—oh, never mind. Go on."

"So—why not settle in Seattle?"

She snorted. "Are you crazy? I'm trying to get away from Montgomery Inns."

"I know, but maybe that's a mistake." He stretched out on the bed, and Marnie was aware of how good he looked. Freshly shaven, with clean clothes, his body long and lean against the slate blue spread, he smiled up at her, and her heart melted.

"A—a mistake?"

"You're killing the golden goose. I bet your father would hire you as a freelance publicist. You could have the Montgomery Inn account, as well as drumming up your own business. You could cultivate other accounts, start your own little empire."

"My father demands absolute loyalty."

"You wouldn't be disloyal."

She hurled him a glance that called him a liar. "He doesn't like sharing."

"You're freelancing. It's not a matter of sharing. Besides, what better way to build client confidence than by snagging one of the best accounts in the business?"

"Because I'm Victor's daughter. Back to square one." She yanked hard on the blinds, drawing them open before sitting on the window ledge and staring out at the warm afternoon. From her vantage point, she saw the glittery waters of the bay and the fishing boats and sailing vessels moving along the horizon. "So where do you come in? What was all this talk of a partnership?" She glanced over her shoulder.

His eyes locked with hers, and an indecent flame flickered in those sienna orbs. "I can think of a few ways," he said, smoothing a wrinkle from the quilt.

"Name them."

"I'd hire you."

"As what?" she asked suspiciously, while dragging her eyes away from the seductive movement of his hand against the bedspread.

"As a publicist for the first Hotel Drake."

"Which doesn't yet exist," she pointed out.

"It will, once I've settled a few things."

"And this fictitious hotel—will it be located in Seattle?"

"It would be easiest for me. After all, I already live there."

She knew that he resided in Seattle in a condominium on the shore of Lake Washington, complete with a mooring for his own boat—the boat he'd probably left in Port Stanton when he'd stowed away on the *Marnie Lee.* "And if you never get this hotel off the ground—"

"I will," he said emphatically, then sighed. "Look, I know a lot of people—more than you," he added, when she was about to point out that she'd been around people in the hotel business for years. "Contacts that could get you off your feet and away from the golden handcuffs of Montgomery Inns."

"I'm already there," she said.

"But you've got to start somewhere."

That much was true.

"And if things don't work out in Seattle, you're no worse off than you are now."

Except you'll be near Dad again. That part she could handle, as long as she was her own boss. *And Kent?* She'd avoid him. And wouldn't it be pleasant showing him that she could make it on her own? Without a man.

Adam Drake's a man.

Dealing with Adam would be the hardest part in all of this. She'd just have to find a way to keep him at arm's length. "This would be strictly business?" she asked.

"Whatever you want."

Her voice wouldn't work for a second. "Our relationship would have to be only professional."

"What else?"

She blushed, damn it, but managed a cool, sophisticated loft of her brow. "There isn't anything, is there?"

"Just the fact that you still owe me one."

"Don't remind me."

Slowly he rolled off the bed, crossed the small expanse of carpet and placed one hand on either side of the windowsill, holding her prisoner. "Then we have a deal?"

Nodding, she tried to shrink away, but was drawn by the magnetism in his eyes. "We have a deal." She thrust out her hand, expecting him to take it, but a crooked smile slowly curved his mouth.

"I think we should seal this bargain with a kiss." Before she could answer, his mouth found hers again and she didn't even try to stop him. She felt her body molding to his of its own accord, and she lost herself in the feel and taste of him.

A partnership with Adam Drake would be no better than dealing with the devil, but right now, wrapped in his arms, Marnie didn't care.

CHAPTER NINE

TRYING TO FORGET the memory of making love to Adam, Marnie hammered another nail into the freshly painted wall of her new office and carefully hung a painting she'd picked up at a local gallery.

Why couldn't she forget him? she wondered, surveying her work with a critical eye. It had been two weeks since she'd awoken in the hotel room alone in Port Chinook. Though she hadn't slept with him, his image had lingered in her mind and had been imprinted on her heart. She'd forced herself to leave him, but she hadn't gone far. In fact, she'd taken his advice and located her new business in Seattle, less than a mile from the corporate headquarters of Montgomery Inns. And she couldn't stop thinking about him.

Shoving the hammer into an empty desk drawer, she muttered, "You're hopeless, Montgomery." Sighing, she flopped onto the edge of the credenza, clasped her hands between her knees and remembered their goodbyes.

"I'll call you," Adam had said, gathering her into his arms, smelling so earthy and male.

"Give me time to settle in—think things through," she'd replied. "Remember, I'm not really convinced that moving in next to my father is the smartest thing I've ever done."

"No," he'd agreed, his eyes twinkling as he looked down at her. "Linking up with me is the smartest thing you've done."

She'd laughed. "I'm afraid linking up with you will be the end of me."

"Never." He'd lifted her up, twirled her off her feet, and when she'd slid back to the floor, kissed her with such breathless passion that, even now, seated in the office, she tingled.

"Remember, we're partners," he'd reminded her.

"But I need time to be my own person before I can be partners with anyone," she'd replied, and she'd left without him, wondering if he would return to Seattle.

Now, two weeks later she knew he, too, was living somewhere near the city. He'd tried to contact her, but she hadn't been ready to talk to him or deal with the conflicting emotions that he always seemed to ignite. Their meetings had been brief. Sometimes she was sure she loved him. In other, more rational hours, she thought she hated him, or should hate him.

She brushed her hands on her skirt and stood in the middle of her office. It was small, even cramped, but was located in a decent part of town. It also came with a part-time secretary and wasn't too expensive.

Marnie had found it herself after a week of reading the paper, talking to realtors and touring available sites. She'd repainted the walls, bought a desk, chairs and a credenza, and set out a few plants near the window. A skylight offered a view of the clouds shifting in the sky. "Home, sweet home," she told herself.

So now all she had to do was drum up business. Her first appointment this afternoon was with her father.

"Fitting," she muttered, checking her watch as her

stomach clenched. She'd already approached two other hotel chains, the marina and a local restaurant without much success, but today she was scheduled to walk back through the hallowed halls of Montgomery Inns.

Adam's idea. Right now, she wasn't convinced working for the company again was such a great plan. As for Adam, she'd seen him briefly a couple of times when he'd stopped by the office, but she'd declined any chance to spend much time with him. Her feelings about him were still confused. She didn't know whether she hated him or loved him, but she told herself that she couldn't trust him.

So why did you take his advice and come back here? Because you "owed him one"? Because you want to start a business relationship with him, become "partners"? Get real, Marnie.

"Oh, shut up!" she grumbled at the nagging note of conscience that had been hounding her since she returned to Seattle.

"You talkin' to me?" Donna's voice carried through the partially opened door. Donna came with the building and was secretary-receptionist for Marnie, an accountant and an interior designer, all of whom occupied this floor of the Maynard Building.

"Just to myself," Marnie sang back.

Grabbing her briefcase and purse, Marnie walked briskly through the door to her office. Donna, offbeat compared to the secretaries who pledged allegiance to Montgomery Inns, was bent over the keyboard of her computer terminal and fiddling with the keys. Somewhere close to twenty, with spiky red hair and outlandish jewelry, she managed to juggle her workload and keep all three offices running smoothly, though she spent a lot of time drinking coffee and smoking cigarettes. So far, though, Marnie had no complaints. Donna was refreshing, outspoken and incredibly efficient.

"Damned thing," Donna muttered, her pretty face a knot of frustration as she poked a long, bloodred finger between the keys of the keyboard.

The computer bleeped angrily.

"Problems?" Marnie asked.

"Always. Can't get the printer to work. I've called the company a million times and they can't seem to find the bug in the system." She leaned back in her chair and lit a cigarette, blowing smoke to the ceiling and scowling at the machine as if she could will it to turn on and hum companionably.

"Wish I could help, but I'm definitely on the 'user unfriendly' list," Marnie joked. "I'll be at Montgomery Inns for a couple of hours. If it takes longer, I'll give you a call."

"I'll be here," Donna replied, wrinkling her nose at the terminal. "Probably all night if I can't get this thing to work."

Marnie waved and walked outside, bracing herself for the battle that she was sure would erupt when she came face-to-face with her father again.

"Marnie!" Kate Delany clasped her hands together and grinned broadly as Marnie walked toward her desk. Piped-in music played softly from hidden speakers and recessed lighting offered soothing tones in the administrative offices of Montgomery Inns. "It's good to see you again!" Kate enthused. "You know, it hasn't been the same here without you—and him—" she motioned to the closed door of Victor's private suite "—he's been an absolute bear!"

"I can imagine," Marnie drawled.

"Please, for the rest of us, reconsider and come back," Kate begged, though her dark eyes sparkled with a teasing light. "If you were around, things would go *sooo* much smoother."

Marnie laughed. She was surprised, but it felt good to be in familiar surroundings again. She relaxed a little as Kate rapped softly before shoving open one of the twin mahogany doors. "She's here," Kate said, closing the door behind Marnie and leaving father and daughter alone.

Victor was seated on the couch, pretending interest in a sailing magazine. "You're late."

"I don't think so—"

He looked up then, his face a little paler than she remembered. "God, it's good to see you."

"You, too, Dad." And she meant it. They stood staring at each other for a few seconds, and all the horrible words and accusations that had kept them apart seemed to fade away. She knew she should still be angry with him; he had, after all, encouraged Kent to lie to the press about their engagement, but despite all Victor's faults, Marnie knew he loved her. Everything he did was simply because he was trying to make her life easier. "Oh, Dad," she whispered, her throat suddenly tight.

Tossing his magazine aside, he rose to his feet and hugged her so fiercely she nearly cried. "Sorry about all that business with Kent," he said, his voice unusually gruff. "Kate advised me to 'butt out of your love life.'"

"A wise woman, Ms. Delany. Maybe you should marry her," Marnie said, lifting her head and swallowing back her tears. She held her father at arm's length and cocked her head to one side. "What d'ya think?"

Victor chuckled as he released her and smoothed his jacket. "Far as I'm concerned, I am married."

"Dad, Mom's been gone a long time."

"I know. And when I die, I'm going to be put into the ground right next to her." He shoved his hands into his pockets and jangled his keys. "Well, have you come to your senses, yet?"

She felt a knot of anxiety tighten her nerves. "About what?"

"About coming back, that's what! I thought you were here to talk business!"

"Yes and no," she hedged. "Come on, Dad, let's sit down." She motioned toward his desk, and Victor, casting her a suspicious glance, settled into his wide leather chair.

"What's this all about?"

"I do want to work for you," she said, "but not as an employee. This is what I think we should do…" She launched into her speech, explained about her new business, how she wanted to freelance, and how she hoped to develop her own set of clients. *And become publicist for the Hotel Drake?* she thought guiltily.

As she spoke, rapidly at first, her father said nothing, just tented his hands under his chin and, while his expression turned dark, stared at her over his fingertips.

When she finally finished, his lips were pursed tightly, and his nostrils had flared. With worried blue eyes, he continued staring at her, and the clock mounted on one wall struck three.

Marnie's insides twisted. She couldn't stand the suspense. "Well?"

He hesitated, but only slightly, and Marnie's heart sank. "The answer is no."

"No?" All her soaring hopes nose-dived back to earth and crashed on the stones of cold reality. What had she expected? She was, after all, still dealing with Victor Montgomery.

"You either work for me or you don't. Period."

"But, Dad—"

He shook his head. "I'll not be used, and I won't allow this corporation to be a springboard for you. This company has been good to you, and so have I. I'm willing to pay you top dollar to work for me as an executive, but I'm not going to subsidize your talent so that you can go out and work for the competition."

"I'm only working for myself. Like you."

"Bull." His fist crashed onto the desk, jarring his humidor and photographs. "Unless I miss my guess, this has something to do with Drake, doesn't it?"

"Adam's not involved—"

"Like hell!" Victor's face suffused with color. "That miserable bastard. First the company, then you. What's the man got against me?"

"Maybe he doesn't like the way you convicted him without a trial," she said sharply, surprised at her quick defense of a man she, herself, didn't completely trust.

"So now you're on his side. When he practically kidnapped you and God only knows what else?"

"He didn't kidnap me, Dad. If anything, I took him where he didn't want to go. And as for sides, I'm not on his or your—"

Her father made a dismissive sound just as Kate knocked and poked her head into the office. "Mr. Simms would like to see you. He asked that I interrupt."

"Not now," Victor snapped, but Kent had already brushed past Kate and strode into the office.

"You're back?" Kent asked, his handsome face breaking into a smile of relief.

Marnie had to grit her teeth to be civil to him. "It doesn't look that way."

Kent stared from Marnie to Victor and back again. "But you're here and…" He gestured toward her briefcase and she noticed him staring at her clothes—the neat black suit and royal blue silk blouse.

"I'm here on business, yes," Marnie replied, lifting her chin, "but your boss isn't interested."

"Victor?" Kent asked.

Victor grumbled as he reached for his pipe and humidor. "She's here because of Drake."

"No, Dad. This is *my* business."

"Humph." He unscrewed the lid of the humidor and filled his pipe with his favorite blend of tobacco.

"Drake?" Kent repeated. "What's he got to do with this?"

"Nothing!" Marnie insisted.

"Everything. He's behind this, you know." Victor struck a match and puffed furiously as he tried to light his pipe. The flame burned his fingers, and he cursed around the stem of his pipe, waving the match out before lighting another. "He's concocted some harebrained scheme about Marnie going out on her own, starting her own publicity business, for crying out loud, and then holding this company up for ransom while working for my competitors! Well, I won't have it!" He shook out his match.

Marnie climbed to her feet and leaned over her father's desk. Her temper was slowly getting the better of her. "You haven't even heard me out," she said, ignoring Kent. "You have no idea what I'd charge. Hiring me freelance would be cheaper than paying me all those employee benefits and taxes you keep complaining about."

"Hey—slow down. You want to work here?" Kent inquired, his gaze as skeptical as her father's.

"On my terms."

"Out of the question." Victor tried to hand her back her proposal, but she reached for her briefcase, snapped it closed and turned her back on the neatly typed pages in her father's fingers.

"Read it, Dad. You might find it interesting." She crossed to the door, and Kent, with a high-sign to Victor, followed her past Kate's desk and down the hall.

"Let me talk to him for you," he suggested, once they were out of Kate's earshot.

"No, thanks. I can speak for myself." Kent was a good reason to be glad she didn't have to work with Montgomery Inns. She wasn't sure she could stand being around him.

"I know, but I think we could work something out." When she didn't reply and kept marching toward the elevators, Kent grabbed her arm and tried to twirl her around. "Marnie, if you'll just listen—"

"Let go of me!" She yanked her arm back as the doors of the elevator opened. Why had she come here? She'd known how her father would react. Now she had to deal with Kent! Shooting him a withering glare, she climbed into the waiting elevator and pressed the button for the lobby. Kent slid between the closing doors.

She was trapped alone with Kent. Damn Adam Drake and his stupid ideas! She should've known this would blow up in her face. She stood in one corner of the car, watching as the lights to the floors flickered on and off. Fourteen…thirteen…twelve…

"Marnie," Kent said softly.

Eleven…ten…

"I want you back."

She uttered a sound of disbelief. "No." Nine…

"I want to see you again."

"It's over, Kent." Eight…seven… Come on, come on, elevator, she thought, wishing it would land in the lobby or some other soul would stop its downward descent and climb on board.

"It doesn't have to be."

She held her silence and heard him swear softly before he slammed his palm on the "stop" button. The elevator jerked to a halt somewhere between the fourth and third floors. Her feet nearly slipped out from under her, and her briefcase banged against the walls of the car. "What are you doing?" she nearly screamed.

"I'm going to talk, damn it, and you're going to listen!"

"No way!" She reached behind him, trying to press the control panel, but he caught her wrist and shoved her back against the wooden panels of the elevator car. "Are you out of your mind?" she whispered, shocked at his nerve. Who did he think he was? "Let go of me!"

"You're the one who should come to your senses."

"About what?"

"Us, Marnie. We could be good together."

"Oh, *pleeease*." She couldn't believe he still thought she cared. What an incredible ego! She pulled hard on her arm, but he didn't release her. "Let go of me, Kent," she warned, wondering if she should scream or kick.

Screaming would attract attention—probably the wrong kind—and kicking him might make him all the more violent.

"I mean it," he persisted, his face close to hers. "We've got so much going for us already. Your dad approves of me, he bought us the boat—"

"A big mistake. We've got nothing, Kent. Release me immediately and I won't cause a scene."

He didn't hear her, but rambled on. "I'm sorry for Dolores and for talking out of turn to the press. I made some mistakes, and don't you think I've paid for them?" For a second a glimmer of intense pain surfaced in his hazel eyes.

She didn't buy it.

"Come on, Marnie. Why don't you and I take the boat for a cruise, try to patch things up?"

"I don't want to hear this, Kent," she said, her voice edged in steel as she glared at him. Motioning toward the control panel with her briefcase, she said, "You've had your little drama, now take your hands off me and let's get going. I have another appointment."

"With whom?"

"It doesn't matter."

"Drake?" Kent demanded, and his fingers tightened around her wrist, pinching her skin. Her stomach roiled.

"Stop it—"

"He doesn't care for you, you know. You saw that up on the island." Kent's face was so close to hers she could see the beads of sweat on his upper lip. "He's using you, Marnie. To get back at your father, or me, or whoever else he thinks hurt him. He doesn't care for you and he never will."

He voiced all her own insecurities, but she managed

to lift her chin a fraction and stare into his eyes. "Let me go, you bastard. Or I'll call security."

Kent sneered, and his breath was hot against her face. For the first time since entering the car with him she felt real fear. "You think he loves you, don't you? Oh, God, Marnie, you're such a fool." He laughed coldly before his lips crashed down on hers with a possessive force that repelled her. Her stomach roiled again, and she struggled, pushing against his shoulders and trying to kick him in the shins. But he sidestepped her blow and kissed her all the harder, groaning low in his throat and pinning her hard against the elevator wall. His mouth ground down on hers with a savagery that scared her to death. She stopped struggling, went absolutely rigid in his arms.

He tried to turn her on. His hands moved against her back, his lips played across hers, but she remained stiff and unresponsive as a statue, knowing instinctively that if she fought him, he'd misconstrue her struggle for passion. When he lifted his head for a second, she moved quickly, biting his lip, then lunging past him and hitting the control panel with both hands.

He yipped. The car jolted, nearly toppling them both before resuming its downward flight.

"Don't you *ever* touch me again," she warned furiously, brandishing her briefcase as if she'd hit him with it. "If you ever, *ever* lay so much as one finger on me, I'll have you up on charges so fast your head will spin."

Blood surfaced at the corner of his mouth, but she didn't feel a shred of remorse. He reached into his pocket for his handkerchief and dabbed at the corner of his mouth. "You're making a big mistake," he said, his eyes narrowing as he attended his wound.

"Not as big as the one I made when I got engaged to you."

His face twisted as if he really were in pain. He blinked hard, and his voice cracked when he whispered, "I love you, Marnie," but he didn't try to reach for her again.

"No, Kent," she replied as the elevator hit ground level. "You love yourself. And my father's money. And the boat. Nothing else really matters to you." She turned and left him, pretending she didn't hear when he called after her.

"That boat is half mine! I've still got my things, *my* things on board," he yelled.

Marnie didn't bother turning around. She crossed the tiled foyer of the hotel, walked through a revolving door and took big gulps of rain-washed air. She was shaking all over and she thought she might throw up at the thought of Kent's hands on her. She went to the nearest phone booth and dialed Adam's number. If only she could see him, touch him…but that was crazy. She was lucky to be rid of Kent; she couldn't rush things with Adam. She wasn't even sure that she wanted Adam as part of her life.

But he already was.

With that disturbing thought, she hung up the unanswered phone, walked back into the building and ran down the stairs to the parking lot.

IT TOOK ANOTHER WEEK for Victor to call. In that time Marnie hadn't seen much of Adam, but that was her choice. No men. No complications. "And no fun," Donna informed her when she heard about Marnie's philosophy. "You know what they say about all work and no play."

"'They,' whoever they are, could be wrong," Marnie replied.

She and Donna had just finished lunch—take-out Chinese food—and Donna was getting ready for an afternoon of typing late tax returns for the accountant by touching up her fingernails with a coat of raspberry-ice polish. Why Donna polished her nails before typing was a mystery to Marnie, but she didn't complain because Donna's work was flawless and they were fast becoming friends.

"Who are these guys anyway?" Donna said, motioning with her head toward a stack of phone messages in Marnie's mail slot. "Victor, Kent, Adam and some guy named Ryan Barns. They never leave you alone."

Marnie grinned impishly, and she threw back her head. "They're all my lovers," she teased, glancing at Donna from the corners of her slitted eyes.

"Sure. The career woman who wants no complications." Donna's plucked brows raised expectantly. "Tell me another one."

"I thought you knew that Victor's my father."

"I'd guessed that much," Donna admitted.

"And Kent—he works for Dad." She purposely left out the fact that they had once been engaged. It was over. No reason to bring up the sorry past.

"He sounds desperate." Her gray eyes appraised Marnie. "And he keeps talking about some boat. Your boat?"

"Believe me, it's a long and boring story," Marnie said, stuffing her empty chow mein carton into a white sack.

"What about Adam Drake?" Donna asked, blowing on her nails.

Good question. What about Adam? She couldn't

spend a waking hour without thinking about him. "Adam used to work for my father. Maybe you read about him. It was in all the papers a year ago."

"A year ago I was in Santa Barbara."

"Another long and boring story," Marnie assured her as she tossed the sack into the trash. "Let's just say he and my dad are mortal enemies."

"Sounds interesting. Besides, I don't think anything about *that* man could be boring. He stopped by yesterday."

"He did?" Marnie was flabbergasted.

Donna read the expression on her face and frowned. "You know, I should've told you, but you were gone at the time and he said it wasn't important, that he'd come back in a few days and then I got busy with tax reports for Miles and—"

"It's all right," Marnie assured her, though she wasn't up to another meeting with Adam. Not yet. She needed more time for her emotions to settle. If that were possible.

"If he shows up again, what should I tell him?"

"That I'm busy...well, no," she retracted. She couldn't avoid him forever, and she really didn't want to. Sooner or later she'd have to confront him as well as her own feelings. "Tell him I'd be glad to see him," Marnie said against her better judgment. There was a part of her that couldn't resist Adam Drake, no matter how many times she told herself that being with him was only inviting disaster.

Two hours later, her father called. "I've reconsidered," he said, and Marnie, sitting precariously on the corner of her desk, nearly fell over. Victor Montgomery wasn't known for changing his mind once he'd taken a stand.

"And?" she said.

"I spoke to several people on the board who want to give you a chance, and it goes without saying that Kent is in your corner. He tells me I'm a fool to let pride stand in my way."

"I don't know what to say." Instantly, Marnie's defenses were up.

"You don't have to say anything. Just show up at the meeting next Monday morning, 9:00 a.m. sharp and lay out your proposal. I want Simms, Byers, Anderson and Finelli to see what you've come up with. Then I'll let you know."

"Fair enough, Dad," she said, trying to keep the smile from her voice. Maybe doing business with Montgomery Inns would work out after all. This might just be the first step to reconciling with her father. She and Victor were the only members of the Montgomery family. And she never doubted that her father loved her; he was just misguided in his attempt to control her life. Finally it looked as if he was about to treat her as an independent woman.

"But I think we should be clear on one point," Victor said, his voice taking on that old familiar ring of authority.

Here it comes—the bomb. "What's that?"

"Adam Drake."

Her heart nearly stopped. "What about him?"

"I never want to hear his name mentioned again."

"Don't you think you're being a little theatrical?" Marnie asked. "He was your employee once. His name is bound to come up."

"Not from you."

"I can't promise that, Dad. But I'll try," she conceded.

"Fair enough. I miss you, Marnie. We all do."

"And I miss you, Dad." She hung up feeling better than she had in weeks. Most of her anger had cooled, and she was ready to deal with him as businesswoman to businessman. She wasn't sure just how she would handle the father/daughter relationship yet, but she was buoyed that Victor had taken the first step toward mending fences.

"One step at a time," she told herself firmly.

THE AFTERNOON SUN was pale behind a hazy layer of clouds. The smells of diesel and dead fish floated on the air and in the water. Adam shoved his sunglasses onto his head and lifted his binoculars, focusing on *Elmer's Folly,* a charter fishing boat churning toward the docks of Ilwaco with Gerald Henderson on board.

It had taken him nearly a week to track down Henderson, who had fled Seattle the day after Adam crashed the party at the Puget West. The way Adam figured it, Gerald had read about Adam being thrown out of the hotel in the *Seattle Observer,* realized there was going to be trouble and decided to disappear for a while.

Unfortunately for Henderson, Adam knew about his sister's beach cabin in Longview and also knew that Henderson enjoyed deep-sea fishing and usually reserved space on the same charter boat which moored in Ilwaco, a small fishing village located on the Washington shore of the mouth of the Columbia River. *Elmer's Folly* chugged into the small marina, located not far from the fish-processing plant, where you could buy anything from clams to salmon or have your trophy gutted, skinned and canned or smoked, depending upon your preference.

Adam spied Henderson on board with eight other men. Good.

Lowering his binoculars, content to wait until all the fishermen disembarked, he leaned against the sun-bleached rail and shoved his sunglasses onto the bridge of his nose.

Gerald Henderson took his time about getting off the boat, but finally he appeared on the dock, wearing worn jeans, flannel shirt, jacket and a hat decorated with fishing lures and hooks. He hauled a couple of fishing poles and a tackle box with him.

"Any luck?" Adam asked, once he'd closed the distance between himself and Henderson. He'd waited around most of the afternoon and now he wanted answers.

"Nah, not even a nibble," Henderson replied before looking up and realizing Adam wasn't just another interested fisherman asking about the salmon run. Henderson's face fell. "What're you doing here?"

"Waiting for you."

"Why? I've already told you everything I know."

"Have you?" Adam surveyed the smaller man. Henderson was nervous, glancing over his shoulder and gnawing at his lip.

"I just want to know how deeply Simms was involved in the embezzling mess."

"Kent?" Henderson shrugged. "We went over this, Drake. I'm not sure who was involved. It could've been you."

"But it wasn't."

"Probably not," Henderson admitted, reaching into the inside pocket of his jacket for a crumpled pack of cigarettes. "Kate and I found the discrepancies on the books and brought them to Kent's attention. He took it from there. But he seemed as surprised as I was that there was something wrong." He tried to shake out a single cigarette, but three or four dropped onto the dock. Swearing, Henderson bent over and picked them up.

"Maybe Kent was just surprised that you figured it out," Adam offered.

Henderson stuck one cigarette between his lips and shoved the others back in the pack. "Maybe." He began walking again, toward the sandy parking lot.

"And you were paid to keep your mouth shut."

"I wasn't paid a dime." He cupped his cigarette against the wind and clicked his lighter to the tip.

"Then how're you surviving?"

"Disability."

"What?"

"And my pension. You should've stayed on with the company a few more years. Great benefits."

"If you say so."

"I do." Henderson took a deep drag on his cigarette. "Look, Drake, I don't know why you think I'll say something more than you don't already know, but I won't. You know everything I do, so why don't you just bug off?" With that he stalked across the lot to a dusty red pickup and threw his fishing gear behind the seat back.

Adam was right on his heels. "There's more that you're not telling me."

Henderson tossed his cigarette into the gravel where the butt burned slowly, a curling thread of smoke spiraling into the clear air. "I don't *know* anything. I just have hunches."

"What are they?"

"Nothing that I can prove." He started to climb into the cab of the pickup, but Adam grabbed his arm and spun him around, slamming him up against the back fender.

"I'll do the proving," he said, shoving his face next to Henderson's and seeing a drip of perspiration as it slid from beneath the smaller man's hatband. "Who agreed to pay your disability?"

Henderson gulped. "The old man himself."

"Montgomery?"

"Yeah."

Adam didn't let go of Henderson's lapels. "And who told you that you'd be paid?"

"My boss. Fred."

"Fred Ainger?"

"Right."

Adam's hard gaze pinned Henderson to the fender. Henderson was shaking by this time, sweat running down his neck in tiny streams. "You think he was involved?"

"I told you, man, I *don't* know." Henderson's gaze slid away, and he smoothed the front of his jacket. "Fred has money problems—I don't know how serious."

"What kind of money problems?"

Chewing on a corner of his lip, Henderson said, "Fred's still paying off Hannah for their divorce—she took half of everything they owned and even got part of his pension, I think. Good old community property." Gerald lifted his hat and wiped the sweat from his brow. "And now he's got Bernice for a wife. She's the daughter of some bigwig doctor back east. Used to expensive things. Fred tries to get them for her. And she's hell-on-wheels with a credit card. Seems to think credit means free money."

Bernice Ainger was thirty years younger than Fred. He'd met her at a convention, become obsessed with her and divorced Hannah to marry the younger woman. He'd been in his early fifties at the time and he'd been paying for that mistake ever since. So how did Fred connect with Simms?

"Funny," Adam drawled, though he wasn't the least in the mood for humor, "but every time I'm around Simms, he seems nervous—like he knows more than he's telling. The thing is, I don't believe that he'd intentionally get caught up in anything that might ruin his career."

"Sometimes people do things on impulse."

"No, this was planned for a long time. Otherwise the money would've been recovered."

Gerald's gaze shifted again, and Adam got the feeling he was wrestling with his conscience. For that, Adam respected him. Ratting on his friends didn't come easy to Henderson. Or else he was just trying to save his own neck.

"I heard something once," Henderson admitted, as the scent of dead fish wafted across the parking lot.

"What?"

"It was Simms, I'm sure it was, though he didn't know that I was on the other side of the partition in the accounting room. I'd been in the vault, and when I came out I didn't say anything. Simms was on the other side of that partition that separated Fred's office from mine...you know the one I mean."

Adam nodded, his heartbeat accelerating slightly. Now, finally, he was getting somewhere.

"Well, anyway, Simms was angry, really angry, telling someone off, but I didn't see who it was. They were walking out the door."

Adam could hardly believe his good luck. For the first time he was learning something new, that Simms *was* directly involved, but that he had an accomplice. Adam had to force himself not to shake every detail out of Henderson.

"Who was in Fred's office when you went into the vault?"

"No one."

"Not Fred?"

"Nope, he'd gone home for the day. Saw him leave myself."

"And Kent?"

Henderson shook his head slowly. "He wasn't there either, but I was in the vault for a good five or ten minutes. And when I came out, Simms and whoever he was talking to were on their way out."

"And you don't think Fred came back? Couldn't he have returned to the office for something he'd forgotten, his keys or wallet or something?"

Henderson took off his hat and slapped it against his thigh. A ring of sweat curled his thin sandy hair. "I don't think so. But I don't know."

"So you think Kent, with or without Fred's help, took some of the Puget West funds?"

"I can't say. I don't know much about Simms. He's kind of a pretty boy, and I doubt he'd do anything to jeopardize his job. After all, he's engaged to the boss man's daughter."

"*Was* engaged," Adam said quickly, irritated that anyone, even Gerald Henderson, who probably had been out of touch with the gossip at Montgomery Inns for a while, would think that Marnie and Kent were still an item. "Past tense."

Henderson stuck out his lower lip and shrugged. "Well, then, who knows. He might have got himself into a heap of debt somehow. That's what happened to Fred. He's hurtin' for cash." He hesitated a second, but then, like so many men when they can finally get something off their chest, Henderson added, "This might sound strange, but...well, I got the feeling that Simms was talking to a woman—not by what he said, but by the scent in the room. You know, like some kind of expensive perfume."

Adam's heart nearly stopped. "Would you recognize it again?"

"I..." Henderson shrugged, then shook his head. "Probably not."

"But who do you *think* it was?" Henderson's intuition might naturally come up with the right suspect.

"I said I don't know. There's got to be seventy-five women working in that building. Simms was probably on a first name basis with half of 'em. I couldn't begin to guess."

"Linda Kirk works in accounting," Adam ventured, turning his thoughts away from a dark possibility.

"But she was home sick that day. In fact, she was gone for over a week with the flu."

Marnie. She'd been going out with Simms at the time... But she had no reason to embezzle funds. Just because Marnie was involved with Simms wasn't any reason to think that she would steal from her own father…no, that line of thinking was preposterous.

Henderson was obviously thinking he'd said too much. His face was flushed; his eyes showed a hint of panic. "Look, Drake, that's all I know. Really."

This time Adam believed him and stepped away from the truck.

Climbing quickly into the cab, Henderson flicked on the ignition. The engine sparked, died, then caught with a roar and a plume of foul-smelling exhaust. Above the rumble of the engine Henderson said, "Fred's not such a bad guy, you know. Just got himself into a little trouble. And Simms—hell, what can you say about that guy?"

"And the woman?"

"*If* there was one. I'm not sure…" He rammed the truck into first, pulled the door closed and took off, spraying gravel and dust behind him.

Adam didn't know if Henderson's information had helped him or not. All along he'd thought Kent Simms was responsible for framing him and that he'd done it alone. Had he been wrong? Was Ainger or a mystery woman involved? Or was Henderson just blowing smoke? Trying to save his own tail?

Adam didn't think so. The man was terrified that he'd slipped up by spilling his guts. So now, he had to try to locate a woman…a woman involved with Kent. But *not* Marnie!

Angrily Adam stomped out Henderson's still-smoldering cigarette and watched as Gerald's pickup wound down the dusty road. Without any answers, he walked across the gritty parking lot and slid into the interior of his rig. Spinning the steering wheel, he headed north to Seattle.

Next stop: Marnie's place. She'd been avoiding him for too long. She'd had enough time to think things through. Besides, he needed her to help him get to the bottom of this.

And you want her. Scowling, he twisted on the radio, hoping to drown out the voice in his head. A jazzy rendition of an old Temptations song came on the air. Yes, he wanted Marnie. Damn it to hell, he'd wanted her from the second he'd seen her trying to helm that boat in the middle of the storm. And wanting her was all right. Making love to her was okay. But falling in love with her could never happen.

Falling in love? Now, why the hell did he think of that?

CHAPTER TEN

As she walked out of the boardroom, Marnie couldn't believe her good luck! After all his blustering and blowing about company loyalty, Victor had actually signed a contract with her. Of course, he'd tried to talk her into coming back to the company and she'd declined. And, of course, Kent had tried to maneuver her into a quiet corner to convince her that they should get back together.

Now Kent tagged after her. As if their last encounter hadn't been violent and revolting. "Let's just take a boat ride Saturday," Kent suggested with that same all-American smile Marnie had once been dazzled by. "We can try and work things out while we're sailing the *Marnie Lee* together. Come on, Marnie, what d'ya say?"

The man didn't understand the word "no." She didn't bother answering, just continued down the hallway from the boardroom toward her father's office.

"You're still mad at me, aren't you?" Kent insisted, touching her lightly on the arm.

"Mad doesn't begin to describe how I feel," she said furiously, jerking away from him, her shoulder banging against the wall.

"You know, the boat's half mine."

"I'll send you a check."

"But the *Marnie Lee* was a gift. You can't just buy me out. I won't sell."

"I don't think you'll have much of a choice, unless you want to buy my half."

"I don't have that kind of money!"

"Then you'll have to borrow it, or we're at an impasse." She started down the hall again.

Kent swore under his breath as he raced to catch up with her.

"This has gone far enough, Marnie. You've had your chance at being independent. Hell, you've even had your little fling with Drake. But now I'm tired of playing your little games and—"

"How many times do I have to say it?" she declared vehemently. "It's over!"

"Why? You seeing someone else?"

"None of your business."

"Drake?"

"Leave me alone." But he grabbed her arm, spinning her around. She braced herself for the same kind of assault as in the elevator. "Touch me and I'll scream or worse," she warned, and he must've believed her for he dropped his hand to his side and didn't blow up as she'd expected. Instead he became deadly calm, his mouth tightening into a thin line of fury, his hazel eyes frigid as he stared at her. A chill slid down her spine.

"There you are!" Victor, who had been delayed by one of the architects, flagged her down. Ignoring Kent, he strode to Marnie and patted her on the back. "Nice presentation," he said, finally noticing his executive vice president. "Went well, didn't you think, Kent? Now, Marnie, if this doesn't work out, you can always have your old job back."

"If this doesn't work out, we're both in real trouble," she joked back.

Kent didn't crack a smile.

"Come on, drinks are on me," her father insisted. "We'll celebrate our new partnership."

Marnie's stomach did a peculiar flip at the mention of partnership, but she indulged her father. They sipped champagne and nibbled on hors d'oeuvres at a French restaurant with a view of Elliott Bay, and Victor wasn't satisfied until the three of them had toasted their new alliance.

The fact that Kent had come along as well made Marnie uncomfortable, but she suffered through it because of Victor. She loved her father, and finally he'd really tried to give her the freedom she so desperately needed.

Two hours later, Victor drove her back to the parking lot where she'd left her car.

"It was like old home week with you here today," he said, a hint of nostalgia in his voice.

"Dad, I've only been gone a little while."

"Seems like forever. Oh, well, we'll just look to the future, right?"

"Right."

He opened the door of her Ford and chuckled. "This isn't your BMW, but I guess it's better than the twenty-year-old Volkswagen I thought you'd purchase."

"It'll have to do. Looks like I'll have to buy out Kent's half of the *Marnie Lee*."

"Don't be too hasty, Marnie."

"Or else he has to buy me out," she said, lacing her fingers through her father's. "I think Kent finally understands that I don't love him, probably never did, and that I'll never marry him. Now, if I could just convince you…"

"Ahh, Marnie," her father said, smiling sadly. "I was

only thinking of you, you know." As she slid into the driver's seat, he leaned over and kissed her cheek. "It's good to have you as part of the team."

"Thanks, Dad."

She started the ignition, but Victor hesitated before closing the door. "I don't suppose you've heard anything from Drake, have you?"

"I thought you didn't want his name mentioned."

"I don't."

"Well, since you brought up the subject, you may as well know. I will be seeing him," Marnie said, deciding that she had to be honest with her father from the beginning. Not that it was any of his business, but she wanted to start off on the right foot.

Her father's face drooped. "I was afraid of that."

"Trust me, Dad. I'm a big girl now."

Glancing over the hood of the car, Victor sighed. "Whatever you do, Marnie, just don't let that bastard hurt you." He slammed the door shut, and as Marnie backed out of her parking space, she caught a glimpse of him in the rearview mirror. He looked older and paler than he had earlier, as if all his vigor had been drained by the mere mention of Adam's name.

She steered the car out of the lot and joined the thread of late-afternoon traffic clogging the city streets. Mist seemed to rise like ghosts from the streets as fog settled over the bay and crept steadily up the steep hills of Seattle.

Pleased that she finally had a paying client, she nevertheless felt a little niggle of guilt. Just how far away from Victor's influence had she really gotten? And was she making her own decisions or allowing Adam to manipulate her? Seeking Montgomery Inns for a client had been Adam's idea. Maybe, like the fog settling against the hillside, she was clinging to the past.

Refusing to be glum, she flipped on the radio and hummed along to soft rock as she followed the line of taillights leading out of the heart of the city. Pulling into the reserved carport of her apartment unit, she switched off the engine, her thoughts turning once more to Adam and her father. Oil and water. Suspect and victim. Her lover and her next of kin.

Raincoat tucked under her arm, she hurried up the exterior stairs to her second-story unit.

Adam was waiting for her.

She saw him seated against the wall, arms folded over his chest, and she nearly dropped through the floor. He glanced up at her. A warm grin stretched slowly across his face, and his eyes seemed a shade darker with the coming night. His black hair gleamed an inky blue in the glow from the security lights, and Marnie's heart leaped at the sight of him.

"'Bout time you showed up," he drawled, rising to stand next to her as she unlocked the door.

"I wasn't expecting company." She slid a glance his way, and her pulse skyrocketed at the sight of his angular jaw and sensual lower lip. "But that's how you operate, isn't it? Always showing up where you're not expected."

"Keeps people off guard."

"Keeps you in trouble." She shoved the door open. "Come on inside. You'll talk your way in anyway. And this way maybe we can keep from being the gossip of Pine Terrace Apartments." Inviting him inside wasn't the greatest idea she'd ever come up with, but she felt like celebrating and the fact that he was here, sitting in the dark, waiting for her, touched a very feminine and romantic side of her nature.

He followed her inside. She heard his footsteps, and her heart thrilled at the familiar sound. "I thought I'd take you out to dinner."

"A bona fide date?" she mocked, glimpsing him over her shoulder.

His grin slashed white against his dark jaw. "That surprises you?"

"More like knocks me off my feet."

"Well, true, our relationship has hardly been flowers, wine, poetry—"

"Oh, *pleeease*..." She tossed her raincoat over the back of the couch and turned to face him. Her tongue was loosened by the champagne, and she was in a mood for honesty. "We don't even have a 'relationship,' remember? Just 'sex.' Isn't that what you said?"

He had the decency to frown. "I was oversimplifying."

"Oh." She lifted her brows, silently inviting him to explain himself.

"We're partners."

"Unwilling," Marnie reminded him, but he touched her then, his fingers surrounding her nape as he drew her to him.

"Why do you keep fighting me?" he whispered.

Staring into his intense gold-brown eyes, she hesitated only a second. "It might be because you have a history of lies," she managed, her voice trembling a little. "I have a long memory, Adam, and it seems that you hang around me whenever it's convenient for you. Most of the time I think you're interested in me because I'm Victor Montgomery's daughter."

His eyes searched her face. "It would be easier if I hated you."

"Don't you?"

"What do you think?" he said, his gaze delving deep into hers.

"I wish I knew, Adam."

"Unfortunately, I find you the most fascinating woman I've ever met."

"Unfortunately?"

"I never wanted to care about you, Marnie. Not even a little." His eyes swept her lips, and her stomach knotted at the thought that he might kiss her. "Believe that I never intended to hurt you."

"You couldn't," she lied easily, though her pulse was fluttering wildly. "I don't care enough."

"Good," he replied with a knowing smile that accused her of the lie. "Then you'll go out with me."

Of course she would. Was there any doubt that, if she saw him again, she'd go along with any of his wild schemes? When Adam Drake was around, it seemed as if all of her hard-fought independence disappeared, that she willingly cast away any vestiges of being her own self-reliant woman. "Why not?" she said. "Just give me time to change."

"You don't have to. You've dressed perfectly for what I have in mind."

"I hate to ask," she said, but decided that her white dress with a wide leather belt looked professional and tailored, dressy enough for a nice restaurant but a little too sophisticated for corn dogs on the beach.

Adam took her arm and whirled her around, propelling her back down the stairs to his car, some sort of four-wheel-drive rig that looked as if it should be tearing up some winding mountain road rather than racing from red light to red light only to idle in the city.

He threw the truck into gear and drove south, through the hilly streets toward the waterfront. Curling fingers of fog climbed over the water and into the alleys, creating a gauzy mist that seemed opalescent as it shimmered beneath the street lamps. Neon signs winked through the thin veil of fog, and the city seemed to shrink in upon itself.

Adam drove to the waterfront and they dined in a funky old restaurant located on one of the piers. Adam had requested a specific table with a window that offered a panoramic view of the dark waters of the bay. The bowed glass was angled enough that through the rising mist some of the city was visible. The tower of Montgomery Inns, Seattle, with its glass-domed ceiling, rose like a thirty-story cathedral on the shores of the sound.

"You must've hunted all over the city for this view," she remarked as the waiter poured white wine into their glasses.

"Nope. I used to come here often when I worked there." He hooked a finger toward the corporate headquarters of Victor's empire. "Remember?"

She didn't bother answering, just sipped her wine as the waiter concentrated on other diners. They ordered salmon, clams and crab, drank Riesling wine, and avoided any reference to Montgomery Inns. Some of Adam's hard edges seemed to retreat in the flickering light from the sconces on the wall. Or was it the wine that caused her perception of him to change? Or maybe the cozy restaurant with its rough cedar walls and eccentric antiques caused her to be a little less critical, slightly nostalgic, more forgiving.

"I saw Henderson today," he finally said, after the waiter had cleared their plates and they were left with two mugs of Irish coffee.

"And? Did he help you, 'unravel the mystery'?" she quipped, unable to keep a trace of scorn from her voice.

Adam scoffed, swigged from his cup and swallowed slowly, his Adam's apple moving sensually in his neck. Marnie tore her gaze away from his throat, but not before her stomach tightened a fraction and the shadows of the darkened restaurant seemed to close around them. She heard the clink of silver, the rattle of dishes, the soft laughter of other patrons. There was also the sound of soft-rock music drifting from the bar and the hint of smoke lingering in the air, but she was so aware of Adam that everything else seemed distant and faded.

Adam's gaze touched hers for a heart-stopping second, and without thinking, she took a swallow of her drink, then licked a lingering dab of whipped cream from her lips.

A fire sparked in his eyes, and she cleared her throat. "You were talking about Henderson?" she prodded, hating the breathless quality of her voice. If only she could feel cool and sophisticated and completely immune to his earthy sensuality.

"Right. Henderson." He swallowed again, his eyes shifting to the window and the dark night beyond. "Well, Henderson's not as much help as I'd hoped he'd be." He told her about his meeting with the man at Ilwaco, purposely omitting Henderson's hunch about a woman, wanting to wait a few minutes before he dropped that particular bomb.

"He thinks Fred Ainger took the money?" Marnie shook her head. "No way. The man's too loyal."

"But to whom? Victor or Bernice?"

"I don't believe it." She drained her mug.

"You don't believe anyone at Montgomery Inns would steal," he said, then amended, "except maybe for me."

"No," she said slowly, running a finger over the still-warm rim of her empty cup, "I don't think you took the cash."

"Well, someone did."

"I know." She sighed, hating to think about it, wishing the money could just be found—discovered to be only misplaced—and they could all get on with their lives.

She glanced up at him sharply and caught him examining her with such absorbed concentration that her skin prickled. She looked quickly away.

Adam paid the bill and they walked outside, along the wet docks into the deep purple night. The wind teased her hair, and along with the odor of the sea, it carried the very real and masculine scent of Adam Drake.

When he stopped before they reached the car and his fingers laced with hers, her heart began to pump more wildly than she ever thought possible. Beneath the hazy glow of a street lamp, with the vapor swirling around them, he caught her around the waist, lowered his head and kissed her, hard and fast, his lips seeking hers with such hunger that she felt dizzy.

Lord, why was it always this way with him? What was it about him that literally took her breath away? She felt the fog clinging to her hair and skin, tasted the coffee and whiskey still clinging to his lips, heard the thunder of blood rushing through her ears.

"Come home with me, Marnie," he whispered against her ear.

She trembled, trying to find the strength to say no. "I don't think I can."

"Sure you can."

"This is dangerous, Adam."

"Why?"

She gathered all her courage and tried to break free of his restraining embrace. "I—I can't be involved with a man just for sex. There has to be more."

"Moonlight and roses? Champagne and promises?" he asked, his eyes darkening with the night. "Diamonds and gold bands?"

"Trust and love," she said, her voice quavering. "That's hard to have when your entire relationship— excuse me, *non*-relationship—is centered around one person using another," she said, disentangling herself so that she could breathe, so that she could think.

His jaw grew hard and she could see from his expression that he was fighting an inner battle. "You know I care about you. Damn it, it wasn't what I wanted, what I'd planned, but I *do* care." He jammed both hands into his pockets. "I can't tell you what you want to hear. I can't make you promises, Marnie. And I can't pretend to be something I'm not. You just have to accept me for what I am."

"And what's that?" she asked.

His lips twitched. "A man who can't seem to keep his hands off you."

Her heart melted and she wanted to fling herself back into his arms, but she resisted, knowing that loving him would only cause more heartache. All of a sudden loving him seemed so easy. Or was it a lie—was she confusing love with sexual desire? She'd thought she had once loved Kent, but that had been a fantasy and her feelings for Kent hadn't scratched the surface of her emotions for this man. As for Adam, at least he wasn't pretending to feel undying passion and love for her. But was his brutal honesty about his very reserved feelings any better?

She sucked in her breath and gathered her courage before she poured out her heart. "I'm too old-fashioned for quick affairs or one-night stands or any of the above," she said, smiling faintly at this ridiculous maidenly retreat after their nights of passion. But she couldn't lie.

"You want me to marry you?"

The question echoed off the bay and through her heart. "No!"

His dark brow arched insolently, silently accusing her of lying through her teeth.

"I—I just need more of a commitment than that I'll wake up with you in the morning and then, maybe, never see you again. Call me old-fashioned, but that's the way I feel."

He sighed, frustrated. "I don't think it's possible to consider you a one-night stand or a quick affair, Marnie. But I'm in no position to promise you a future that just doesn't exist—and that's because of your father. I don't even know what my future will be. I can't promise you anything. Come on." Without waiting for a response, he grabbed her hand and pulled her across the street to his rig.

They drove in tense silence back to her apartment.

He flicked the radio on, and tunes from the "fabulous fifties, sensational sixties and spectacular seventies" filtered through the interior between blasts of some inane radio announcer trying to be a comedian. Marnie was in no mood for jokes.

She was in no mood for arguing with Adam.

She rested her head against the passenger window and caught a glimpse of Adam, his features drawn, his mouth tight as he drove. To avoid an issue that had no answers, she changed the course of the conversation. "Tell me more about Henderson."

Adam's expression changed as he switched mental gears. "Henderson. Boy there's one nervous guy. He really couldn't confirm that Fred Ainger was part of the setup."

She turned to face him. "I thought you were convinced that he was the man."

"Just one suspect. But there may be others." He downshifted, rounded a corner and glanced at her from the corner of his eye. "Henderson overheard an argument, well, from the sounds of it, more like a dressing down, right after the embezzling. Simms was really telling someone off, but Henderson, who had just come out of the accounting-room vault and was on the other side of the partition, couldn't see who it was."

"He doesn't have an idea?"

"He thinks it might be a woman."

"A woman? Why?" Marnie asked, her mind spinning with the names of a dozen women who worked at the hotel and had access to the accounting records. "Linda Kirk?" she said, thinking of the petite middle-aged woman with a quick smile and sharp mind. "I don't believe it!"

"Neither does Henderson. Linda was out sick that week." Adam told her about Henderson's hunch and the perfume.

"That's not much to go on," she said when Adam finished. "Just because Kent was arguing with someone in the accounting department isn't any big news. At least I don't think it's enough to indict anyone."

Adam flinched at her sarcasm.

"Sorry. Sore subject," she said.

"You have any idea who would be involved with Simms?"

"Besides me?" she said smartly, then sighed and ran her fingers through her hair. She thought about Dolores Tate. And Stephanie Bond. And Lila Montague, all women whom Kent had dated. "I'm afraid the list is miles long."

"Good thing I'm so patient," he replied, smothering a cynical smile, and Marnie almost laughed.

"Right."

"Just think about it."

"I will," she promised as he stopped at a red light. When the light changed, he stepped hard on the throttle, sped through the intersection and turned into the small drive leading to her apartment building.

He pulled into a vacant space, threw the rig into park, clicked off the headlights and turned off the ignition before turning all his attention in her direction. The cab of the truck seemed suddenly intimate. Mist drizzled down the windshield and the warmth of their bodies was beginning to cloud the glass. Adam's presence seemed to fill the interior, and she knew that she had to escape before she made the same mistake with him that she had in the past.

Her voice was scarcely a whisper. "Thanks for dinner. I—"

"I want to come up."

Her throat went dry. "You never give up, do you? You just keep pushing and pushing and never stop."

"When something's important, I go for it."

She knew he wasn't speaking of her, couldn't be. He'd made that perfectly clear. "And when something's dangerous, I leave it alone," she said. "You know the old saying 'once burned, twice shy'?"

"You don't have to be shy with me." He touched her hand, and she felt a shiver of delight. "As for that business about the danger, I don't believe it."

"Well, you're wrong!" she argued, as his fingers wrapped over hers and she felt the pads of his fingertips, warm and enticing against the underside of her arm. *Think, Marnie, think!* But she didn't pull her arm away. "Look, Adam, I don't mountain climb, or play with rattlesnakes, or run into burning buildings."

"But you do sail a boat in the middle of a storm, you do stand up to one of the most intimidating men in the state—"

"Meaning you?"

"Meaning your father. And you are willing to take a few risks, if you feel strongly about something."

She blushed in the deep interior and reached for the door handle, pulling up on the lever and getting nowhere. Adam had electronically locked the door by means of some sort of child-protection device and she was trapped inside the rig with him.

"You barely knew me and you stood up to your father, as well as the board, in my defense." With his left hand, he withdrew the keys from the ignition, and the only sound inside the four-wheel-drive vehicle was the soft jangle of metal. "You were willing to take a risk then."

"That was before I knew that you'd use me or anyone else to get what you want."

"All I want is the truth."

The keys clinked softly—like wind chimes disturbed by a stealthy breeze. "I don't see how I can help you," she said, suddenly aware of a knot in her throat and the restless energy that seemed to radiate from him.

"It's simple really. You've been hired by your father's company, right? As a freelance publicist."

"Yes, but how did you find out?"

"I still have a few friends at Montgomery Inns."

"Spies, you mean," she said, flabbergasted. Hadn't her father always been suspicious of disloyal people within the tight fabric of Montgomery Inns? Marnie had always thought that Victor was jumping at shadows, that his paranoia over the embezzlement was playing tricks in his mind. Apparently she had been wrong.

"No one 'spies' for me." But the look he sent her caused her to shiver.

"Yet." Cold certainly settled in the pit of her stomach.

"Yet."

Oh, God! "But now you're hoping that I'll do your dirty work for you," she guessed, sickened.

"Of course not."

"I won't betray my own father!"

He tugged at her arm, so swiftly she didn't see him move. Dragging her close so that his nose was touching hers, he growled, "Let's get a couple of things straight, Marnie. I'm not asking you to betray anyone or spy on anyone. And I'm not going to put either your personal career or your physical well-being in jeopardy. That's not the way I work. Whether you believe me or not, I don't expect you to plunder the company files, or sabotage the computer system, or be involved in any other corporate espionage b.s."

She gulped, but managed to meet his gaze with her own. "Then what is it you want from me?"

"Nothing," he ground out, then swore loudly and violently. "Or everything. I can't decide which." His gaze burned like molten gold as he glared down at her. "Damn it, Marnie, you've got me so messed up, sometimes I don't know up from sideways. But I do know this much. I have never, *never* wanted a woman the way I want you!"

"And it frightens you," she surmised with sudden clarity.

"It scares the living hell out of me!"

His fingers tangled in the pale strands of her hair, and his lips descended upon hers skillfully. He groaned as he felt her yield and give herself to him. She wound her arms around his neck and, lifting her face from his, managed a tremulous smile. She wanted him as much as he wanted her. If not more. "What're we gonna do about this?" she wondered aloud, breathless.

"Give me twenty minutes, and I'll show you," he vowed, reaching behind him and unlocking the doors.

"That quick?"

His grin turned wicked. "Or two hours. Your choice, Miss Montgomery. Your every wish is my command."

Once inside, he carried her into the bedroom and laid her gently on the bed. Marnie quivered as he kissed her, removing clothing and brushing his lips intimately against her skin.

She was on fire. All the emotions of the last few weeks running rampant through her willing body. Her skin aflame, her breasts aching for his touch, her lips anxious as they melded to his.

He took his time with her, touching her and running his hands and mouth against her skin, teasing her and waiting until she was ready, until she took his hand and pressed it to her breast, until she felt as if the hot, aching vortex within her would be forever empty.

Stripping him of his clothes, she closed her mind to all doubts, opened her eyes and watched as slowly his hard body found hers. She gasped at his entrance, and words of love sprouted to her lips, only to be lost as he began to move and she could no longer control her tongue or voice.

"Oh, Marnie," he whispered against her ear, his skin slick with sweat. "Sweet, sweet Marnie."

CHAPTER ELEVEN

"IT'S GOOD TO HAVE you back, even if it's only temporary." Kate Delany set a cup of coffee on the corner of
Marnie's desk, the desk she'd occupied while she still
worked full-time for the firm, in the office that she'd
come to look upon as a prison.

"Thanks. I need this." She picked up the mug, let the
steam drift toward her nostrils and sighed. "You know,
I never thought I'd admit it, but it's good to be back."
Despite her bid for independence, Marnie surprised herself by missing some of the people she'd worked with.
She'd also had trouble adjusting to the slower pace of
her own office. Now, working at Montgomery Inns,
she discovered she enjoyed the bustle and energy of a
hotel swarming with hundreds of guests and employees.

Cradling her own cup of coffee, Kate dropped into
one of the chairs near the desk. "So how's it going for
Montgomery Public Relations? Any new accounts?"
She crossed one slim leg over the other.

"A couple. But this one—" she tapped the eraser end
of her pencil on a press release she was working on for
Montgomery Inns "—takes up most of my time."

"Your father will be pleased." Kate's dark eyes twinkled. "He's never gotten over the fact that you walked
out on him."

Marnie shifted uncomfortably in her chair. She didn't

expect a reprimand, not even a gentle one, from Kate. "I only needed a little breathing space."

"I think he understands that now."

"You talked to him about it?" Marnie guessed, sipping the strong, hot coffee.

Kate laughed. "For hours. It takes a long while to convince your father of anything." At that her laughter died, and a cloud appeared in her eyes. Marnie guessed she was thinking of Victor's reluctance to remarry.

Marnie said, "Well, since you championed my cause, maybe I can champion yours."

"I wish *someone* could," Kate admitted, "but I don't think it's possible. Oh, well, no one can say I didn't try." She took a long swallow of coffee and seemed lost in her thoughts—nostalgic thoughts from the expression on her face. "I'd convinced myself after Ben and I divorced that I'd never find anyone else. Not that I was still in love with him or anything like that. Ben was far from perfect, a little boy who never grew up. Didn't like the responsibility of marriage, wasn't ready to support a wife, and wouldn't hear of starting a family." She smiled sadly. "But he was fun. The kind of boy you'd love to date but hate to marry. Anyway, it didn't work out and I came to work here and I met your father and he was everything Ben wasn't. Strong, dependable, steady as a rock. I couldn't believe it when he noticed me, plucked me out of the secretarial pool…" Kate's voice trailed off, and she cleared her throat. Tiny lines of disappointment surrounded her lips. "Well, that was a long time ago."

Marnie hated to see Kate so defeated. "Don't give up on him just yet," she said.

"Never say never, right?" Kate asked, finishing her coffee.

"Right!"

"Okay. So enough of me crying in my beer—or coffee. What about you, Marnie?" Kate asked as she stood. "Why don't you give Kent a second chance?"

Another little push from Kate. Marnie was surprised. "I'm not a glutton for punishment."

"Was it that bad?"

"Worse, but it doesn't matter," Marnie said, uncomfortable at the turn in the conversation.

"Is there someone else?"

Marnie thought of Adam and his reluctance to commit to her. Yes, she was falling in love with him. They were treading water, waiting for the tidal wave that would eventually drive them apart. "No one serious," she said when she caught Kate's probing gaze.

Kate lifted a skeptical brow. "Victor told me you were seeing Adam Drake."

Marnie didn't comment, but Kate sighed and drummed her fingers on her empty cup. "Take my word for it, Marnie. That man's trouble with a capital *T*. And if you ever want to hurt your father to the point that he'll never forgive you, then I suppose you can just keep on seeing Adam. When Victor finds out, he'll be devastated."

"My father can't choose whom I date."

"Or marry?" Kate asked, and Marnie's head snapped up. For a second a fleeting look of understanding passed between them and Marnie realized that she was much like Kate, caught in a love affair that could only end badly, emotionally tied to a man, who, for reasons of his own, couldn't or wouldn't allow himself to be tied down forever. Depression weighted her heart.

Kate stood, rounded the desk and touched her lightly

on the shoulder. "Kent's a good man, Marnie, though I know he has his faults. But he knows he hurt you, and I believe he'd never hurt you again. As for Dolores—"

Marnie's eyes widened. *Kate knew?* Her cheeks flushed hot with embarrassment. How many other employees knew or guessed that Kent had two-timed the boss's daughter? What about her father?

Her anxiety must have registered, because Kate said, "Victor doesn't know. And not that many people in the firm had any idea that he was…seeing anyone while you were engaged. In fact, the only reason I knew was that I came upon Dolores crying in the ladies' room one day and I took her back to my office to calm her down. She let everything out. She was nearly hysterical, sobbing and carrying on. Kent had told her he didn't want to see her again and she didn't believe him. She wanted to quit Montgomery Inns, but I convinced her to stay, at least for a while. But, from the looks of it, Kent broke up with her for good."

"Doesn't matter," Marnie heard herself saying. She didn't love Kent. Never had. And in the past few weeks she'd seen a side to him that was frightening.

"Probably not. I doubt if I'd ever forgive him, if I were in your shoes. But I thought you should know the full story. Done with that?" she asked, flicking her finger toward Marnie's nearly empty cup.

"Yes. And thanks."

"Don't mention it. I'm just glad you're back and back on your own terms. See ya later." She swept out of the room, leaving Marnie restless and concerned.

She spent the better part of the first week working with the Montgomery Inns account and spending more time at the hotel than she did at her own office.

Donna, ever efficient, swore that she had the situation under control, but the most difficult part of Marnie's job was being so removed from Adam. After Kate's rebuff, when he'd tried and failed to contact Victor, he'd decided not to call Montgomery Inns. Marnie had to content herself with seeing him in the evenings at her place. At the thought of their nights together, she smiled.

At the hotel, she worked with Todd Byers, who had assumed her position for the few weeks she'd been gone. Todd was about twenty-seven, with unruly blond hair and round, owlish-looking glasses.

"That about does it," he said, flopping back in a chair near her desk and resting his heels on another chair. "We should have all the publicity for Puget Sound West done for the next six months."

Marnie rubbed her chin. She couldn't afford to blow this account. "You're right, but I'll follow up just in case."

Todd shrugged, obviously thinking she was overly careful. "The next project's in California. San Francisco. Renovations are half finished," Todd said. "Victor wants us to go there next month."

"I know," Marnie admitted, remembering her conversation with her father about her schedule and wondering how she was going to juggle her time as it was. She thought about leaving Adam, and her heart tugged a little, but she ignored that tiny pain.

"Well, I've got a few loose ends to tie up, then I'm outta here," Todd said, dropping his feet to the floor and slapping his hands on his legs. "It's almost seven."

The time had gone by so quickly, Marnie had barely noticed. "I'll see you tomorrow," she said as Todd smiled, saluted her, and exited.

Twenty minutes later, as she was leaving, she bumped into Rose Trullinger in the hallway. "Just the person I wanted to see," Rose said, though she was wearing a full-length coat and was tugging on a pair of gloves as if she were heading outside to her car. "I don't have time to go into it right now, but I want the Puget West brochure changed. The pictures of the suites don't do justice to the design."

Marnie couldn't believe it. "But you approved those shots." A courtesy, since Rose really had no authority over publicity. But Marnie had tried to please everyone.

"I know, I know. I made a mistake." She finished with the glove and met Marnie's gaze levelly, as if she were daring Marnie to challenge her.

"The brochures are already being printed."

Rose smiled thinly. "Then get them back," she said. "I'll talk to you tomorrow."

"You bet you will," Marnie said under her breath. She headed toward her father's office, but discovered that he and Kate were already gone for the day. In fact, the executive offices were practically deserted. She should go home, work on the Jorgenson Real Estate account, her latest client, but she was in no hurry, as Adam was out of town, meeting with some investors from Los Angeles.

Rose's strange attitude had reminded her of her conversation with Adam. Hadn't he said one of the accomplices could be a woman? She hesitated as an idea occurred to her—maybe she could help find the culprit. She was alone in the building, with access to all the computer files… This might be her only chance to prove, once and for all, that Adam was innocent.

She walked down a corridor, turned right and en-

tered the accounting area for the entire hotel chain.
There were twenty desks, none currently occupied, in
the bookkeeping area and three offices, partitioned off
from the rest of the workers: a cubicle for Fred Ainger,
one for Linda Kirk and one for Desmond Cipriano, the
man who had replaced Gerald Henderson.

Feeling a little like a thief, she walked straight to
Fred's desk, and using her own code, accessed the computer files for the Puget West hotel. She printed out
scores of records, accounting as well as construction
and research, hoping for some clue as to who took the
money. She believed Adam was innocent. There were
times when she didn't trust him, but she really believed
that he hadn't taken a dime from her father. If he had,
why would he want to dig up all the evidence again?
No, Adam was a man hell-bent to clear his name, and
to that end, Marnie decided, she could help him.

For the next three nights, she pored over the docu-
ments, making notes to herself, reading all the information until the figures swam before her eyes, but she
found nothing, not one shred of evidence concerning the
missing funds. True, she wasn't trained in accounting,
and a dozen lawyers and accountants and auditors had
gone over the books when the discrepancy was discovered, but she'd hoped…fantasized…that she would be
able to unearth the crucial evidence that would prove
Adam's innocence, absolve him of the crime, and give
him back his sterling reputation.

"You are a fool," she told herself on Saturday morning as she dressed. Adam was due back in town later in
the afternoon, and she planned on using the morning to
visit the *Marnie Lee*. There was still the matter of Kent's
belongings on the boat, a point he'd made several times

since she'd started work at the hotel, and she wanted all trace of him out of her private life. Of course, she'd have to find a way to buy out his half of the vessel, but that would have to wait until she had a little more cash or could talk to her banker. A loan would probably be impossible, though. She'd just started her own business, didn't own her own home and her car was worth only a few thousand dollars. Her savings had to be used to keep her afloat until the receipts for the business exceeded the expenses.

The only person who would loan her enough money to buy out Kent was Victor, and she'd sell the boat rather than crawl back to her father and beg for money just when she was trying to prove she could make it on her own. It looked as if the *Marnie Lee* would soon be on the auction block. Kent had already indicated that he couldn't afford to buy Marnie out—so there was no other option.

She drove to the marina and walked along the waterfront. The sun was bright, the air brisk and clear, the sky a vivid blue. Only a few wispy clouds dared to float across the heavens.

Marnie zipped up her jacket and watched as sails and flags snapped in the brisk breeze. She was almost to the *Marnie Lee*'s berth when she heard her name. "Miss Montgomery!"

Turning, she spied Ed, the caretaker for the marina, scurrying toward her. He was small and wiry, not any taller than she. "Miss Montgomery. I need to talk to you!" he said, a trifle breathless.

"Hi, Ed."

"Hey, you told me to tell you if anyone asked about your boat, you want to know about it."

Marnie grinned. So someone wanted the *Marnie Lee!* Just when she needed the cash! "Did he leave his name and number?"

"Nope. But I know the guy," Ed said uncomfortably. "Name's Kent Simms."

"Oh." All her hopes were crumpled, and anger coursed through her blood. "And what did he want?"

"On board. But I said, 'No dice. Not unless you're with Miss Montgomery.' He left, but he was none-too-pleased about the situation."

"I'll bet not. When was he here?"

"Just yesterday around noon, and once before." Ed explained that Kent had been trying to get aboard the *Marnie Lee* for nearly three weeks, off and on. Marnie was annoyed before she realized that maybe he wanted more than the few belongings stashed aboard the yacht. Maybe he wanted more. Perhaps he thought he owed her one by stealing the boat, just to get back at her for taking the *Marnie Lee* the night of the party.

She didn't really blame him because she knew that Kent, right or wrong, considered the boat his. He'd had a strange attachment to the *Marnie Lee* from the first time he'd seen the boat, as Victor had proudly presented his gift to the two of them for "sailing along life's choppy waters and calm seas." Victor had walked them grandly through the cabins and decks, showing off a boat that was equal to his pride and joy, the *Vanessa*. Nonetheless, half the boat was hers, and the sooner Kent accepted that fact, the better for them both.

What if Kent balked when she put the sleek yacht up for sale? What if he refused to sign the papers?

After thanking Ed for his eagle eye and fierce loyalty, she walked down the sun-bleached planks of the pier and boarded the gently rocking boat. The *Marnie Lee* was a source of pride to her, as well. She rubbed a hand over the rail and eyed the teak decking and polished chrome fittings. Yes, it was beautiful and, now, after discovering Adam aboard this very boat, she had a special attachment to the craft as well. Unfortunately, she couldn't afford the upkeep.

Running her hands down the polished rail, she entered the main salon and started rifling through drawers and cupboards, pulling out Kent's personal chessboard, his brass compass, his deck of cards, a few sailing magazines and a couple of paperback murder mysteries. She checked the galley and packed up his gourmet coffee, popcorn and exotic teas. She didn't want him to have any reason to return. She boxed everything she recognized as Kent's and realized how little, she, herself, had added to the belongings on the boat.

In the main cabin, she tossed Kent's clothes, shoes, swimsuit, slippers, cuff links, shaving kit and date book into a box. She started packing his laptop computer, but hesitated, then turned on the machine. Waiting until the tiny monitor warmed up, she wondered what she hoped to find. Her stomach knotted. What if this computer was the key, the proof of Kent's duplicity? As the access screen glowed in front of her, she worked with the various menus, and spent two hours scanning the files. Nothing. Not one shred of incriminating evidence against him. She didn't know whether to be disappointed or relieved.

She unplugged the laptop and packed it in a box with Kent's clothes. After double-checking the bureau a second time, she opened the closet and noticed the wall safe. She'd almost forgotten about it. The combination was easy; the numbers were a sequence of dates, the day, month and year of Kent's birth. Grimly she turned the dial, listening for the tumblers to click.

Nothing. The lock didn't budge.

She tried again, convinced she'd fouled up the number sequence in her haste.

Again the lock held.

"What the devil? Come on, you!" she muttered to the lock.

With renewed concentration, she redialed the combination three more times, giving up when she realized that Kent had changed the code. Probably after she'd broken up with him.

"Well, that's great," she muttered, hands on her hips, perspiration dotting her brow. "Just super!" Now she'd have to get the damned combination from Kent and return to the boat before she could be sure that nothing on board belonged to him. Frustrated, she threw the last of his belongings—a picture of the two of them, their arms wound around each other as if they were really in love—into a box.

It took most of the morning to clean out the boat and, with Ed's help, carry all Kent's belongings to her car, but when she was finished and was driving home she felt a sense of accomplishment, as if she'd managed to break the last remaining link of the chain that bound her to Kent. "Except you still have to dispose of the boat," she reminded herself as she parked in her assigned parking space at her apartment. And there was the small but irritating matter of the wall safe.

As for Kent's belongings, she'd leave them in her locked car and take them to the office on Monday, where in the basement parking lot of Montgomery Inns, they would separate once and for all.

THROUGH THE WINDOW, Adam noticed the sprawling suburbs of Seattle as the plane descended at SeaTac airport. He'd had two drinks on the way back from L.A., where his talk with Brodie hadn't gone any better than the last time. Yes, Brodie and his investment group were interested, but, as before, if Adam couldn't completely clear his name, the investors just weren't able to do business with him.

He'd spoken to another man as well, Norman Howick, an oil man, a millionaire with a reputation for taking risks on new ventures. Howick had been interested, but hadn't been able to commit. He'd been too much of a gentleman to mention Adam's unsavory past, but the inference had hung in the air between them like a bad smell.

"Back to square one," he muttered to himself as the 747 touched down with a chirp of tires and a bump. The big plane screamed as it slowed before taxiing toward the terminal.

Closing his eyes, pleasant thoughts of Marnie rippled through his mind. He realized his feelings for her had changed and deepened. He no longer viewed her as Victor's daughter, and that was probably a mistake, but he couldn't help himself.

Being with her brought a certain brilliance to his otherwise austere world. She was the light and he was night, she was a smile and he was a frown. Not that she didn't have her own dark side and her temper—he'd been on the wrong end of that a time or two. He chuckled softly as he remembered her fury—the scarlet tinge on her cheeks, the fiery spark in her blue eyes, the rapier cut of her words and the haughty toss of her flaxen hair when she was truly angry.

"You've got it bad, Drake," he chastised as he walked along the jetway and through the terminal. It took half an hour to locate his baggage and his car, and then he was speeding along the freeway and back to Marnie.

At her apartment, he took the steps two at a time, rang the bell and scooped her into his arms when she opened the door. She let out a startled squeal as he twirled her back across the threshold and into her living room.

"Miss me?" she asked, her blue eyes laughing.

"Just a little." He kissed her eyes, her throat, her neck...and she giggled like a delighted child. The scent of her was everywhere, and he buried his face in her hair and breathed deeply.

"I missed you, too," she said, caressing his cheeks before she kissed him on the lips.

He couldn't stop. So sensual yet innocent, Marnie unwittingly created a fever in him that raged through his blood, licking like fire to heat his loins and drive all thoughts—save the primal need to make love—from his mind. He kicked the door shut with one foot and carried her straight into the bedroom, then fell with her onto the bed.

"But I have dinner ready—"

"It'll wait." Her skin was warm to his touch, her smell intoxicating.

"So can we."

"Speak for yourself," he said, working on the buttons of her blouse as his lips and tongue touched the soft shell of her ear. She responded by moaning his name.

"Adam, oh, Adam…" Her eyes glazed over, but she smiled and said, "You're incorrigible, you know."

"Probably." Her blouse parted.

"And totally without scruples. Oh!"

"Mmm." He pressed hot, wet lips against the hollow between her breasts and felt the fluttering beat of her heart. "Not even one lousy scruple?"

"None," she said, her voice breathy, a thin sheen of perspiration beginning to glow against her skin as he shoved the silky fabric of her blouse over her shoulder.

"Ah, what a lonely, unscrupulous life I lead," he said, his breath whispering across her bare skin as he unclasped her bra and her breasts spilled forward, dusty pink nipples stiffening in the shadowy light.

He sucked in his breath, willing himself to take it slow, while the fire in his loins demanded release. All he wanted to do was thrust deep into her and get lost in the warmth of her body. She moved against him, rocking slightly, reaching up and linking her fingers behind his head, only to draw him downward so that his open mouth surrounded her waiting nipple.

He took that precious bud in his mouth and suckled, hard and long, drawing on her breast as she writhed against him. His fire had spread to her and she held him tight, breathing in shallow gasps, her skin slick with sweat.

She wanted him as much as he wanted her, and he wasted no time ripping off his clothes and ridding her of her jeans and panties. When at last he was over her, poised for entry, he hesitated only slightly, staring at her fair hair, feathered around her face like an angel's halo, her innocent blue eyes staring up at him with infinite trust and hunger, her lips parted in desire.

At that precarious moment he hated himself. For what he'd done to her, for what he'd done to himself, for that frightening and overpowering need to claim her in a way as primitive as the very earth itself.

Yet he couldn't stop himself. In that heartbeat when he should have told her that they would never have a future together, that their lives would soon part forever, he squeezed his eyes shut against her beauty, swore silently at himself, then plunged deep into the moist warmth and comfort that she so willingly offered.

SOMETHING HAD CHANGED. Marnie felt it. Ever since Adam had returned, he'd seemed different—desperate, but she didn't understand why. They'd made love, and there'd been a savagery to their lovemaking that bordered on despair. As if Adam felt they would never make love again.

"I cleaned out the boat," she said, once they were seated at the small table in her kitchen.

He looked at her, his brows raised.

"All Kent's things. I'm taking them with me to work on Monday." She took a bite of chicken-and-pasta salad. "He must really want them. He's been hanging around the docks trying to get on board the *Marnie Lee.*"

"What was on board?" Adam asked. He'd eaten half his salad and was drinking from a long-necked bottle of beer.

"Nothing special. Just the usual male paraphernalia. You must've seen most of it when you were rooting around the boat looking for supplies." Memories of the storm and rain running down the windowpanes as they'd made love in Deception Lodge floated through her mind. She swished her wine in her glass and studied the clear liquid. "But I don't think he wanted his things. There wasn't anything that valuable on board, though I couldn't get into the safe—he changed the combination." At that, Adam's head jerked up. "I don't think there's anything really important in there, it's too risky. Remember I had keys to the boat. Oh, and he left his laptop computer—or one of them. I think he has a couple. But I checked it out. Nothing."

Adam scowled in frustration, and Marnie rambled on. "I think Kent really wanted back on the boat to steal it from me. You know, tit-for-tat, since I took the boat from him. Fortunately Ed, the caretaker, caught him and threw him out."

"Why would Kent steal the boat?" Adam asked, his gaze keen as he took a long swallow of his beer.

"To get back at me." She explained about Kent's feeling of ownership for the *Marnie Lee*.

Eyeing her pensively, he finally asked, "What happened between you two?"

Marnie swallowed hard, then set her fork carefully on her plate. This, she felt, was a moment of truth. Could she trust her secret with Adam, the man who had so callously used her once before, a man with whom she knew she was falling in love? She cleared her throat, wondering if she had the courage to tell him the entire embarrassing story and deciding that he deserved the truth. Whether he admitted it or not, they *were* involved in a relationship. "Kent cheated on me," she finally admitted, struggling with the damning words. Though Kent meant nothing to her anymore, her pride was still damaged. "Not just once, not just a fling, but he had an affair with his secretary for the entire duration of our engagement."

"His secretary?"

"Dolores Tate," she said, then felt foolish, like a common gossip. "It doesn't matter, and I guess he did me a favor."

Adam rotated his near empty bottle in his hands. "You loved him?"

Shrugging, she avoided his eyes and stared out the window near the table. Outside, a robin flew into the lacy branches of a willow tree. "I thought I did at the time." She played with her fork. "But I think I was just caught up in the excitement of it all. Dad was so thrilled and the whole office congratulated us."

"Except Dolores?"

"She and I were never close." Clearing her throat, she looked up at him. "What about you? Any near brushes with the altar?"

"Nope."

"That's hard to believe."

It was his turn to glance away. "Any time a woman got too pushy and started talking about settling down, I always found an excuse to end it."

"Why?"

"I just never saw any reason for it."

"No family pressure to get married and father grandchildren?"

"No family."

She bit her lip as she had a sudden insight into the man. She'd never heard him talk about his life, and thought he'd just been a private person, never thinking that his childhood might have been painful.

"Can't remember my folks. My mother never told anyone who my father was, and she left when I was three. Never heard from her again. I was raised by Aunt

Freda—really my mother's aunt. She died a couple of years back." He drained his beer, concluding the conversation.

Marnie swallowed hard. For the first time she understood some of the anger and pain she'd felt in Adam. "I'm sorry."

"Don't be. It's all ancient history."

"Didn't you ever want to find your parents?" she asked.

"Never!" His face grew hard, and his eyes narrowed in barely repressed fury. "I never want to see the face of a woman who could walk away from her child."

"Maybe she couldn't afford—"

"What she couldn't afford was an illegal abortion."

She swallowed hard. "You don't know…" Her voice trailed off.

"I do know. And I guess you couldn't blame her. She had nothing but a mistake in her gut. But that's not why I don't want to find her."

Tears burned the backs of Marnie's eyes, and her throat clogged, but Adam, staring intently at his hands, didn't seem to notice. "When I was three, she left with a sailor. A man she'd known two and a half days. Took off for L.A., and neither Freda nor I ever heard from her again. That's why she's as good as dead to me."

Oh, God. She wanted to reach forward, to place her hand on his, instead she asked softly, "But what about your grandparents?"

"Never met 'em. They were older—my grandfather fifty-five, my grandmother forty at the time my mother was born. According to Freda, they never really understood my mother and disowned her when she turned up pregnant and unmarried at seventeen. Believe it or not, my grandfather was a minister. He couldn't accept that his daughter ended up a sinner." His voice was bitter and distant, as if it took all his willpower to speak at all. "And I was a part of that sin. Proof that his daughter had fallen. They never even saw me. Freda was the only decent relative in the whole family tree. And she's gone now, so, no, I have no family."

"Does it bother you?" she whispered.

"I don't let it." Scraping his chair back, he carried his plate to the sink. "I don't even know why I told you all this," he said, frowning darkly and hooking his thumbs in the front pockets of his jeans.

Marnie crossed the kitchen, wrapped her arms around his neck and smiled up at him through her tears. "I wish I could say something, anything, that would change things."

"No reason to," he said harshly, but didn't push her away. In fact, his hands moved from his pockets to surround her and hold her close. Marnie held back the sobs that burned deep inside for the little abandoned boy who'd never known a mother's love.

If only he would let her close to him, let her take away some of the pain. She listened to the steady beat of his heart and she knew that she loved him, would always love him, no matter what.

"Marnie," he whispered hoarsely into her hair as the first tears trickled from the corners of her eyes. "Oh, Marnie... Marnie... Marnie." His voice sounded desperate, and Marnie clung to him as he swept her off her feet and carried her to the bedroom.

CHAPTER TWELVE

"YOU HAD THE NERVE to remove my things from the boat?" Kent accused, his voice cracking and his face turning white beneath his tan. He grabbed her arm and propelled her down a corridor.

"Let go of me." Marnie jerked back her arm and glared at him. "I'm sick of you manhandling me. Don't ever touch me again! Got it?" When he didn't respond, she added, "I just thought you'd want to know about your things."

"But you had no right—"

"It's all in my car," she cut in, disregarding his protests of injustice. "I'd be glad to transfer them to yours, if you give me the keys."

"You want the keys to the Mercedes? Are you out of your mind? Do you know what it's worth? You think I'd trust you with it after that stunt with the boat?" He was nearly apoplectic.

Marnie didn't care. "Do you want your stuff or not?"

"Of course!"

"Then let's transfer it now."

Kent checked his Rolex. "I have a meeting in seventeen minutes."

"It won't take long." He hesitated while Marnie walked to the elevator and pushed the button. "No problem. I'll leave it on your hood."

"What the hell's gotten into you?" he growled, but followed her to the bank of elevators, straightening the cuffs of his jacket and tie. "You used to be sane."

"When I was engaged to you?" She almost laughed. Most of the pain had faded with time. And the fact that now she knew what a real relationship between a man and a woman could be, she hardly believed that she had once considered herself in love with Kent. "Let's not talk about it. All right? In fact, let's not talk about anything." She considered the last time she'd been trapped in an elevator alone with Kent, but she wasn't worried. She could handle herself.

The doors to the elevator opened, and she stepped inside, joining Todd Byers, the hotel-services manager and two men from the sales team. She smiled at the other occupants, and Kent made a failed attempt to hide the fact that he was vastly perturbed with her and the entire situation.

Marnie, on the other hand, talked and chatted with Todd, laughed with the men from sales, and was still chuckling when she and Kent landed in the first sub-basement, where the executives parked their cars.

The luster of Kent's black sports car gleamed under the overhead lights, in sharp contrast to her used Ford. She didn't care. Unlocking the trunk, she motioned to the three stacked boxes. "Didn't you miss any of this stuff?"

She thought he blanched and swallowed hard, but she only caught a glimpse of his profile as he unlocked his car. "Some of it," he said, lifting one of the flaps and peering inside the largest carton. "You found my computer?"

"Right where you left it—humming and clicking and

spinning out information left and right," she said, unable to stop from baiting him.

"What?" he asked, horrified. "But it has an automatic shutoff..." He stopped short, finally realizing that she was joking with him.

"Relax, Kent. Your computer and all you other precious belongings are safe."

"You brought them straight from the boat?"

"After a short layover at my apartment."

"Oh." He yanked at his tie as he carried the first box to his car. It was too large to stuff in his trunk, so he had to place it behind the front seat. "Did, uh, did anyone else see any of this?"

"What do you mean?"

Kent looked at her over the shiny roof of the Mercedes, and she noticed tiny beads of sweat at his hairline. He licked his lips. "I mean Drake. Did he see it?"

She shrugged and thought about lying to him, but couldn't. Instead, she said simply, "He didn't rifle through anything. Why?"

Kent seemed relieved. "It's private, Marnie. That's all. Just between you and me. It's got nothing to do with him."

Suspicious, she dropped a small box into his open trunk. "Well, I hope you didn't have anything specific that you didn't want him to see, because he spent a lot of time alone on the boat."

"On *our* boat? Damn it, Marnie, you won't even let me near the *Marnie Lee* and I own half of it! But that loser, he's allowed to snoop around anywhere he wants! I can't believe you, Marnie." He slammed the passenger door of the car shut. "After what that jerk did to your father, how can you even think of allowing him anywhere near you or the yacht!"

"You knew he was on it," she pointed out, then waved her hands to forestall any further protests. She wasn't going to get into an argument with Kent. "Have you got everything?"

"You tell me. Since I'm not allowed on *my* boat, I can't tell if everything's here."

"If I find anything else, I'll send it to you," she replied, turning toward the elevators but catching a glimpse of the hard set of Kent's mouth.

A WOMAN. Henderson had said he'd thought Simms was in cahoots with a woman. But which woman? Seated at a bar stool in Marnie's apartment, Adam stared at the printouts Marnie had brought from the accounting department. In the corporate headquarters of Montgomery Inns there were over seventy employees, fifty-two of whom were women.

Crossing off those who didn't have access to computer terminals and accounting records, the number dwindled to thirteen; though with Kent's authority, the woman involved could merely have been an accomplice. She could have been the one pulling the strings behind Kent, even though she didn't have the power or wherewithal to actually move the funds. Leaving Kent in charge. No, that didn't work. Unless Kent really was the brains behind the operation.

Adam tapped his pencil against his teeth in frustration. Four women had easy access to the computer terminals as well as authority to access delicate information: Linda Kirk in accounting, Rose Trullinger

in interior design, Kate Delany, Victor's assistant, and
Marnie.

There were other women who worked in bookkeeping and records, and a few secretaries who were high
enough on the corporate ladder to dig into the files. But
to create an intricate embezzling scheme? Not likely.

However, he couldn't discount the men. Henderson
thought Fred Ainger was involved. And what about Desmond Cipriano? The man who had taken over Henderson's office was young, brash and hungry. He'd had
a lesser job during the time of the embezzlement and
had been promoted after Henderson left the company.
Only with the corporation a few years, Desmond didn't
have all that much loyalty or time invested in Montgomery Inns.

A headache began to pound at Adam's temples and
he rubbed his eyes. He threw his pencil down in disgust. Who? Who? Who?

MARNIE FELT LIKE a traitor as she walked toward Kate's
desk. Of course, no one knew she had taken company
records home, but nonetheless she was uncomfortable
and she felt like talking with her father, maybe gaining
some insight from him or maybe even convincing him
to speak with Adam.

No doubt Victor would hit the roof when he found
out she'd misused her authority, but better he learn it
from her than find out on his own.

"Is he in?" she asked as Kate set the receiver of the
phone back in its cradle.

Kate shook her head, and her auburn curls swept
the shoulders of her linen suit. "Had to meet with the
lawyers. I thought he said something about seeing you

later…" She thought for a minute. "Something about dinner?"

"That's news to me."

Kate seemed puzzled. She ran her fingers down her appointment book and sighed loudly. "Nothing here, but I could've sworn…"

"Then you're not going out with him?" Marnie asked, knowing that her father and Kate often had dinner together.

"Not tonight." Kate closed the appointment book. Her lower lip trembled a little.

"Trouble?" asked Marnie.

"Not really."

"But…"

Kate sniffed and cleared her throat. "Your father is… preoccupied right now. Lots going on. The Puget West just opened, the architects are working on the blueprints for Deception Lodge, and the California projects…well, I don't have to tell you about them. San Francisco's due to reopen in October and—"

Marnie held up her hands, palms out, as if in surrender. She understood only too well how easily Victor Montgomery could bury himself in his work. "Enough said. It sounds as if my father has put his personal life on hold for a while and something should be done about it."

"Oh, no!" Kate shook her head vehemently. "He's just busy and he needs that—being busy, I mean. He can't slow down. It would kill him. And besides, this isn't the first time I've been shoved to the back burner. We'll get through it," Kate predicted, but tears shimmered in her eyes, and she suddenly reached forward and grabbed Marnie's hand. "If I can give you one piece of advice, Marnie, it's don't get involved with a man who isn't ready to commit. You could spend the rest of your life waiting." The phone rang, and Kate, obviously embarrassed by her outburst, let go of Marnie's hand and waved her off. "I'll be all right," she mouthed before turning her attention to the phone and saying, "Mr. Montgomery's office."

Feeling totally depressed, Marnie moved quickly down the corridor. Did Kate know about her dead-end relationship with Adam? But how? Just a lucky guess? Or from bits and pieces, snatches of conversation?

Inside her office she shivered and rubbed her arms while surveying this room that she had once claimed; the plush carpet, the expensive furniture, the panoramic view. Did she want it back?

No. Beautiful as the office was, it was made up of carpet and ceiling tile and antiques and brass lamps and piped-in music. Things. Just material goods. And material goods had never seemed less appealing. Especially now that she was forced to consider a life without Adam, or worse yet, to be strung along like Kate, always waiting, while knowing in her heart that the man she loved could never let go of the past or offer her a future. "Oh, Lord." With a sigh, she took off her earrings and dropped them into her purse.

She considered her father's fervent loyalty to a wife who had been gone over a decade. To what purpose? Why wouldn't he marry again?

And Adam. Would he never marry? Would he never find a woman on whom he was willing to take a chance? Well, if he did, his future wife certainly wouldn't be the daughter of a man who had tried to put him behind bars.

But she loved him, Marnie thought painfully. And

that was the pure, naked truth. Of all the men in the world, she was senseless enough to fall in love with the one she couldn't have. So, could she live with him and forget about marriage, about children, about a mate for life?

Perhaps her romantic notions were nothing more than dusty fantasies left over from a childhood without a mother, a child who was read stories about beautiful princesses and castles and dragons and knights on white steeds who wanted to do nothing more than live happily ever after with the girl of their dreams.

"Idiot," she chided, as she punched out the number of her own publicity firm.

Donna answered on the second ring. "Montgomery Publicity."

"Hi. How's it going?" Marnie asked, balancing a hip against the desk in her old office at the hotel.

"Mmm. Busy," Donna said, and Marnie could almost imagine her polishing her nails, swigging coffee and smoking a cigarette while manning the phones and typing out complicated corporate tax returns for Miles Burns, the accountant in 301. "You got a couple of call backs from Andrew Lorenzini at Sailcraft. He liked your proposal and wants to meet again next week."

"Good." With a few accounts like Sailcraft, Marnie wouldn't be so dependent upon Montgomery Inns.

"Andrew Lorenzini," Donna repeated. "He sounds interesting."

"He sounds married," Marnie replied.

"Oh, well, too bad," Donna replied with a loud sigh. "Anything else?"

"Nope. As I said it's a real killer today."

"Well, don't work too hard."

"Wouldn't dream of it," Donna replied, before saying, "Oh, yes, there was one more message. Adam called. Couldn't get through to you at Montgomery Inns, and said he'll meet you tonight at the usual spot. Now *he* sounds interesting *and* romantic. I've seen him, you know. Total hunk."

"What you've seen is too many movies."

"Not enough. And definitely not with the right men."

Marnie laughed as she rang off. Her mood improved as she thought of an evening alone with Adam. So they weren't planning to walk down the aisle together, so they didn't have a future all mapped out for them, so her father thought he was as crooked as a pig's tail. So what? The new Marnie Montgomery could take a relationship and her life one spontaneous step at a time! The old Miss Ellison-trained Marnie was long buried. The new Marnie was taking over!

She hummed to herself as she grabbed her briefcase and started for the elevator. Then the thought struck. Hadn't Kate said that her father wanted to take her to dinner? And Adam had left a message saying he and she were to meet at the usual spot, meaning her apartment. So there was a chance that Victor, if he planned on picking up his daughter for dinner at her place would come face-to-face with the man he hated.

Marnie sucked in her breath. The thought of the two men she loved confronting each other at her place chilled her to the bone. She dashed back into her room and dialed the number of her father's mobile phone. A monotone voice told her that the phone wasn't in service. Quickly she punched out her father's extension and Kate answered. Without explaining why, she asked Kate to try and reach Victor and make sure that tonight's dinner plans were rescheduled. "Anytime later this week," she instructed, and felt a little better when Kate told her she was expecting Victor to call in to the office at any moment.

Marnie's relief was short-lived. How long could she sustain this juggling act? she wondered, her good mood chased away by the horrid memory of Adam and her father, fists clenched, squaring off at Deception Lodge.

"It won't happen. It can't," she told herself as she took the elevator to the employee cafeteria, grabbed a doughnut and poured herself a cup of coffee. She talked with a few of the women from the marketing department, people she'd worked with at Montgomery Inns. Within minutes she caught up with several women— their lives, their children's trials and tribulations and their grandchildren's accomplishments.

"So, now that we've bored you to death. What about you, Marnie?" Helen Meyers asked. "How was your grand adventure in the San Juans?"

"So it's hit the local gossip mill?" she countered.

"And a three-county area," Roberta Kendrick agreed.

Marnie laughed, enjoying the company. She told them bits about her trip in the storm but didn't mention Adam's name and was blindsided by Helen's next remark.

"I heard Adam Drake kidnapped you." Helen's graying brows arched over her rimless glasses.

"Stowed away," Roberta interjected. Picking up her teacup, she shook her head at Helen. "Don't change things around."

"I'm just repeating what I heard."

"He was on the boat," Marnie conceded. "And I hate to admit it, but it was a good thing. The storm was worse than anyone would have guessed. And Adam's a pretty good sailor."

Helen swiped at a stain on the table. "Well, I know it's not popular to say, but I, for one, and I think I speak for everyone in the marketing department, miss Mr. Drake."

"Do you?" Marnie was surprised to hear such anarchy from one of Victor's loyal employees.

"If you ask me, he got the shaft!"

"Helen!" Roberta cried, then made quick, apologetic motions with her hands. "Please, don't listen to her, she's just angry with Mr. Simms today."

"That know-nothing! You were right to break off with him, Marnie. He's useless!"

One side of Marnie's mouth lifted, and Roberta tried to pour oil on rough waters. "We all miss Mr. Drake," she admitted, throwing a speaking glance in Helen's direction meant to still the little woman's tongue. "He was fair and had a sense of humor, and no one worked harder for the company than he did. It looks bad for him, but…well, most of us don't believe that he took any money from your father. It just doesn't make sense." Helen looked as if she were about to add her two cents, and Roberta put in quickly, "However, we all are doing our best to work with Mr. Simms. If your father trusts him, then we—"

"Bull!" Helen cut in, and Roberta rolled expressive green eyes. "The man's a dimwit, and you know it, Roberta Kendrick!"

Somehow Marnie managed to channel the conversation and turn it to a less disastrous course. She listened for a few minutes while Roberta caught her up on the details of her trip to Hawaii the previous February. Finally Marnie escaped.

She spent the next couple of hours with Todd, who assured her that Rose Trullinger's request to change the brochure was out of the question. "You could double-check with your dad on that one," he said, polishing his glasses with a handkerchief as he stood over her desk, eyeballing the pictures in question, "but I've never seen your father change something like this unless there was a good reason."

"I agree. Besides, I think I'm supposed to make that kind of final decision," Marnie replied.

Todd pushed his glasses onto the bridge of his nose. "Right you are. Besides, you can't believe everything Rose tells you these days."

"No?"

Todd shook his head. "She's going through some pretty heavy stuff right now. Her husband isn't getting any better. One of Rose's daughters dropped out of school to help her take care of him, but it looks like he might have to go in for open-heart surgery, and there's some hassle about insurance benefits. So Rose is real tense these days, and everyone around here is trying to cut her a little slack while being as supportive as possible."

"I wish I'd known this earlier," Marnie said, trying to remember her conversation with the slender woman.

"Don't worry about it. She's probably already forgotten the entire issue. My guess is that within a week or two she won't know this shot—" he thumped a finger on the picture "—from the one she says she wanted." He glanced at his watch and scowled. "Are we done for the day? I gotta run."

"Sure. I'll see you Monday."

Todd left, shutting the door behind him. Marnie leaned back in her chair, swiveling to stare through the bank of windows to the Seattle skyline. Skyscrapers loomed upward, seeming to slash through a summer-blue sky. Only a few clouds hung on a lazy, summer breeze. At the sound, boats chugged across the gray blue waters, leaving foaming wakes and reflecting a few of the sun's afternoon rays.

Everyone working for Montgomery Inns seemed to have more than his or her share of problems. Kate Delany and Rose Trullinger were just a few.

And what about you? What about your relationship with Adam? Talk about going nowhere!

"Oh, stop it," she said, mentally chewing herself out and refusing, absolutely refusing, to be depressed. Deciding to call it a day herself, she stuffed some work into her briefcase, grabbed her jacket and swung open the door. One of the elevators was out of order, and a crowd of employees milled around the remaining operable lifts.

Marnie took the stairs, concluding that a little exercise wouldn't hurt her. Her heels rang on the metal steps as she descended, passing each floor quickly. She didn't see the girl huddled on the landing of the eighth floor until she almost tripped over her.

Marnie froze. The girl was a woman. Dolores Tate— and she was sobbing loudly. Her curly brown hair was wilder than ever, her eyes red. A handkerchief was wadded in her fist, and her skin was flushed from crying. She gasped as she recognized Marnie and looked as if she wanted to disappear as quickly as possible.

A tense silence stretched between them before Marnie managed to ask, "Are you okay?"

Dolores sniffed and cleared her throat. "Do I look okay?" Her voice dripped sarcasm.

Disregarding Dolores's unconcealed contempt, Marnie asked, "What's wrong?"

"You?" Dolores responded, blinking hard. "*You* want to know what's wrong with me? God, that's choice!" Her purse, lying open, was shoved into a corner. Dolores pawed through the oversize leather bag. "I need a cigarette." She found a new pack and worked with the cellophane while her hands trembled. Finally she lit up. "You want to know what's wrong with me? Why don't you take a wild guess?"

Marnie knew the woman was baiting her, but she couldn't resist. "This probably has something to do with Kent."

"Bingo!" Dolores threw back her head and shot a plume of smoke toward the ceiling many stories above. "But I don't suppose I have to tell you about Kent. He did a number on you, too."

"Doesn't matter."

"Not to you, maybe." Tears trickled from the corners of Dolores's eyes. She swiped at the telltale drops with her fingers. "But I actually loved the bum." Laughing bitterly, Dolores found her handkerchief again and wiped her nose. "How's that for stupid?"

"We all make mistakes," Marnie replied, wishing she didn't sound so clichéd.

"Yeah, well, I made my share." Suddenly her gaze was fixed on Marnie's. "And, well, for what it's worth— I didn't mean to hurt you. I was just in love with the wrong man. But apparently—" her voice cracked, and she drew up her knees, bowing her head and holding her cigarette out in front of her as the smoke curled lazily into the air "—apparently, Mr. Simms doesn't feel the same about me." She blinked rapidly. "In fact, that bastard told me he never even cared about me! I guess I was only good for one thing. He broke it off with me, you know. A couple of weeks ago, but I thought I could change his mind. Obviously I was wrong about that, too."

Marnie was aware of footsteps ringing on the steps a few stories up. "Look, you want to go somewhere and talk about it?" she said, feeling suddenly sorry for a woman who had so many hopes wrapped up in a man like Kent.

"With you? Are you out of your mind? That's why he broke up with me, you know. He blamed *me* for him losing you. Can you believe it? Like it was *my* fault!" She finally seemed to hear the clattering ring of footsteps closing in on them and she struggled to her feet, crushing out her cigarette with the toe of a tiny shoe.

"If it's any consolation," Marnie offered, "I think you did me a big favor."

"Why?" Dolores asked, attempting to compose herself as a few men from the personnel department edged passed them and continued down the stairs. Marnie waited until the noise faded and, from far below, a door slammed, echoing up the staircase before silence surrounded them again. "Oh, I get it," Dolores said, her eyes turning bright. "This is all because of Adam Drake, right?" She smiled a little. "That really burned Kent, you know. That you would be interested in Drake."

"Because he was supposed to have embezzled from

"One Minute" Survey

You get up to **FOUR books** <u>and</u> Mystery Gifts...

ABSOLUTELY FREE!

See inside for details.

YOU pick your books –
WE pay for everything.
You get up to FOUR new books and TWO Mystery Gifts.
absolutely FREE!
Total retail value: Over $20!

Dear Reader,

Your opinions are important to us. So if you'll participate in our fast and free "One Minute" Survey, **YOU** can pick up to four wonderful books that **WE** pay for!

As a leading publisher of women's fiction, we'd love to hear from you. That's why we promise to reward you for completing our survey.

IMPORTANT: Please complete the survey and return it. We'll send your Free Books and Free Mystery Gifts right away. **And we pay for shipping and handling too!** *We pay for EVERYTHING!*

Try **Essential Suspense** featuring spine-tingling suspense and psychological thrillers with many written by today's best-selling authors.

Try **Essential Romance** featuring compelling romance stories with many written by today's best-selling authors.

Or TRY BOTH!

Thank you again for participating in our "One Minute" Survey. It really takes just a minute (or less) to complete the survey… and your free books and gifts will be well worth it!

Sincerely,

Pam Powers

Pam Powers
for Reader Service

"One Minute" Survey

GET YOUR FREE BOOKS AND FREE GIFTS!

✓ Complete this Survey ✓ Return this survey

1 Do you try to find time to read every day?
☐ YES ☐ NO

2 Do you prefer stories with happy endings?
☐ YES ☐ NO

3 Do you enjoy having books delivered to your home?
☐ YES ☐ NO

4 Do you share your favorite books with friends?
☐ YES ☐ NO

YES! I have completed the above "One Minute" Survey. Please send me my Free Books and Free Mystery Gifts (worth over $20 retail). I understand that I am under no obligation to buy anything, as explained on the back of this card.

☐ I prefer
Essential Suspense
191/391 MDL GNT4

☐ I prefer
Essential Romance
194/394 MDL GNT4

☐ I prefer BOTH
191/391 & 194/394
MDL GNUG

FIRST NAME | LAST NAME

ADDRESS

APT.# | CITY

STATE/PROV. | ZIP/POSTAL CODE

my father?" Marnie countered, and Dolores sucked in a sharp breath. Her throat worked, before she tried to pull herself together.

"You know something about it?" Marnie asked, reading Dolores's abrupt change of attitude. No longer the scorned, broken woman, Dolores was now looking guilty as sin. All the subterfuge came together in Marnie's mind.

Dolores must be the very woman they were looking for—the woman Kent was talking to when Gerald Henderson overheard the conversation in the accounting department. "You know that Fred Ainger was involved, and Kent?" she asked as Dolores, one hand on her purse, the other hanging desperately onto the rail, began to back down the stairs.

"I don't know anything about it," Dolores responded, denial and guilt flaring in her eyes.

"Oh, come on, Dolores! It's written all over your face! And Gerald Henderson overheard you and Kent in the accounting office."

"Not me!" Dolores shook her head. "I was never near the accounting department with Kent!"

"Then who was?" Marnie asked, following Kent's lover down the stairs and feeling a little like a predator. Dolores was obviously terrified that she'd said too much.

"I—I don't know," she squeaked.

Marnie clasped Dolores's wrist, stopping the other woman cold. "What are you afraid of?" When Dolores didn't immediately respond, Marnie said, "You must be involved."

"No!"

For a minute she stared at her, and slowly Marnie believed her. Stark terror streaked through Dolores's red-rimmed eyes. Yet there was something she was holding back, something important. Marnie gambled. "I have to go to my father with this."

"Oh, God, no," Dolores pleaded. "Really, I don't know anything."

Marnie's conscience nagged her, but she pressed on. This was, after all, her one chance to absolve Adam of a crime he didn't commit and prove his innocence. "Then you won't mind telling that to my father or the board or the police?"

Dolores nearly fainted. Her entire body was shaking, and for a terrifying instant Marnie was afraid the girl might lose her footing and fall down the stairs.

"Listen, Dolores, why don't you just tell me everything you know about the theft? Then I'll decide if my father has to know about your part in it."

"I wasn't part of it!" she cried.

"Then who're you protecting? Kent?" Marnie scoffed. "After what he did to you? Believe me, Dolores, he's not worth it."

Dolores wavered. Chewing on her lip, she said, "If I help you…?"

"I'll talk to my father, explain that you were basically an innocent bystander—a victim. But you have to tell me the truth—all of it—and I can't promise that you won't be prosecuted if it turns out that you're involved more than you say you are."

Dolores gulped, but her eyes held Marnie's, and for the first time since they'd met, Marnie felt as if a glimmer of understanding passed between them. "You have to believe me, I didn't do anything and I never got a cent," she whispered, licking her lips nervously.

"But you did know what was going on?"

"I—uh—I found out when I caught Kent fiddling with the books." Dolores sank to the step and dropped her head into her hands. "It's all such a mess and I loved Kent so much that…that I didn't…couldn't blow the whistle on him."

"Was Fred involved?" Marnie asked softly.

"I don't know. I don't think so." Dolores shook her head slowly. "I think there was someone else, but I really don't know who. Kent kept me in the dark as much as possible. That's the way he was." Her pouty lips compressed, and anger caused her pointed chin to quiver. "And he never cared about me. Not at all." Her hands curled into tiny fists of outrage.

"Would you be willing to testify against him?"

Dolores stared at Marnie a long time. "I can do better than that," she said at last, finally throwing in her lot with Marnie. "I can tell you where the records are— the books that show how the money was skimmed off the project funds."

Marnie was floored. "Where?"

Dolores smiled through her tears. "In the boat."

"The boat?"

"The damned boat. Your boat. The *Marnie Lee*. Everything you need to prove that Kent's the thief is in the safe in your boat!"

CHAPTER THIRTEEN

THE PHONE RANG in Marnie's apartment, but Adam let the answering machine take the call. He made it a practice not to answer her phone or do anything that might suggest that they were a couple. He respected Marnie's privacy, true, but there was another reason. He couldn't get too tied into this woman, much as he cared for her. It wouldn't be fair to either of them. Until he could prove his innocence, he had nothing to offer her.

On the fourth ring, the answering machine picked up, playing Marnie's tape recording. A few seconds later, Marnie's voice, breathless, rang from the box. "Adam? Are you there?" Marnie asked, her voice ringing with excitement on the telephone recorder. "If you are, pick up. Please! This is important!"

Just the sound of her voice brought a grin to his face. He picked up and drawled, "Gee, lady, sounds like you're in desperate need of a man. What can I do for you?"

"Thank God you're there!" she whispered, relief and delight mingled in her words.

"You know me, just hanging around your place, a kept man," he returned. Her good mood was infectious, and he imagined how she must look, cheeks flushed pink, her flaxen hair tousled, her blue eyes clear and bright.

"Meet me at the *Marnie Lee!* I'll be there in half an hour!"

"Whoa. Slow down a second. Why?"

"I don't have time to tell you now," she said, nearly laughing, her voice bubbling with enthusiasm. "Just meet me there!" With a profound click, she hung up, and Adam slowly replaced the phone. Whatever she was up to, it couldn't wait.

He glanced at the table, where pencils, pens, a calculator and two half-empty cups were scattered over the reports from Montgomery Inns. After hours of poring over the personnel and accounting records, Adam had come up with nothing that even remotely hinted at who was behind the embezzlement and consequent frame-up. He was tired, his back and neck ached and his mouth tasted stale from cup after cup of coffee. He was getting nowhere fast.

A boat ride with Marnie sounded like just the ticket to get his mind off this mess.

Scooping up his keys from the table, he stuffed them into the pocket of his jeans and saw Simms's name on a personnel report. "You son of a bitch," Adam muttered. "I'll get you yet." But he wasn't as convinced as he once had been. Though Henderson's hearsay tied Kent to the crime, it was just Henderson's word against Simms's. No, he needed more proof: cold, hard facts. Adam had foolishly underestimated Simms and whoever the hell his accomplice was. They were professionals when it came to sliding dollars out of the company accounts. If Kate Delany hadn't noticed the discrepancies, they could have embezzled millions.

He was reaching for his jacket on the curved arm of the hall tree when he stopped short at a sudden thought.

Kate Delany. Of course! He didn't need Victor's help; if he could convince Kate to talk to him, to explain how she'd been tipped off, then he might find the answer to how the money was shuffled, to where, and more importantly, to whom.

Feeling that he was suddenly on the verge of a breakthrough, he shoved his arms through the sleeves of his jacket and projected ahead to an evening of sailing, a dinner with candlelight and wine and a night of lovemaking, with Marnie lying beside him, her pale hair, touched by the moonglow, looking as if it were a silvery fire.

First a night with Marnie, then tomorrow he'd tackle Ms. Delany. If the woman would see him. She'd made it all too clear that she thought he was no better than a weasel.

Well, dammit, she'd just have to deal with him.

The doorbell chimed softly through Marnie's apartment. "Marnie? You ready?" Victor's voice boomed through the panels as Adam pulled open the door.

They stood face-to-face, inches apart, the threshold of Marnie's front door a symbol of the rift between them. Adam on one side, Victor on the other, a year of bitterness, lies and mistrust separating them as surely as the threshold itself.

One side of Adam's mouth lifted into a mocking grin. "Well, Victor," he drawled, as the older man's shock turned to simmering rage. "It's been a long time. I'd invite you in, but I'm just on my way out."

Victor tilted his aristocratic head, and the nostrils of his patrician nose flared slightly. "Where's Marnie?"

"I'm going to meet her."

"She's having dinner with me."

"That's not the way I understand it," Adam replied, then added, "excuse my manners." He glanced pointedly at his watch. "I guess I've got a few minutes. Would you like to come in for a drink?"

Victor snorted. "What the hell do you think you're doing hanging around my daughter? I warned you—"

"I figure Marnie's old enough to make her own decisions."

"Or mistakes," Victor declared, gazing past Adam to the interior of the apartment, as if he expected Marnie to walk out of the kitchen, fling herself into his arms and complain that Adam had been holding her hostage against her will. It amused Adam that Victor really expected him to lie at every turn.

"Well, if you're not interested in coming in and shooting the breeze, then I guess I'd better be off. She's waiting for me at the boat. So if you'll excuse me…"

But Victor stood as if rooted to the porch, his gaze narrowing to some spot beyond Adam, his old eyes fixed on the inside of the apartment. "Oh, my God," he whispered, and his throat worked slightly. His face turned bloodless, as if he'd seen a ghost. "What the devil have you been doing, Drake?" he asked in a voice so low it was nearly lost in the rumble of traffic from the street.

"What do you mean? I told you she's not here…"

Ignoring Adam, Victor pushed past him, strode down the hallway to the table where Adam had been seated, where stacks of computer printouts lay sprawled over the white tabletop. Each heading, in bold inch-high letters, announced that the pages were property of Montgomery Inns.

Adam's stomach tightened. In his fantasies about

being alone with Marnie and his exuberance of thinking
they were about to solve the mystery with Kate Delany's
help, he'd forgotten about the sheaves of paper, damning
and incriminating printouts, strewn all over the kitchen.

Victor picked up the first few pages, scanned the
print and nearly staggered as he slumped into a chair,
dropping his head into his hands, one page of a printout
still wadded in his fingers. Hearing Adam approach,
he looked up, his eyes suddenly old and tired. "You did
it, didn't you? You managed to turn my own daughter
against me."

"No, I—"

"Damn it, Drake, I'm sick of lies! Sick!" With a renewed rush of energy, Victor struck one stack of printouts, and it skidded off the table to pour onto the floor,
sheet after perforated sheet, rolling and folding onto the
tile, condemning Marnie in her father's eyes. "She got
them from corporate headquarters, didn't she? Hell, yes,
she did. She still has access to the files. And then she
brought them back to you, like a dog bringing slippers
to his master for a pat on the head. God, you're incredible. My own daughter!" His voice trembled perilously,
but he didn't break down.

"Marnie was just trying to help me."

"Or ruin Montgomery Inns!" Victor's face had
flushed, and his lips shivered in rage.

"She wouldn't—"

"She already did, Drake, and I'm holding you personally responsible. I know you're trying to put together a
deal to open a rival hotel, right here in downtown Seattle, and you've convinced my daughter to become involved in some sort of corporate espionage against her
own flesh and blood. Well, I won't hear of it! You can

tell Marnie for me that she's fired!" he shouted, slamming his fist on the table and scrambling to his feet. "I'm calling my lawyers immediately to press charges against you for stealing company records. And I'm going to change my will. From this moment forward, Marnie's cut off! Understand? Cut off from any more Montgomery money. As far as I'm concerned, I don't have a daughter anymore."

Adam grabbed hold of the older man's lapels as Victor tried to brush past him. "If you just would have talked to me this never would have happened."

"Talk to you? All you had to do was call for an appointment," Victor raged, his voice becoming louder.

"I tried! But you left word with Kate Delany that you wouldn't see me."

"Enough of your lies! Just give Marnie the message."

"Don't you think you'd better tell her yourself?" Adam suggested, as he dropped the collar of Victor's coat.

"Why? She wouldn't believe me. It's you she trusts now. You've got her under some sort of spell, and when she wakes up, I hope to God she realizes what an incredible mistake she made—that you're just not worth it."

"Marnie can make up her own mind," Adam repeated, his jaw clenched so hard it throbbed.

Victor slammed out of the apartment, and Adam felt a tremendous loss. Not for himself. But for Marnie. Victor was the only family she had in the world, and no matter how angry she became with her father, he was still her own flesh and blood. Adam braced himself for the rift that was to come. He knew she loved the old man and would be devastated when she found out that Victor had branded her a traitor and disowned her.

He'd seen how much Victor meant to her when they'd discussed family ties.

Adam had ruined everything for her. He leaned heavily against the wall. How could he tell her that her father considered her no better than dead?

The phone rang again and the answering machine clicked on. Adam hesitated, half expecting Marnie's voice to be on the phone. "Marnie?" a woman asked. The voice was high-pitched and sluggish, as if she were drunk or drugged. "Marnie? Are you there? Oh, God, please be there! Marnie? This is Dolores…"

Dolores Tate? Adam froze, listening to Dolores's message.

"…look, I, uh, well, Kent knows that you know about the books. He, um, oooh, God! He came over and…and I told him. But somehow—somehow he already knew. I could see it in his eyes." She was crying now. Her voice faltered. "He flipped out and…he hit me, Marnie," she whispered, sniffing loudly. "He *hit* me. And I think he's on the way to the boat. I wouldn't mess with him if I were you… He might have a gun. Oh, Lord…"

Adam rushed back to the phone and picked up the receiver.

"Dolores, this is Adam Drake," he said, only to hear the sound of the connection being severed. A second later a dial tone buzzed in his ear.

What was she talking about? What books? What did it have to do with Marnie? A gun? Did she say a *gun!*

He didn't waste any time trying to call Dolores back. He didn't bother locking the apartment. Taking the steps to the parking lot two at a time, he raced down the stairs and only hoped that he wasn't too late.

IN THE MAIN CABIN of the boat, Marnie twisted the combination lock for the fifth time, but nothing happened. Not one single tumbler had seemed to fall into place. She wasn't just coming up with numbers at random, she'd taken the time to rifle through Kent's desk, and came up with dates, figures, or series of numbers that held special significance for him.

She tried again using his birthdate, her birthdate, the day he was promoted. Nothing, nothing and nothing.

Racking her brain, she came up with a long shot. The date of their engagement. The tumblers clicked, and the heavy door swung open. Maybe Kent did care for her more than she believed. She reached into the safe and withdrew a small velvet box. Inside was a diamond ring—the engagement ring she'd given back to him. Beneath the box were several stock certificates, and at the very bottom was a ledger book. Marnie opened the book and a computer disk fell out.

She heard brisk footsteps on the deck above. Adam. "Down here," she called, still reading the entries in the ledgers. They were coded, but she could see that vast amounts of money had been moved around the various accounts of Montgomery Inns—or at least that's what she suspected.

Adam's footsteps sounded on the stairs. "We've got it!" she yelled, her voice bubbling. She was practically beaming when he walked through the cabin door. "Look, it's all here—" she said, before her words died in her throat and she met Kent's all-knowing gaze.

"Ah, Marnie," he said, clicking his tongue and sighing. His face was cold and set. A tiny sliver of fear pricked her heart.

"Where's Adam?" she demanded.

"Don't know." He lifted one shoulder. "You expecting him?"

She knew she had to be careful. If she lied, Kent would see right through her. "I *hoped* you were him."

Kent winced. "So what am I going to do with you?"

"I think the question is, 'What are the police going to do to you, Kent?'" she said bravely, though she was cold inside. The glint in his eye was deadly, the determined set of his jaw rock-hard and his mouth was a thin, cruel line.

"That does pose a problem," he admitted, and for a fleeting second his iciness seemed to thaw and he looked again like the man she'd almost married. "I never wanted to hurt you." He glanced down at the books, still lying open in Marnie's hands. "But I got caught up in all this…well, it's over and done with," he said, his regret giving way to harsh reality. "Now, we've got to figure out where we go from here."

"You have to tell my father the truth. You have to give yourself up."

Kent snorted, as if she were a fool. "And spend the next twenty years in jail? I don't think so."

"If you don't tell him, I will."

"Oh, Marnie," he said, shaking his head again. "I don't think you're in a position to bargain." With that, he reached into his pocket and pulled out a small but deadly pistol. Marnie's heart stopped.

"You couldn't—"

"Maybe not. But I don't have many choices left, do I? If only Drake had butted out, this all would've worked."

"You mean if he'd taken the fall."

He motioned with his gun to the door. "Hand me the

books, then climb on deck. I think we should take a little cruise until I figure out what I've got to do."

"You're going to kidnap me?" she cried, fear giving way to stark terror. Alone on the open sea with Kent. But it was better than having Adam show up here and innocently walk into the barrel of Kent's gun.

"No, Marnie," he said as surely as if he could read her mind, "I'm not going to kidnap you. You're going to come with me willingly. Otherwise, I might have to find a way to kill your boyfriend and plant some evidence on him that proves without a doubt that he was the man who embezzled from your father."

"I'd never go along with that story," she said, her throat squeezing together so that it was hard to speak.

"Hopefully you won't have to. Maybe I'll bargain with Drake. If he cares anything for you, he might be willing to confess in order to spare your life and his."

Marnie could barely believe her ears. Did Kent actually think that Adam would claim responsibility for a crime he didn't commit, just to save her? Though Kent's pistol worried her, she couldn't accept the fact that he would actually shoot her. Embezzling was one kind of crime; murder was an entirely different story. Though cold fear crawled up her spine, she didn't really believe that Kent was capable of murder. This was all a bluff; it had to be.

Aware of Kent right behind her, she climbed the stairs to the deck, where the wind had picked up speed and sails were snapping loudly. "This is crazy, Kent. You're no killer. You couldn't hurt anyone."

"Tell that to your friend, Ed."

"Ed?" she repeated, her dread and adrenaline causing her heart to beat triple-time. "You didn't—"

"He never knew what hit him, but, no, he's not dead. Just sleeping for a while."

Only then did she realize just how desperate Kent had become. "What did you do to him?" she demanded, turning to face him, though her hair swept in front of her eyes. She thought she caught a movement of something on the bridge, another person, and her heart plummeted. Kent had brought along his accomplice.

"Don't worry about Ed. He'll survive," Kent assured her again. "Now, come on. You're so good at stealing this boat and sailing off into the sunset, why don't you do the honors and man the helm?"

A smug smile toyed at his lips, and Marnie never wanted to strike a person so much as she did just then. Her hand drew back to slap him.

"Don't even think about it," he warned.

From the corner of her eye, she caught a flash of movement. She turned and discovered Adam hurling himself from the bridge, flying through the air and straight at Kent.

"What—" Kent whirled, aimed his pistol, but Marnie, already poised to strike, hit his hand and the gun, flashing fire, spun out of his hand. Adam landed on Kent and sent them both sprawling along the smooth planks of the deck.

The accounting books were knocked from Kent's grasp. They fluttered upward and caught on the wind before dropping and sliding across the deck to drop into the sea. The computer disk followed, and Marnie raced to the rail, trying vainly to capture the evidence before it settled into the cold, dark waters. But the disk settled quickly beneath the surface. Devastated, she dared one look over her shoulder and grinned inwardly.

Adam was on top of Kent, one fist clenched around the front of Kent's expensive shirt, the other poised over his face, ready to pummel Kent's perfect features to a bloody mass.

Marnie didn't hesitate. Kicking off her shoes, she climbed onto the rail, poised for half a second, then dived neatly between the *Marnie Lee* and the boat tethered next to her.

"Marnie! Wait!" Adam's voice rang across the sound as ice-cold water rushed over her in a frigid wave. She swam downward, through the murky water, trying to see the books and the computer disk, hoping to keep some shred of evidence against Kent.

But the water was dark between the boats, and though she searched, she found nothing, not one paper drifting through the depths. Her lungs burned and she swam upward breaking the surface and gasping for air.

She glanced up at the *Marnie Lee* and watched as Adam dived into the water beside her. He surfaced a minute later, treading water and wiping water from his eyes.

"Anything?" he asked.

"Nothing."

He dived again, and Marnie followed suit, hoping against hope that not all of the evidence was lost. But she saw nothing, *nothing* and she knew in her heart that by this time, the pages that hadn't settled to the floor of the sound would be ruined and indecipherable. As for the computer disk, what were the chances that it, if discovered, was still operable?

Something slithered by her toes and she inwardly cringed at the thought of what kind of fish or eel had passed. She kicked toward the surface again.

With a loud roar, the engines of the *Marnie Lee* caught fire and the propeller started to churn in the dark water creating a whirlpool that sucked everything in its current. Marnie felt herself being pulled with papers, flotsam and kelp toward the craft. She struggled, swimming toward the shore against the drag of the frigid water, but the stern of the boat swung hard, coming closer. She managed to break the surface and gulp for air, but caught a mouthful of water.

"Watch out!" Adam cried, swimming toward her in quick, sure strokes. He wrapped one strong arm around her waist and swam with all his might toward the dark piers and the protection of the docks as she coughed and retched.

He only stopped when they were safely beneath the wharf and he could hold on to the barnacled pilings for support. "You okay?' he asked, and genuine concern etched his face.

"I—I'm fine," she gasped, her throat still squeezing shut against the onslaught of foul-tasting water. "But Kent. He's getting away!" Disappointment weighted her down. They'd lost the evidence they so sorely needed!

"He won't get far," Adam predicted. She turned in the water, so that her body was pressed to his.

"Why not?"

Tenderly Adam brushed aside a lank lock of hair that was plastered to her cheek. "I figured he'd make a run for it. I already called the Coast Guard. He'll be picked up before you and I get dried off."

"You didn't!"

"Oh, yes, I did." His brown eyes appeared darker in the shifting shadows beneath the dock. "Besides," he said, his voice thick, "it doesn't matter."

"Doesn't matter? Are you kidding? Do you know what those papers were?"

Adam's arm tightened around her. "If I were a betting man, I'd say they were the records explaining where all the missing funds went."

"Right, and now they're gone!" Her lips trembled from the cold. "And—and Kent, he won't admit to anything."

"Don't worry about it," Adam advised, his face closing the small distance between them.

"Why not?"

"Because it doesn't matter. When I saw Kent with that gun pointed at you, I realized that nothing mattered but your safety. God, I've been a fool." He kissed her then, his lips pressing possessively to hers, his mouth molding along the yielding contours of hers. She wrapped her arms around his neck, and despite the icy cold water, she felt warm and secure. As long as she was with Adam, *nothing else mattered.*

CHAPTER FOURTEEN

As soon as they climbed out of the water, Adam located a phone in the office of the marina and called an ambulance for Ed. The ambulance arrived within fifteen minutes, and Ed, arguing his health, was whisked off to the nearest hospital. After drying off with a couple of towels, courtesy of the locker room of the marina, Adam drove Marnie to the hospital, where they waited until Ed's doctor assured them that he'd be all right. Ed was suffering from a minor concussion. The doctor, a very distinguished man in his sixties whose authority brooked no argument, insisted, over Ed's very vocal protests, on keeping him in the hospital overnight for observation.

Two hours later, after witnessing Ed's cantankerous ribbing with one of the nurses, Marnie and Adam were satisfied that he would manage one night at Eastside General.

"Let's go to my place and clean up," Adam suggested as they climbed back into his car.

"So my apartment isn't good enough?" Marnie teased.

"Not tonight." Adam considered the printouts still strewn across Marnie's kitchen table and his conversation with Victor. He didn't want any reminders of the afternoon. Besides, until he'd heard that Kent was apprehended and locked up, he wanted to keep Marnie safe. The picture in his mind, of Kent pointing a pistol at Marnie's chest, kept returning in vivid and terrifying clarity.

Though Kent might know where Adam lived, he'd be less likely to try to surprise them there.

Adam's condominium was located on the eastern shore of Lake Washington, planted on a wooded hillside with steps that wound down to a private dock where his boat was anchored—remnants of the good life courtesy of Victor Montgomery.

He'd brought Marnie here a couple of times in the past few weeks, but they'd never stayed long and not once had she spent the night. Tonight would be different.

"First dibs on the shower," she said as they walked into the entry hall and gazed through a double bank of ceiling high windows with a view of the flint-colored waters of the lake. The bedrooms were downstairs, and Marnie walked confidently through Adam's room to the master bath, where she peeled off her clothes and stepped under the shower's steamy spray. The hot water rinsed the grit and briny smell from her skin. She washed her hair as well, trying to clean away the memory of Kent, his gun, and the pages of the accounting records as they floated just out of her reach.

She didn't hear Adam enter the bathroom, but felt the cold rush of air as he shoved aside the glass shower door and joined her in the misty warmth of the shower's spray.

"Couldn't wait?" she teased, glancing back over her shoulder to see his handsome face in the fog.

"That's one way of putting it." But he didn't seem

all that interested in the soap. Standing behind her, he reached forward, his hands surrounding her abdomen as he pulled her closer to him, his fingers spreading over her skin as he drew her tight enough that her buttocks pressed against his thighs.

Her skin tingled, and the water acted as a lubricant, allowing his hands to move silkily against her skin, as he turned her toward him. Heat, as liquid as the gentle spray, uncoiled within her.

She felt his hardness and the brush of his lips against her nape as he kissed her damp skin. She moaned low in her throat, and his fingers moved slowly upward, grazing the underside of her breasts, causing her nipples to stand erect.

He captured both her breasts in his hands, and she arched backward as he entered her, driving deeply into that warm womanly void that only he could fill.

I love you, she thought, but didn't dare utter the words. Instead she gasped as he moved within her, long and sure, causing a spasm of delight to ripple through her body as she braced against the wet tiles, receiving all of him eagerly.

"Marnie, love," he whispered against her ear, as he moved faster and faster until she was caught up in a whirlpool of emotion that wound tighter and tighter until she was spinning out of control, her breathing labored, her mind and soul filled with only Adam.

Crying her name, he plunged into her and collapsed and she, too, fell against the tile, her heart pounding in her ears. She didn't want to move, couldn't get enough air.

Finally, when her breathing had slowed to normal,

she coughed and Adam chuckled. "We'd better get out of here before we drown."

"Or before the water turns cold," she agreed with a laugh.

They spent the rest of the evening sipping wine, eating wedges of cheese and bread and making love. As if their narrow escape had heightened Adam's need to be with her, he barely let her out of his sight. Even when she insisted on rinsing out her dress and hoping it would dry, he was right at her side, assuring her she looked stunning in his faded old bathrobe.

They were settled on the couch, staring at the sunset when Marnie stretched and smiled at Adam. "I guess it's time to do my daughterly duty."

"What's that?" he asked warily.

"I think I'd better call Dad and tell him what happened."

"Maybe you should wait on that," he suggested, taking her hand and drawing her into the circle of his arms. She was half lying against him, his legs surrounding hers, her back pressed to his chest, and his face was nestled next to hers.

"Until when? Kent calls up and asks for bail money?"

She glanced sideways to catch his gaze. Adam's golden brown eyes held hers, and for the first time a premonition of fear slid down her spine. "There's something you're not telling me."

"I saw your father today," Adam said slowly, as if the words were hard to find. "He stopped by your apartment—seemed to think that you had dinner plans with him."

Marnie's stomach knotted. "Oh. I didn't have any

plans with him, but Kate thought the same thing. She was supposed to get hold of him and cancel."

At the mention of Kate's name, Adam's brows quirked. "She must've forgotten. Anyway, the upshot is that he not only found me in your apartment but he also saw the printouts."

"Oh, God," she whispered, a dull roar starting in her ears.

"He leapt to the wrong conclusions—"

"—that I was betraying him!" The dull roar seemed louder, more deafening; it beat through her brain and created a dark cloud at the corner of her vision.

"I tried to explain that it was all my fault, but he wouldn't listen. You know how he can get."

"Oh, yes," she said silently, waiting for the ax to fall. Victor would've been outraged that his only daughter had turned Judas on him. "He fired me, didn't he?"

"For starters."

"Worse?" Her insides crumbled. She'd never meant to hurt her father, and yet she'd done the one thing Victor could not handle. "Don't tell me. He disowned me."

"Something like that," Adam said, and there was naked pain in his eyes. As if he really did care what happened to her.

The glorious evening turned into a nightmare. Yes, she'd wanted her independence; yes, she'd wanted to follow her own path; but she'd never intended to wound her father, only to show him the truth—that Adam was innocent.

Tears stung the backs of her eyes, and she pulled out of Adam's embrace, as if in so doing she could change the past.

"I'm sorry," he whispered.

She laughed bitterly through the tears. "Don't be. It wasn't your fault," she said, flinging his own words back at him when she'd once tried to solace him.

"Yes. But this time it's a lie. This is all my fault. I knew involving you was a mistake, but it seemed the only logical way." Sighing, he threw back his head and stared at the ceiling. "I should never have put you into this kind of a position."

"But you did and I went into this with my eyes open."

"I pushed you."

"Well, maybe a little on the island. You weren't invited. But not since we've been back. Since we landed in Seattle, I chose to see you. I could just have easily chosen not to." *Except that I was beginning to fall in love with you,* she thought desperately, unable to utter the words. She didn't want to chase him out of her life by bringing up an emotion he didn't believe in, and now, after she'd learned that she'd lost her father, Adam was speaking as if he, too, were going to disappear from her life. Shivering, she rubbed her arms and felt the cozy warmth of terry cloth that smelled like him.

"There's more," he finally said as the shadows lengthened across the room.

"What could it possibly be?"

"I think I know who Kent's accomplice is."

"You do?" She was skeptical, and a headache was building behind her eyes. It wasn't every day a girl lost her family in one fell stroke.

"Kate Delany," he said.

"Kate?" She almost laughed. "You're out of your mind! No one is more loyal to my father than Kate."

He looked at her long and hard. "You like her, don't you?"

"Yes! She's like—well, not a second mother, but a big sister to me. Don't tell me she's a part of this mess, because I won't believe you!" Marnie said, her voice rising an octave as a wave of hysteria hit her. Too much had happened in one day and she couldn't believe that Kate, faithful, steady Kate, had stolen from the man she loved.

She scrambled to her feet and began to pace. "I've got to go, Adam. I've got to straighten all this out—"

"No."

"Yes, I—" God, why couldn't she think clearly? He was on his feet and gathering her into his arms.

"Stay with me."

"I can't, not tonight, but—"

"Not tonight," he whispered against her hair. "Stay with me forever."

His words stopped her protests. "I—I don't understand."

"Sure you do, Marnie. Marry me."

Then she understood. His desperation. His guilt. He felt responsible for her because Victor had disowned her. It was sweet and noble, but not a gesture of love.

"You don't mean this," she said.

"I want you to be my wife, Marnie," he whispered, and if she hadn't known better, she almost would have believed him.

The phone rang, and Adam answered. The conversation was long and one-sided. She only heard snatches of it, but guessed that Kent had been apprehended. Lord, what a mess. Her father would be devastated to find that Kent and Kate had betrayed him as well as his only daughter.

Shoving her hands in her pockets, she walked onto

the deck and stared at the stars winking high in the sky. She ached inside, ached from the pain of losing her father and worse yet, ached with the thought that she was losing Adam.

Oh, yes, he'd proposed, but out of a sense of duty. Never once had he said he loved her.

She heard the sliding glass door open. "It's over," he said, coming up behind her and standing so close she could almost feel him. But he didn't touch her. "Kent's confessed to everything and Kate's in custody."

"And Dad?"

"He's at police headquarters."

"He must be destroyed."

"Your father has a way of bouncing back."

Marnie curled her fingers over the rail. "Not this time," she whispered, then turned, feeling the warmth of Adam's arms surround her. He kissed her so gently she thought her heart would break. She drowned herself in the smell and feel and taste of him for this one last night. Tomorrow they would both have to deal with reality and the very genuine probability that they'd never see each other again.

"IT'S NOT EASY for me to say I was wrong," Victor allowed, standing near the windows in his office, his hands clasped behind his back. "But I was, and I guess an apology is in order. Adam, Marnie... I'm sorry."

They were standing in his office together because they'd both been summoned. Adam's countenance was grim, and he stared at Victor long and hard. Marnie was nervous. Though her spine was stiff, her chin lifted defiantly, her heart screamed forgiveness. Victor was her father.

"I misjudged you, Adam. Listened to the wrong people and I...well, I was convinced that you were a traitor to the company." Victor took in a long breath. "To that end, I did you a horrible disservice and I intend to make a public statement to that effect. And, if you want it, I'd be glad to offer you a job, a full vice presidency with stock options. If you'll consider it."

"Never."

Victor clamped his mouth shut and nodded stiffly. "You could name your price."

"My price would be too high, Victor," Adam said with quiet authority. "I'd want it all. Including your daughter."

Marnie had to brace herself against the desk for support. *Don't do this,* she thought, *not now.* "No, Adam, I don't think you understand," she said trying to place a hand on his arm. He shook it off.

"I just don't trust anyone who would throw his only daughter out of his life."

Victor sucked in his breath. Marnie knew this was difficult for her father. The past few days, with the arrest of Kent and Kate, along with a few other people who had known about the embezzlement, had been hard on Victor. His usually firm face was lined, his eyes bagged. He reached across his desk and grabbed his pipe, which he stuffed with tobacco.

As he lit his pipe, he stared through the smoke at his only daughter. Marnie felt her heartstrings tug.

"Adam's right. Again. I've been especially rough on you," Victor admitted, his voice coarse from emotion. "I mistreated you, Marnie, and I wouldn't blame you if you never forgave me."

His hands trembled slightly and once again he hid

them behind his back. His teeth clamped down on the stem of his pipe as he continued, "I never really listened to you, didn't believe you could make it on your own, threw a fit when you linked up with Adam and then, when you were only trying to help him, I did the worst thing a father can do. I acted as if you didn't exist. I wouldn't blame you if you never spoke to me again." He lowered himself heavily into his chair, broken and lost.

Marnie could barely get any words past the knot in her throat. "I—I love you, Dad," she whispered, sniffing loudly, and Victor's head snapped up.

"I love you, too, precious. I'm so sorry."

All at once he was standing, and Marnie rushed into his arms, crying uncontrollably as she clung to him. Her poor father. According to the police, Kate Delany had admitted swindling the funds because she felt she was in a dead-end situation with Victor. He'd never marry her, and she wasn't even certain he wouldn't eventually tire of her and pick out a younger, prettier secretary to become his next mistress.

Kent, jealous of Adam's influence with Victor, had found out about Kate's scheme. He had agreed to help her work out the movement of the funds and had made sure everything went through Adam's department, transferring the money from account to account and skimming off enough to eventually add up to half a million dollars. When an auditor had started nosing around, Kate, herself, had made the "discovery" of the embezzlement and with Kent's help, thrown the suspicion on Adam.

Now Kent and Kate were facing prosecution, Dolores was turning state's evidence and even Gerald Henderson was testifying.

"Things will be all right," she told her father, smiling through her tears. "You'll see."

"God, I hope so." Victor swiped at his eyes, then pulled out a handkerchief and blew his nose loudly.

Marnie turned to Adam, but discovered that he'd left. The room was empty except for her father and herself.

"You'd better go find him," her father advised with a grin. "If I were you, I wouldn't let that one get away."

"I won't. But I don't know when I'll be able to work on the publicity for San Francisco—"

"Don't worry about it," her father said. "Just patch things up with Adam. The rest will work out."

She believed him. She ran through the hotel and impatiently waited for an elevator. "Come on, come on," she whispered as the lift eventually stopped and dropped her into the parking lot.

Running to the *B* level, her heart in her throat, she had the horrible thought that Adam didn't want her any longer. That, upon seeing her embracing her father, he assumed she would always be a spoiled little rich girl, Victor's daughter. But he was wrong—so wrong. She loved Adam with all her heart and nothing, *nothing* was going to keep her from pledging her love for him and making him understand that she didn't care about marriage, the future, or the past. She only wanted Adam. For as long as he would have her.

THE CALL FROM BRODIE came in too late. After speaking to Victor Montgomery directly, Brodie had finally come to understand that Adam had nothing to do with the embezzlement. Victor had called Brodie himself and given Adam a personal recommendation to the California lawyer.

Too late. Much too late. Adam had been pleased to give Brodie the news that he didn't need him or his financing. Norman Howick, the rogue oilman, had promised him a deal that was perfect. Adam already had his plane ticket on the first flight tomorrow morning. He wondered if he'd hear from Marnie, and his heart wrenched at the thought.

If this deal with Howick worked out—and it looked good—Adam would be packed and leaving Seattle by the end of the week. Alone. Without her.

Well, that's what you wanted, wasn't it? You used her. To get what you wanted. So now that you're off the hook for the embezzling scam and she's back with Daddy, everything's just as you planned.

"Dammit all to hell," he growled, grabbing a bottle of Scotch from his liquor cabinet and walking outside to the deck of his condominium. The day was clear and bright and he'd planned on taking a boat ride. A warm summer sun spangled the water with golden light, and sailboats and skiffs were skimming the surface of Lake Washington. He'd even loaded a few supplies into his boat when the phone had rung and he'd raced back to the condo where he'd been able to tell Brodie where to stuff his offer.

But the satisfaction he should have felt, when he'd told Brodie where to get off, wasn't enough. He was still missing Marnie in his life and he felt hollow inside.

He uncapped the bottle and took a long pull before screwing on the cap and walking down the overgrown path to the deck where his small cabin cruiser lay docked. Unwinding the ropes from the pilings, he scanned the cliff where his condominium stood one last time—as if he expected Marnie, with her bright eyes and tinkling laughter to suddenly appear.

Forget her.

Impossible. He climbed aboard, pushed off and started the engine. It coughed, sputtered, then caught with a roar. He gunned the throttle, and the boat picked up speed, slicing across the water while the wind tore at his face.

Marnie... Marnie... Marnie... Her face swam before his eyes and he knew it would take forever to forget her.

"Where're we going?"

Even her voice seemed to follow him. Stupidly, he looked over his shoulder and there she was. Just as he'd pictured her. He blinked once to believe what could only be an apparition, and she laughed. Braced against the railing, the wind singing through her hair, her smile beguiling and bright, she tossed back her head. "Well? The San Juans? The Caribbean? Maybe Alaska? Where?"

He was momentarily tongue-tied as Marnie reached over and quickly switched off the ignition. The engine died. The boat slowed to a stop and floated on the gentle roll of the lake.

"How'd you get here?" he demanded, finally comprehending that she'd fooled him somehow.

"I'm a stowaway," she said, laughing. "Just like you were."

She'd been in the small cabin below-decks? "But how did you know I'd go out today?" He was beginning to smile, he felt a familiar tug on his lips.

"I watched you. I pulled up to the front of the house and spied you carrying things on board. So I snuck down the hill and hid."

"But why?"

Her smile faded, and her blue eyes turned the color of the sea. "Because I want you, Adam," she said with obvious difficulty. "I can't bear the thought of you leaving. When I turned around in Dad's office and you'd disappeared, it seemed as if a part of me had left with you." She looked away from him now, as if afraid that he would reject her, and he realized how difficult this was for her.

"When you proposed to me, I knew it was because my father disowned me, that you felt guilty and responsible." When he tried to interrupt, she held out a quivering hand to stop him. "And you thought I was one of those women in your life pushing for a commitment. But that's not true." When she faced him again, tears stood in her eyes. "I want you for as long as we can be together, and then, when it's over, I'll leave. I won't pressure you."

Adam laughed out loud. This beautiful, incredible woman was willing to give him everything and so much, much more. "Pressure me?" He grabbed her around the waist and kissed the tears from her eyes. "Are you crazy? You're the one who's going to get all the pressure, lady. I *want* you to marry me. I didn't propose out of some sense of duty, Marnie. I proposed because I want you to be my wife. The only reason I didn't drag you to a preacher kicking and screaming is that I thought you should resolve your relationship with your father as well as become your own woman. Isn't that what you've been screaming about for the past month?"

"You're serious?" she said, disbelief clouding her eyes.

"More serious than I've ever been in my miserable life," he assured her, his hands brushing a strand of pale hair from her eyes. "Believe me, Marnie. I want you. Today. Tomorrow. Forever. From the moment I saw you standing at the helm, battling the storm and barking orders at the sight of me, I knew you were the one. I just couldn't admit it. Not to you and not to myself."

He watched her swallow hard.

"I love you, Marnie Montgomery. If you don't believe anything else in this world, believe that I love you."

She blinked back her tears. "Does this mean that I'm still in the running for the publicist of Hotel Drake?"

"And anything else that has to do with me," he replied, kissing her soundly on the lips. "Will you marry me?"

"Absolutely."

"This won't interfere with your independence?" he teased.

"I am my own woman, Mr. Drake. And I know my own mind. And all I want is you."

"But you're a businesswoman now."

She smiled coyly. "Then I'll just have to move my business wherever you want. I'll have your children and tend your house. But, believe me, I will be my own woman."

"And my wife?" he asked skeptically.

"I think I can be both."

"You'd better be," he said, his mouth coming down to claim hers possessively, as if he already were her husband. She nearly dropped the keys to the boat into the water, but he didn't care. He had everything he needed in his arms.

Lifting his head, he asked, "Where do you want to go for a honeymoon?"

She grinned slowly. "Anywhere you take me." One

of her eyebrows lifted saucily. "You know, we could start right now."

"Now?"

"Well, you do have a cabin downstairs and...if we want to, we can just sail away together."

"You're sure?"

"More sure than I've ever been in my life."

"Miss Montgomery, you've got yourself the deal of a lifetime." One arm around her waist, he plucked the keys from her palm with his free hand, started the engine, rammed the boat into gear, and set on a course that would hold them steady for the rest of their lives.

* * * * *

EXPECTING TROUBLE

Delores Fossen

To Tom, thanks for all the support.

PROLOGUE

A DEAFENING BLAST shook the rickety hotel and stopped Jenna cold.

With her heart in her throat, Jenna raced to the window and looked down at the street below. Or rather what was left of the street, a gaping hole. Someone had set shops on fire. Black coils of smoke rose, smearing the late afternoon sky.

"Ohmygod," Jenna mumbled.

There was no chance a taxi could get to her now to take her to the airport. And worse were rebel soldiers, at least a dozen of them dressed in dark green uniforms. She'd heard about them on the news and knew they had caused havoc in Monte de Leon. That's why by now she'd hoped to be out of the hotel, and the small South American country. She hadn't succeeded because she'd been waiting on a taxi for eight hours.

One of the soldiers looked up at her and took aim with his scoped rifle. Choking back a scream, Jenna dropped to the floor just as the bullet slammed through the window.

She scurried across the threadbare rug and into the bathroom. It smelled of mold, rust and other odors she didn't want to identify, and Jenna wasn't surprised to see roaches race across the cracked tile. It was a far cry from the nearby Tolivar estate, where she'd spent the past two days. Of course, there'd been insects of a different kind there.

Paul Tolivar.

Staying close to the wall, Jenna pulled off one of her red heels so she could use it as a weapon and climbed into the bathtub to wait for whatever was about to happen.

She didn't have to wait long.

There was a scraping noise just outside the window. She pulled in her breath and waited. Praying. She hadn't even made it to the please-get-me-out-of-this part when she heard a crash of glass and the thud of someone landing on the floor.

"I'm Special Agent Cal Rico," a man called out. "U.S. International Security Agency. I'm here to rescue you."

A rescue? Or maybe this was a trick by one of the rebels to draw her out. Jenna heard him take a step closer, and that single step caused her pulse to pound in her ears.

"I know you're here," he continued, his voice calm. "I pinpointed you with thermal equipment."

The first thing she saw was her visitor's handgun. It was lethal-looking. As was his face. Lean, strong. He had an equally strong jaw. Olive skin that hinted at either Hispanic or Italian DNA. Mahogany-brown hair and sizzling steel-blue eyes that were narrowed and focused.

He was over six feet tall and wore all black, with various weapons and equipment strapped onto his chest, waist and thighs. He looked like the answer to her unfinished prayer.

Or a P.S. to her nightmare.

"We need to move now," he insisted.

Jenna didn't question that, but she still wasn't sure what she intended to do. Yes, she was afraid, but she wasn't stupid. "Can I trust you?"

Amusement leapt through his eyes. His reaction was brief, lasting barely a second before he nodded. And that was apparently all the reassurance he intended to give her. He latched on to her arm and hauled her from the tub. He allowed her just enough time to put back on her shoe before he maneuvered her out of the bathroom and toward the door to her hotel room.

"Extraction in progress, Hollywood," he whispered into a black thumb-size communicator on the collar of his shirt. "ETA for rendezvous is six minutes."

Six minutes. Not long at all. Jenna latched on to that info like a lifeline. If this lethal-looking James Bond could deliver what he promised, she'd be safe soon. Of course, with all those rebel soldiers outside, that was a big *if*.

Cal Rico paused at the door, listening, and eased it open. After a split-second glance down the hall, he got them out of the room and down a flight of stairs that took them to the back entrance on the bottom floor. Again, he looked out, but he must not have liked what he saw. He put his finger to his lips, telling her to stay quiet.

Outside, Jenna could still hear the battery of gun- fire and the footsteps of the rebels. They seemed to be moving right past the hotel. She was in the middle of a battle zone.

How much her life had changed in two days. This should have been a weekend trip to Paul's Monte de Leon estate. A prelude to taking their relationship from friendship to something more. Instead, it'd become a terrifying ordeal she might not survive.

Jenna tried not to let fear take hold of her, but adrenaline was screaming for her to run. To do something. *Anything.* It was a powerful, overwhelming sensation. Fight or flight. Even if either of those options could get her killed.

Cal Rico touched his fingers to her lips. "Your teeth are chattering," he mouthed.

No surprise there. She didn't have a lot of coping mechanisms for dealing with this level of stress. Who did? Well, other than the guy next to her.

"Try doing some math," he whispered. "Or recite the Gettysburg Address. It'll help keep you calm."

Jenna didn't quite buy that. Still, she tried.

He moved back slightly. But not before she caught his scent. Sweat mixed with deodorant soap and the faint smell of the leather from his combat boots. It was far more pleasant than it should have been.

Stunned and annoyed with her reaction, Jenna cursed herself. Here she was, close to dying, only hours out of a really bad relationship, and her body was already reminding her that Agent Cal Rico smelled pleasant. Heaven help her. She was obviously a candidate for therapy.

"I'll do everything within my power to get you out of here," he whispered. "That's a promise."

Jenna stared at him, trying to figure out if he was lying. No sign of that. Just pure undiluted confidence. And much to her surprise, she believed him. It was probably a reaction to the testosterone fantasy he was weaving around her. But she latched on to his promise.

"All clear," he said before they started to move again.

They hurried out the door and into the alley that divided the hotel from another building. Cal never even paused. He broke into a run and made sure she kept up with him. He made a beeline for a deserted cantina. They ducked inside, and he pulled her to the floor.

"We're at the rendezvous point," he said into his communicator. "How soon before you can pick up Ms. Laniere?" A few seconds passed before he relayed to her, "A half hour."

That was an eternity with the battle raging only yards away. "We'll be safe here?" Jenna tried not to make it sound like a question.

"Safe enough, considering."

"How did you even know I was in that hotel?"

Cal shifted his position so he could keep watch out the window. "Intel report."

"There was an intelligence report about me?" But she didn't wait for him to answer. "Who are you? Not your name. I got that. But why are you here?"

He shrugged as if the answer were obvious. "I'm a special agent with International Security Agency— the ISA. I've been monitoring you since you arrived in Monte de Leon."

Still not understanding, she shook her head. "Why?"

"Because of your boyfriend, Paul Tolivar. He is bad news. A criminal under investigation."

Judas Priest. This was about Paul. Who else?

"My ex-boyfriend," she corrected. "And I wish I'd known he was bad news before I flew down here."

Maybe it was because she was staring craters into him, but Agent Rico finally looked at her. Their gazes met. And held.

"I don't suppose someone could have told me he was under investigation?" she demanded.

He was about to shrug again, but she held tight to his shoulder. "We couldn't risk telling you because you might have told Paul."

Special Agent Rico might have added more, if there hadn't been an earsplitting explosion just up the street. It sent an angry spray of dirt and glass right at them. He reacted fast. He shoved her to the floor, and covered her body with his. Protecting her.

They waited. He was on top of her, with his rock-solid abs right against her stomach and one of his legs wedged between hers. Other parts of them were aligned as well.

His chest against her breasts. Squishing them.

The man was solid everywhere. Probably not an ounce of body fat. She'd never really considered that an asset, but she did now. Maybe all that strength would get them out of this alive.

Since they might be there for a while, and since Jenna wanted to get her mind off the gunfire, she forced herself to concentrate on something else.

"I believe Paul might be doing something illegal. He uses cash, never credit cards, and he always steps away from me whenever someone calls him on his cell. I know that's not really proof of any wrongdoing."

In fact, the only proof she had was that Paul was a jerk. When she refused to marry him, he'd slapped her and stormed out. Jenna hadn't waited around to see if he'd return with an apology. She hadn't even waited when Paul's driver had refused to take her into town. She'd walked the two miles, leaving everything but her purse behind.

Agent Rico smirked. "Tolivar was under investigation for at least a dozen felonies. The Justice Department thought you could be a witness for their case against him."

"Me?" She'd said that far louder than she intended. Then she whispered, "But I don't know anything." Oh, mercy. She hadn't thought things would be that bad. "What did Paul want with me? Not a green card. He's already a U.S. citizen."

Cal nodded. "The Justice Department believes he wanted your accounting firm so he could use it to launder money."

"Wait, he can't have my accounting firm. According to the terms of my father's will, I'm not allowed to sell or donate even a portion of the firm to anyone that isn't family."

He had no quick response, and his hesitation had her head racing with all sorts of bad ideas.

"We believe Paul Tolivar planned to marry you one way or another this evening," Cal said. "He had a phony marriage license created, in case you turned down his proposal. Intel indicates that after the marriage, he planned to keep you under lock and key so he could control your business and your money."

A sickening feeling of betrayal came first. Then anger. Not just at Paul, but at herself for believing him and not questioning his motives. Still, something didn't add up. "If Paul planned to keep me captive, then why didn't he come after me when I left his estate?"

"He had someone follow you. I doubt he intended to let you leave the country. He contacted the only taxi service in town and told them to stall you."

So she'd been waiting for a taxi that would never

have shown up. And it was probably just a matter of time before Paul came after her.

"I slept with him," Jenna mumbled. Groaned. She pushed her fists against the sides of her head. "You must think I'm the most gullible woman in the world."

"No. I think you're an heiress who was conned."

Yes. Paul had given her the full-court press after she'd met him at a fund-raiser. Phone calls. Roses. *Yellow* roses, her favorite. And more. "He told me he was dying of a brain tumor."

Rico shook his head. "No brain tumor."

It took Jenna a moment to get her teeth unclenched. "The SOB. I want him arrested. I want—"

"He's dead."

She had to fight through her fit of rage to understand what he'd said. "Paul's dead?"

Cal Rico nodded. "He was murdered about an hour ago. That's why I'm here—to stop the same thing from happening to you."

Her heart fell to her knees. "Wh-what?"

"We have reason to believe that Paul left instructions. In the event of his death, he wanted others dead, too. You included. Those rebel soldiers out there are after you. And they have orders to kill you on sight."

CHAPTER ONE

International Security Agency Regional Headquarters
San Antonio, Texas
One year later

SPECIAL AGENT CAL RICO checked his watch—again.
Only three minutes had passed since the last time he'd
looked. It felt longer.

A lot longer.

Of course, waiting outside his director's door had a
way of making each second feel like an eternity.

"Uh-oh," he heard someone say. Cal saw a team
member making his way up the hall toward him. Mark
Lynch was nicknamed Hollywood because of his
movie-star looks. He was a Justice Department liai-
son assigned to the regional headquarters. "What'd you
screw up, Chief?" Lynch asked.

Chief. Cal had been given his moniker because of his
aspirations to become chief director of the International
Security Agency. Except they weren't just aspirations.
One day he *would* be chief. Since that was his one and
only goal, it made things simple.

And in his mind, inevitable.

"Who said I screwed up anything?" Cal commented.
But he was asking himself the same thing.

Lynch arched his left eyebrow and flashed a Tom

Cruise smile. "You're outside Kowalski's office, aren't you?"

Cal had been assigned to the Bravo team of the ISA for well over a year, and this was the first time he'd ever been ordered to see his director. Since he'd just returned from a monthlong assignment in the Middle East and wouldn't receive new orders within seven duty days, he was bracing himself for bad news.

He'd already called his folks and both of his brothers to make sure all was well on the home front. That meant this had to do with the job. And that made it more personal than anything else could have been.

"If you have a butt left when Kowalski quits chewing it," Hollywood continued, "then show up at the racquetball court at 1730 hours. I believe you promised me a rematch."

Cal mumbled something noncommittal. He hated racquetball, but after this meeting he might need a way to work out some frustrations. Pounding Hollywood might just do it.

The door to the director's office opened, and Cal's lanky boss motioned for him to enter.

"Have a seat," Director Scott Kowalski ordered. There was no mistake about it. His tone and demeanor confirmed that it was an order. "Talk to me about Jenna Laniere."

Cal had geared up to discuss a lot of things with his boss, but she wasn't anywhere on that list. Though he'd certainly thought, and dreamed, about the leggy blonde heiress. "What about her?"

"Tell me what happened when you rescued her in Monte de Leon last year."

That was a truly ominous-sounding request. Still,

Cal tried not to let it unnerve him. "As best as I can recall, I entered the hotel where she'd checked in, found her hiding in the bathroom. I moved her from that location and got her to the rendezvous point. About a half hour later or so, the transport took her away, and I rejoined the Bravo team so we could extract some American hostages that the rebels had taken."

Kowalski put his elbows on his desk and leaned closer. "It's that half hour of unaccounted-for time that I'm really interested in."

Hell.

That couldn't be good. Had Jenna Laniere filed some kind of complaint all these months later? If so, Cal had her pegged all wrong. She had seemed too happy about being rescued to be concerned that he'd used profanity around her.

"Wait a minute," Cal mumbled, considering a different scenario. One that involved Paul Tolivar, or rather what was left of Tolivar's regime. "Is Jenna Laniere safe?"

Translation: had Tolivar's cronies or former business partners killed her?

The FBI had followed Jenna for weeks after her return to the States. When no one had attempted to eliminate her, they'd backed off from their surveillance.

As for Tolivar's regime, there hadn't been enough hard evidence for the Monte de Leon or U.S. authorities to arrest Tolivar's partners or anyone else for his murder. In fact, there hadn't been any evidence at all except for Justice Department surveillance tapes that couldn't be used in court since they would give away the identities of several deep-cover operatives. A move that would almost certainly cause the operatives to be executed. The Justice Department wasn't about to lose key men to further investigate a criminal's murder. Especially one that'd happened in a foreign country.

"Ms. Laniere's fine," Kowalski assured him.

The relief Cal felt was a little stronger than he'd expected. And it was short-lived. Because something had obviously happened. Something that involved her. If Jenna had indeed filed a complaint, there'd be an investigation. It could hurt his career.

The one thing he valued more than anything else.

He would not fail at this. He couldn't. Bottom line— being an operative wasn't his job, it was who he was. Without it, he was just the middle son of a highly decorated air force general. The middle son sandwiched between two brothers who'd already proven themselves a dozen times over. Cal had never excelled at anything. In his youth, he'd been average at best and at worst been a screwup—something his father often reminded him of.

His career in the ISA was the one way he could prove to his father, and more important to himself, that he was worth something.

"After you rescued Ms. Laniere, the Justice Department questioned her for hours. Days," Kowalski corrected. "She didn't tell them anything they could use to build their case against Tolivar's business partners. In fact, she claims she never heard Tolivar or his partners speak of the rebel group that they'd organized and funded in Monte de Leon. The group he ordered to kill her. She further claimed that she never heard him discuss his illegal activities."

"And the Justice Department believes she was telling the truth?"

Kowalski made a sound that could have meant anything. "Have you seen or spoken with her in the past year?"

"No." Cal immediately shook his head, correcting that. "I mean, I tried to call her about a month ago, but she wasn't at her office in Houston. I left a message on her voice mail, and then her assistant phoned back to let me know that she was on an extended leave of absence and couldn't be reached."

The director steepled his fingers and stared at Cal. "Why'd you try to call her?"

Cal leaned slightly forward as well. "This is beginning to sound a little like an interrogation."

"Because it is. Now back to the question—why did you make that call?"

Oh, man. That unnerving feeling that Cal had been trying to stave off hit him squarely between the eyes. This was not something he wanted to admit to his director. But he wouldn't lie about it, either.

No matter how uncomfortable it was.

"I was worried about her. Because I read the investigation into Tolivar's business partners had been reopened. I just wanted to see how things were with her."

Judging from the way Director Kowalski's smoke-gray eyes narrowed, that honest answer didn't please him. He muttered a four-letter word.

"Mind telling me what this is about?" Cal asked. "Because last I heard it isn't a crime for a man to call a woman and check on her."

But in this case, his director might consider it a serious error in judgment.

Since Jenna had a direct association with an international criminal like Paul Tolivar, no one working in the ISA should have considered her a candidate for a friendship. Or anything else.

Kowalski aimed an accusing index finger at Cal. "You know it violates regulations to have intimate or sexual contact with someone in your protective custody. And for those thirty minutes in Monte de Leon, Jenna Laniere was definitely in your protective custody."

That brought Cal to his feet. "Sexual contact?" Ah, hell. "Is that what she said happened?"

"Are you saying it didn't?"

"You bet I am. I didn't touch her." It took Cal a few moments to get control of his voice so he could speak. "Did she file a complaint or something against me?"

Kowalski motioned for him to take his seat again. "Trust me, Agent Rico, you'll want to sit down for this part."

Cal bit back his anger and sank onto the chair. Not easily, but he did it. And he forced himself to remain calm. Well, on the outside, anyway. Inside, there was a storm going on, and he could blame that storm on Jenna.

"As you know, I'm head of the task force assigned to clean up the problems in Monte de Leon," Kowalski explained. "The kidnapped American civilians. The destruction of American-owned businesses and interests."

Impatient with what had obviously turned into a briefing, Cal spoke up. "Is any of this connected to Ms. Laniere?"

"Yes. Apparently, she's still involved with Paul Tolivar's business partners. That's why we started keeping an eye on her again."

That took the edge off some of Cal's anger and grabbed his interest. "Involved—how?"

Kowalski pushed his hands through the sides of his

graying brown hair. "She's been staying in a small Texas town, Willow Ridge, for the past couple of months. But prior to that while she was still in Houston, one of Tolivar's partners, Holden Carr, phoned her no less than twenty times. They argued. We're hoping that during one of their future conversations, Holden might divulge some information. That's why the Justice Department has been monitoring Ms. Laniere's calls and emails."

In other words, phone and computer taps. Not exactly standard procedure for someone who wasn't a suspected criminal. Of course, Hollywood would almost certainly have been aware of that surveillance and monitoring, and it made Cal wonder why the man hadn't at least mentioned it. Or maybe Hollywood hadn't remembered that Cal had rescued Jenna.

"What does all of this have to do with alleged sexual misconduct?" Cal insisted.

Kowalski hesitated a moment. Then two. Just enough time to force Cal's anxiety level sky-high. "It's come to our attention that Jenna Laniere has a three-month-old daughter."

Oh, man.

It took Cal a few moments to find his breath, while he came up with a few questions that he was afraid even to ask.

"So what does that have to do with me?" Cal tried to sound nonchalant, but was sure he failed miserably.

"She claims the baby is yours."

CHAPTER TWO

CAL FINALLY SPOTTED HER.

Wearing brown pants and a cream-colored cable-knit sweater, Jenna came out of a small family-owned grocery store on Main Street. She had a white plastic sack clutched in each hand. But no baby.

One thing was for sure—she didn't look as if she'd given birth only three months earlier.

But she did look concerned. Her forehead was bunched up, and her gaze darted all around.

Good. She should be concerned about the lie she'd told. It probably wasn't a healthy thought to want to yell at a woman. But for the entire hour-long drive from regional headquarters to the little town of Willow Ridge, Texas, he'd played around with it.

She claims the baby is yours.

Director Kowalski's words pounded like fists in Cal's head. Powerful words, indeed.

Career-ruining words.

That's why he had to get this situation straightened out so that it couldn't do any more damage. Before the end of the week, he was due for a performance review, one that would be forwarded straight to the promotion board. If he had any hopes of making deputy director two years early, there couldn't even be a hint of negativity in that report.

And there wouldn't be.

That's what this visit was all about. One way or another, Jenna was going to tell the truth and clear his name. He'd worked too damn hard to let her take that early promotion away from him.

Cal stepped out of his car, ducked his head against the chilly February wind and strolled across the small parking lot toward her. He figured she was on her way to the apartment she'd rented over the town's lone bookstore. Judging from the direction she took, he was right.

Even though she kept close to the buildings, she was easy to track. Partly because there weren't many people out and about and partly because of her hair. Those shiny blond locks dipped several inches past her shoulders. Loose and free. The strands seemed to catch every ray of sun.

That hair would probably cause any man to give her a second look. Her body and face would cause a man to stare. Which was exactly what he was doing.

She must have sensed his eyes on her because she whirled around, her gaze snaring him right away.

"It's you," she said, squinting to see him in the harsh late afternoon sun. She sounded a little wary and surprised.

However, Cal's reactions were solely in the latter category.

First, there were her eyes. That shock of color. So green. So clear. He hadn't gotten a good look at her eyes when he rescued her in that dimly lit hotel, but he did now. And they were memorable. As was her face. She wore almost no makeup. Just a touch of peachy color on her mouth. She looked natural and sensual at the same time. But the most startling reaction of all was that he wasn't as angry at her as he had been five minutes before.

Well, until he forced himself to hang on to that particular feeling awhile longer.

"We have to talk," Cal insisted. And he wasn't about to let her say no. He took one of her grocery sacks so he could hook his arm through hers.

She looked down at the grip he had on her before she lifted her eyes to meet his. "This is about Paul Tolivar's business partner, isn't it? Is Holden Carr the one who's having me followed?"

That stopped Cal in his tracks. There was a mountain of concern in her voice and expression. Much to his shock, he wasn't immune to that concern.

He didn't like this feeling. The sudden need to protect her. This sure as heck wasn't an ISA-directed mission.

He repeated that to himself. "Someone is following you?" he asked.

She gave a surreptitious glance around, and since their arms were already linked, she maneuvered him into an alley that divided two shops.

"I spotted this man on my walk to the grocery store. He stayed in the shadows so I wasn't able to get a good look at him." Her words raced out, practically bleeding together. "Maybe he's following me, maybe he's not. And there's a reporter. Gwen Mitchell. She introduced herself a couple of minutes ago in the produce aisle."

Cal made note of the name. Once he was done with this little chat, he'd run a background check on this Gwen Mitchell to see if she was legit. "What does she want?"

Jenna dismissed his question with a shrug, though

tension was practically radiating from her. The muscles in her arm were tight and knotted. "She claims she's doing some kind of investigative report on Paul and the rebel situation in Monte de Leon."

That in itself wasn't alarming. There were probably lots of reporters doing similar stories because of the renewed investigation. "You don't believe her?"

"I don't know. Since the incident in Monte de Leon, I've been paranoid. Shadows don't look like shadows anymore. Hang-up calls seem sinister. Strangers in the grocery line look like rebel soldiers with orders to kill me." She shook her head. "And I'm sorry for dumping all of this on you. I know I'm not making any sense."

Unfortunately, she was making perfect sense. Cal had never met Paul's business partner, the infamous Holden Carr, but from what he'd learned about the man, Holden wasn't the sort to give up easily. Maybe he wanted to continue his late partner's quest to get Jenna's accounting firm and trust fund. Jenna's firm certainly wasn't the only one enticing to a potential money launderer, but Holden was familiar with it, and it had all the right foreign outlets to give him a quick turnover for the illegal cash.

Or maybe this was good news, and those shadows were Justice Department agents. Except Director Kowalski hadn't mentioned anything about her being followed. It was one thing to monitor calls and emails, but tailing a person required just cause and a lot of manpower. Since Jenna wasn't a suspect in a crime, there shouldn't have been sufficient cause for close surveillance.

And that brought them right back to Holden Carr.

"You've heard from Holden recently?" he asked. A

lie detector of sorts since he knew from the director's briefing that she'd been in contact with the man in the past twenty-four hours.

"Oh, I've heard from him all right. Lucky me, huh? He's called a bunch of times, and right after I got back from Monte de Leon, he visited my office in Houston. And get this—he says he's always been in love with me, that he wants to be part of my life. Right. He's in love with my estate and accounting firm, and what he really wants is to be part of my death so he can inherit it." She paused. "Please tell me he'll be arrested soon."

"Soon." But Cal had no idea if that was even true.

"Good. Because as long as he's a free man, I'm not safe. That's why I left Houston. I thought maybe if I came here, Holden wouldn't be able to find me. That he'd stop harassing me. Then yesterday afternoon he called me again, on my new cell phone." She moistened her lips. And looked away. "He threatened me."

That didn't surprise Cal. Holden wouldn't hesitate to resort to intimidation to get what he wanted. Still, that was a problem for the back burner. He had something more pressing.

"Holden didn't make an overt threat," Jenna continued before Cal could speak. "He implied it. It scared me enough to decide that I need professional security. A bodyguard or something. But I don't know anyone I can trust. I don't know if the bodyguard I call might really be working for Holden."

Unfortunately, that was a real possibility. If Holden knew where she was, then he would also know how to get to her.

She paused and blew out a long breath. "Okay, that's enough about me and my problems. Why are you here?"

She conjured a halfhearted smile. "Gosh, that's a déjà vu kind of question, isn't it? I remember asking you something similar when you were rescuing me in Monte de Leon. Is that why you're here now—to rescue me?"

"No." But why the heck did he suddenly feel as if he wanted to do just that?

From that still panicked look in her eyes, it wasn't a good time to bring up his anger, but Cal wasn't about to let her off the hook, either.

"Why did you lie about who your baby's father is?" he demanded.

Jenna blinked, and then her eyes widened. "How did you know?"

"Well, it wasn't a lucky guess, that's for sure. This morning my director called me into his office to demand an explanation as to why I slept with someone in my protective custody."

"Ohmygod." Jenna leaned against the wall and pulled in several hard breaths. "I had no idea. How did your director even find out I'd had a baby?"

Because she already had a lot to absorb, Cal skipped right over the Justice Department eavesdropping on her, and gave her a summary of what Director Kowalski had relayed to him. "You told Holden Carr that the baby was mine."

Jenna nodded, and with her breath now gusting hard and fast, she studied his expression. It was as icy as the Antarctic. "This could get you into trouble, couldn't it?"

"It's *already* gotten me into trouble. Deep trouble. And it could get worse."

He would have added more, especially the part about Director Kowalski demanding DNA proof that Cal wasn't the baby's father. But he caught some movement from the corner of his eye. A thin-faced man in a dark blue two-door car. He drove slowly past them.

"That's the guy," Jenna whispered, tugging on the sleeve of Cal's leather jacket. "He's the one who followed me to the grocery store."

The words had hardly left her mouth when the man gunned the engine and sped away. But not before Cal made eye contact with him.

Oh, hell.

Cal recognized him from the intel surveillance photos.

He cursed, dropped the grocery bag and slipped his hand inside his jacket in case he had to draw his gun. "How long did you say he's been following you?"

Jenna shook her head and looked to be on the verge of panicking. "I think just today. Why? Do you know him? Is he a friend of yours?"

There was way too much hope in her voice.

"Not a friend," Cal assured her. "But I know *of* him." He left it at that. "Where's your baby?"

"In the apartment. My landlord's daughter is watching her. Why?"

Cal didn't answer that. "Come on. We'll finish this conversation there."

And once they had finished the discussion about the paternity of her child, he'd move on to some security measures he wanted her to take. Maybe the Justice Department could even provide her with protection or a safe house. He'd call Hollywood and Director Kowalski and put in a request.

Cal tried to get her moving, but Jenna held her ground. "Tell me—who's that man?"

Okay, so that wasn't panic in her eyes. It was determination. She wasn't about to drop this. Not even for a couple of minutes until they could reach her apartment.

"Anthony Salazar," Cal let her know. "That's his real name, anyway. He often uses an alias."

She stared at him. "He works for Holden Carr?"

"He usually just works for the person who'll pay him the most." Cal hadn't intended to pause, but he had to so he could clear his throat. "He's a hired assassin, Jenna."

CHAPTER THREE

JENNA WAS GLAD the exterior wall of the café was there to support her, or her legs might have given way.

First, there was Cal's out-of-the-blue visit to deal with.

Then the news that he knew about the lie she'd told.

And now this.

"An assassin?" she repeated.

Somehow she managed to say aloud the two little words that had sent her world spinning out of control—again. She'd had a lot of that lately and was more than ready for it to stop.

Cal cursed under his breath. He picked up the grocery bag he'd dropped and then slipped his arm around her waist.

Jenna thought of her baby. Of Sophie. She couldn't let that assassin get anywhere near her daughter.

She started to break into a run, but Cal maneuvered her off the sidewalk and behind the café. They walked quickly into the alley that ran the entire length of Main Street. So they'd be out of sight.

"You didn't know that guy was here?" she asked as they hurried.

"No."

That meant Cal had come to confront her about naming him as Sophie's father. That alone was a powerful reason for a visit. She owed him an explanation.

And a Texas-size apology.

But for now, all Jenna wanted to do was get inside her apartment and make sure that hired gun, Anthony Salazar, was nowhere near her baby. And to think he might have been following her on her entire walk to the grocery store. Or even longer. He could have taken out a gun and fired at any time, and there wouldn't have been a thing she could do to stop it.

He could have hurt Sophie.

Maybe because she was shaking now, Cal tightened his grip around her, pulling her deeper into the warmth of his arm, while increasing the pace until they were jogging.

"I didn't name you as my baby's father to hurt your career," she assured him. "I didn't think anyone other than Holden would hear what I was saying."

A deep sound of disapproval rumbled in Cal's throat. He didn't offer anything else until they reached the bookstore. Her apartment was at the back and up the flight of stairs on the second floor.

"You have a security system?" he asked as they hurried up the steps.

"Yes."

She unlocked the door—both locks—tossed the groceries and her purse on the table in the entry and bolted across the room. The sixteen-year-old sitter, Manda, was on the sofa reading a magazine. Jenna raced past her to the bedroom and saw Sophie sleeping in her crib. Exactly where she'd left her just a half hour earlier at the start of her afternoon nap.

"Is something wrong?" Manda asked, standing.

Jenna didn't answer that. "Did anyone come by or call?"

Manda shook her head, obviously concerned. "Are you okay?"

"Fine," Jenna lied. "I just had a bad case of baby separation. I had to get back and make sure Sophie was all right. And she is. She's sleeping like…well, a baby."

Still looking concerned, Manda nodded, and her gaze landed on Cal.

"He's an old friend," Jenna explained. She purposely didn't say Cal's name. Best not to give too much information until she knew what was going on. Besides, she'd already caused Cal enough trouble.

Jenna took the twenty-dollar bill from her pocket and handed it to Manda. "But I was barely here thirty minutes," the teen protested. "Five bucks an hour, remember?"

"Consider the rest a tip." Jenna put her hand on Manda's back to get her moving. She needed some privacy so she could find out what was going on.

"Why didn't the alarm go off when we came in?" he wanted to know as soon as Manda walked out with her magazine tucked beneath her arm. It wasn't a question, exactly. More like the start of a cross-examination.

"It's connected to the bookstore." She shut the door and locked it. "The owner turns it on when she closes for the evening."

That didn't please him. His disapproving gaze fired around the apartment, but it didn't have to too far. It was one large twenty-by-twenty-five-foot room with an adjoining bath and a tiny nursery. The kitchenette and dining area were on one side, and the living room with its sofa bed was on the other. It wasn't exactly quaint and cozy with the vaulted, exposed beam ceiling, but it was a far cry from her massive family home near Houston.

"Why this place?" he asked after he'd finished his assessment.

"It has fewer shadows," she said, not wanting to explain about her sudden fear of bogeymen, assassins and rebel fighters.

She could still hear the bullets.

She'd always be able to hear them.

Cal nodded and eased the grocery bag onto the tile-topped table.

"You want a drink or something?" Jenna motioned to the fridge.

"No, thanks." There was an unspoken warning at the end of that. That was her cue to start explaining this whole baby-daddy issue.

She was feeling light-headed and was still shivering, so Jenna snagged the trail mix from her grocery bag and went to the sofa so she could sit down.

"First of all, I didn't know what I said about the baby would even get back to you. To anyone." She popped a cashew into her mouth and offered him some from the bag. He shook his head. "Yesterday, when Holden called, I'd just returned from Sophie's three-month checkup with the pediatrician. Right away, he started yelling, saying that he knew that I'd had a child."

"How did he know?"

"That's the million-dollar question." But then, Jenna rethought that. "Or maybe not. I stopped by my house on the outskirts of Houston to pick up some things before I went to the appointment. Holden probably had someone watching the place and then followed me. I was careful. You know, always checking the rearview mirror and the parking lot at the clinic. But he could have had that Salazar guy following me the whole time."

In hindsight, she should have anticipated Holden would do something like this. In fact, she should have known he would. He was as tenacious as he was ruthless.

"So Holden confronted you about the baby?" Cal asked.

"Oh, yes. Complete with yelling obscenities. And that was just the prelude. No more facade of being in love with me. He demanded to know if Paul was Sophie's father. If so, he said he would challenge me for custody."

"Custody?" Cal didn't hide his surprise very well.

"Apparently, Paul had some kind of provision in his will that would make Holden the legal guardian to any child that Paul might have—if I'm proven unfit, which Holden says he can do with his connections. After he threatened me with that, I stalled him, trying to think of what I should say, and your message was still in my head. It made the leap from my brain to my mouth before I could stop it, and I just blurted out your name."

Cal walked closer and slid onto the chair across from her. Close enough for her to see all the scorching blue in his eyes. And close enough to see the emotion and the anger, too. "My message?"

She swallowed hard. "The one you left on my voice mail at my office about a month ago. My assistant sent it to me, and I'd recently listened to it."

A lot. In fact, she'd memorized it.

She'd found his voice comforting, and that's why she'd replayed it. Night after night. When she couldn't sleep. When the nightmares got the best of her. But his voice wasn't comforting now, of course. Coupled with his riled glare, there wasn't much comforting about him or this visit.

Well, except that he'd put his arm around her when he thought she was cold.

A special kind of special agent.

He still looked the part, even though he wasn't in battle gear today. He wore jeans, a dark blue button-down shirt that was almost the same color as his eyes and a black leather jacket.

"Anyway, after I realized it was stupid to give Holden your name," she continued, "I thought about calling him back and making something up. But I figured that'd only make him more suspicious."

Because Cal wasn't saying anything and because she suddenly didn't know what to do with her hands, Jenna offered him the trail mix again, and this time he reached into the bag and took out a few pieces.

"I've done everything to keep my pregnancy and delivery quiet. *Everything*," Jenna said, aware that her nerves were causing her to babble. It was either that, humming or reciting something, and she didn't want to launch into a neurotic rendition of the Preamble to the Constitution. "I don't have any family, and none of my friends know. No one here in Willow Ridge really knows who I am, either."

She didn't think it was her imagination that he was hesitant to say anything. Under the guise of eating trail mix, Cal sat there, letting her babble linger between them.

Since she had to know what was going on in his head, Jenna just went for the direct approach. "How did your director find out that I'd told Holden about my baby?"

His jaw muscles began to stir against each other. "The Justice Department has kept tabs on you."

"Tabs?" She took a moment to consider that. "That's an interesting word. What does it mean exactly?"

More jaw muscles moved. "It means they were keeping track of you in case Holden decided to divulge anything incriminating they could use in their case against him."

So it was true. Her fears weren't all in her head. The authorities thought Holden might be a danger as well.

Or maybe they didn't.

Maybe they were just hoping Holden would do something stupid so they could use that to arrest him.

"I was bait?" she asked.

"No." But then he lifted his shoulder. "At least I don't think so."

Jenna prayed that was true. The thought wasn't something she could handle right now.

"The baby is Paul Tolivar's?" Cal asked.

She nodded. And waited for his reaction. She didn't get one. He put on his operative's face again. "Just how much trouble will this cause for you?" she wanted to know.

"The ISA has a morality clause." His fingers tightened around a dried apricot, squishing it. "Plus, the regs forbid personal contact during a protective custody situation."

That was not what she wanted to hear. "You could be punished."

Again, it took him a moment to answer. "Yeah."

"Okay." Jenna took a deep breath, and because she

couldn't stay still, she got up to pace. There was a solution to this. Not necessarily an appetizing solution, but it did exist. "Will my statement that I lied be enough to clear you, or will you need a paternity test?"

"My director wants a test." He stood as well, and caught her arm when she started to go past him. His fingers were warm. Surprisingly warm. She could feel his touch all the way through her thick sweater. "But I think that's the least of your worries right now."

"Because of Anthony Salazar." Jenna nodded. "Yes. He's definitely a worry. His being here means I'll need to leave Willow Ridge and go into hiding."

"You're already in hiding," Cal pointed out. "And he found you. He'll find you again. He's very good at what he does. You need more protection than a bookstore security system or a hired bodyguard can give you. I'll make some calls and see what I can do."

Pride almost caused her to decline his offer. But she knew that it wouldn't protect her baby. And that was the most important thing right now. She had to stay safe because if anything happened to her, it would happen to her precious daughter as well.

"Thank you," Jenna whispered. She repeated it to make sure he heard her. "I really am sorry about dragging you into my personal life."

"We'll get it straightened out," he assured her. But there was a lot of skepticism in his voice.

And annoyance, which she deserved.

"Okay, while you make those calls, I'll arrange to have the paternity test done," Jenna added.

Somehow, though, she'd have to keep the results a secret from anyone but Cal and his director.

Because she didn't want Holden to learn the truth.

Jenna moved away from Cal and started to pace again, mumbling a poem she'd memorized in middle school. She couldn't help it. A few lines came out before she could stop them.

"What you must think of me," she said. "For what it's worth, Paul and I only had sex once, and we used protection. But I guess something went wrong…on a lot of levels. Honestly, I don't really even remember sleeping with him." Jenna mumbled that last part.

"You don't remember?" he challenged.

She shook her head. "One minute we were having dinner, and the next thing I remember was waking up in bed with him. I obviously had too much to drink. Or else he drugged me. Either way, it was my stupid mistake for being there. Then I made things so much worse by telling Holden that you're my daughter's father. And here we didn't even have sex. Heck, we never even kissed on the floor of that cantina."

A clear image formed in her mind. Of that floor. Of Cal on top of her to protect her from the explosion. It wasn't exactly pleasurable. Okay, it was. But it wasn't supposed to be.

Not then.

Not now.

She'd already done enough damage to Cal's career without her adding unwanted sexual attraction that could never go beyond the fantasy stage.

He opened his mouth to say something, but didn't get past the first syllable. There was a knock at the door, the sudden sound shattering the silence.

Cal reacted fast. He reached inside his jacket and pulled out a handgun from a shoulder holster. He motioned for her to move out of the path of the door.

Jenna raced across the room and took a knife from the cutlery drawer. It probably wouldn't give them much protection, but she didn't intend to let Cal fight alone. Especially since the battle was hers.

With his hands gripped around his weapon, he eased toward the door. Every inch of his posture and demeanor was vigilant. Ready. Lethal.

Cal didn't use the peephole to look outside, but instead peered out the corner of the window.

He cursed softly.

"It's Holden Carr."

CHAPTER FOUR

THIS WAS NOT how Cal had planned his visit.

It was supposed to be in and out quickly. He was only on a fact-finding mission so he could get out of hot water with the director. Instead, he'd walked right into a vipers' nest. And one viper was way too close.

Holden Carr was literally pounding on Jenna's door.

Cal glanced back at her. With a butcher knife in a white-knuckled death grip, Jenna was standing guard in front of the nursery. She was pale, trembling and nibbling on her bottom lip. *Bam!* There were his protective instincts.

There was no way he could let her face Holden Carr alone. From everything Cal had read about the man, Holden was as dangerous as Paul, his former business partner. And Paul had been ready to commit murder to get his hands on Jenna's estate.

"Go to your daughter," Cal instructed while Holden continued to pound.

She shook her head. "You might need backup."

He lifted his eyebrow. She wasn't exactly backup material. Jenna Laniere might have been temporarily living in a starter apartment in a quaint Texas cowboy town, but her blue blood and pampered upbringing couldn't have prepared her for the likes of Holden Carr.

"I'll handle this," Cal let her know, and he left no room for argument.

She mumbled something, but stepped back into the nursery.

With his SIG Sauer drawn, Cal stood to the side of the door. It was standard procedure—bad guys often like to shoot through doors. But Holden probably didn't have that in mind. It was broad daylight and with the door-pounding, he was probably drawing all kinds of attention to himself, but Cal didn't want to take an unnecessary risk.

Once he was in place, he reached over. Unlocked the door. And eased it open.

Cal jammed his gun right in Holden's face.

Holden's dust-gray eyes sliced in the direction of the SIG Sauer. There was just a flash of shock and concern before he buried those reactions in the cool composure of his Nordic pale skin and his Viking-size body. He was decked out in a pricy camel-colored suit that probably cost more than Cal made in a month.

"I'm Holden Carr and I need to see Jenna," he announced.

Cal didn't lower his gun. In fact, he jabbed it against Holden's right cheek. "Oh, yeah? About what?"

"A private matter."

"It's not so private. From what I've heard you're threatening her. It takes a special kind of man to threaten a woman half his size. Of course, you're no stranger to violence, are you? Did you murder Paul Tolivar?"

Holden couldn't quite bury his anger fast enough. It rippled through his jaw muscles and his eyes. "Who the hell are you?"

"Cal Rico. I'm Jenna's...friend." But he let his tone indicate that he was the man who wouldn't hesitate to pull the trigger if Holden tried to barge his way in. "Anything you have to say to Jenna, you can say to me. I'll make sure she gets the message."

"The message is she can't hide from me forever." Holden enunciated each word. "I know she had a baby. A little girl named Sophie Elizabeth. Born three months ago. That means the child is Paul's."

It didn't surprise Cal that Holden knew all of this, but what else did he know? "Paul, the man you murdered," Cal challenged.

There was another flash of anger. "Not that it's any of your business, but I didn't murder him. His housekeeper did. She was secretly working for a rebel faction who had issues with some of Paul's businesses."

"Right. The housekeeper." Cal made sure he sounded skeptical. He'd already heard the theory of the runaway housekeeper known only as Mary. "I don't suppose she confessed."

Holden had to get his teeth apart before he could respond. "She fled the estate after she killed him. No one's been able to find her."

"Convenient. Now, mind telling me how you came by this information about Jenna's child?"

"Yes. I mind."

Cal hadn't expected him to volunteer that, since it almost certainly involved illegal activity. "Hmmm. I smell a wire tap. That kind of illegal activity can get you arrested. Your dual citizenship won't do a thing to protect you, either. If you hightail it back to Monte de Leon, you can be extradited."

Though that wasn't likely. Still, Cal made a note to discover the source of that possible tap.

Holden looked past him, and because they were so close, Cal saw the man's eyes light up. Cal didn't have to guess why. Holden was aiming his attention in the direction of the nursery door and had probably spotted Jenna. He tried to come inside, but Cal blocked the door with his foot.

"She'll have to talk to me sooner or later," Holden insisted. "Call off your guard dog," he yelled at Jenna.

"What do you want?" Jenna asked. Cal silently groaned when he heard her walking closer. She really didn't take orders very well.

"I want you to carry out Paul's wishes. In his will, he named me guardian of his children. He didn't have any children at the time he wrote that, but he does now."

"You only want my daughter so you can control me," Jenna tossed out.

Holden didn't deny it. "I've petitioned the court for custody," he said.

Jenna stopped right next to Cal, and she reached across his body to open the door wider. "No judge would give you custody."

"Maybe not in this country, but in Monte de Leon, the law will be on Paul's side. Even in death he's still a powerful man with powerful friends."

"Sophie's an American," Jenna pointed out. "Born right here in Texas."

"And you think that'll stop Paul's wishes from being carried out? It won't. If the Monte de Leon court deems you unfit—and that can easily happen with the right judge—then the court will petition for the child to be brought to her father's estate."

"Sophie is not Paul's child." She looked Holden right in the eye when she told that lie.

But Holden only smiled. "I've seen pictures of her. She looks just like him. Dark brown hair. Blue eyes."

Pictures meant he had surveillance along with taps. This was not looking good.

Cal could hear Jenna's breath speed up. Fear had a smell, and she was throwing off that scent, along with motherly protection vibes. But that wouldn't do anything to convince this SOB that he didn't have a right to claim her child.

From the corner of his eye, Cal spotted a movement. There was a tall redheaded woman with a camera. She was about forty yards away across the street and was clicking pictures of this encounter. Gwen Mitchell no doubt. And she wasn't the only woman there. He also spotted a slender blonde making her way up the steps to Jenna's apartment.

"That's Helena Carr," Jenna provided.

Holden's sister and business partner. Great. Now there was an added snake to deal with, and it was all playing out in front of a photographer with questionable motives. Cal could already hear himself having to explain why he was in small-town America with his standard-issue SIG Sauer smashed against a civilian's face.

"This meeting is over," Cal insisted. He lowered his gun, but he kept it aimed at Holden's right kneecap.

"It'll be over when Jenna admits that her daughter is Paul's," Holden countered.

"We just want the truth." That from Helena, who was a feminine version of her brother without the Viking-wide shoulders. Her stare was different, too. Nonthreatening. Almost serene. "After all, we know she slept with Paul, and the timing is perfect to have produced Sophie."

Cal hoped he didn't regret this later, but there was one simple way to diffuse this. "I have dark brown hair, blue eyes. Just like Sophie's." He hoped, since he hadn't actually seen the little girl.

Helena blinked and gave him an accusing stare. Holden cursed. "Are you saying you're the father?" he asked.

"No," Jenna started to say. But Cal made sure his voice drowned her out.

"Yes," Cal snarled. "I'm Sophie's father."

"Impossible," Holden snarled back.

Cal gave him a cocky snort. "There is nothing impossible about it. I'm a man. Jenna's a woman. Sometimes men and women have sex, and that results in a pregnancy."

And just in case Jenna was going to say something to contradict him, Cal gave her a quick glance. She was staring at him as if he'd lost his mind.

"You won't mind taking a DNA test," Holden insisted.

"Tell you what. You send the request for a DNA sample through your foreign judge and let it trickle its way through our American judicial system. Then I'll get back to you with an answer."

Of course, the answer would be no.

Still, that wouldn't stop Holden from trying. If he controlled Jenna's child, then he would ultimately have access to a vast money-laundering enterprise. Then he could fully operate his own family business and the one he'd inherited from Paul.

"This isn't over." Holden aimed the threat at Jenna as he stalked away.

Cal was about to shut the door and call his director so he could start some damage control, but Helena eased her hand onto the side to stop it from closing.

"I'm sorry about this." Helena sounded sincere. Or else she'd rehearsed it enough to fake sincerity. Maybe this was the brother-sister version of good cop/bad cop. "I just want the truth so I can make sure Paul's child inherits what she deserves."

Jenna didn't even address that. "Can you stop your brother?"

Cal carefully noted Helena's reaction. She glanced over her shoulder. First at her brother who was getting inside their high-end car. Then at the photographer.

"Could I step inside for just a moment?" That sincerity thing was there again.

But Cal wasn't buying it.

Jenna apparently did. With the butcher knife still clutched in her hand, she stepped back so Helena could enter.

"That reporter out there might have some way to eavesdrop on us," Helena explained. "She has equipment and cameras with her."

Maybe. But Cal hadn't seen anything to suggest long-range eavesdropping equipment. Still, it was an unnecessary risk to keep talking in plain view. Lipreading was a possibility. Plus, anything said here could ultimately put Jenna in more danger and get him in deeper trouble with the director. Not that her paternity claims were exactly newsworthy, but he didn't want to see his and Jenna's names and photos splashed in a newspaper.

"Well?" Cal prompted when Helena continued to look around and didn't say anything else.

"Where do I start?" She seemed to be waiting for an invitation to sit down, but Cal didn't offer. Helena sighed. "My brother is determined to carry out Paul's wishes. They've been friends since childhood when our parents moved to Monte de Leon to start businesses there. Holden was devastated when Paul was killed."

Cal shrugged. "Paul isn't the father of Jenna's child, so there's no wish to carry out."

The last word had hardly left his mouth when he heard a soft whimpering cry sound coming from the nursery.

"Sophie," Jenna mumbled.

"Go to her," Cal advised. "I'll finish up here."

Jenna hesitated. But not for long—the baby's cries were getting louder.

"I do need to talk to Jenna," Helena continued. She opened her purse and rummaged through it. "Do you have a pen? I want to leave my cell number so she can contact me."

That was actually a good idea. He might be able to get approval to trace Helena's calls and obtain a record of her past ones.

Cal didn't have a pen with him, and he looked around before spotting one and a notepad on the kitchen countertop. He got it and glanced into the nursery while he was on that side of the room. Jenna was leaning over the crib changing Sophie's diaper.

"Someone was following Jenna." Cal walked back to Helena and handed her the pen and notepad.

She dodged his gaze, took the pen and wrote down her number. "You mean that reporter across the street?

She approached us when we drove up and said she was doing an article about Paul. She said she recognized Holden from newspaper pictures."

Cal shook his head. "Not her. Someone else. A man." He watched for a reaction.

Helena shrugged and handed him the notepad. "You think I know something about it?"

"Do you? The man's name is Anthony Salazar."

Her eyes widened. "Salazar," she repeated on a rise of breath. "You've seen him here in Willow Ridge?"

"I've seen him," Cal confirmed. "Now, mind telling me how you know him?"

Her breath became even more rapid, and she glanced around to make sure it was safe to talk. "Anthony Salazar is evil," she said in a whisper.

He caught her arm when she turned to leave. "And you know this how?"

She opened her mouth but stopped. "Are you wearing a wire?" she demanded.

"No, and I'm not going to strip down to prove it. But you *are* going to give me answers."

Her chin came up. Since he had hold of her arm, he could feel that she was trembling. "You're trying to make me say something incriminating."

Yeah. But for now, Cal would settle for the truth. "What's your connection to Salazar? Does he work for your brother? For you?"

She reached behind her and opened the door. "He worked for Paul."

He hadn't expected that answer. "Paul's dead."

"But his estate isn't."

"What does that mean?" Cal asked cautiously.

"Yesterday was the first anniversary of Paul's death.

Early this morning his attorney delivered emails of instruction to people named in his will. I saw the list. Salazar got one."

Cal paused a moment to give that some thought. "Are you saying Paul reached out from the grave and hired this man to do something to Jenna?"

"That's exactly what I'm saying." Helena turned and delivered the rest from over her shoulder as she started down the steps. "Neither Holden nor I can call off Salazar. No one can."

CHAPTER FIVE

AFTER JENNA CHANGED Sophie's diaper, she gently rocked her until her daughter's whimpers and cries faded. It took just a few seconds before her baby was calm, cooing and smiling at her. It was like magic, and even though it warmed her heart to see her baby so happy, Jenna only wished she could be soothed so easily.

Not much of a chance of that with Holden, his sister and that assassin lurking around. She kept mumbling the poem "The Raven," and hoped the mechanical exercise would keep her calm.

She heard Cal shut and lock the door, and Jenna wanted to be out there while he was talking to Helena. After all, this was her fight, not Cal's. But she also didn't want Holden or Helena anywhere near her baby.

With Helena gone, Jenna went into the kitchen so she could fix Sophie a bottle. Cal glanced at her, but he had his phone already pressed to his ear, so he didn't say anything to her.

"Hollywood, I need a big favor," Cal said to the person on the other end of the phone line. "The subjects are Holden Carr, Jenna Laniere and Anthony Salazar." He paused. "Yes, the Holden and Jenna from Monte de Leon. I need to know how he found out where she's living. Look for wiretaps first and then dig into her employees. I want to know about any connection with anyone who could have given him this info or photos of Jenna Laniere's baby."

Well, that was a start. Hopefully Cal's contacts would give them an answer soon. It wouldn't, however, solve her problem with Salazar.

She and Sophie needed protection.

And she needed to clear up the paternity issue with Cal's director. And amid all that, she had to make arrangements to move. The apartment was no longer safe now that Holden and Helena Carr knew where she was. Packing wouldn't take long—for the past year, she'd literally been living out of a suitcase, anyway.

With Sophie nestled in the crook of her arm, Jenna warmed the formula, tested a drop on her wrist to make sure it wasn't too hot, and carried both baby and bottle to the sofa so she could feed her. Sophie wasn't smiling any longer. She was hungry and was making more of those whimpering demands. Jenna kissed her cheek and started to feed her.

Once it was quiet, it was impossible to shut out what Cal was saying. He was still giving someone instructions about checking on the reporter and where to look for Holden Carr's leak, and Cal wanted the person to learn more about some emails that might have recently been sent out by Paul's attorney.

She didn't know anything about emails, but a leak in communication could mean someone might have betrayed her. There was just one problem with that. Before the trip to the pediatrician, no one including her own household staff and employees had known where she was.

Now everyone seemed to know.

Cal ended his call and scrubbed his hand over his

face. He was obviously frustrated. So was Jenna. But she had to figure out a way to get Cal out of the picture. He didn't deserve this, and once she was at a safe location, she could get the DNA test for Sophie.

"So, this is Sophie," he commented, walking closer. "She's so little for someone who's caused a lot of big waves."

"I'm the one who caused the waves," Jenna corrected.

Cal shrugged it off, but she doubted he was doing that on the inside. "She seems to like that bottle."

"I couldn't breast-feed her. I got mastitis—that's an infection—right after she was born. By the time it'd run its course and I was off the antibiotics, Sophie decided the bottle was for her." Jenna cringed a little, wondering why she'd shared something so personal with a man who was doing everything he could to get her out of his life.

Cal walked even closer, and Sophie responded to the sound of his footsteps by turning her head in his direction. She tracked him with her wide blue-green eyes and fastened her gaze on him when he sat on the sofa next to them. Even with the bottle in her mouth, she smiled at him.

Much to Jenna's surprise, Cal smiled back.

It was a great smile, too, and made him look even hotter than he already was. That smile was a lethal weapon in his arsenal.

"She looks like you," Cal said. "Your face. Your eyes."

"Paul's coloring, though," she added softly. "But when I look at her, I don't see him. I never have. I loved her unconditionally from the first moment I realized I was pregnant." Sheez. More personal stuff.

Why couldn't she stop babbling?

"Helena left you her cell number," Cal said, dropping the notepad onto the coffee table, switching the subject. "She said you're to call her."

Jenna glanced at it and noticed that it had a local area code. "What does she want?"

"Honestly? I don't know. All I know is I don't trust her or Holden." Sophie kicked at him, and he brushed his fingers over her bare toes. He smiled again. But the smile quickly faded. "Helena said that early this morning Salazar received an email from Paul's estate. It might have something to do with why he's here."

Paul again. "It doesn't matter why he's here. I plan to call the Willow Ridge sheriff and see if he can arrest him."

"That's one option. Probably not a good one, though. Salazar won't be easy to catch."

"But we both saw him, right there on Main Street," Jenna pointed out.

Cal nodded. "Unless the local sheriff is very good at what he does, and very lucky, he could get killed attempting to arrest a man like Salazar."

Oh, mercy. She hadn't even considered that. "Then I have to move sooner than I thought. As soon as Sophie's finished with her bottle, I'll—"

But she stopped there because it involved too many steps and a lot of phone calls.

Where should she start?

"We'll have some information about Holden soon," Cal finished for her. "Once we have that, we'll go from there. It's best if we arrange for someone else to pick up Salazar, not the local sheriff."

"We?" she challenged, wondering why he wasn't excusing himself from this situation.

He kept his attention on Sophie and reached out and touched one of her dark brown curls. "We, as in someone assigned from the International Security Agency."

But not him. A coworker, maybe.

Jenna thought about that for a moment and wondered about the man sitting next to her. She hadn't forgotten the way he'd bashed through a window to save her. "Are you a spy?"

He didn't blink, didn't react. "I'm an operative."

"Is that another word for a spy?"

"It can be." Still no reaction. "The ISA is a sister organization to the CIA. We have no jurisdiction on American soil. We operate only in foreign countries to protect American interests, mainly through rescues and extractions in hostile situations." He took his eyes off Sophie and aimed them at her. "I'm not sure how much I can get involved in your situation."

"I understand." Sophie was finished with her bottle, and Jenna put her against her shoulder so she could burp her. "Besides, I've caused you enough trouble."

He didn't disagree. But there was some kind of debate stirring inside him. "I hadn't expected to want to protect you," he admitted.

Oh. She was surprised not just by his desire to help her, but also by the admission itself. "Why?"

"Why?" he repeated.

She searched his eyes, looking for an answer. Or at least a way to rephrase the question so that it didn't imply the attraction she felt for him. An attraction he probably didn't feel.

"Why did you call my office in Houston last month?" It was something Jenna had wanted to ask since she'd received the message.

Cal shrugged. "The ISA was reopening the investigation into Paul's business dealings and murder. I wanted to make sure you were okay."

"And that's all?" She nearly waved that off. But something in his eyes had her holding her tongue. She wanted to know the reason.

He didn't dodge her gaze. "I was going to see if you'd gotten over Paul. I'd planned to ask you out."

Jenna went still. So maybe the attraction was mutual after all.

She doubted that was a good thing.

"I was over Paul the moment he slapped me for refusing his marriage proposal," Jenna let him know.

His jaw muscles went to war again. "I heard that slap. I was monitoring you with long-distance eavesdropping equipment."

She felt her cheeks flush. It embarrassed her to know that anyone, especially Cal, had witnessed that. The whole incident with Paul was a testament to her poor judgment.

"I've been a screwup most of my life," she admitted.

He made a throaty sound of surprise. "You think that slap was your fault?"

"I think being at Paul's estate was my first mistake. I should have had him investigated before I went down there. I shouldn't have trusted him."

He leaned closer. "Is this where I should remind you

about hindsight and that Paul was a really good con artist?"

"It wouldn't help. I've been duped by two other losers. One in college—my supposed boyfriend stole my credit cards and some jewelry. And then there was the assistant I hired right before this mess with Paul. He sold business secrets to my competition." She paused, brought her eyes back to his. "That's why I'm not jumping for joy that you wanted to ask me out."

Cal flexed his eyebrows. "You think I'm a loser like those other guys?"

"No." Shocked that he'd even suggest it, she repeated her denial. "I know you're not. But I have this trust issue now. On top of the damage I've caused your career, I know I'd be bad for you."

He didn't say a word, and the silence closed in around them. Seconds passed.

"Remember when you were lying beneath me in that cantina?" he asked.

"Oh, yes." She winced because she said it so quickly. And so fondly.

"Well, I remember it, too. Heck, I fantasize about it. I was hoping once I saw you, once I got out my anger over the lie you told, that the fantasies would stop."

Oh, my. Fantasies? This wasn't good. She'd had her own share of fantasies about Cal. Thankfully, she didn't say or do anything stupid. Then Sophie burped loudly, and spit up. It landed on Jenna's shoulder and the front of her sweater.

The corner of Cal's mouth lifted. There was relief in his expression, and Jenna thought he was already regretting this frank conversation.

She glanced down at Sophie, who was smiling now.

Jenna wiped her mouth, kissed her on the forehead, put her in the infant carrier seat on the coffee table and buckled the safety strap so that she couldn't wiggle out.

"Could you watch her a minute while I change my top?" Jenna asked.

"Sure." But he didn't look so sure. It was the first time he'd ever seemed nervous. Including when he'd faced gunfire during her rescue.

Jenna stood. So did Cal, though he did keep his hand on the top edge of the carrier. "Forget about that fantasy stuff," he said.

"I will," she lied. "I don't want to cause any more problems for you."

But she had already caused more problems. Jenna could feel it. The attraction was stirring between them. It was a full-fledged tug deep within her belly. A tug that reminded her that despite being a mom, she was still very much a woman standing too close to a too-attractive man.

She fluttered her fingers toward the nursery. "I won't be long." But even with that declaration, she gave in to that tug and hesitated a moment.

Cal cursed softly under his breath. "We'll talk about security plans after you've changed your top."

That should have knocked her back to reality. But while his mouth was saying those practical words, his eyes seemed to be saying, *I want to kiss you.*

Maybe that was wishful thinking.

Either way, Jenna turned before she said something they'd both regret.

She hurriedly grabbed another sweater from the suitcase in the nursery. She shut the door enough to give herself some privacy, but kept it ajar so she could hear if

Sophie started to cry. Jenna peeked out to see Cal playing with her daughter's toes while he made some funny faces. The interaction didn't last long—Cal's phone rang, and he answered it.

"Hollywood," Cal greeted. "I hope you have good news for me."

So did Jenna. They desperately needed something to go their way.

She peeled off the soiled sweater, stuffed it into a plastic bag and put it in the suitcase. It would save her from having to pack it in the next hour or two. Then she put on a dark green top and grabbed some other items from around the room to pack those as well.

When she'd finished cramming as much in the suitcase as she could, she took a moment to compose herself. And hated that she didn't feel stronger. But then, it was hard to feel strong when her past relationship with Paul might endanger her daughter.

She peeked out to make sure Sophie was okay. She was. So Jenna waited, listening to Cal's conversation. It was mostly one-sided. He grunted a few responses, and started to curse, but he bit it off when he looked down at Sophie. The profanity and his expression said it all.

"Bad news?" Jenna asked the moment he hung up.

"Some." He looked at Sophie and then glanced around the room. "It's best if you stay put while arrangements are being made for you and Sophie to move."

She walked back to the sofa and sat down across from her daughter. Just seeing that tiny face was a reminder that the stakes were massive now. "Staying put will be safe?"

Cal nodded. "As safe as I can make it."

"You?" she questioned. Not we. "Your director approves of this."

"He approves."

Which meant the situation was dangerous enough for the director to break protocol by allowing her to be guarded by Cal despite the inappropriate conduct that he believed had happened between them.

"How bad is the bad news?" she asked.

He pulled in his breath and walked closer. "Our communications specialist is a guy we call Hollywood. He's very good at what he does, and he can't find an obvious leak, so we don't know how Holden located you. Not yet, anyway. But we were able to get more information about the emails sent out by Paul's attorney. Each one was sent from a different account, and one went to your office in Houston. Holden, Helena and Anthony Salazar each got one. The final one went to your reporter friend, Gwen Mitchell."

Gwen Mitchell? So Paul had known her. Funny, the woman hadn't mentioned that particular detail when she'd introduced herself at the grocery store.

Jenna reached for the phone. "Well, my email didn't come to my private or business addresses. I check those several times a day. I'll call my office and see if it arrived in one of the other accounts."

Cal caught her arm to stop her. "The ISA has already retrieved it and taken it off your server. It's encrypted so we'll need the communications guys to take a look at it."

That sounded a bit ominous, so she settled for nodding. "What's in these emails?"

"We've only gained access to yours and Salazar's. His email was encrypted as well, but we decided to focus on it first. The encryption wasn't complex, and the computer broke the code within seconds. We're not sure if all the emails are similar, but this one appears to be instructions that Paul left with his attorney shortly before his death."

"Instructions?" The content of that email was obviously the bad news that had etched Cal's face with worry. "Paul gave Salazar orders to kill me?"

"Not exactly."

His hesitation caused her heart rate to spike.

"Then what?" she asked, holding her breath.

"We're piecing this together using some files we confiscated from Paul's estate and the email sent to Salazar. Apparently before you rejected Paul's proposal and he decided to kill you, he tried to get you pregnant."

Oh, mercy. She'd known Paul was a snake, but she hadn't realized just how far he'd gone with his sinister plan.

"Paul used personal information he got from your corrupt assistant, the one who sold your business secrets," Cal continued. "With some of that information, Paul invited you to his estate when he estimated that you'd be ovulating. He drugged you. That's why you don't remember having sex with him."

She groaned. This just kept getting worse and worse. Everything about their relationship had been a cleverly planned sham. "Paul ditched the plan after I said there was no way I'd marry him."

Cal shrugged. "He intended to kill you, but he also planned for your refusal and your escape."

Jenna felt her eyes widen. "He knew I might escape?"

"Yeah." He let that hang in the air for several seconds. "He also took into account that he might have succeeded in getting you pregnant. In his email to Salazar,

Paul instructed the man to tie up loose ends, depending on how your situation had turned out."

"So what exactly is Salazar supposed to do?" Jenna didn't even try to brace herself.

Cal glanced at Sophie. Then stared at her. "In the event that you've had a child, which you obviously have, Salazar has orders to kidnap the baby."

CHAPTER SIX

CAL WAITED FOR a call while Jenna bathed Sophie. Jenna was smiling and singing to the baby, but he knew beneath that smile, she was terrified.

A professional assassin wanted to kidnap her baby and do God knows what to both her and Sophie in the process. They'd dodged a bullet—Salazar had indeed followed Jenna to the grocery store and hadn't just headed for the apartment to grab Sophie. Maybe he hadn't had the address of the apartment. Or perhaps he wanted to get Jenna first. Maybe he thought if he eliminated the mother, then it'd be a snap to kidnap the child.

That plan left Jenna in a very bad place. She couldn't go on the run, though every instinct in her body was shouting for her to do just that. Running was what Salazar hoped she would do.

She'd be an easy catch.

Cal didn't intend to let that happen. Correction. He had to arrange for someone else to make sure that didn't happen. For the sake of his career, he was going to take these initial steps to keep Sophie and Jenna safe, and then he was going to extract himself from the picture.

He checked his phone to make sure it wasn't dead. It wasn't. And there was still no call from headquarters or Hollywood, who was on the way with some much needed equipment. Cal needed some answers. They were seriously short on those.

Sophie made an "ohhh" sound and splashed her feet and hands in the shallow water that was dabbed with iridescent bubbles. Cal glanced at her to make sure all was okay, and then turned his attention back to the phone.

"Ever heard the expression a watched pot doesn't boil?" Jenna commented. "It's the same with a cell phone. It'll never ring when you're sitting there holding it."

She lifted Sophie from the little plastic yellow tub that Jenna had positioned on the sole bit of kitchen counter space, and she immediately wrapped the dripping wet baby in a thick pink terry-cloth towel.

Cal stood from the small kitchen table and slipped his phone into his pocket in case Jenna needed a hand. But she seemed to have the situation under control. She stood there by the sink, drying Sophie and imitating the soft baby sounds her daughter was making.

He went closer to see the baby's expression. Yep, she was grinning a big gummy grin. Her face was rosy and warm from the bath, and she smelled like baby shampoo. Cal had never thought a happy, freshly bathed baby could grab his complete attention, but this little girl certainly did.

Deep down, he felt something. A strange sense of what it would actually be like to be her father. It would be pretty amazing to hold her and feel her unconditional love.

When he came out of his daddy trance, he realized Jenna was looking at him. Her right eyebrow was slightly lifted. A question: what was he thinking? Cal had no intention of sharing that with her.

"Want to hold her while I get her diaper and gown?" Jenna asked.

Cal felt like someone had just offered to hand him a live grenade. "Uh, I don't want to hurt her."

Jenna smiled and eased Sophie into his arms. He looked at Jenna. Then Sophie, who was looking at him with suddenly suspicious eyes. For a moment, he thought the baby was going to burst into tears. She didn't, though he wouldn't have blamed her. Instead, she opened her tiny mouth and laughed.

Cal didn't know who was more stunned, Jenna, him or Sophie. Sophie jumped as if she'd scared herself with the unexpected noise from her own mouth. She did more staring, and then laughed again.

"This is a first," Jenna said, totally in awe. Cal knew how she felt. It was like witnessing a little miracle. "I'll have to put it in her baby book." She disappeared into the bedroom-nursery for a moment and came back with Sophie's clothes. "First time you've ever held a baby?" she asked.

He nodded. "My brother, Joe, has a little boy, Austin. He's nearly two years old, but I was away on assignment when he was born. I didn't see him until he was already walking."

"You missed the first laugh, then." She took Sophie from him and went to the sofa so she could sit and dress the baby. "You're close to your family?"

"Yes. No," he corrected. "I mean, we keep in touch, but we're all wrapped up in our jobs. Joe's a San Antonio cop. My other brother is special ops in the military. I started out in the military but switched to ISA."

Jenna had her attention fastened on diapering Sophie and putting on her gown, but Cal knew where her attention really was when he noticed she was trembling. He caught her hand to steady it and helped her pull the gown's drawstring so that Sophie's feet wouldn't be exposed. Sophie didn't seem to mind. The bath had relaxed her, and it seemed as if she was ready to fall asleep.

"Why is Paul sending Salazar after us now?" Jenna asked. She stood and started toward the nursery. "Why wait a year?"

Cal tried not to react to the emotion and fear in her voice. "Could be several reasons," he whispered as he followed her. "Maybe it took this long for his will to get through probate. The courts don't move quickly in Monte de Leon. Or maybe he figured the emails would cause a big splash, something to make sure everyone remembers him on the first anniversary of his murder."

"Oh, I remember him." She eased Sophie into the crib, placing the baby on her side, and then after kissing her cheek, Jenna covered her lower body with a blanket. "I didn't need the emails or Salazar to do that."

She kissed Sophie again and walked just outside the door, and leaned against the door frame.

A thin breath caused her mouth to shudder.

There was no way he could not react to that. Jenna was hurting and terrified for her daughter. Cal was worried for her, too. The ISA might not be able to stop Salazar before he tried to kidnap Sophie.

Since Jenna looked as if she needed a hug, Cal reached out, slid his arm around her waist and pulled her to him. She didn't resist. She went straight into his arms.

She was soft. *Very* soft. And it seemed as if she could

melt right into him. Cal felt his hand move across her back, and he drew her even closer.

Her scent was suddenly on him. A strange mix of baby soap and her own naturally feminine smell. Something alluring. Definitely hot. As was her body. He'd never been much of a breast man, but hers were giving him ideas about how those bare breasts would respond to his touch.

"This isn't a good idea," she mumbled.

Cal knew exactly what she meant. Close contact wasn't going to cool the attraction. It would fuel it.

But it felt right soothing her on a purely physical level. When he was done here, after Jenna and Sophie were no longer in danger, he needed to spend some time getting a personal life.

He needed to get laid.

Too often he put the job ahead of his needs. Jenna had a bad way of reminding him that the particular activity shouldn't be put off.

She pulled back and met his gaze. The new position put their mouths too close. All he had to do was lean down and press his lips to hers, and Cal was certain the result would be a mind-blowing kiss that neither of them would ever forget.

Which was exactly why it couldn't happen.

Still, that didn't stop his body from reacting in the most basic male way.

With their eyes locked, Jenna put her hand on his chest to push him away. Her middle brushed against his. She froze for a split second, and then went all soft and dewy again. He saw her pupils pinpoint. Felt her warm breath ease from her slightly open mouth. Her pulse jumped on her throat.

She was reacting to his arousal. Her body was preparing itself for something that couldn't happen.

"I'm flattered," she said, her voice like a silky caress on his neck and mouth.

Uh-oh. She probably meant it to be a joke, a way of breaking the tension. But it didn't break anything. That breath of hers felt like the start of very long French kiss. A kiss he had to nix. He didn't have the time or inclination to deal with a complicated relationship.

Besides, she wasn't his type.

He didn't want a woman who was fragile, so prissy. No, he wanted a woman like him, who liked sex a little rough and with no strings attached. A relationship with Jenna would come with strings longer than the Rio Grande. And he couldn't see her having down-and-dirty sex with him whenever the urge hit.

Her breath brushed against his mouth again, and Cal nearly lost the argument he was having with himself. Knowing he had to do something, fast, he stepped away from her.

In the same instant, there was a knock at the door.

His body immediately went into combat mode, and he drew his gun from his shoulder holster.

"It's me, Hollywood," their visitor called out.

He pushed aside the jolt of adrenaline. "He works for the ISA," Cal clarified to Jenna.

However, he didn't reholster his weapon until he looked out the side window to verify that it was indeed his coworker and that Hollywood wasn't being held at gunpoint. But the man was alone.

Cal opened the door and greeted him. "Thanks for coming." He checked the area in front of the bookstore but didn't see Gwen, the reporter, or either of the Carrs.

"No problem." Hollywood stepped inside and handed Cal a black leather equipment bag. "I brought a secure laptop, a portable security system, an extra weapon and some clothes. I didn't know how long you'd be here so I added some toiletries and stuff."

"Good." Cal didn't know how long he'd be there, either. "Has anyone picked up Salazar?"

"Not yet. We're still looking." Hollywood's attention went in Jenna's direction, and with his hand extended in a friendly gesture, he walked toward her. "Mark Lynch," he introduced himself. "But feel free to call me Hollywood. Everyone does."

"Hollywood," she repeated. She sounded friendly enough, but she was keeping her nerves right beneath the surface.

Cal hoped to do something to help with those nerves, something that didn't involve kissing, so he took out the laptop and turned it on. They needed information, and he would start by reviewing the message traffic on Salazar to see if anyone had spotted him nearby. By now, Salazar knew who Cal was. He would know that the ISA was involved. However, Cal seriously doubted that would send the man running. Salazar wasn't the type.

"We're working on trying to contain Anthony Salazar," Cal heard Hollywood tell Jenna.

"And I'm to stay put until that happens?" she spelled out. She shoved her hand into the back pockets of her pants.

Cal frowned and wondered why he suddenly thought he knew her so well. Jenna and he were practically strangers.

Hollywood glanced at him first and then nodded in response to Jenna's question. "The local sheriff has been alerted to the situation, and the FBI is sending two agents to patrol through the town. Cal can keep things under control here until we can make other arrangements." He took out a folder from the bag and handed it to Cal.

Cal opened it and inside was a woman's picture. "Kinley Ford?" he read aloud from the background investigation sheet that he took from the envelope. He glanced through the info but didn't recognize anything about the research engineer.

"That file is a little multitasking," Hollywood explained. "The FBI sent her info and picture over this afternoon. She's not associated with Jenna or Salazar, but she's supposedly here in town. She disappeared from Witness Protection, and there are lot of people who want to find her."

Cal shook his head. "Please don't tell me I'm supposed to look for her."

"No. But if anyone asks, that's why you're here. It's the way the director is keeping this all legitimate. He can tell the FBI that you're here in Willow Ridge to try to locate Kinley Ford, as a favor for a sister agency. Don't worry. I'll be the one looking for the missing woman, but your name will be on the paperwork."

Cal breathed a little easier. He wanted to focus on Jenna and Sophie right now.

"I'll set up this temporary security system," Hollywood continued. "And then I'll get out of here so I can stand guard until the FBI agents arrive."

Cal approved of that. The local sheriff would need help with Salazar around. "What about the background check on Gwen Mitchell?"

"Still in progress, but Director Kowalski found some

flags. According to her passport, she was in Monte de Leon during Jenna's rescue."

That grabbed Cal's attention. "Interesting."

"Maybe. But it could mean nothing. She is a reporter, after all. There's nothing to link Gwen to Paul or the Carrs. She appears to have been doing a story on one of the rebel factions."

"And she got out alive." That in itself was a small miracle. Unless Gwen had had a lot of help. The ISA hadn't rescued her, that was for sure, so she must have had other resources to get her out of the country.

"We'll keep digging," Hollywood explained. His voice was a little strained as if he was tired. He rummaged through the bag and came up with several pieces of equipment. "Are these the only windows?" he asked, tipping his head to the trio in the main living area.

"There's a small one in the bathroom," Jenna let him know.

Hollywood nodded and went in that direction to get started. Cal was familiar with the system Hollywood was using. It would arm all entrances and exits so that no one could break in undetected, but it could also be used to create perimeter security to make sure Salazar didn't get close enough to set some kind of explosive or fire to flush them out.

Once the laptop had booted up, Cal logged in with his security code and began to scan through the messages. One practically jumped out at him.

"Here's the email that Paul sent you," Cal told her. "ISA retrieved it and kept it in our classified in-box so I could look at it."

She took a step toward him, but then turned and

checked on the baby first. "Sophie's sleeping," Jenna let him know, as she hurried to the sofa to sit beside him.

Cal was positive this email was going to upset her, but he was also positive that they needed to read it. Besides, there might be clues in it that only she would understand, and they might finally make some sense of all of this.

"Jenna, if you've received this email, then I must be dead," she read aloud. "I doubt my demise has caused you much grief, but it should. Once I have a plan, I don't give up on it. Ever. Our heir will inherit your vast wealth and mine, and will continue what I've started here in Monte de Leon. What the plan doesn't include is you, my dear."

She stopped, took a deep breath and continued. "So put your affairs in order, Jenna. I'll be the first person to greet you in the hereafter. See you in a day or two. Love, Paul."

There were probably several Justice Department and ISA agents already examining the email, but it appeared to be pretty straightforward. A death threat, one that Salazar had probably been paid to carry out.

She groaned softly. "Paul planned for all possibilities. Like a baby. I'm sure the email would have been different if I hadn't had a child." Jenna scrubbed her hands over her face. "And when I woke up this morning, I thought my biggest threat was Holden Carr."

Maybe he still was. Cal was eager to get a look at those other emails. All he needed was some kind of evidence or connection that could prompt the FBI to arrest Holden or his sister.

Cal glanced at the notepad on the coffee table. Helena's number was there, and she'd wanted Jenna to call her. While it wouldn't be a pleasant conversation, it might be a necessary one.

Jenna must have followed his gaze. She reached for the notepad and retrieved her cell phone from her purse on the table next to the front door. But before she could press in the numbers, Hollywood came back into the room.

"All secure back there," he informed them. He went to the windows at the front of the apartment and connected a small sensor to each. He put the control monitor on the kitchen table and checked his watch. "I'll be parked on the street near here until I get the okay from the FBI."

Cal stood and went to him to shake his hand. "Thanks, for everything."

"Like I said, no problem. If you need anything else, just give me a call."

Cal let Hollywood out, then closed and locked the door. While he set the security monitor to arm it, Jenna sat on the sofa, dialed the call to Helena and put her cell on speaker.

The woman answered on the first ring. "Jenna," Helena said, obviously seeing the name on her caller ID. Cal made a note to switch Jenna to a prepaid phone that couldn't be traced.

"Why did you want to talk to me?" Jenna immediately asked.

Helena's answer wasn't quite so hasty. She paused for several long moments. "Is your friend, Cal, still there with you?"

"He's here," Cal answered for himself.

It was a gamble. Helena might not say anything important with him listening. But he also didn't want Helena to think that Jenna was alone. That might prompt her to send in Salazar for Sophie—if the man was actually working for Helena, that is. But perhaps the most obvious solution was true—that Salazar was being paid by Paul's estate.

Helena paused again, longer than the first time. "Why didn't you tell us you're an American operative?"

Cal groaned softly. She shouldn't have been able to retrieve that information this quickly. "Who said I am?"

"Sources. *Reliable* ones."

"There are no reliable sources for information like that," Cal informed her. She or Holden had paid someone off. Or else there was a major leak somewhere in the ISA.

"What did you want to talk to me about?" Jenna prompted after a third round of silence.

"Holden," Helena readily answered. "The Justice Department and the ISA have contacted me. They want me to give them evidence so they can arrest my brother for illegal business practices and for Paul's murder."

Jenna glanced at him before she continued. "Is there evidence?"

"For his business dealings. Holden isn't a saint. But there couldn't be evidence for Paul's murder. The housekeeper's responsible for that."

Ah, yes. That mysterious housekeeper again. Cal had monitored Paul's estate for the entire two days of Jenna's visit, and while he'd heard the voices of many of Paul's employees, he hadn't heard of this housekeeper named Mary. Not until after Paul's body had been found with a single execution-style gunshot wound to the head. It'd been the local authorities who'd pointed the finger at the housekeeper, and they had based that on the notes they'd found on Paul's computer. He'd apparently been suspicious of the woman and had decided to fire her. But those notes had been made weeks before his death.

"Did you agree to help the Justice Department and the ISA?" Cal asked, though he was certain he knew the answer.

But he was wrong.

"Yes. I intend to help the authorities bring down my brother," Helena announced.

Jenna's eyes widened, but Cal figured his expression was more of skepticism than surprise. "Are you doing that to get Holden out of the way so you can inherit both Paul's and his estates?"

"No." She was adamant about it. That didn't mean she was telling the truth. "I want the illegal activity to stop. I want the family business to return to the way it was when my parents were still alive."

"Admirable," Cal mumbled. He didn't believe that, either, though he had to admit that it was possible Helena was a do-gooder. But he wasn't about to stake Jenna's and Sophie's safety on that.

"What was in Paul's email to you?" Jenna asked the woman. Cal moved closer to the phone and grabbed the notepad so he could write down the message verbatim.

"The email was personal," Helena explained. "Though I'm sure it won't stay that way long. Cal will see to that."

Yes, he would. "If that's true, then you might as well tell me what it says."

This was the longest silence of all. "Paul said he would see me in the hereafter in a day or two."

Almost identical wording to Jenna's email, but Cal

jotted it down anyway. "Why would Paul want you dead?"

"I don't know." Helena sighed heavily, and it sounded as if she had started to cry. "But he obviously believes I wronged him in some way. Maybe Paul wanted Holden to inherit everything, and this is his way of cutting me out of his estate."

Or maybe Holden had gotten a death threat, too. But then with plans to have Sophie kidnapped, that left Cal with a critical question. Whom had Paul arranged to raise the child? Certainly not an assassin like Salazar.

He thought about that a moment and came full circle to the fifth recipient of one of Paul's infamous emails.

Gwen Mitchell.

He needed a full background report on her ASAP. It was possible that she was connected to Paul.

"Jenna, we're both in danger," Helena continued. "That's why we have to work together to stop this person that Paul has unleashed on us."

"Work together, how?" Jenna asked.

"Meet with me tomorrow morning. Alone. No Holden and no Cal Rico."

That wasn't going to happen. Still, Cal had to keep this channel of communication open. "Jenna will get back to you on that," he answered.

"Be at the Meadow's Bed-and-Breakfast tomorrow morning at ten," Helena continued as if this meeting was a done deal. "It's a little place in the country, about twenty miles from Willow Ridge. I'll see you then." And with that, she hung up.

Jenna clicked the end-call button. She wasn't trembling like before. Well, not visibly, anyway. "Do you think she wants to kill me, too?"

He considered several answers and decided to go with the truth. "Anything's possible at this point." But he did need to get a look at all the emails to get a clearer picture.

"I'm scared for Sophie," she whispered.

Yeah. So was he. And being scared wasn't good. It meant he'd lost his objectivity. He blamed that on holding Sophie. On that first laugh. Oh, and the cuddling session with Jenna. None of those things should have happened, and they'd sucked him right in and gotten him personally involved.

Jenna swiveled around to face him, blinking back tears, and moved closer into his arms.

And Cal let her.

"I'm not a wimp," she declared. "I run a multimillion-dollar business. And if the threats were aimed just at me, I'd be spitting mad. But my baby is in danger."

Cal couldn't refute that. Heck, he couldn't even reassure her that Salazar wouldn't make a full-scale effort to kidnap Sophie. All he could do was sit there and hold Jenna.

A single tear streaked down her cheek, and Cal caught it with his thumb, his fingers cupping her chin. And he was painfully aware that he was using his fingers to lift her chin. Just slightly.

So he could put his mouth on hers.

And that's exactly what he did.

The touch was a jolt that went straight through him like a shot. It didn't help that Jenna made a throaty, feminine sound of approval. Or that she slid her arms around his neck and drew him closer.

Cal cursed himself for starting this. And worse, for continuing it and deepening the kiss. French-kissing

Jenna was the worst idea he'd ever had, but that jolt of fire that her mouth was creating overruled any common sense he had left. She tasted like silk and sin, and he wanted a whole lot more.

He heard a ringing sound and thought it was another by-product of the jolt. But when the ringing continued, Cal realized passion wasn't responsible. His cell phone was. He untangled himself from Jenna and checked the caller ID screen.

It was Director Kowalski.

"Hell," he mumbled. Cal quickly tried to compose himself before he answered it. "Agent Rico."

"We might have a problem," the director started. That wasn't the greeting Cal wanted to hear. "First of all, I just read the email that Paul Tolivar supposedly sent Jenna. You think it's legit?"

Cal had given that some thought. He should have given it more. "I'm not sure. Anyone close to Paul could have composed those emails and sent them out. Anyone with an agenda." He glanced at Jenna. There was no surprise in her eyes, which meant she'd already come up with that theory.

"You have someone in mind?"

This was easy. Cal didn't even have to think about it. "Helena or Holden Carr. Both inherited a lot of money from Paul. Also, those flags on Gwen Mitchell might turn out to be a problem."

"Yes, we're working on her. But something else has popped up." The director took in an audible breath. "We might be wrong, but there are new flags. Ones within the department."

Everything inside Cal went still. This was worse than bad news. "What's wrong?"

"We think we might have a leak in communications who could have been responsible for alerting Gwen Mitchell and the Carrs as to Jenna Laniere's whereabouts."

"A leak might not have been necessary for that. Holden or Helena Carr could have been watching Jenna's estate and then followed her when she went there." Of course, that didn't explain how they'd known about Sophie, unless the person watching the estate had seen the baby in the car. That was possible, but it sounded as if the director thought someone or something else might have been responsible. "Who do these flags point to?"

"Not to anyone specific, but if it's true, the source of the information has to be in ISA."

Oh, man. The bad news just kept getting worse. They might have a traitor within the organization. "Who in ISA would have access to the pool of information that would affect all the players in this case?"

Kowalski blew out an audible breath. "Mark Lynch is a possibility."

That was not the name he'd expected to hear the director say. "Hollywood," Cal mumbled.

"I know he's on the way there with equipment. And I know you two are friends. I didn't learn about the flags until a few minutes ago."

And that in itself could be a problem because it meant someone was trying to cover their tracks. Or else set someone up. "What exactly are these flags?"

"Hollywood monitored the message traffic pertaining to Jenna Laniere. Faxes, emails, telephone calls. The info in question went from Paul Tolivar to his lawyer. It was her detailed financial data, including passwords and codes for her business accounts."

Cal knew about those messages that'd been sent a year ago while Jenna was in Monte de Leon. Paul had gotten into Jenna's laptop the first day she was at his estate and had copied her entire hard drive. Though Paul had only sent those messages to his lawyer, it didn't mean that someone else couldn't have learned the contents, saved them and now sent them out again. But why do it now, especially since the information was a year old?

That led Cal to his next question. "Why do you think Hollywood's the one who compromised this information?"

"Because we intercepted an encrypted message that was meant for him. The message was verification of receipt of Ms. Laniere's info and details about the payment for services rendered. We checked, and there has been money sent to an account in the Cayman Islands."

Cal tried not to curse. He didn't want a gut reaction to make him accuse his friend of a crime he might not have committed. "That still doesn't mean Hollywood's guilty. One or both of the Carrs could be trying to set him up to make it look as if he sold Jenna's financial information. And they might be doing that to get us to focus on Hollywood and not them."

"Could be." But the director didn't sound at all convinced of that. "It's a lot of money, Cal. If the Carrs had wanted to set someone up, why wait until now?"

That timeline question kept coming up, and Cal still didn't have an answer for it. Was it tied to Sophie? And if so, how?

"There's a final piece to this mess," the director continued. "We accessed Hollywood's personal computer, and we found several encrypted messages from Anthony Salazar. In the most recent one, Salazar asks Hollywood to help him with the kidnapping."

Cal couldn't fight off the gut reactions any longer. He felt sick to his stomach. Yes, it could all be a setup, but it was a huge risk to take if it wasn't. Hell. Had he been that wrong about a man he considered a friend?

"We tried to stop Hollywood before he left to go see you. But when he gets there, tell him he's to report back to me immediately. Don't let him in," Kowalski warned.

Cal groaned. "He's already been here. He installed the equipment and left."

The director cursed. "He wasn't supposed to be there yet. He had instructions to arrive at 9:00 p.m."

Cal got to his feet and glanced around. At the equipment bag. At the laptop he'd used to read the email Paul sent Jenna. At the security systems that Hollywood had activated a full hour ahead of schedule.

"What are my orders?" Cal asked. He motioned for Jenna to get Sophie.

"We might have a rogue agent on our hands. Get Ms. Laniere and her daughter out of there," the director ordered. *"Now."*

CHAPTER SEVEN

THE NIGHTMARE WAS BACK.

This time, she wasn't in Monte de Leon, and there were no rebel soldiers. Jenna knew this was much worse—her precious baby was in danger.

"Bring as little as possible," Cal instructed in a whisper. He stuffed diapers and some of Sophie's clothes into her bag and added a flashlight. "Hurry," he added.

Not that she needed him to remind her of that. Everything about his movements and body language indicated they had to move fast.

"What kind of flags did you say the director found on Hollywood?" Jenna whispered. Cal had told her that Hollywood might have bugged the place. He might be listening to their every word.

"They don't have a full picture yet." Cal looped the now full diaper bag over his shoulder and motioned for her to pick up Sophie. "You'll have to carry her. I need at least one hand free."

So he could shoot his gun if it became necessary.

"Does your car have an infant seat already in it?" he mouthed.

She nodded and scooped the sleeping baby into her arms. Thankfully, Sophie didn't wake up. "I'm parked just behind the bookstore. The keys are in my purse."

Jenna wanted to ask if it was safe to take her car.

But maybe it didn't matter. They had to take the risk and get out of there.

Cal drew his gun while she swaddled Sophie in a thick blanket. The moment she finished, she motioned for them to go. He paused a moment at the door. Then he opened it and glanced around outside.

"Let's go," he ordered.

Jenna grabbed her purse. She stuffed her cell phone into it, extracted her keys and stepped out into the cold night air. It was dark, and there was no moon because of the cloudy sky, but the bookstore had floodlights positioned on the four corners of the building.

Cal kept her behind him while they made their way down the stairs. He stopped again and didn't give her the signal to move until he'd glanced around the side of the store. Once he had them moving again, he kept them next to the exterior wall.

It seemed to take a lifetime to walk the twenty yards or so to her car. She unlocked the door with her keypad, but instead of letting her get in, Cal motioned for her to stand back. She did. And he used the flashlight to check the undercarriage for explosives.

God. What a mess they were in.

After Cal had gone around the entire perimeter of the car, he caught onto her and practically shoved them in through the passenger's side. Jenna turned to put Sophie in the rear-facing car seat, but a sound stopped her cold.

Footsteps.

Standing guard in front of her, Cal lifted his gun and took aim.

"Don't shoot," someone whispered. It was a woman's voice, and Jenna expected to see Helena step from the shadows.

Instead, it was Gwen Mitchell.

She lifted her hands in a show of surrender. She didn't appear to be armed and unlike the meeting in the grocery store, the woman didn't have a camera.

"I have to talk to you," Gwen said.

"This isn't a good time for conversation." Cal kept his gun aimed at Gwen, and he shut the car door. However, he didn't leave her side to get in. He stood guard, and Jenna made use of his body shield. She leaned over and put Sophie in the infant seat. She strapped her in and then climbed into the backseat with her in case she had to do what Cal was doing—use her body as a final defense.

"It's important," Gwen added.

Everything was important right now, especially getting out of there. Jenna glanced around and prayed that Salazar wasn't using Gwen as a diversion so he could sneak up on them and try to kidnap Sophie.

"We should go," Jenna reminded Cal.

Gwen fastened her attention on Jenna. "A few minutes ago I sent you a copy of the email that I got from Paul. Read it and you'll know why it's important that we talk. Then get in touch with me."

Jenna hadn't brought her laptop, but she thought maybe her BlackBerry was in her purse. Once they were on the road and away from there, she'd check and see if the email had arrived into her personal account. But for now, she continued to keep watch and wished that she had a weapon to defend Sophie and herself with.

"Keep your hands lifted," Cal instructed Gwen, and he began to inch his way to the driver's side of the car.

"Don't trust anyone," Gwen continued. "There's something going on. I don't know what. But I think

Paul's left instructions for someone to play a sick game. I think he wants to pit each of us against the other."

Then Paul had succeeded. Five emails. Five people. And there wasn't any trust among them. It was too big of a risk to start trusting now.

"Did he say anything about me in the email he sent to you?" Gwen asked.

"No," Jenna assured her.

"You're sure? Because I'm trying to figure out why he contacted me. Do you have any idea?"

Cal didn't answer. He'd had enough, and got into the car and started the engine. He drove away, fast, leaving Gwen to stand there with her question unanswered.

"The way she said Paul's name makes me think she knew him well," Jenna commented. She kept her eyes on the woman until she was no longer in sight.

"How well she knew him is what I need to find out. Right after I get you and Sophie to someplace safe."

With all the rush to leave her apartment, she hadn't considered where to go. First things first, they had to make sure no one was following them, or there wouldn't be any safe place to escape to.

Cal sped down Main Street. Thankfully, there was no traffic. It wasn't unusual for that time of night—Willow Ridge wasn't exactly a hotbed of activity. He took the first available side road to get them out of there.

Jenna continued to keep watch around them. She wanted to get her BlackBerry, but that could wait until she was sure they weren't in immediate danger. However, maybe she could get some answers to other questions. After all, her baby's life was in danger, and Jenna wanted to know why.

"What made your director think we couldn't trust Hollywood?" she asked.

Like her, Cal was looking all around. "He thinks Hollywood transferred some information he obtained through official message traffic that he was monitoring."

"Information about me?"

"Yeah," he answered as if he was thinking hard about that.

She certainly was. "I met Hollywood for the first time tonight. He doesn't even know me." But that didn't mean he couldn't be working for one of the other players in this. "You don't think Paul got to him, too?"

"I don't know. He was in Monte de Leon during your rescue, and he had access to any and all information flowing in and out of Paul's estate. There are plenty of people who would have paid for that information."

She considered that a moment while she stared back at the dark road behind them. The lights of Willow Ridge were just specks now. "Do you trust Hollywood?"

"Before tonight I thought I did." He shook his head. "But I can't risk being wrong. It's possible he got greedy and decided to sell your financial information to someone. If he's innocent, then what we're doing is just a waste of time."

But it didn't feel like a waste. It felt like a necessity.

"I changed all my passwords and account information after Paul was killed," Jenna explained. "So, unless someone's gotten their hands on the new info, those old codes won't do them any good." Of course, maybe Hollywood didn't know they were old.

"If someone were using this to set him up, it wouldn't

matter if the codes were outdated. The unauthorized message traffic is enough to incriminate him."

So Hollywood could be innocent. Still, they were on the run, and that meant someone had succeeded in terrifying her.

"Any idea where we're going?" she asked.

Cal checked his watch and the rearview mirror. "I'm sure the director is making arrangements for a safe house. All previous arrangements will be ditched because Hollywood would have had access to the plans."

"So it could take a while." Jenna believed Cal would do whatever it took to keep Sophie safe, but she wasn't certain that would be enough.

"How far is your estate?" he asked.

She'd hoped there wouldn't be any more surprises tonight. "About two hours." But Jenna shook her head. "You're thinking about going there?"

"Temporarily."

Oh, mercy. She hated to point out the obvious, but she would. "The reason I'm not there now is the threats from Holden."

"Holden might be the least of our worries," Cal mumbled. And she knew it was true. "How good is the estate's security system?"

"It's supposed to be very good." Her surprise was replaced by frustration. "In hindsight, I should have stayed put there, beefed up security and told Holden where he could shove his threats. Then we wouldn't be running for our lives."

Cal met her gaze in the mirror. "You were scared and pregnant. I don't think your decision to leave was based solely on logic."

"Pregnancy hormones," she said under her breath.

She couldn't dismiss that they hadn't played a part in her going on the run. But hiding had made her pregnancy more bearable, and it'd saved her from having to explain to her friends that she'd gotten pregnant by an accused felon.

"I've spent a lot of my life running," she commented. Why she told him that she didn't know. But she suddenly felt as if she owed him an explanation as to why she'd left the safety of the estate and headed for a small town where she knew no one. "Before my parents were killed in a car accident, when we'd have an argument, I'd immediately leave and take a long trip somewhere."

He shrugged. "There's nothing wrong with traveling."

"This wasn't traveling. It was escaping." Heck, she was still escaping. And this time, she might not succeed. Sophie might have to pay the ultimate price for Jenna's bad choices. "I have to make this right for Sophie. I can't let her be in danger. She's too important to me."

"I understand," he said. "She's important to me, too."

And for some reason, that wasn't like lip service. He wasn't just trying to console her.

Cal had only known Sophie a few hours. There was no way he could have developed such strong feelings for her. Was there? Maybe the little girl had brought out Cal's paternal instincts. Or maybe he was just protecting them. Either way, it was best not to dwell on it. Once they got to her estate, Cal would leave. After all, he had a career to salvage.

Jenna checked on Sophie again. She was still asleep and would probably stay that way for several hours. With no immediate threat, it was a good time to check for that BlackBerry. Jenna climbed over the seat, buckled up and grabbed the purse that she'd tossed onto the floor.

It took several moments for the BlackBerry to load and for her to scroll through the messages. There was indeed one that Gwen had forwarded to her.

"Gwen, I expect you're surprised to hear from me," Jenna read aloud. *"When I was considering whom to give this particular task, I thought of several candidates, but you're the best woman for the job. Yes, this is a job offer. You see, I've been murdered, and if you're reading this, then my killer is still out there. I want you to use your skills as an investigative journalist and find proof of who that person is. Once you have the proof, contact Mark Lynch at the International Security Agency."*

"Mark?" Cal repeated. "Why would Paul want her to contact Hollywood?"

Jenna exchanged puzzled glances with him. "Obviously, Paul knew him. Or knew *of* him. But why would Paul trust Hollywood with that kind of information? Why not just turn it over to Holden or Salazar?"

Cal didn't say anything for several seconds. "Maybe he's giving each person one task. Or maybe Gwen is right and this is his way of dividing and conquering. If you're all at odds and suspicious of each other, then he'll get some kind of postmortem satisfaction. He sends Salazar after Sophie. Gwen, after the person who murdered him. And he somehow turns Helena against her own brother."

Yes. Jenna would have loved to know what Paul had written to Helena. Or to Holden. If they had all the e-mails, they might be able to figure out what Paul was really trying to do.

"Did you read the entire email?" Cal asked.

"No. There's more." She scrolled down the tiny screen. *"If you find my killer, then my attorney will wire the sum of one million dollars to a bank account of your choice. I'm giving you one week. If you don't have the proof, the job will go to someone else."*

So this wasn't going to stop. If Gwen failed, then the investigation would continue.

"Maybe Hollywood will be offered the job," Cal speculated. "Or Salazar."

She heard him, but her attention was on the last lines of the email. *"To make things easier for you, I want you to focus your efforts on my number-one suspect,"* she continued reading aloud. *"Actually, she's my only suspect. Her name is Jenna Laniere."*

That was it. The end of Paul's instructions.

Jenna had to take a moment to absorb it. "Paul obviously didn't trust me right from the start, or he wouldn't have written this email."

"If he's the one who wrote it."

She turned in the seat to face Cal. "What are you thinking?"

"I'm thinking Gwen, Holden or Helena could be behind these messages from the grave." He hissed out a breath. "Even Hollywood could have done it. This could all be some kind of ploy to get Paul's estate."

Maybe. After all, Holden and Helena had shared Paul's money. Maybe one of them wanted it all. Or if Gwen was the culprit, maybe this was her way of ferreting out a story.

But how did Hollywood fit into this? Unless the man was just an out-and-out criminal, she couldn't figure out a logical scenario where he'd be collecting any of Paul's money.

"Maybe your friend's innocent," Jenna said, thinking out loud. "What if someone is setting him up so you can't trust him? That way, it would be one less person you could turn to for help."

Cal lifted his shoulder. "It's possible, I suppose. Once the director has gone through all the message traffic, we should know more."

Yes, but would that information stop her daughter from being in danger? Jenna couldn't shake the fear that Sophie was at the core of all of this.

Something caught her eye.

Headlights in the distance behind them.

Cal noticed it, too. His attention went straight to the rearview mirror. Neither of them said anything. They just sat there, breaths held, waiting to see what would happen.

He kept his speed right at fifty-five, and the headlights got closer very quickly. The other car was speeding. Still, that in itself was no cause for alarm. Combined with everything, however, her heart and mind were racing with worst-case scenarios.

"Get in the backseat and stay down," Cal insisted.

Jenna tried to keep herself steady. This could be just a precaution, she reminded herself, but she did as he asked. She climbed onto the seat with Sophie and positioned her torso over the baby so that she could protect her still-sleeping baby. But she also wanted to keep watch, so she craned her neck so she could see the side mirror.

The car was barreling down on them.

Jenna prayed it would just pass them and that would

be the end to this particular scare. She could see Cal's right hand through the gap of the seats, and because of the other car's bright headlights, she could also see his finger tense on the trigger of his gun. He had the weapon aimed at the passenger's window.

The lights got even brighter as the car came upon them. Too close. It was a dark SUV, much larger than her own vehicle. Jenna braced herself because it seemed as if the SUV was going to ram right into them.

"Is it Salazar?" she asked in a raw whisper. Her heart was pounding now. Her breath was coming out in short, too-fast jolts.

"I can't tell. Just stay down."

Jenna didn't have a choice. She had to do whatever she could to protect Sophie. As meager as it was, her body would become a shield if the driver of that vehicle started shooting.

The headlights slashed right at the mirror when the car bolted out into the passing lane. She prayed it would continue to accelerate and go past them.

But it didn't.

With her heart in her throat, Jenna watched as the car slowed until it was literally side by side with them. Cal cursed under his breath and aimed his gun.

"Brace yourself," he warned her a split second before he slammed on the brakes.

She saw a flash of red from the other car. The driver had braked as well, and the lights lit up the darkness, coating their shadows with that eerie shade of bloodred.

Cal threw the car into Reverse and hit the accelerator. She didn't know how he managed, but he spun the car around so they were facing in the opposite direction, and gunned the engine.

There was another flash of brake lights from the SUV. The sound of the tires squealed against the asphalt. Jenna squeezed her eyes shut a moment and prayed. But when she looked into the mirror, her worst fear was confirmed.

The SUV was coming at them again.

If it rammed them or sideswiped them, it'd be difficult for Cal to stay on the road. It was too dark to see if there were ditches nearby or one of the dozens of creeks that dotted the area. But Jenna didn't need to see things like that to know the danger. If the SUV driver managed to get them off the road, he could fire shots at a stationary target. They wouldn't be hard to hit.

"Should I call the sheriff?" she asked. She had to do something. *Anything.*

"He wouldn't get here in time."

The last ominous word had hardly left Cal's mouth when there was a loud bang. The SUV rammed into the back of her car, and the jolt snapped her body. Jenna caught Sophie's car seat and held on, trying to steady it and brace herself for a second hit.

It came hard and fast.

The front bumper of the SUV slammed into them. The motion jostled Sophie, and she stirred, waking.

"Get all the way down," Cal instructed. "Put your hand over Sophie's ears and cover her as much as you can with the blanket."

She did, though Jenna had to wonder how that would help. A moment later, she got her answer. He didn't slow down. Didn't try to turn around again. He merely turned his gun in the direction of the back window and the SUV. Cal used the rearview mirror to aim.

And he fired.

The blast was deafening. Louder than even the impact of the SUV. That sound rifled through Jenna, spiking her fear and concern for her child. Even though she had clamped her hands around Sophie's ears, the sound got through and her baby shrieked.

Cal fired again and again.

The bullets tore through the back window, the safety glass webbing and cracking, but it stayed in place. Thank God. Even though the glass wasn't much protection, she didn't want it tumbling down on Sophie.

Cal fired one more shot and then jammed his foot on the accelerator to get them out of there.

CHAPTER EIGHT

CAL SPED THROUGH the wrought-iron gates that fronted Jenna's estate.

He'd spent most of the trip watching the road, to make sure that SUV hadn't followed them. As far as he could tell, it hadn't, even though they had encountered more traffic the closer they got to Houston. And then the traffic had trailed off to practically nothing once he was on the highway that led to Jenna's house.

Though the estate was only twenty miles from Houston city limits and there were other homes nearby, it felt isolated because it was centered on ten pristine acres.

The iron gates were massive, at least ten feet tall and double that in width. Fanning off both sides of the gate was a sinister-looking spiked-top fence that appeared to surround the place.

Even though there was no guard in the small redbrick gatehouse to the left, the builder had obviously planned for security, which made Cal wonder why Jenna had ever left in the first place. Yes, she'd told him she had a tendency to take off when things got rough, but the estate was as close to a stronghold as they could get. Somehow, he'd have to make Jenna understand that this was their best option. For now. He'd have to try to soothe her flight instinct so she wouldn't be tempted to run.

He stopped in the circular drive directly in front of the house and positioned the car so that Jenna would only be a few steps away from getting inside. He didn't want her exposed any longer than necessary. Salazar had expert shooting skills with a long-range assault rifle.

Like the rest of the property, the house was huge. There was a redbrick exterior and a porch with white columns that stretched across the entire front and sides. The carved oak front door opened, and he immediately reached for his gun.

"It's okay," Jenna assured him. "That's Meggie, the housekeeper. She's worked here since I was a baby."

The woman was in her mid-sixties with graying flame-red hair. Short, but not petite, she wore a simple blue-flowered dress. She didn't rush to greet them, but she did give them a warm smile when Jenna stepped from the car with a sleeping Sophie cradled in her arms.

"Welcome home. I have rooms made up for all of you," Meggie announced. Her words came out in a rushed stream of excitement. "When you called and said you were on the way, I got the crib ready in the nursery. The bedding is already turned down for the little angel. And I put your guest in the room next to yours."

"Thank you," Jenna muttered.

Once they were inside and the door was shut, Meggie patted Jenna's cheek and eased back the blanket a bit so she could see Sophie. She smiled again, and her aged blue eyes went to Cal. "She looks like you."

He wasn't sure what to say to that, so he didn't say anything. Meggie thought Sophie was his.

Cal forced himself to assess his surroundings. He'd expected luxury, and wasn't disappointed. Vaulted ceilings. Marble floors. Victorian antiques. But there were also a lot of windows and God knows how many points of entry. It would be a bear to keep all of them secure.

"We're exhausted," Jenna said to the woman, her voice showing her nerves. Maybe the nerves were from Meggie's comment about Sophie's looks but more likely from the inevitable adrenaline crash. "We'll get settled in for the night and we can talk tomorrow. There are things I should tell you."

Meggie nodded, and lightly kissed Sophie's cheek.

"Where's the main security panel?" he asked before Meggie could walk away.

She pointed to a richly colored oil landscape painting in the wide corridor just off the foyer. "The access code is seven, seven, four, one." Then she made her exit in the opposite direction.

Jenna let out a deep breath. A shaky one. Now that she was safe inside, the impact of what'd happened was hitting her. She was ready to crash, but Cal needed to take a few security measures before he helped her put Sophie to bed.

He aimed for some small talk so he could get some information about the place. And maybe get her mind off the nightmare they'd just come through.

"You were born here?" Cal asked, going to the monitor. The painting had a hinged front, and he opened it so he could take a look at what he had to work with.

"Literally. My mother didn't trust hospitals. So my dad set up one here. In fact, he set up a lot of things here, mainly so that we'd never have to leave."

"They were overly protective?" Cal armed the system and watched as the lights flashed on to indicate the protected areas.

"Yes, with a capital Y. My mother was from a wealthy family, and she'd been kidnapped for ransom when she was a child. Obviously it was a life-altering experience for her. She was obsessed with keeping me safe, and over the years, Dad began to share that obsession. What they failed to remember was that my mother had been kidnapped from her own family's house."

Jenna followed his sweeping gaze around the room before her eyes met his. "There really is no place that's totally safe. Sometimes this estate felt more like a prison than a home."

That explained her wanderlust and maybe even the reason she'd gone to Monte de Leon. For months Cal had seen that trip as a near fatal mistake, but then he glanced at Sophie. That little girl wouldn't be here if Jenna hadn't made that trip. Maybe it was the camaraderie he'd developed with Jenna as they'd waited on that cantina floor. Whatever it was, that bonding had obviously extended to the child in her arms.

"Is the security system okay?" she asked.

"It looks pretty good." The back of the faux painting had the layout of the estate and each room was thankfully labeled not just for function but for the type of security that was installed. "The perimeter of the fence is wired to detect a breach. You have motion detectors at every entrance and exit. And all windows. This is a big place," he added in a mumble.

"Yes," she said with a slight tinge of irony. "Any weak spots you can see?"

"Front gate," he readily supplied. "Is it usually open the way it was when we came in?"

She nodded. "But it can be closed by pressing the button on the monitor or the switch located just inside the grounds." Jenna reached over and did just that. "There's an automatic lock and keypad entry on the left side of the gate."

Which wasn't very safe. Keypads could be tampered with or bypassed. Hollywood certainly knew how to do those things. Salazar likely did, too.

"What's this?" he asked, tapping the large area on the south side of the house that was labeled Gun Room.

"My father was an antique gun collector. He built an indoor firing range to test guns before he bought them."

Interesting. He hadn't expected that, but he would add it to his security plan. "You can shoot?"

"Not at all. The noise always put me off. But I'm willing to learn. In fact, I want to learn."

He just might teach her. Not so he could use her as backup. But it might make her feel more empowered. Plus, the room might come in handy, because it was almost certainly bulletproof. If worse came to worst, then he might have to move them in there. For now, though, he looked for a more comfortable solution.

"Where are the rooms we're supposed to stay in?" he asked. When Jenna shifted a little, he realized that Sophie was probably getting heavy. He holstered his gun and gently took the baby from her. The little girl was a heavy sleeper. She didn't even lift an eyelid.

"Thanks." Jenna touched her index finger to a trio of rooms on the east side of the house. "That's the nursery, my room's next to it and that's the guest room."

He put his finger next to hers. Touching her. She didn't move away. In fact, she slipped her hand over his. It was such a simple gesture. But an intimate one. It was a good thing Sophie was between them, or he might have done something stupid like pull Jenna into his arms.

"There's a problem," he let her know.

The corner of her mouth lifted for just a second. "I think we're too tired to worry about another kissing session."

There was no such thing as being too tired to kiss. But Cal didn't voice that. Instead, he moved his hand away to avoid further temptation. "Your bedroom has exterior doors."

"Two of them. And another door leads to the pool area. The guest room has an exterior door as well."

From a security perspective, that wasn't good. "How about the nursery?"

"No exterior doors. Four windows, though."

He'd take the windows over the doors. "That's where we'll be spending the night."

She didn't question it. Jenna turned and started walking in that direction. Cal followed her, trying to keep his steps light so he wouldn't wake Sophie. Jenna led him down a corridor lined with doors and stopped in front of one.

"Don't turn on the lights," Cal told her when she opened the door. It was possible that Holden or someone else was doing some long-range surveillance, and Cal didn't want to advertise their exact location in the estate.

He took a moment to let his eyes adjust to the darkness, and he saw the white crib placed against an interior wall well away from the windows. That was good. Cal went that direction and eased Sophie onto the mattress. She moved a little and pursed her lips, sucking at a nonexistent bottle, and he braced himself for her to wake up and cry. But her eyes stayed closed.

"There isn't a bed in here," Jenna whispered. "Just that."

He spotted a chaise longue in the small adjacent sitting room just off the nursery. The chaise wasn't big enough for two people, but hopefully it would be comfortable enough for Jenna to get some sleep.

"I can have a bed brought in," she suggested.

"No. Best not to have any unnecessary movement." Nor did he want to alert anyone else in the household to their sleeping arrangements. Tomorrow, they'd work out something more comfortable.

Jenna walked mechanically to a closet and took out two quilts. The rooms were toasty warm, but she handed him one and draped the other around herself. Since she didn't seem steady on her feet, Cal helped her in the direction of the chaise.

"Get some sleep," he instructed.

She moved as if she were about to climb onto the chaise, but then she stopped. There was just enough moonlight coming through the windows that he could easily see her troubled expression.

"I've really made a mess of things," she said.

Oh, no. Here it was. The adrenaline crash. Reality was setting in, and she started to shake. He couldn't see any tears, but he had no doubt they were there.

She moved again. Closer to him. Until they were touching, her breasts against his chest. That set off Texas-size alarms in his head, and the rest of his body, but it didn't stop him from putting his arms around her.

She sobbed softly, but tried to muffle it by putting her mouth against his shoulder. Her warm breath fluttered against his neck.

"You'll get through this," he promised, though he

knew it wouldn't be easy. She was in for a long, hard night. And so was he.

"You're not trembling," she pointed out.

"I'm trained not to tremble. Besides, I only shot an SUV tonight. Trust me, I've done worse." He tried to make it sound light. Cocky, even. But he failed miserably. The attack couldn't be dismissed with bravado.

She pulled back and blinked hard, trying to rid her eyes of the tears. "Have you ever killed anyone?"

Cal was a little taken aback with the question, and he kept his answer simple. "Yeah."

"Good."

"Good?" Again, he was taken aback.

Jenna nodded. "I want you to stop Salazar if he comes after Sophie."

Oh. Now he got it. Cal pushed her hair away from her face. "I won't let him hurt her. Or you."

Hell. He hadn't meant to say that last part aloud. It was too personal, and it was best if he tried to keep some barrier between them.

Her mouth came to his, and all that barrier stuff suddenly sounded like something he didn't want after all. He wanted her kiss.

Since it was going to be a major mistake, Cal decided to make the most of it. Something they'd both regret. And maybe that would stop them from doing it again. So he took far more than he should have.

He hooked his arm around her, just at the top of her butt. He drew her closer so that it wasn't only their chests and mouths that were touching. Their bodies came together, and the fit was even better than his fantasies.

The soft sound Jenna made was from a silky feminine moan of pleasure. A signal that she not only wanted this but wanted more. She wrapped her arms around him and gently ground her sex against his.

While the body contact was mind-blowing, Cal didn't neglect the kiss. This last kiss. Since he'd already decided there couldn't be any more of them, he wanted to savor her in these next few scorching moments. To brand her taste, her touch, the feel of her into his memory.

The kiss was already hot and deep. He deepened it even more. Because he was stupid. And because his stupidity knew no boundaries, he followed Jenna's lead.

Oh, man. Their clothes weren't thick enough. A wall wouldn't have been thick enough.

He could feel the heat of her sex. And his. The brainless part of him was already begging him to lower Jenna to that chaise and strip off her pants. Sex would follow immediately. Great hot sex. Which couldn't happen, of course. Sophie was just in the adjoining room and could wake up at any minute.

Cal repeated that, and he forced himself to stop. When he stepped back from her, both of them were gasping for breath.

"Good night," he managed to say.

"That was your idea of a good-night kiss?" Jenna challenged.

No. It was his idea of foreplay, but it was best not to say that out loud. "We can't do it again."

Why did it sound as if he was trying to convince himself?

Because he was.

Still, he was determined to make this work. He was

a pro. A rough-around-the-edges operative. He could stop himself from kissing a woman.

He hoped.

She trailed her fingers down his arm and then withdrew her touch. "I wanted to kiss you on the floor of that cantina," she admitted. "Why, I don't know." Jenna shook her head. "Yes, I do. You're hot. You're dangerous. You're all the things that get my blood moving."

His pulse jumped. "So you like hot dangerous things?" he asked.

"I like you," she said, her voice quivery now. She sank down onto the chaise and looked up at him. "But liking you isn't wise. I've made a lot of bad choices in my life, and I can't do that anymore now that I have Sophie. If I fall for a guy, then it has to be the right guy, you know?"

"Sure." He wouldn't tell her that soon his job wouldn't be that dangerous. If he got that deputy director promotion, he'd be doing his shooting from behind a desk. On some level Cal would miss the fieldwork, but the deputy director job was the next step in his dream to be chief. Maybe it was best that Jenna thought his dangerous work would continue. Maybe this was the barrier they needed between them.

"Sleep," he reminded her.

Jenna lay down on the chaise and covered up. Cal was about to do the same on the floor, but his cell phone rang. He yanked it from his pocket and answered it before it could ring a second time and wake up Sophie.

"It's Kowalski," his director greeted. "What's your situation?"

Cal got up, walked across the room and stepped just outside the door and into the hall. "Is this line secure?"

"Yes. I'm using the private line in my office."

Good. That meant if there was a leak or threat from Hollywood, then at least this call wouldn't be overheard. Cal had called Kowalski right after the SUV incident, but he hadn't wanted to say too much until he knew the info would stay private.

"I'm at Ms. Laniere's estate. Were you able to get anything on that SUV that tried to run us off the road?"

"Nothing. The Texas Rangers are investigating. There was a team of them nearby searching for that missing woman, and they got there faster than the FBI."

Well, Cal wasn't holding his breath that they'd find anything related to Salazar. If the assassin had been the driver, then the first thing he would have done was ditch the vehicle. He wouldn't have wanted to drive it around with bullet holes in it.

"And what about Salazar?" Cal asked, hoping by some miracle the man had been picked up.

"He's still at large."

Cal didn't bother to groan since that was the answer he'd expected. "What about the plates?" He had made a note of them and had asked the director to run them.

"The plates weren't stolen. They were bogus."

Strange. A pro like Salazar would normally have just stolen a vehicle and then discarded it when he was done. Bogus plates took time to create. "And Hollywood? Anything new to report?"

"Nothing definitive on him, either."

Cal was afraid of that. "How did he take the news that he's under investigation?"

The director took several moments to answer. "He doesn't know."

"Excuse me?" Cal was certain he'd misunderstood the director.

"Lynch doesn't know he's being monitored. I want to let him have access to some information and see what he does with it. If he does nothing, then maybe someone has set him up."

Or maybe Hollywood knew about the monitoring and was going to play it clean for a while.

"How's Ms. Laniere?" Kowalski asked, pulling Cal's thoughts away from all the other questions.

She's making me crazy. "She's shaken up, of course." Cal used his briefing tone. Flat, unemotional, detached. Unlike the firestorm going on inside him. "My plan was to stay here with her and her child until we can make other arrangements."

"Of course." The director paused, which bothered Cal. Was Kowalski concerned about this whole paternity issue? Was he worried that Cal was going to sleep with her? Cal was worried about that, too.

"Ms. Laniere is the main reason I'm calling," Kowalski explained. "We might have another problem."

This didn't sound like a personal issue. It sounded dangerous. Besides, they didn't need another problem, personal or otherwise. They already had a boatload of them. "What's wrong now?"

"The Ranger CSI unit is at Ms. Laniere's apartment in Willow Ridge now. About a half hour ago they found a listening device near the front door. It wasn't government issue. It was something you could buy at any store that sells security equipment. Still, Lynch could have put it there."

Holden or Helena could have done the same. All

three had been there. Or maybe even Gwen had done it after Jenna and he had left.

"There's more," the director continued. "I had the CSI check your car as well, and they just called to say they'd found a vehicle tracking system taped to the undercarriage."

Cal cursed. "Someone wanted to follow me." He carried that through one more step. "And that means someone could have done the same to Jenna's car."

"Probably."

"But I checked the undercarriage when I looked for explosives." Cal started for the front of the house.

"You could easily have missed it. It's small, half the size of a deck of cards. But don't let the size fool you. It might be wireless and portable, but it's still effective even at long range."

"Stay put," he called out to Jenna. "I have to go outside and check on something."

Cal hurried toward the front of the house, disengaged the security system, unlocked the front door. He drew his weapon before he hurried out into the cold night. No one seemed to be lurking in the shadows waiting to assassinate him, but he rushed. He didn't want to leave Jenna and Sophie alone for too long.

Thankfully, the overhead porch lights were enough for him to clearly see the car. Staying on the side that was nearest to the house, he stooped and looked underneath. There was no immediate sign of a tracker. But then he looked again at a clump of mud. He touched it and realized it was a fake. Plastic. He pulled it back and looked at the device beneath.

His heart dropped.

"Found it," Cal reported. "Someone camouflaged it."

"So someone wired both cars," the director concluded. "The bad news is that anyone with a laptop could have monitored your whereabouts."

Cal's heart dropped even further. Because that meant someone had tracked them to Jenna's estate.

Salazar and maybe God knows who else knew exactly where they were.

CHAPTER NINE

JENNA CHECKED HER WATCH. It was nearly 6:00 a.m. Soon, Sophie would wake up and demand her breakfast bottle.

She took a moment to gather her thoughts and to reassure herself one last time that everyone was okay. The security alarm hadn't gone off. No one had fired shots into the place. That SUV hadn't returned.

But all of those things might still happen.

Cal hadn't come out and said that, but after he'd discovered the tracking device on her car, they both knew anything was possible. He'd considered moving them again, but had decided to stay put and hope their safety measures were enough to keep out anyone who might decide to come after them.

After Cal had disarmed and removed the tracking device, every possible function of the security system had been armed. Cal had even alerted all three members of the household staff, and the gardener, Pete Spears, had assured them that he'd keep watch from the gatehouse.

All those measures had been enough. They were still alive and unharmed. But the day had barely started.

With that uncomfortable thought, Jenna eased off the chaise and moved as quietly as she could so she wouldn't wake Cal. He hadn't slept much. She knew that because he'd been awake when she finally fell asleep around midnight. He was still awake when she'd gotten up at 2:00 a.m. to feed a fussing Sophie. He'd even gone with them to the kitchen when she fixed the bottle, and he'd taken his gun with him.

But he was thankfully asleep now.

He was sitting with his legs stretched out in front of him, so his upper back and neck were resting on the chaise. His face looked perfectly relaxed, but he had his hand resting over the butt of the gun in his shoulder holster.

She reached for her shoes, but Cal's hand shot out. Before Jenna could even blink, he grabbed her wrist, turned and used the strength of his body to flatten her against the chaise.

Their eyes met.

He was on top of her with his face only several inches away from hers. In the depths of those steel-blue eyes, she saw him process the situation. There was no emotion in those eyes. Well, not at first. Then he cursed under his breath.

"Sorry. Old habits," he mumbled.

It took her a moment to get past the shock of what'd just happened. "You mean combat training, not intimate situations?" She meant it as a joke, but it came out all wrong. Of course it did. His kisses could melt paint, and he was on top of her in what could be a good starting position for some great morning sex.

But there wouldn't be any.

Cal got off her with difficulty. He dug his knee into the chaise to lever himself up, but that created some interesting contact in their midsections.

"Dreams," he explained when he noticed that she was looking at the bulge behind the zipper of his jeans.

About me? she nearly asked but thankfully held

her tongue. It was wishful thinking. Yes, he'd kissed her, but he hadn't wanted to. It'd been just a primal response. Now he wanted some distance between them. He wanted Sophie and her safe so he wouldn't feel obligated to help. And after all the trouble she'd caused for him, she couldn't blame him one bit.

Sophie's soft whimpers got her moving off the chaise but not before Cal and she exchanged uncomfortable glances. She really needed to make other security arrangements so he could leave. But that was the last thing on earth she wanted.

"Good morning, sweetheart," she greeted Sophie.

Jenna scooped her up into her arms and stole a few morning kisses. Sophie stopped fussing and gave her a wide smile. It wouldn't last, though. Soon her baby would want her bottle, so Jenna started toward the kitchen.

Cal was right behind her.

Meggie was ahead of them in the hall. The woman was walking straight toward them. "A fax just arrived for you." She handed Cal at least a dozen pages, but her attention went straight to Sophie. "I've got a bottle waiting for you, young lady."

Sophie looked at her with curious eyes and glanced up at Jenna. Jenna smiled to reassure her, and it seemed to work because Sophie smiled, too, when Meggie took her and headed for the kitchen.

Since Cal had stopped to look at the fax and since it seemed to have grabbed his complete interest, Jenna stopped as well. "Bad news?"

"It could be." He glanced through the rest of the pages and then handed her the first one. "These are reports I requested from my director. I asked for a background on Gwen Mitchell and I also wanted him to look for any suspicious activity that could be linked back to you."

She skimmed through the page and groaned. "There was a break-in at the pediatrician's office. Sophie's file was stolen." Jenna smacked the paper against the palm of her hand. "Holden is responsible for this. He's trying to prove that Paul's the father."

"What would have been in that file?" Cal asked.

"Well, certainly no DNA information, but her blood type was listed. It's O-positive."

Cal actually looked conflicted. "O-positive is the most common. It's my blood type."

Jenna immediately understood his mixed emotions. This might make Holden think she was telling the truth about Cal being Sophie's father. But this would also make his director have more doubts. She really did need to get a DNA test done right away.

Cal made his way toward the kitchen while he continued to read the fax. "Gwen Mitchell's been a free-lance investigative reporter for ten years." He shuffled through the pages. "She's gotten some pretty tough stories, including one on a mob boss. And a Colombian drug dealer."

So they weren't dealing with an amateur. "She doesn't sound like the type of person to back off."

"She's not," Cal confirmed. He stopped again just outside the kitchen entrance. "According to this, when Gwen was working on that story in Colombia, a woman was killed."

Jenna nearly gasped. "Gwen murdered her?"

"Not exactly, but she was responsible for the woman's death. Gwen made the drug lord believe this woman had revealed sensitive information. The drug lord had her killed. Gwen managed to record the actual murder and that became the centerpiece of her story."

"Oh, God." So this was what they were up against. A ruthless woman who'd do whatever was necessary to get her story. And in this case her story was getting Jenna. Gwen would do anything to collect the one million dollars that Paul had offered her.

Cal walked ahead of her and checked the security system. It was identical to the check he'd made before and after Sophie's 2:00 a.m. feeding. When he was satisfied that everything was still secure, they went to the kitchen.

Meggie had Sophie in the crook of her arm and was trying to feed her a bottle while she checked something on the stove. Jenna went to take the child, but Cal caught her.

"I'll take her. You need to eat something."

Jenna's stomach chose that exact moment to growl. She couldn't argue with that. But she was more than a little surprised when Cal so easily took Sophie from Meggie. He sat down at the kitchen table and readjusted the bottle so there'd be an even flow of formula.

Jenna and Meggie exchanged glances.

"You're sure you haven't done baby duty before?" Jenna asked. She poured herself a cup of coffee, and Meggie dished her up some scrambled eggs.

"Nope," he assured her.

He was a natural. He seemed so at ease with Sophie. And willing to help. It made Jenna feel guilty—his willingness could be costly for him. If she hadn't told that lie to Holden, Cal would never have come to Willow Ridge, and he wouldn't be in this dangerous situation now. Of course, Jenna was thankful he was there. For Sophie's sake. But she hated what she'd done to him.

Jenna had only managed to eat one bite of the eggs when a shrill beep pulsed through the room. It brought Cal to his feet. He handed Sophie to her and drew his gun.

Just like that, her heart went into overdrive, and her stomach knotted. Jenna passed her daughter to Meggie so she could go with Cal and see what had happened to trigger the surveillance system.

Cal hurried to the security panel just as his cell phone rang. He answered it while he opened the panel box.

"You're here at the estate?" he asked a moment later. That sent him to the side windows by the front door, and he looked out. "Something's wrong."

It wasn't a question, but he must have gotten an answer because he hung up.

"Director Kowalski just arrived," Cal relayed to her. "He found Holden and Helena Carr outside. They were trying to get in the front gate."

CAL HAD HOPED that today wouldn't be as insane as the day before, but it wasn't off to a good start. Here it was, barely dawn, his director had arrived for an impromptu visit, and two of their suspects were only yards away. Cal didn't want those two in the same state with Jenna and Sophie, yet here they were.

Had they been the ones to put the tracking devices on Jenna's and his vehicles? Maybe. Or maybe they'd merely benefited from what someone else had done.

"Can your director arrest Holden and Helena?" Jenna asked.

"Probably not. I'm sure they'll have a cover story for their attempt to get through the front gate."

But maybe they could call the local authorities and have them picked up for trespassing. It wouldn't keep the duo in jail long since they'd have no trouble making bail, but it would send a message that they couldn't continue to intimidate Jenna without paying a consequence or two.

Cal grabbed his jacket and disarmed the security system so he could go outside and *greet* their visitors. Jenna picked up her jacket as well.

"I want to talk to them," she said before he could object to her going with him.

"That wouldn't be wise."

"On the contrary. I want them to know I won't cower in fear or hide. I want them out of my life."

Cal wasn't sure this was the way to make that happen, but he didn't want to take the time to argue with her. Director Kowalski might need backup.

"Wait on the porch," he instructed. "That way, they can see you, but you can get back inside if things turn ugly."

He hoped like the devil that she obeyed.

Cal walked down the steps and spotted the gardener, Pete, in the gatehouse. He was armed with a shotgun. Good. He'd take all the help he could get.

There were three cars just on the other side of the gate. Two were high-end luxury vehicles, no doubt belonging to Holden and Helena. Cal wondered why they hadn't driven together. The third vehicle was a standard-issue four-wheel-drive from ISA's motor pool.

The three drivers were at the gate, waiting. Cal didn't like the idea of his director being locked out with the

Carrs, but he couldn't risk Sophie's and Jenna's safety. He needed to keep that gate closed until he was sure this visit wasn't going to lead to an attack.

Before he approached the gate, Cal glanced over his shoulder. Amazingly, Jenna was still on the porch. He doubted she'd stay there, but he welcomed these few minutes of safety.

"I didn't try to break in," Helena volunteered. "I merely wanted to speak to Jenna, and I was trying to find an intercom or something when that man with the shotgun sounded the alarm."

Kowalski was behind her. He had his weapon drawn in his right hand and held an equipment bag in his left. He rolled his eyes, an indication he didn't buy Helena's story.

Holden's eyes, however, were much more intense. He had his attention fastened to Jenna on the porch. "I need to talk to her, too," he insisted.

I, not *we.* Given the fact that the siblings had arrived in separate vehicles, perhaps they were in the middle of a family squabble. Considering what Helena had said at Jenna's apartment in Willow Ridge, that didn't surprise Cal.

"Jenna's not receiving visitors," Cal said sarcastically. "But I'll pass along any message."

Holden continued to watch Jenna. "The message is that she's in grave danger." His voice was probably loud enough for her to hear.

Cal shrugged. "Old news."

"Not exactly," Holden challenged. He glanced at his sister.

Now it was Helena's turn to show some intensity. Anger tightened the muscles on her face. "My brother broke into my personal computer and read the email Paul's attorney sent me. Holden seems to think that I'd be willing to do whatever Paul wants me to do."

Well, this had potential. "And what does Paul want you to do?"

Helena came closer and hooked her perfectly manicured fingers around the wrought-iron spindles that made up the gate front. "Paul seemed to believe that I would tie up loose ends if Salazar failed."

Holden stepped forward as well. "My sister's orders are to kill us all once Salazar has Sophie."

Oh, hell. Paul really had put together some plan. Kidnapping and murder.

"I'm not a killer," Helena said, her voice shaky now. "I have no idea why Paul thought I would do this."

"Don't you?" Holden again. He aimed his answer at Cal. "My sister was sleeping with Paul. She didn't think I knew, but I did. And I also knew that they had plans to kill Jenna if she turned down his marriage proposal."

"That's not true," Helena protested.

Cal heard footsteps behind him and groaned. A glance over his shoulder confirmed that Jenna wanted to be part of this conversation. He didn't blame her. But he also wanted to keep her safe. He positioned himself in front of her, hoping that would be enough if bullets started flying.

"Paul didn't love me," Helena said to Jenna. She shook her head. "He didn't love you, either."

"I know," Jenna readily agreed. "He wanted my business. And you were in on his plan to get it?"

"Only the business." Helena's face flushed as if she was embarrassed by the admission of her guilt. "I never would have agreed to murder."

Cal wasn't sure he believed her. A flushed face could be faked. "How does Gwen Mitchell fit into the picture?" he asked.

Helena's eyes widened. "The reporter?"

"Yeah. Paul was sleeping with her, too." It was a good guess. After reading Gwen's background, Cal figured she'd do anything to get a story.

Helena shook her head again and a thin stream of breath left her mouth. "I didn't know."

"So Paul slept around," Holden snarled. If he had any concern for his sister's reaction, he didn't show it. "I don't think that's nearly as important as the fact that he's put bounties on our heads." Holden cursed. "He was my friend. Like a brother to me. And this is what he does?"

Kowalski came closer. "What exactly did Paul say in the email he sent you?" he asked Holden.

Holden sent a nasty glare the director's way. "Well, he didn't ask me to kill anyone, that's for sure. He asked me to check on some accounts and old business connections. Nothing illegal. Nothing sinister. Obviously, Helena can't say the same. Paul made some kind of arrangement with my sister—"

"He didn't," Helena practically shouted. "And I didn't agree to do what he asked." She caught her brother's arm and whirled him around so he was facing her. "Have you ever considered that he could be doing this for some other reason? To get us at each other's throats? Paul had a sick sense of humor, and this might be his idea of a joke."

"My daughter is in danger," Jenna said, drawing everyone's attention back to her. "It's not a joke. Salazar is out there, and Paul is the one who sent him after Sophie."

Cal glanced at Holden and Helena to see their reactions. They were still hurling daggers at each other. It was a good time to interject some logic in this game of pointing fingers.

"If Paul wanted Sophie, but he also wanted all of you dead, then who would be left to raise her?" the director challenged. "Who would be left to manage his estate? Why would he want to eliminate the very people who could give him some postmortem help?"

Dead silence.

"Maybe he expected Gwen Mitchell to help him," Jenna mumbled. "Maybe they were more than just lovers."

That was exactly what Cal was considering. Gwen's ruthlessness would have endeared her to Paul. And for that matter, the emails could be a hoax. A way to drive them all apart. Gwen could have further instructions that Paul could have given her before he was murdered.

And that brought Cal back to something he wanted to ask. "How exactly did you two know that Jenna would be here?"

Holden shrugged and peeled off the leather glove on his left hand. "It wasn't a lucky guess, was it, Helena?"

The woman's shoulders snapped back, but she didn't answer her brother. She looked at Cal instead. "Salazar called me a few hours ago to tell me that he'd put a tracking device on Jenna's car. He said she was here."

Cal silently cursed and glanced around to make sure Salazar wasn't lurking somewhere. "Go back in the house," he instructed Jenna in a whisper. "Arm the security system."

"But if it isn't safe for me, it isn't safe for you," Jenna pointed out, also in a whisper.

"I won't be long," he promised, knowing that didn't really address her concerns. Still, he had some unfinished business. Concerns about his personal safety could wait.

"What else did Salazar say?" Kowalski demanded from Helena once Jenna started for the house.

"Nothing. I swear. He told me about the tracking device, said Jenna was at the estate, and that was it. He hung up." She slid an icy glance at her brother. "I didn't know Holden had tapped my calls. Not until I arrived here and realized that he'd followed me."

Cal stared at Holden, to see if he would add anything, or at least offer an explanation as to why he'd eavesdropped on his sister's conversations. But maybe this was the way it'd always been between them.

"You're not getting into the estate," Cal assured both of them. "You're trespassing."

Holden smacked the glove against the gate. "Arrest me, then. Go ahead. Waste your time when what you should be doing is stopping Salazar."

"Oh, I intend to do that." And he intended to stop Gwen if she was as neck deep in this as he thought she was.

"I don't think it'll be a waste of time if you report to the local FBI office for questioning," the director interjected.

"When there's a warrant for my arrest, I'll show up," Holden snarled. He headed for his car, got in and drove away. His tires squealed from the excessive speed.

"I'll go in for questioning," Helena told Kowalski. Her eyes watered with tears. "I'll do whatever's necessary to keep us all alive."

"Paul asked you to kill us," Cal reminded her. "What makes you think you're in danger?"

She glanced at her brother's car as it quickly disappeared down the road. "Holden won't show me the email he got from Paul. My brother doesn't trust me. And why should he? Because of Paul, Holden thinks I'll try to kill him, and he's no doubt trying to figure out how to kill me first before I can carry through with Paul's wishes."

With that, she walked to her car. Her shoulders were slumped, and she swiped her hand over her cheek to wipe away her tears.

"Any idea what was in Holden's email?" Cal asked once Helena had driven away.

Kowalski shook his head. "We're still working on that. But Helena didn't lie when she said what was in hers. Paul did leave orders to kill Jenna, Holden and anyone else who got in the way of Salazar taking the baby."

Anyone else. That would be Cal. Somehow he would stop Salazar and unravel this mess that'd brought danger right to Jenna's doorstep.

He reached over and hit the control switch to open the gate. Kowalski walked closer and handed him an equipment bag. "I figured you might need this. There's an extra weapon, ammo and a clean laptop."

Cal appreciated the supplies, but knowing Salazar could be out there, he continued to keep watch. So did Pete. The lanky man with sandy blond hair shifted his shotgun and wary gaze all around the grounds. There weren't many places Salazar could take cover and use an assault rifle. Unless he actually made it onto the property. Then there were a lot of places he could use to launch an attack.

Cal glanced down into the unzipped bag and then looked at Kowalski. "Does this mean I'll be here for a while?"

"For now." He paused. "I know it's not protocol. Hell, it's not even legal. That's why you can't be here in a professional capacity. This is personal, understand? You're on an official leave of absence."

"I understand."

It was the truth. This had become personal for Cal.

"Last night after we talked, I worked to set up a safe house for Ms. Laniere and her child," Kowalski explained. "But then the communications monitor at headquarters informed me that my account might have been compromised. There was something suspicious about the way info was feeding in and out of what was supposed to be a secure computer. That means someone might have seen the message traffic on the safe house."

Cal cursed. "Hollywood?"

"Maybe. But it could also be a false alarm caused by a computer glitch. That's why I decided to come in person and tell you to stay put for now."

That's what Cal was afraid he was going to say. "But Salazar knows where Jenna is."

Kowalski nodded. "You might have to take him out if we can't stop him first. The FBI and the Rangers are looking for him. They know he's probably in the area."

Yeah. And for that reason, Cal didn't want to leave Jenna alone for too long. "I'll do what's necessary."

Another nod. The director glanced around uneasily. "What about the paternity issue? Did you get that DNA test done to prove you aren't the baby's father?"

Cal hadn't forgotten about that, but it was definitely on the back burner. "I figured it could wait until all of this is over. Besides, I want Holden and Salazar to believe the child is mine. That might get them to back off."

Though that was more than a long shot. Things had already been set into motion, and it would take a miracle to stop them.

Kowalski met him eye-to-eye. "You're sure that's the only reason you're putting off a DNA test?"

Cal stared at him and tried not to blast the man for accusing him of lying. "I've never given you a reason to distrust me."

"You have now." The director turned and started for his vehicle. "Clear up this paternity issue, Cal, before it destroys everything you've worked so hard to get."

There was just one problem with clearing it up. Well, two.

Jenna and Sophie.

He closed the gate and stood there watching his boss drive away. Cal wondered if his chances at that promotion had just driven away, too. Without Kowalski's blessing, Cal wasn't going to get that deputy director job. Not a chance. He wouldn't even have a career left to salvage.

Cal grabbed the equipment bag and went back to the house. Jenna was there, waiting for him just inside the door. A few feet behind her was Meggie. She had Sophie cradled in her arms. The little girl smiled at him. She was too young and innocent to know the danger she was in.

Seeing Jenna and the baby was a reminder that his career was pretty damn small in the grand scheme of things.

"So, are we going on the run again?" Jenna began to nibble on her bottom lip.

"No." He hoped that was the right thing to do.

Still, he wasn't going to put full trust in his director's decision for them to stay put because Hollywood might still be getting access to any-and everything.

"I need backup," Cal mumbled to himself. More than just a gardener with a shotgun.

And it had to be someone he trusted.

His brother Max was his first choice. If Max was on assignment, then he'd call a friend who owned a personal protection agency. One way or another he wanted someone reliable on the grounds ASAP, and these were men he could trust with his life.

"So we stay put," Jenna concluded. She paused. "And then what?"

"We prepare ourselves for the worst."

Because the worst was on the way.

CHAPTER TEN

"RULE ONE," CAL said to Jenna. He slipped on her eye goggles and adjusted them so they fit firmly on her face. "Treat all firearms as if they're loaded."

He positioned the Smith & Wesson 9 mm gun in her hand and turned her toward the target. It was the silhouette of a person rather than a bull's-eye. Jenna didn't like the idea of aiming at a person, real or otherwise, but she also knew this was necessary. Cal was doing everything humanly possible to keep her and Sophie safe. She wanted to do her part as well.

"Rule two," he continued. "Never point a weapon at anything or anyone you don't intend to destroy."

There it was in a nutshell. Her biggest fear. She'd have to kill someone to stop all of this insanity.

Every precaution was being taken to prevent anyone, especially Salazar, from gaining access to the estate. Cal's friend Jordan Taylor had arrived an hour earlier. He was an expert in security. Jenna hadn't actually met or seen the man because he'd immediately gotten to work on installing monitoring equipment around the entire fence. Jordan had brought another man, Cody Guillory, with him, and the two were going to patrol the grounds. In the meantime, Director Kowalski and the FBI had assured Cal they were doing everything to catch Salazar and neutralize the threat.

However, Cal had insisted she learn how to shoot, just in case.

Jenna hadn't balked at his suggestion, but she had waited until Sophie was down for her morning nap. Meggie and the baby were in the nursery with the door locked, Meggie was armed and the rest of the house was on lockdown. No one was to get in or out.

"Rule three—don't hold your gun sideways. Only stupid people trying to look cool do that. It'll give you a bad aim and cause you to miss your target." Cal moved behind her.

Touching her.

Something he'd been doing since this lesson started. Of course, it was impossible to give a shooting lesson without touching, but the contact made it hard for her to concentrate. It reminded her of their kiss and the fact that she wanted him to touch her. She needed therapy. How could she be thinking about such things at a time like this?

Quite easily, she admitted.

It was Cal and his superhero outfit. Camo pants, black chest-hugging T-shirt. Steel-toed boots. The clothes had been in the equipment bag that the director had delivered, and in this case, the clothes made the man. Well, they made her notice every inch of his body, anyway.

"Okay, here we go," he said, pulling her attention back to the lesson. "Feet apart." He put his hand on the inside of her thigh, just above her knee, to position her.

A shiver of heat went through her.

"Left foot slightly in front. Right elbow completely straight. Since you're new at this, look at the target with your right eye. Close your left one. It'll make it easier to aim." He stopped with his hand beneath her straight elbow and his arm grazing her breasts. "You're shaking a little. Are you cold?"

The room was a little chilly, but that wasn't it. Jenna knew she should just lie. It was right there on the tip of her tongue, but she made the mistake of glancing at him. Even through the goggles, he had no trouble seeing her expression.

"Oh," he mumbled. "Some women get turned on from shooting. All that power in their hands."

Jenna continued to stare at him. "I don't think it's the gun." She probably should have lied about that, too.

Cal chuckled. It was husky, deep and totally male. He dropped his hands to her waist to readjust her stance. At least that's how it started, but he kept his hands there and pressed against her. His front against her back.

That didn't help the shaking. Nor did it cool down the heat.

He grabbed two sets of earmuffs, put one on her and slipped the other on himself. "Take aim at the center of the target," he said, his voice loud so that she could hear him. "Squeeze the trigger with gentle but steady pressure."

Which was exactly what he was doing to her waist.

"Now?" she asked.

"Whenever you're ready." He brushed against her butt.

Sheez. Since this lesson was turning into foreplay, Jenna decided to go ahead. She thought through all of Cal's instructions and then pulled the trigger. Even with the earmuffs, the shot was loud, and her entire right arm recoiled.

She pulled off the earmuffs and goggles and had a look at where her shot had landed.

"That'll work," Cal assured her.

Jenna looked closer at the target and frowned. "I hit the guy in his family jewels."

Cal chuckled again. "Trust me, that'll work."

She replaced the earmuffs and goggles so she could try more shots. She adjusted her aim but the bullet went low again. It took her three more tries before she got a shot anywhere near the upper torso.

"I think you got the hang of it," Cal praised. He took off his own muffs and laid them back on the shelf. He did the same to hers and then took the gun from her. It wasn't easy—her fingers had frozen around it.

"You did good," he added, making eye contact with her.

His hand went around the back of her neck, pulling her to him, and his mouth went to hers.

Yes! she thought. *Finally!*

Maybe it was the fact she was a new mother and had learned to appreciate what little free time she had, but Jenna wanted to make the most of these stolen moments.

Cal obviously did, too. He kissed her, hungry and hot, as if he'd been waiting all morning to do just that.

He ran his hand into her hair so that he controlled the movement of her head. She didn't mind. He angled her so that he could deepen the kiss. And just like that, she was starved for more of him.

With his hands and mouth on her, Jenna's back landed against one of the smooth, square floor-to-ceiling columns that set off the firing lane. Cal landed against her. All those firm sinewy muscles in his chest played havoc with her breasts. It'd been so long since she'd been in a man's arms, and this man had been worth the wait.

His mouth teased and coaxed her. The not so gentle pressure of his chest muscles and pecs made her latch on to him and pull him even closer, until they were fitted together exactly the way a man and woman should fit. They still had their clothes on, but Jenna had no trouble imagining what it would be like to have Cal naked and inside her.

Her need for him was almost embarrassing. She'd never been a sexually charged person. She preferred a good kiss to sex, probably because she'd never actually had good sex. But something told her that she wouldn't have to settle for one or the other with Cal. He was more than capable of delivering both.

He slid his hand down her side, to the bottom of her stretchy top, and lifted it. His fingers, which were just as hot and clever as his mouth, were suddenly on her bare skin, making their way to her breasts and jerking down the cups of her bra.

Everything intensified. His touch. The heat. That primal tug deep within her.

Cal pulled back from the kiss, only so he could wet his fingertips with his tongue. For a moment, she didn't understand why. But then his mouth came back to hers, and those slick wet fingers went to her nipples. He caressed her, and gently pinched her nipples, bringing them to peaks.

Jenna nearly lost it right there.

Frantically searching for some relief to the pressure-cooker heat, she hooked her fingers through the belt loops of his camo pants and dragged him to her, so that his hard sex ground against the soft, wet part of her body.

It was good. Too good.

Because it only made her want the rest of him.

She reached for his zipper, but Cal clamped his hand over hers. Stopping her. "No condom," he reminded her.

Jenna cursed, both thankful and angry that he'd managed to keep a clear head. She didn't want a clear head. She wanted Cal. But she also knew he was right. They couldn't risk having unprotected sex.

She tried to calm down. She'd been ready to climax, and her body wasn't pleased that it wasn't going to get what it wanted.

Cal, however, didn't let her come down. He pinned her in place against the column and shoved down her zipper. He didn't wait to see how she would react to that. He kissed her again. And again, the heat began to soar.

While he did some clever things with his mouth, he tormented her nipples with his left hand. But it was his right hand that sent her soaring. It slid into her jeans. Underneath her panties. He wasn't gentle, wasn't slow. His middle and index fingers eased into the slippery heat of her body and moved.

It didn't take much. Just a few of those clever strokes. Another deep French kiss. He nipped her nipple with his fingertips.

Their kiss muffled the sound she made, and his fingers continued to move, to give her every last bit of pleasure he could.

CAL CAUGHT HER to make sure she didn't fall. Jenna buried her face against the crook of his neck and let him catch her. Her breath came out in rough, hot jolts. Her body was trembling, her face, flushed with arousal.

She smelled like sex.

It was a powerful scent that urged his body to do a lot more than he'd just done. Of course, what he'd done was too much. He'd crossed lines that shouldn't have been crossed. In fact, he'd gone just short of what his director already suspected him of doing.

A husky laugh rumbled in Jenna's throat, and she blinked as if to clear her vision. Cal certainly needed to clear his. He made sure she was steady on her feet, and then he zipped up her jeans so he could step away from her.

She blinked again. This time, she looked confused, then embarrassed. "Oh, mercy. You could get into trouble for that."

He shrugged and left it at that.

"I keep forgetting that this has much stiffer consequences for you than it does for me." Still breathing hard, she pushed the wisps of blond hair from her face. A natural blonde. He'd discovered that when he unzipped her pants and pushed down her panties.

Now he needed to forget what he'd seen.

Hell. He just needed to forget, period.

"Of course, I'll get a broken heart out of this," she mumbled, and fixed her jeans.

A broken heart?

Did that mean she had feelings for him?

"Forget I said that," she mumbled a moment later. She looked even more embarrassed. "I'm not making sense right now."

So no broken heart. But still Cal had to wonder....

He didn't have long to wonder because his phone rang. The caller ID screen indicated it was Jordan.

"I was beefing up security by the front gate when a car pulled up," Jordan explained in the no-nonsense tone that Cal had always heard him use. "You have a visitor. She says her name is Gwen Mitchell and that she *must* talk to you."

"Gwen Mitchell's out front," Cal relayed to Jenna.

He wasn't exactly surprised. Everyone seemed to know where they were. But how should he handle this visit? He needed to question Gwen, but he didn't want to do that by placing Jenna and Sophie at risk.

"She says she has some new information you should hear," Jordan added. "She's refused to give it to me, but I can get it if you like. What do you want me to do with her?"

From Jordan, it was a formidable question. If Gwen had any inkling of the dangerous man that Jordan could be, she probably would have been running for the hills. Jordan was loyal to the end. He and Cal were close enough that he would trust Jordan to kill for him. Of course, he hoped killing Gwen wouldn't be necessary.

"Make sure she's not armed," Cal instructed. "And then escort her to the porch. I'll meet you at the front door."

"You're not going to let her in the house?" Jordan challenged.

"Not a chance."

Cal believed Gwen wanted one thing. A story. And even though he could relate to her devotion to duty, he was beginning to see that as a huge risk.

"You're meeting with her?" Jenna asked, following right behind him.

Cal locked the gun room door, using the key that Jenna had given him earlier. "I have a hunch that Gwen knows a lot more than she's saying. Plus, I want to hear what she considers to be important information."

"It could be a trap," Jenna pointed out.

"It could be, but if so, it's suicide. Jordan won't let an armed suspect make it to the door. Still, I want you to wait inside."

She huffed. For such a simple sound, it conveyed a lot. Jenna didn't like losing control of her life. But one way or another he was going to protect her.

"I'll stay in the foyer," she bargained. "Because you aren't actually going outside, are you?" She didn't wait for him to confirm that. "Besides, any information she has would pertain to me. Paul sent her after me because he thought I planned to murder him. I deserve to hear what she has to say."

He stopped at the front door, whirled around and stared at her. He had already geared up for an argument about why she shouldn't be present at this meeting, but Jenna pressed her fingers over his mouth.

"Don't let sexual attraction for me get in the way of doing what's smart," she said. Except it sounded like some kind of accusation.

"The sexual attraction isn't making me stupid."

"If you didn't want me in your bed," Jenna continued, "then you wouldn't be so protective of me. You'd let me confront Gwen." She frowned when he scowled at her. "Or you'd at least let me listen to what she has to say. I can do that as safely as you can. You already pointed out that Jordan will make sure Gwen isn't armed."

True. So why did he still feel the need to shelter Jenna from this conversation?

Hell. The attraction he felt for her could really complicate everything.

Cal scowled and threw open the front door.

Gwen was there, looking not at all certain of what she might have gotten herself into. Jordan probably had something to do with that. At six-two and a hundred and ninety pounds, he was no lightweight. He stood behind Gwen, looming over her. He was armed and had an extra weapon on his utility belt. In addition, he had a small communicator fitted into his left ear. He was no doubt getting updates from an associate somewhere on the grounds.

Jordan seemed to be doing a good job of neutralizing any threat from Gwen, but Cal took it one step further and made sure he was in front of Jenna.

"There's someone else waiting by the gate," Jordan informed them. "Archie Monroe. His ID looks legit. Says he's from Cryogen Labs."

Cal went on instant alert, and motioned for Jordan to come inside. He shut the door, leaving Gwen standing outside, and lowered his voice to a whisper. "Could it be Salazar?"

"Not unless he's had major cosmetic surgery. This guy's about sixty, gray hair and he's got a couple of spare tires around his middle."

"It's not Salazar," Jenna provided. Jordan and Cal stared at her. "He's a lab technician. I called Cryogen this morning and asked them to send out someone to do a DNA test on Sophie."

Cal choked back a groan and geared himself up for an argument.

Jenna beat him to it. "The DNA issue is hurting your career. I can't let it continue."

Cal opened his mouth. Then he closed it and tried to get hold of his temper. "I will not let you put my job ahead of Sophie's safety. Got that?" Then he turned to Jordan. "Tell him there's been a misunderstanding, that his services are not needed."

Jordan nodded and opened the door to hurry toward the front gate. Jenna didn't say anything else, but she did send Cal a disapproving look. He knew she didn't want this test. Not really. She wouldn't want to do anything to increase the risk of danger for Sophie. That's what made it even more frustrating.

She was doing this for him.

That attraction had *really* screwed up things between them.

"Is there a problem?" Gwen asked, glancing over her shoulder at Jordan, who was making his way to the lab tech.

"You tell me," Cal challenged. "Why are you here?"

Gwen's attention went to Jenna. "I know you didn't murder Paul."

Not exactly a revelation.

"That's why you came?" Jenna stepped closer. "To tell me something I already know?"

"I have proof. I got Paul's attorney to email me surveillance videos. There's not any actual footage of Paul being killed, but there is footage of you leaving the estate. Fifteen minutes later, there's footage of Paul coming out of his office to get something and then returning."

Cal knew all about that surveillance. The ISA had studied and restudied it. Well, Hollywood had. And Cal had reviewed it to make sure Jenna hadn't been the killer. The surveillance hadn't captured images of the person who'd entered Paul's office and shot him in the back of the head. Thermal images taken with ISA equipment had shown a person entering through a private entrance. No security camera had been set up there. Of course, the killer had to have known that.

"You could have called Jenna to tell her this," Cal pointed out.

Gwen shook her head. Her eyes showed stress. They were bloodshot and had smudgy dark circles beneath. "I think someone's listening in on my conversations. Someone's following me, too. I think it's because I'm getting close to unraveling all of this."

"Or maybe you're faking all this to cover your own guilt," Jenna countered.

Gwen didn't look offended. She merely nodded. "I could be, but I'm not." She gave a weary sigh. "I think there's a problem with the emails Paul wanted us all to receive."

"I'm listening," Cal said when she paused.

"I've been talking to Paul's attorney, and he told me that Paul wrote many emails and left instructions as to which to send out. For instance, if Jenna had had a baby, he was to send out set three. If any one of us, Jenna, Holden, Helena or Salazar, was dead by the time of the send-out date, then a different set was to be emailed."

"So?" Cal challenged. This wasn't news, either.

"So it wasn't the lawyer who determined which set was to go out. It was Holden."

"Holden?" he and Jenna said in unison. Whoa. Now *that* was news.

"I asked him, and he confirmed it. But he said he had no idea what was in the other emails. He claims that they were encrypted when they went out and that in Paul's instructions to him, he asked Holden not to try to decode them, that he wanted each email to be personal and private."

Well, that added a new twist, not that Cal needed this information to suspect Holden. Holden had a lot to gain from this situation, especially if he wanted to make sure he didn't have to share Paul's estate with his sister or any potential heirs.

But then, Gwen had motive, too. It could be that she just wanted a good story from all of this, but Paul had offered her a million dollars to find his killer. That was a lot of incentive to put a plan together. And there was another possibility: that Gwen hadn't just been involved in Paul's life but also his death.

Cal decided to go with an old-fashioned bluff.

"You didn't have any trouble getting Paul's lawyer to cooperate." He made a knowing sound. "Did you meet him when you were pretending to be Paul's maid? Are you the infamous Mary? And before you think about lying to me, you should probably know that I just read a very interesting intel report from an insider in Monte de Leon." That was a lie, of course, but Cal thought it would pay off.

Gwen's eyes widened, and she went a little pale. "Yes, I was Mary. I faked a résumé to get a job at Paul's estate, but he quickly figured out who I was."

The bluff had worked. Cal continued to push. "Is that when you killed him?"

"No." More color drained from her face, and she repeated that denial. "I didn't kill Paul."

"And why should I believe you?" Cal pressed.

"Because killing him wouldn't have helped me get

a story. I wanted the insider's view to Paul's business. With him dead, my story was dead, too."

"Now you've resurrected it with a new angle. You don't care that you're putting Jenna and her daughter in danger?"

"I don't know what you mean." Gwen's voice wavered. "I haven't put them in danger."

"Haven't you?" Jenna asked, stepping closer so that she was practically in Gwen's face.

"Not intentionally." She seemed sincere. Of course, she was a reporter after a story, so Cal wasn't buying it.

Cal saw something over Gwen's shoulder, and he re-aimed his gun. But it was Jordan, who was quickly making his way back to the porch.

"Hell. It's like Grand Central Terminal around here," Jordan grumbled. "I sent the lab guy on his way, but someone else just drove up. He says his name is Mark Lynch. Hollywood. And he wants to see all three of you."

Gwen flattened her hand on her chest. "Me?"

"Especially you."

CHAPTER ELEVEN

JENNA DIDN'T KNOW which surprised her more—that Hollywood had shown up or that he wanted to see Gwen. It was definitely a development that she hadn't seen coming. It could be very dangerous.

Her first instinct was to tell Jordan to stop Hollywood from getting any closer to the house. Sophie would be waking from her nap at any minute, and even though Meggie had instructions not to leave the nursery until she checked with them, if they let Hollywood in the gate, he would be too close to her baby.

Gwen was already too close.

"We could take this meeting to the gatehouse," Jenna suggested. That way, they could ask Hollywood how he knew Gwen and why he wanted to see her. Or why he wanted to see Cal and her, for that matter. Even though he didn't know it, he was a suspect.

Cal glanced at her. She knew that look. He was trying to figure out how to make this meeting happen so that she wasn't part of it.

"Hollywood asked to see me, too," Jenna reminded him.

"People don't always get what they want," Cal responded.

Before Jenna could challenge that, Gwen interrupted. "I don't want to see him." She managed to look indignant. Angry, even. "He's going to tell you that I'm behind the attempt to kill you. It's not true."

"Why would he tell us that?" Jenna demanded.

Silence. Gwen glanced over her shoulder as if to verify that Hollywood's car was indeed there.

"We'll go to the gatehouse," Cal insisted. "I'm interested in what Hollywood has to say about you. And himself." He turned to Jenna and took his backup weapon from an ankle holster. Cal handed it to her. "Stay close to me."

She nodded, taking the weapon as confidently as she could. Jenna didn't want Gwen to know that she didn't have much experience handling a gun.

Jenna also silently thanked Cal for not giving her a hassle about attending this impromptu meeting. That couldn't have been easy for him. His training made him want to keep her tucked away so she'd be safer. Part of Jenna wanted that, too. But more than her own safety, she wanted to get to the truth that would ultimately get her daughter out of danger.

Cal locked the front door before they stepped away from it. The chilly wind whipped at them as they went down the porch steps and across the front yard. Both Cal and Jordan shot glances around the estate, both of them looking for any kind of threat. However, Jenna felt their biggest threat was the man waiting on the other side of the gate.

Hollywood was there with his hands clamped around the wrought-iron rods. He stepped back when Jordan entered the code to open the gate.

"Thanks for seeing me," Hollywood greeted Cal. He volleyed glances at all of them, except for Gwen. He tossed her a venomous glare.

Jordan stepped forward, motioning for Hollywood to lift his arms, and searched him. He extracted a gun from a shoulder holster hidden beneath Hollywood's leather jacket. Hollywood didn't protest being disarmed. He merely followed Cal's direction when Cal motioned for him to go inside the gatehouse.

The building was small. It obviously wasn't meant for meetings, but Cal, Gwen and Jenna followed Hollywood inside. Jordan waited just outside the door with his body angled so that he could see both them and the house. Good. Jenna didn't want anyone trying to sneak in.

Hollywood aimed his index finger at Gwen. "Anything she says about me is a lie."

"Funny, she said the same thing about you," Cal commented.

"Of course she did. She wants to cover her butt."

"And you don't?" Gwen challenged.

Jenna decided this was a good time to stand back and listen. These two intended to clear the air, and that could give them information about what the heck was going on.

"I slept with her last year in Monte de Leon," Hollywood confessed to Cal. "And when I told her it couldn't be anything more than a one-night stand, she didn't take it well. I figured she'd be out to get me. She's the one who's setting me up. She wants to make it look as if I've been feeding information to Salazar."

"Don't flatter yourself." Gwen took a step closer and got right in Hollywood's face. "I wasn't upset about the breakup. I was upset with myself that I let it happen in the first place."

Hollywood cursed. "You planned it all. You came on

to me with the hopes I'd give you information about the ISA's investigation into Paul's illegal activities."

"I slept with you because I'd had too much to drink," Gwen tossed back.

Hollywood didn't have a comeback for that. He stood there, seething, his hands balled into fists and veins popping out on his forehead.

"So you slept with both Paul and Hollywood around the same time?" Jenna asked the woman.

Gwen nodded and had the decency to blush, especially since her affair with Paul had been a calculating way to get her story. That meant Hollywood might be telling the truth about Gwen's motives. But he still could have leaked information.

"How exactly could Gwen have set you up?" Cal asked, taking the words out of Jenna's mouth.

"I think she stole my access code and password while she was in my hotel room in Monte de Leon."

Jenna looked at Gwen, who didn't deny or confirm anything. But she did dodge Jenna's gaze.

"You reported that the code and password could have been compromised?" Cal asked.

"No. I didn't know they had been. Not until yesterday when I figured out that someone was tapping into classified information. I knew it wouldn't take long for Kowalski to think I was the one doing it."

"And you aren't?" Jenna asked point-blank.

"I'm not." There was no hesitation. No hint of guilt. Just frustration. But maybe Hollywood was true to his nickname—this could be just good acting.

"There's a lot going on," Hollywood continued. "Someone is pulling a lot of strings to manipulate this situation. Gwen wants a story, and she wants it to be big. That's why she's stirring the pot. That's why these crazy things are happening to all of us."

"Someone is out to get us," Cal clarified. "Someone tried to run me and Jenna off the road last night. And someone planted a tracking device on her car. You think Gwen is responsible for that?"

"Well, it wasn't me. I stayed back in Willow Ridge to look for that missing woman, Kinley Ford. Heck, I even called the FBI from town to let them know I'd learned the woman had been there. You can check cell tower records to confirm that."

Not really. Because with Hollywood's expertise, he could have figured out a way around that.

Hollywood swore under his breath and shook his head. "Gwen has the strongest motive for everything that's happening. She wants that story."

Gwen stepped forward, positioning herself directly in front of Hollywood. "Holden or Helena could be paying you big bucks for information. For that matter, the money could be coming directly from Paul's estate."

"I wouldn't take blood money," Hollywood insisted, ramming his finger against his chest. "But you would. So would Holden or Helena."

So this could all come down to money. That didn't shock Jenna, but it sickened her to know that her daughter could be in danger simply because someone wanted to get rich.

Cal glanced at Jordan to make sure the area was still safe. He waited until Jordan nodded before he continued the conversation with Hollywood. "Any reason you didn't tell me yesterday that you'd had sex with a person of interest in this investigation?"

The frustration in Hollywood's expression went up

a significant notch. His chest pumped with his harsh breaths. "Before you judge me, I think you should remind yourself why you're here. You slept with Jenna while she was in your protective custody."

Jenna wanted to set the record straight for Cal's sake, but he caught her hand and gave it a gentle warning squeeze.

"I can't trust either of you," Cal said to Hollywood and Gwen. "I don't care what your motives are. I want you to back off and leave Jenna and Sophie alone."

"You should be telling the Carrs this," Gwen pointed out.

"Maybe you'll do that for me." Cal didn't continue until Gwen looked him in the eye. "You can also tell them that Jenna, Sophie and I are leaving the estate within the hour. We're already packed and ready to go."

Jenna went still. Had Cal really planned that, or was this a ruse to get everyone off their trail?

"You think that's a wise move?" Hollywood asked.

"I think it's a *safe* move. And this time, I'll check and make sure there aren't any tracking devices on the vehicle we use."

Gwen turned and faced Jenna. Her expression wasn't as tense as Hollywood's, but emotion tightened the muscles in her jaw. "No matter where you go, the Carrs will find you."

"And you, too?"

Gwen shrugged and folded her arms over her chest. "I plan to write a story about Paul's murder."

"Then this meeting is over," Cal insisted. He put his hand on Hollywood's shoulder to get him moving out the door.

"I'm innocent," Hollywood declared. "But I don't

expect you to trust me. Just hear this, I'll do whatever's necessary to clear my name."

"If you do that, I'll be overjoyed. But for right now, I don't want you anywhere near Jenna or Sophie. Got that?" It was an order, not a request.

Hollywood nodded and walked out. So did Gwen. Both went to their respective vehicles, but Jordan didn't return Hollywood's gun until the man had started his engine and was ready to leave. Jenna and Cal stood inside the gatehouse and watched the duo drive away.

"Are we really leaving the estate?" Jenna asked.

"No," he whispered. "But I want to make it look as if we are. Then I can continue to beef up security here, and we can stay put until all of this is resolved."

Cal's plan seemed like their best option. She didn't like the idea of traveling anywhere while her daughter was a target.

They walked out of the gatehouse and started for the estate. After the battle they'd just had with their visitors, Jenna suddenly had a strong need to check on Sophie.

"You think Hollywood and Gwen will believe we're leaving?" She checked over her shoulder to make sure they were gone. Jordan was keeping watch to make sure they didn't double back.

"Jordan's employee will drive out of here in a couple of minutes," Cal explained. He caught her arm and picked up the pace to get them to the porch. "He'll be using a vehicle with heavily tinted windows. As an extra precaution we won't use any of the house phones. They might be tapped, and I don't want anyone to know we're here. We can use the secure cell phone that Director Kowalski gave to me."

Jenna hoped that would be enough. And that Kowalski hadn't given Cal compromised equipment. After all, someone had managed to put those tracking devices on their cars.

"Get down!" she heard Jordan yell.

Jenna started to look back at him to see what had caused him to shout that, but Cal didn't give her a chance. He hooked his arm around her waist and dragged her between the flagstone porch steps and some shrubs.

Jordan dove into the gatehouse. His eyes were darting all around, looking for something.

But what?

Jenna didn't have to wait long for an answer.

"Salazar's on the grounds," Jordan shouted.

CHAPTER TWELVE

IF SALAZAR WAS on the grounds, he had come there for one reason: to get Sophie. If the assassin had to take out Jenna and Cal, that wouldn't matter. A man like Salazar wouldn't let anything get in the way of trying to accomplish his mission.

Later, after Cal had gotten Jenna out of this mess, he'd want to know just how Salazar had managed to get through what was supposed to be the secured perimeter of the estate. But for now, he had to focus on keeping Jenna and Sophie safe.

He lifted his head a little and assessed their situation. Jordan was in the doorway of the gatehouse, but he hadn't pinpointed Salazar's position. But someone had. Probably Jordan's assistant, Cody Guillory. The man had spotted Salazar and relayed that info through the communicator Jordan was wearing. Since Cal didn't know the exact location of Jordan's assistant, that meant Salazar could be anywhere.

Cal glanced at the front door. It was a good twenty feet away. It wasn't that far, but they'd literally be out in the open if he tried to get Jenna inside. Besides, it was locked and it would take a second or two to open it. That'd be time they were in Salazar's kill zone. Not a good option. At least if they stayed put, the stone steps would give them some protection.

Unless Salazar planned to launch explosives at them.

"Call Meggie," Cal said, handing Jenna his cell phone. "Make sure she's okay. Then tell her to set the alarm and move Sophie to the gun room."

He didn't risk looking at Jenna, though he knew that particular instruction would be a brutal reminder of the danger they were in. Jenna already knew, of course, but by now she probably had nightmarish images of Salazar breaking into the house.

With her voice trembling and her hands shaking, Jenna made the call. Cal shut out what she was saying and focused on their surroundings. He tried to anticipate how and where Salazar would launch an attack. There were more than a dozen possibilities. Salazar might even try to take out Jordan first.

A shot cracked through the air and landed in one of the porch pillars.

Cal automatically shoved Jenna farther down just in time. The next shot landed even lower. It sliced through the flagstone step just above their heads. Salazar had gone right for them. Cal prayed that Meggie had managed to set that alarm and get Sophie into the gun room.

The third shot took a path identical to the second. So did the fourth. Each bullet chipped away at the flagstone and sent jagged chunks of the rock flying right at them. Hell. Maybe staying put hadn't been such a good idea after all. Now they were trapped in a storm of shrapnel.

Cal pushed aside the feeling that he'd just made a fatal mistake and concentrated on the direction of the shots. Salazar was using a long-range assault rifle from somewhere out in the formal garden amid the manicured shrubs and white marble statues. There were at least a hundred places to hide, and nearly every one of them would be out of range for Cal's handgun.

Another shot sent a slice of the flagstone ripping across Cal's shirtsleeve. Since the rock could do almost as much damage as a bullet, he crawled over Jenna, sheltering her as much as he could. She was shaking, but she also had a firm grip on the gun he'd given her earlier. Yes, she was scared, but she was also ready to fight back if she got the chance. This wasn't the same woman he'd rescued in Monte de Leon. But then, the stakes were higher for her now.

She had Sophie to protect.

His only hope was that Salazar would move closer so that Cal would have a better shot or Jordan could get to him. One of them had to stop the man before he escalated the attack.

There was another spray of bullets, and even though Cal sheltered his eyes from the flying debris, he figured Salazar had succeeded in tearing away more layers of their meager protection. Cal couldn't wait to see if Salazar was going to move. He had to do something to slow the man down.

Cal levered himself up just slightly and zoomed in on a row of hedges that stretched between two marble statues. He fired a shot in that direction.

A shot came right back at Cal, causing him to dip even lower. From the gatehouse, Jordan fired a round. He was as far out of range as Cal. But between the two of them, they might manage to throw Salazar off his own deadly aimed shots. Not likely, though. Plus, they couldn't just randomly keep firing or they'd run out of ammunition.

But there was a trump card in all of this. Jordan's

assistant. Maybe Cody Guillory was working his way toward Salazar so he could take him out.

The shots continued, the sound blasting through the chilly air and tainting it with the smells of gunpowder, sulfur and smoke. The constant stream of bullets caused his ears to ring. But the ringing wasn't so loud that he didn't hear a sound that sent his stomach to his knees.

The alarm. Someone had tripped the security system.

Which meant someone had broken in. Salazar or his henchman. Salazar normally worked alone, but this time he obviously hadn't come solo. There must be two of them. One firing at them while the other broke inside. Both trained to the hilt to make sure this mission was a success.

Jenna tried to get up. Cal shoved her right back down. And not a moment too soon. A barrage of bullets came their way. Each of the shots sprayed them with bits of rock and caused their adrenaline levels to spike. As long as those shots continued, it'd be suicide to try to get to the door and into the house.

But that was exactly what Cal had to do.

Meggie and Sophie were probably locked in the gun room, but that didn't mean Salazar wouldn't try to get to them. Hell, he might even succeed. And then he could kidnap Sophie and sneak her out, all while they were trapped out front dodging bullets.

"I'm going in," Cal told her. "Stay put."

She was shaking her head before he even finished. "No. I need to get to Sophie."

"I'll get to her. You need to stay here."

It was a risk. A huge one. Salazar could have planned it this way. Divide and conquer. Still, what was left of the steps was better protection than dragging Jenna onto the porch. Cal took a deep breath and got ready to scramble up the steps.

But just like that, the shots stopped.

And that terrified him.

Had the shooter left his position so he, too, could get into the house?

"Cover me," Cal shouted to Jordan, knowing that the man couldn't do a lot in that department. Still, fired shots might cause a distraction in case the gunman was still out there and ready to strike.

Cal didn't bother with the house keys. That would take too long. He'd have to bash in the door and hope that it gave way with only one well-positioned kick.

Jordan started firing shots. Thick blasts that he aimed at the hedges and other parts of the formal garden.

"I'm going with you," Jenna insisted.

Cal wanted to throttle her. Or at least yell for her to stay put. But he couldn't take the time to do either. Jordan's firepower wouldn't last. Each shot meant he was using up precious resources.

"Now," Cal ordered since it seemed as if he would have a partner for this ordeal.

He climbed over the steps, making sure that Jenna stayed to his side so that she wouldn't be in the direct line of fire from anyone who might still be in those hedges. Cal reached the door and gave it a fierce kick. It flew open, thank God. That was a start. But it occurred to Cal that he could be taking Jenna out of the frying pan and directly into the fire.

Cal shoved her against the foyer wall and placed himself in front of her. He disarmed the security system to stop the alarm. Then he paused, listening. He tried to

pick through the sounds of Jordan's shots and the house.
And he heard something he didn't want to hear.

Footsteps.

Someone was running through the house. Hopefully
Meggie was in the gun room. The obvious answer was
Salazar.

"I have to get to Sophie," Jenna said on a rise of
breath. She broke away from him and started to run
right toward those footsteps.

JENNA BARELY MADE IT a step before Cal latched on to
her and dragged her behind him.

Her first instinct was to fight him off. To run. So she
could get to her baby to make sure she was safe. But
Cal held on tight, refusing to let her go.

"Shhh," he warned, turning his head in the direction
of those menacing footsteps.

Salazar had managed to break through security, and
he was probably inside, going after Sophie.

Cal started moving quietly, but quickly. He kept her
behind him as he made his way down the east corridor
toward the gun room.

"Keep watch behind us," he whispered.

Jenna automatically gripped her gun tighter, and slid
her index finger in front of the trigger. It was ironic that
just an hour earlier she'd gotten her first shooting lesson, and now she might have to use the skills that Cal
had taught her. She hoped she remembered everything
because this wouldn't be a target with the outline of a
man. It would be a professional assassin.

That was just the reminder she needed. It didn't matter if she had no experience with a firearm. She'd do
whatever was necessary to protect Sophie.

Cal's footsteps hardly made a sound on the hard-wood floors of the corridor. Jenna tried to keep her steps light as well, but she knew she was breathing too hard. And her heartbeat was pounding so loudly that she was worried someone might be able to hear it. Though with Cal bashing down the door, the element of surprise was gone. Still, she didn't want Salazar to be able to pinpoint their exact location.

Just in case, she lifted her gun so that she'd be ready to fire.

She and Cal moved together, but it seemed to take an eternity to reach the L-shaped turn in the corridor. Cal stopped then and peered around the corner.

"All clear," he mouthed.

No one was anywhere near the door to the gun room. Of course, that didn't mean that someone hadn't already gotten inside.

Her heart rate spiked, and she held her breath as they approached the room. The door was shut, and while keeping watch all around them, Cal reached down and tested the knob.

"It's locked," he whispered.

She released the breath she'd been holding, only to realize that Salazar could still have gotten inside and simply relocked the door.

Cal pressed the intercom positioned on the wall next to the door. "Meggie, is everything okay?" he whispered.

"Yes," the woman immediately answered.

Relief caused Jenna's knees to become weak. She had to press her left hand against the wall to steady herself. "Sophie's okay?"

"She's fine. What's going on?"

But there was no time to answer.

Movement at one end of the hall made Cal pivot in that direction. "Get down," he ordered her.

Jenna ducked and glanced in that direction. She saw the dark sleeve of what appeared to be a man's coat. Salazar.

Cal fired, the shot blistering through the corridor.

She didn't look to see what the outcome of that shot was because she saw something at the other end of the hall.

With her heart in her throat, she took aim. Waited. Prayed. She didn't have to wait long. A man peered around the corner. He had a gun and pointed it right at her.

Jenna didn't even allow herself time to think. This man wasn't getting anywhere near her daughter.

She squeezed the trigger and fired.

CHAPTER THIRTEEN

CAL FORCED JENNA to sit on the leather sofa of the family room.

He didn't have to exert much force. He just gently guided her off her feet. She wasn't trembling. Wasn't crying. But her blank stare and silence let him know that she was probably in shock.

Once the director was finished with the initial investigation and reports, Cal needed to talk her into getting some medical care. She'd already refused several times, but he'd keep trying.

Two men were dead.

Cal was responsible for one of those deaths. He'd taken out Salazar with two shots to the head. Jenna had neutralized Salazar's henchman. Her single shot had entered the man's chest. Death hadn't been immediate—he'd died while being transported to the hospital. Unfortunately, the man hadn't made any deathbed confessions.

Cal got up, went to a bar that was partly concealed behind a stained-glass cabinet door and poured Jenna a shot of whiskey. "Drink this," he said, returning to the sofa to sit next to her.

As if operating on autopilot, she tasted it and grimaced, her eyes watering.

"Take another sip," he insisted.

She did and then finished off the shot. She set the glass on the coffee table and folded her hands in her lap. "Does killing someone ever get easier?" she asked.

"No."

He hated that this was a lesson she'd had to learn. What she'd done was necessary. But it would stay with her forever.

She glanced around the room as if seeing the activity for the first time. Director Kowalski was there near the doorway, talking to two FBI agents and a local sheriff. They were all lawmen with jurisdiction, but Kowalski was unofficially leading the show. This had international implications, and there were people who would want to keep that under wraps.

Jenna's eyes met his. The blankness was fading. She was slowly coming to terms with what had happened, but once the full impact hit her, she'd fall apart.

But Cal would be right there to catch her.

"Sophie," she said, sounding alarmed. She started to get up. "I need to check on her again."

Cal caught her. "I just checked on her a few minutes ago. Sophie's fine. Jordan's still with her and Meggie in the nursery. Even though there's no way she'd remember any of this, I didn't want her to be out here right now."

His attention drifted in the direction of the corridor, where federal agents were cleaning up the crime scene.

Cal didn't want Sophie anywhere around that.

Jenna nodded. "Thank you."

He saw it then. Jenna's bottom lip trembled. He slid his arm around her and hoped this preliminary investigation would end soon so her meltdown wouldn't happen in front of the others.

"You did a good thing in that corridor," Cal reminded her. "You did what you needed to do."

The corner of her mouth lifted, but there was no humor in her smile. "You gave me a good shooting lesson."

Yeah. But he'd given her that lesson with the hopes that she'd never have to use a gun.

Kowalski stepped away from the others and walked toward them. He stopped, studied Jenna and looked at Cal. "Is she okay?"

"Yes," Jenna answered at the exact moment that Cal answered, "No."

The director just nodded. "I don't want any of this in a local report," he instructed Cal. "The sheriff has agreed to back off. No questions. He'll let us do our jobs, and the FBI will file the official paperwork after I've read through and approved it."

"I'll need to give a statement," Jenna concluded. Emotion was making her voice tremble.

"It can wait," Kowalski assured her. "But I don't want you talking to anyone about this, understand?"

"Yes." This would be sanitized and classified. No one outside this estate would learn that an international assassin had entered the country to go after a Texas heiress. The hush-up would protect Jenna and Sophie from the press, but it wouldn't help Jenna deal with the aftermath.

"Any idea how Salazar got onto the grounds?" Cal wanted to know.

"It appears he was here before your friend Jordan Taylor even put his security measures into place. There's evidence that Salazar was waiting in one of the storage buildings on the property."

Smart move. That meant Salazar had used the tracking device on Jenna's car to follow them to the estate, and he'd hidden out for a full day, waiting for the right time to strike. But why hadn't Salazar attacked earlier, when he and Jenna were outside meeting with the others? The only answer that Cal could come up with was that he had wanted as few witnesses as possible when he went after Sophie.

"Salazar and his accomplice broke in through French doors in one of the guest suites," Kowalski continued. "We believe the plan was to locate the child, kill anyone they encountered and then escape."

Jenna pressed her fingertips to her mouth, but Cal could still hear the soft sob. He tightened his grip on her, and it didn't go unnoticed. Kowalski flexed his eyebrows in a disapproving gesture.

Cal ignored him. "What about all the rest? Any idea who hired Salazar or if Hollywood had any part in this?"

The director shook his head. "There's no evidence to indicate Agent Lynch is guilty of anything. He might have been set up."

That's what Hollywood was claiming, and it might be true. Still, Cal wasn't about to declare anyone's innocence just yet. "Who was paying Salazar?"

"The money was coming from Paul's estate, but his attorney will almost certainly say that he was unaware the payment was going to a hired killer."

"He might not have known," Cal mumbled.

Kowalski shrugged. "The ISA will deal with the attorney. But the good news is that Ms. Laniere and her child seem to be out of danger."

Jenna looked at the director. Then at Cal. He saw new concern in her eyes.

"I'm not leaving," Cal assured her.

That got him another flexed-eyebrow reaction from the director. "Tie things up around here," Kowalski ordered. "I want you back at headquarters tomorrow."

Cal got to his feet. "I'd like to take some personal time off."

"I can't approve that. Tomorrow, the promotion list should be arriving in my office. You'll know then if you've gotten the deputy director job." Kowalski's announcement seemed a little like a threat.

Choose between Jenna and the job.

"I'm sorry," Jenna whispered. She stood, too, and this time moved Cal's hand away when he tried to catch her. "I'm going to check on Sophie."

No. She was going to fall apart.

"I'll be at headquarters tomorrow," Cal assured the director. "But I'm still requesting a personal leave of absence." Without waiting to see if Kowalski had anything else to mandate, Cal went after Jenna.

She was moving pretty fast down the corridor, but he easily caught up with her. She didn't say anything. Didn't have to. He figured she was already trying to figure out how she was going to cope without him there.

Cal was trying to figure out the same thing.

Jordan stood in the doorway of the nursery. His gun wasn't drawn, but it was tucked away in a shoulder holster. "Everything okay?" he wanted to know.

Jenna maneuvered past him and went straight to her daughter. Sophie was awake and making cooing sounds as Meggie played peekaboo with her. Jenna scooped up the little girl in her arms and held on.

"The director and all the law enforcement guys will be leaving within an hour or two," Cal informed Jordan. He didn't go closer to Jenna. He stood back and watched as she held Sophie. "The threat might be over, but I'd like you to stay around for a while."

Jordan followed Cal's gaze to Jenna. "Is this job official?"

"No. Personal."

Jordan's attention snapped back to Cal. "You? Personal?"

"It happens."

Jordan didn't look as if he believed that. He shrugged. "I can give you two days. After that, it'll just be Cody. But he's good. I trained him myself."

Cal nodded his thanks. Hopefully, two days would be enough to tie up those loose ends the director had mentioned. Now if Cal could just figure out how to do that.

"Is she willing to take a sedative?" Jordan asked, tipping his head to Jenna.

Cal didn't have to guess why Jordan had asked that. He could see Jenna's hand shaking. "Probably not." Even though it would make the next few hours easier.

"My advice?" Jordan said. "Liberal shots of good scotch, a hot bath and some sleep."

All good ideas. Cal wondered if Jenna would cooperate with any of them. But when she began to shake even harder, she must have understood that merely holding her baby wasn't going to make this all go away.

Cal went to her and took Sophie. The little girl looked at him as if she didn't know if she should cry or smile. She settled for a big, toothless grin, which Cal realized made him feel a whole lot better. Maybe he'd been wrong about the effects of holding her. He kissed her cheek, got another smile and then handed her to Meggie.

"See to Jenna," Meggie whispered, obviously concerned about her employer.

Cal was concerned, too. He looped his arm around Jenna's waist and led her out of the nursery. She didn't protest, and walked side by side with him to her suite.

"It's stupid to feel like this," Jenna mumbled. "That man would have killed us if I hadn't shot him."

Her words were true. But he doubted the truth would make it easier for her to accept.

"You're so calm," she pointed out, stepping inside the room. It was the first time he'd been in her suite. Like the rest of the house, it was big and decorated in soothing shades of cream and pale blue. He wasn't counting on those colors to soothe her, though. It'd take more than interior decorating to do that.

Cal shut the door. "I'm not calm," he assured her.

"You look calm." Her voice broke on the last word. Cal waited for tears, but she didn't cry. Instead, she moved closer to him. "My baby's safe," she muttered. "We're safe. Salazar is dead. And you'll be leaving soon to go back to headquarters."

He shook his head, not knowing what to say. Yes, he probably would leave for that morning meeting with Kowalski. He opened his mouth to answer, to try to reassure her that he'd be back. But Jenna pressed her hand over his lips.

"Don't make promises you can't keep," she said. She tilted her head to the side and stared at him. "I'm going to do something really stupid. Something we'll regret."

Jenna slid her hand away, and her mouth came to his, kissing him.

The shock of that kiss roared through Cal for just a split second. Then the shock was replaced with the jolt of something stronger—pleasure. His body automatically went from comfort and protect mode to something primal. Something that had him taking hold of her and dragging her to him.

He made that kiss his own, claiming her mouth. Taking her. Demanding all that she had to give.

His hands were on her. Her hands, on him. Their embrace was hungry, frenzied. Both of them wanted more and were taking it.

And then he got another jolt…of reality.

Sex wasn't a good idea right now. Not with Jenna on the verge of a meltdown.

He forced himself to stop.

With her breath gusting, Jenna looked at him. "No," she said. She came at him again. There was another fast and furious kiss. It was hard, brutal and in some ways punishing. It was also what she needed.

Cal felt the weariness drain from her. Or maybe she was merely channeling all her emotions into this dangerous energy. She shoved him against the door, fusing her mouth to his, her hands going after his shirt.

Part of him wanted to get naked and take her right there. But only one of them could get crazy at the same time. Since Jenna had latched on to that role, Cal knew he had to be the voice of reason.

But then her breasts ground against his chest. And her sex pressed against his.

Oh, yeah.

That put a dent in any rational thought.

Still, somehow, he managed to catch her arms and

hold her at bay so he could voice a little of the reasoning he was desperately trying to hang on to.

"You're not ready for this," he insisted.

"I'm ready." There wasn't any doubt in her tone. Her eyes. Her body.

She shook off his grip, took his hand and slid it down into the waist of her loose jeans. Into her panties. She was wet and hot.

Oh, mercy.

Then she ran her own palm over the very noticeable bulge in his pants. "You're ready."

"No condom," he ground out.

Jenna's eyes widened, and she darted away from him. She ran to a dresser on the other side of the room, and frantically began searching through the drawers. Several moments later, she produced a foil-wrapped condom.

Cal didn't give her even a second to celebrate. He locked the door and hurried to her. He grabbed the condom, and in the same motion, he grabbed her. He kissed her and backed her against the dresser.

The kiss continued as they fought with each other's clothes. He got off her top, and while he wanted to sample her breasts—man, she was beautiful—his body was urging him in a different direction.

With her butt balancing her against the edge of the dresser, he stripped off her jeans. And her white lace panties. By then, she was all over him. Her mouth, hungry on his neck. Her hands fighting with his zipper. She won that fight, and took him into her hands.

Cal didn't breathe for a couple of seconds. He didn't care if he ever breathed again. He just wanted one thing.

Jenna.

He opened the condom and put it on. "This is your last chance to say no."

She looked at him as if he were crazy. Maybe he was. Maybe they both were. Jenna hoisted herself up on the edge of the dresser.

"I'm saying yes," she assured him.

To prove it, she hooked her legs around him, thrust him forward and he slid hot and deep into her.

He stilled a moment. To give her time to adjust to the primal invasion of her tight body. He watched her face, looking for any sign that she might be in pain.

Angling her body back, she slid forward, giving him a delicious view of her breasts and their joined bodies.

She wasn't the pampered heiress now. She was his lover. Funny, he hadn't thought she would be this bold, but he appreciated it on many, many levels.

"Don't treat me like glass," she whispered.

"No intention of that," he promised.

He caught her hair and pulled her head back slightly to expose her neck. He kissed there and drove into her.

Hard.

Fast.

Deep.

Her reaction was priceless. Something he'd remember for the rest of his life. She grabbed him by his hair and jerked his head forward, forcing eye contact. And with her hand fisted in his hair, she moved, meeting him thrust for thrust.

Their mouths were so close he could almost taste her, but she was just out of reach. Instead, her breath caressed his mouth while her legs tightened around him.

Their frantic rhythm created the friction that fueled her need. It became unbearable. She closed around him, her body shuddering. The unbearable need went to a whole different level.

She sighed his name. "Cal." Jenna repeated it like some ancient plea for him to join her in that whirl of primitive pleasure.

Cal leaned in, pushing into her one last time. He kissed her and surrendered.

Even with his pulse crashing in his ears and head, he heard the one word that came from his mouth.

Jenna.

SHE WAS HALF-NAKED on a dresser. Out of breath, sweaty and exhausted. And coming down from one of the worst days of her life. Yet it'd been a long time since Jenna had felt this good. She bit back a laugh. Cal would think she was losing her mind.

And maybe she was.

This shouldn't have happened. Being with Cal like this only made her feel closer to him. It only made her want him more. But that wasn't in their future. She was well on her way to a broken heart.

"Hell," Cal mumbled. "We had sex on the dresser."

He blinked as if trying to focus and huffed out short jolts of breath. He was sweaty, too. And hot. Just looking at him made her want him all over again.

"You don't think I'm the sex-on-the-dresser type?" she asked, trying to keep things light for her own sanity. She couldn't lose it. Not now. Because soon, very soon, Cal would begin to regret this, and she didn't want her fragile mental state playing into his guilt.

With his breath still gusting, he leaned in and brushed a kiss on her mouth. It went straight through her, warm and liquid. "I thought you'd prefer sex on silk sheets," he mumbled.

Still reeling a little from that kiss, she ran her tongue over her bottom lip and tasted him there. "No silk sheets required."

Just you. Thankfully she kept that thought to herself.

He withdrew from her, gently. Unlike the firestorm that'd happened only moments earlier. Cal helped her to her feet, made sure she was steady and then he went into the adjacent bathroom.

Jenna took a moment to compose herself and remembered there were a lot of people still in her house. FBI, Kowalski, the sheriff. She started to have some doubts of her own. She should be focusing on the shootings.

But the shootings could wait. Right now she needed to put on a good front for Cal, spend some time with her daughter and try to figure out where to go from here.

Her old instincts urged her to run. To try to escape emotions she didn't want to face. But running would only be a temporary solution. She looked up and could almost hear her father saying that to her. Funny that it would sink in now when her life was at its messiest.

She needed to stay put, and concentrate on getting Helena, Holden and Gwen out of her life. While she was at it, she also needed to hold her daughter. Oh, and she had to figure out how to nurse her soon-to-be-broken heart.

With her list complete, she started to get dressed. She was still stepping into her jeans when Cal returned.

He looked at her with those scorching blue eyes and had her going all hot again. Jenna pushed aside her desire, reminding her body that it'd just gotten lucky. That wasn't going to happen again any time soon.

"You okay?" he asked.

Jenna nodded and was surprised to realize that it was true. She wasn't a basket case. She wasn't on the verge of sobbing. She felt strong because she had been able to help protect her baby.

He shoved his hands into his pockets. "When things settle down, you might want to see a therapist. There are a lot of emotions that might come up later."

She nodded again and put her own hands in her pockets. "Now that Salazar is dead, it's time to clear up Sophie's paternity with your director."

He looked down at the floor. "Best not to do that. We don't know who hired Salazar, and until we do, nothing is clear."

Confused, Jenna shook her head. "But certainly it doesn't matter if everyone knows that Sophie is Paul's biological child."

"It might matter." He paused and met her gaze. "Gwen was having an affair with Paul. Helena, too. Either could be jealous and want to get back at you. Either could have sent Salazar to take Sophie because they feel they should be the one who's raising her."

Oh, God. She hadn't even considered that, and she couldn't dismiss it. Both Helena and Gwen hadn't been on the up-and-up about much of anything.

"Holden could be a problem, too," Cal continued. "Paul might have told him to take any child that you and he might have produced. The child would be Paul's heir, and Holden would like nothing more than to control the heir to a vast estate."

Her chest tightened. It felt as if someone had clamped

a fist around her heart. "So Sophie could still be in danger?"

"It's possible." He took his hands from his pocket and brought out his phone.

Alarmed, she crossed the room to him. "What are you going to do?"

"Something I should have done already." He scrolled through the numbers stored in his phone, located one and hit the call button. "Director Kowalski," he said a moment later. "Are you still at the estate? I need to speak to you."

Jenna shook her head. "No," she mouthed.

But Cal didn't listen to her. He stepped away, turning his back to her. "I'll meet you in the living room in a few minutes." He hung up and walked out the door.

She caught his arm. "What are you going to say to him?"

"I'll tell him that I lied. That Sophie is my daughter. I want to start the paperwork to have Sophie legally declared my child. I'll do that when I get to headquarters in the morning."

Oh, mercy. He was talking about legally becoming a father. Cal would make an amazing dad. She could tell that from the way he handled her daughter. But this arrangement would cost him that promotion.

"You don't have to do this," Jenna insisted. "We'll find another way to make sure she's safe."

"There is no other way." He caught her shoulders and looked her straight in the eye. "This is your chance at having a normal life. This way you won't always be looking over your shoulder."

"But what about you? What about your career?"

A muscle flickered in his jaw, and she saw anger flare in his eyes. "Do you really think I'm the kind of man who would endanger a child for the sake of a promotion?" He sounded disappointed. "I'm going to do this, Jenna, with or without your approval."

And with that, he walked out.

CHAPTER FOURTEEN

CAL HADN'T EXPECTED Kowalski's ultimatum.

But he should have. He should have known the director wasn't going to let him have a happy ending.

He stood at the door and watched Kowalski, the FBI agents and the sheriff drive away. Now that the sun had set, a chilly fog had moved in, and the cars' brakes lights flashed in the darkness like eerie warnings. Jordan was there to shut the gate behind them. He gave Cal a thumbs-up before heading in the direction of the garden. He was probably going to give his assistant some further instructions about security.

The security measures wouldn't be suspended simply because everyone else had left the estate. Jordan, or one of his employees, would stay on as long as necessary. Of course, Cal still had to get out the word, or rather the lie, that Sophie was his child. Once that was done, he would deal with the ultimatum Kowalski had delivered just minutes before he left.

Cal closed the front door, locked it and reset the security system before he went in search of Jenna. He dreaded this meeting with her almost as much as he'd dreaded the one he'd just had with Kowalski. He felt both numb and drained.

He'd killed a man today. It was never easy even when necessary as this one had been. But his difficulty dealing with the death was minor compared to Jenna's. She'd killed a man, too. Her first. In fact, the first time she'd ever fired a gun at another human being.

This would stay with her forever.

Maybe that's why sex had followed. That was a sure-fire way to burn off some of her high-anxiety adrenaline. Cal shook his head.

It had felt real. And that was a big problem.

He'd compounded it by arguing with Kowalski. The conversation had been necessary, and Cal didn't regret it. But that wouldn't make his chat with Jenna any easier. She needed to know what the director had ordered him to do. And then he somehow had to convince her, and himself, that he could follow through and do what had to be done.

Cal found her in the kitchen. Meggie was at the stove adding some seasoning to a great-smelling pot roast. Jenna was seated at the table feeding Sophie a bottle. Jenna looked as tired and troubled as he felt.

Unlike Sophie.

When the little girl spotted him, she turned her head so that the bottle came out of her mouth. And she smiled at him.

He smiled right back.

Weariness drained right out of him. He wasn't sure how someone so small could create dozens of little daily miracles.

Sophie squirmed, pushing the bottle away, and made some cooing sounds.

"I interrupted her dinner," he commented. Cal sat in the chair next to them.

"She was just about finished, anyway." Jenna's tone was tentative, and she studied him, searching his eyes for any indication of how the conversation with Kowalski had gone.

Sophie reached for him, and Cal took her into his arms. He got yet another smile. It filled him with warmth and it broke his heart.

What the devil was he going to do?

How could he give up this child who'd already grabbed hold of him?

"Something's wrong," Jenna said. She touched his arm gently, drawing his attention back to her.

"Uh, I need to check on something," Meggie suddenly announced. She adjusted the temperature on the pot roast and scooted out of the kitchen. She was a perceptive woman.

"Well?" Jenna prompted.

Best to start from the beginning. "Kowalski didn't buy my story about being Sophie's father. The ISA has retrieved one of Sophie's pacifiers from your apartment in Willow Ridge and compared the DNA to mine. Kowalski knows I'm not a match. It's just a matter of time before he learns that Paul is."

"I see." She repeated it and drew back her hand, letting it settle into her lap. "Well, that's good for you. He doesn't still think you slept with me, does he?"

"No." Cal brushed a kiss on Sophie's cheek. "And Kowalski will keep the DNA test a secret."

He hoped. Kowalski had promised that, anyway.

"But?" Jenna questioned.

"I told him I still wanted to do the paperwork to have Sophie declared my child. I want the DNA test doctored. I want anyone associated with Paul to believe she's mine so they'll back off."

Jenna fastened her attention on him. "There's more, isn't there?"

Cal cleared his throat. "In the morning you'll go into temporary protective custody. Kowalski will leak the fake DNA results through official and unofficial channels, and you and Sophie will stay in protective custody until everyone is sure the danger has passed. He thinks it shouldn't be more than a month or two before the ISA finds out who's responsible for this mess and gets that person off the streets."

"The ISA?" she repeated after a long pause. "But you said your organization doesn't normally handle domestic situations."

"Sometimes they make exceptions."

"I see." Jenna paused again, studying him. Worry lines bunched up her forehead. "And what about you? How does all of this affect you?"

Cal took a deep breath. "Kowalski will tell the chief director the truth, that this is all part of a plan to guarantee your safety." Another deep breath. "In exchange for his guarantee of your safety, Kowalski wants me to extract myself from the situation."

Her eyes widened. "Extract?" she questioned. "What does that mean exactly?"

He'd rehearsed this part. "Kowalski thinks I've lost my objectivity with you and Sophie. He thinks I'll be a danger to both of you and myself if I stay." Cal choked back a groan. "It's standard procedure to extract an agent when there's even a hint of any conflict of interest."

Though nothing about this felt standard. Of course, Cal couldn't deny that he'd stepped way over a lot of lines when it came to Jenna.

Sophie batted him on the nose and put her mouth on his cheek as if giving him a kiss.

Cal took yet more deep breaths. "By doctoring the records and the DNA, Kowalski will be protecting you. But he wants me to swear that I won't see you or Sophie until there's no longer a threat to either of you."

Jenna went still. "But the threat might always be there."

Cal nodded and watched the pain of that creep into her eyes.

She quickly looked away. "Okay. This is good. It means you'll probably get your promotion. Sophie will be safe. And I'll get on with my life." Jenna stood, walked across the room and looked out the window. "So when do you leave?"

"Kowalski wanted me to leave immediately, but I told him I'd go in the morning when the ISA agents arrive."

She stood there, silent, with her back to him.

It was because of the sudden silence in the room that Cal had no trouble hearing a loud crash that came from outside the house.

He got to his feet, and while balancing Sophie, he took out his phone to call Jordan. But his phone rang first. Jordan's name and number appeared on the caller ID screen.

"Cal, we've got a problem," Jordan informed him. "Someone just broke though the front gate."

Before Cal could question him, there was another sound. One he definitely didn't want to hear.

Someone fired a shot.

JORDAN'S VOICE WAS LOUD enough that Jenna heard what he said. If she hadn't heard the crash, she might have wondered what the heck he was talking about. But there was no mistaking the noise of something tearing through the metal gates.

And then it sounded as if someone had fired a gun. It was too much to hope that the noise was from a car backfiring.

While Cal continued to talk with Jordan, Jenna reached for Sophie, and Cal reached for his gun.

"Try to contain the situation as planned," Cal instructed Jordan. "I'll take care of things here."

He shoved his phone back into his pocket and turned to her to give her instructions. But Meggie interrupted them when she came running back into the kitchen.

The woman was as pale as a ghost. "I saw out the window," she said, her voice filled with fear. "A Hummer rammed through the gate. Some guys wearing ski masks got out, and one of them shot the man that came here with Jordan Taylor."

Jenna's gaze went to Cal's, and with one look he confirmed that was true. "How many men got out of the Hummer?" Cal asked Meggie. He sounded calm, but he gripped Jenna's arm and got them moving out of the kitchen.

"Four, I think," Meggie answered. "Maybe more. All of them had guns."

Four armed men. Jenna knew what they were after: Sophie. Salazar had failed, but someone else had been sent to do the job.

There was another shot. Then another. Thick blasts that sounded like those that had come from Salazar. Someone was shooting a rifle at Jordan. He was out there and under attack. It wouldn't be long, maybe seconds, before the gunman got past Jordan and into the house.

Cal headed for the gun room. There was no escape route there, and Jenna knew what he planned to do. Cal wanted Meggie, Sophie and her to be shut away behind bulletproof walls while he tried to protect them. But it was four against two. Not good odds especially when her daughter's safety was at stake.

"I'm going to help you," Jenna insisted. She handed Sophie to Meggie and motioned for the woman to go deep into the gun room. Jenna grabbed two of the automatic weapons from the case.

"I need to make sure you're safe," Cal countered. Though he was busy grabbing weapons and ammunition, he managed to toss her a firm scowl. "You're staying here."

Outside, there was a flurry of gunfire.

Jenna shook her head. "You need backup." She wasn't going to hide while Cal risked his life. "If they get past Jordan and you, the gunmen will figure out a way to get into that room. They might even have explosives. Sophie could be hurt."

He shoved some magazines of ammo into his pockets, then stopped and stared at her. "I can't risk you getting hurt."

She looked him straight in the eye. "I can't risk Sophie's life. I'm going, Cal. And you can't stop me."

He cursed, glanced around the room at Sophie and Meggie. If her daughter was aware of the danger, it certainly didn't show. Sophie was cooing.

"Stay behind me," Cal snarled to Jenna.

She didn't exactly celebrate the concession, though

she knew for him, it was a huge one. Jenna looked at Sophie one last time.

"Lock the door from the inside and stay in the center of the room, away from the walls," Cal instructed Meggie. Then he shut it.

Jenna didn't have time to dwell on her decision because Cal started toward the end of the corridor.

"What's the plan?" she asked.

"We go to the front of the house where the intruders are, but we stay inside until we hear from Jordan. He'll try to secure the perimeter."

"Alone? Against four gunmen?" Mercy, that didn't sound like much of a plan at all. It sounded like suicide.

"Jordan knows how to handle situations like these." But Cal didn't sound nearly as convinced as his words would pretend.

Jenna didn't doubt Jordan's capabilities, either. But he was outnumbered and outgunned.

"Jordan knows I have to stay inside," Cal added. He headed straight for the front of the house, and Jenna was right behind him. "I'm the last line of defense against anyone trying to get to Sophie."

However, they only made it a few steps before there was another crash. It sounded as if someone had bashed the front door in.

Oh, God.

Jenna's heart began to pound as alarms pierced through the house. The security system had been tripped.

Which meant someone was inside.

CHAPTER FIFTEEN

THIS COULD NOT be happening.

He and Jenna had already survived one attack from Salazar, and now they were facing another.

He pulled Jenna inside one of the middle rooms off the corridor and listened for any sign that it was Jordan who'd burst through that door. But he knew Jordan would have identified himself. Jordan was a pro and wouldn't have risked being shot by friendly fire.

And that meant it was the gunmen who'd bashed their way in.

So Jenna and he had moved from being backups to primary defense. He sure as hell hadn't wanted her to be in this position, but there was no other choice. They might need both of them to stop the gunmen from getting to Sophie. The gun room was much safer than the rest of the house, but it wasn't foolproof. If the gunmen eliminated them, they'd eventually find their way to Sophie.

Cal was prepared to die to make sure that didn't happen.

He heard movement coming from the foyer. He also heard Jenna's breathing and then her soft mumbling. She was mouthing something, probably meant to keep her calm.

It wouldn't work.

Not with her child at risk. Cal was trained to deal with these types of intense scenarios, and even with all that training, he had to battle his emotions.

And that made this situation even more dangerous.

He forced himself to think like an operative. He was well equipped to deal with circumstances just like this. So what would happen next? What did he need to do to make this survivable?

At least four armed men had invaded the house. Even if they knew the layout, they wouldn't know where Sophie was. Which meant they'd have to go searching for their prize. They wouldn't do that as a group.

Too risky.

Too much noise.

They'd split up in pairs with one pair taking the west corridor. The other would take the east, which was closer to the gun room. The pairs would almost certainly search the entire place, going from room to room. That meant at least two would soon be coming their way. The other two wouldn't be that far behind.

Cal eased out of the doorway so he could see the west corridor entrance. Even though he didn't hear anything, he detected some movement and saw a man in a blue ski mask peer around the corner, so, "Blue" was already in place and ready to strike.

Cal didn't make any sudden moves. For now, he needed to stay put and stay quiet, all the while hoping the doorjamb would conceal him.

A moment later, Blue and his partner quietly stepped into the corridor. Blue ducked into a room to search it, and the other kept watch. ·

Cal was going to have to do this the hard way. He didn't want to start a gun battle in the very hallway of the gun room, but he didn't have a choice. He'd have to take out the guy standing guard, and the moment he did that, it would put his partner and the other pair of gunmen on alert. Of course, they already knew he was in the house. They already knew he was trained to kill.

The question was: how good were they?

And the answer to that depended on who had hired them.

If it was Hollywood, well, Cal didn't want to think about how bad this could get. Hollywood had as much training as he did. They'd be an equal match. And God knows how this would end.

Cal didn't want to risk giving away his position, so he hoped that Jenna would stay put and not make any sounds. He got his primary gun ready, and without hesitating, he leaned out just far enough to get a clean shot.

The one standing guard saw him right away as Cal had expected. And he turned his gun on Cal. But it was a split second too late. Cal fired first. He didn't want to take any chance that this guy would survive and continue to be a threat, so he went with three shots, two to the head, one to the chest.

The gunman fell dead to the floor.

Jenna's breathing kicked up a notch, and he was sure she was shaking. He couldn't take the time to assure her that they'd get out of this alive. Because they might not. Those first shots were the only easy ones he would get. Everything else would be riskier.

Cal volleyed his attention between the room being searched and the other end of corridor. He needed help, and as much as he hated it, it would have to come from Jenna.

He angled himself in the doorway so that he was

partly behind the cover of the doorframe. "Watch," he instructed Jenna in a whisper. "Let me know when the gunmen come around the corner."

It was just a matter of time.

Cal's only hope was to take care of the Blue who was still in the room, and then start making his way toward the other pair. To do that, Jenna and he would have to use the rooms as cover. And then they'd have to pray that the second pair didn't backtrack and take the same path of their comrades. Cal didn't want them to be ambushed.

And there was one more massive problem.

While he watched for Blue to make an appearance from the room, Cal thought through the simple floor plan he'd seen on the security panel door. The east and west corridors flanked the center of the house, but there was at least one point of entry that the pair in the west hall could use to get to the side of the house where he and Jenna were.

The family room.

It could be accessed from either hall.

And if the pair used it, that meant they'd be making an appearance two rooms down on the right. He hoped that was the only point where that could happen. Of course, the floor plan on the security panel could have been incomplete.

But he couldn't make a plan based on what he didn't know. The most strategic place for Jenna and him to be was in that family room. That way they could guard the corridor and guard against an ambush. First, though, he had to neutralize Blue.

There was still no movement near the dead gunman's body. No sound of communication, either. Cal couldn't wait too long or all three would converge on them at once. But neither could he storm the room. Too risky. He had to stay alive and uninjured so he could get Jenna, Meggie and Sophie out of this.

"Go back inside," he instructed Jenna in as soft a whisper as he could manage. "Move to your right and aim at the room where Blue is. Fire a shot through the wall and then get down immediately."

She didn't question him. Jenna gave a shaky nod and hurried to get into position. Cal kept watch, dividing his attention among Blue's position, the family room and the other end of the corridor.

Cal didn't risk looking at Jenna, but there was no way he could miss hearing her shot. The blast ripped through the wall and tore through the edge of the door-frame of the other room.

Perfect.

It was exactly where Cal wanted it to go. And Jenna did exactly as he'd asked. He heard her drop to the floor.

Cal didn't have to wait long for a response. Blue re-turned fire almost immediately, and Cal saw a pair of bullets slam into the wall behind them. He calculated the angle of the shots, aimed and fired two shots of his own.

There was a groan of pain. Followed by a thud.

Even though he knew his shots had been dead-on, Cal didn't count it as a success. Blue could be alive, waiting to attack them. Still, there was a better than fifty-fifty chance that Cal had managed to neutralize him.

"Let's go," Cal whispered to Jenna. He had to get moving toward the family room, and he couldn't leave her alone. As dangerous as it was for her to be with him and out in the open, it would be more dangerous for her to stay put and run into the gunmen.

Jenna hurried to the doorway and stood next to him. She had her weapon ready. He only hoped her aim continued to be as good as that last shot.

"We go out back to back," he said. "You cover that end." He tipped his head toward the dead guy and the room with the bullet holes in the wall. "When we get to the family room, I want you to get down."

Judging from her questioning glance, Jenna didn't approve. Tough. He didn't want to have to worry about her being in the line of fire, and he would have three possible kill zones to cover.

Cal took out a second automatic so he'd have a full magazine, and stepped into the hall. Out in the open. Jenna quickly joined him and put her back to his. He waited just a second to see if anyone was going to dart out and fire at them. But he didn't see or hear anything.

"Let's go," he whispered.

They got moving toward the family room. Cal didn't count the steps, but each one pounded in his head and ears as if marking time. He thought of Sophie. Of Jenna. Of the high stakes that could have fatal consequences. But he pushed those thoughts aside and focused on what he had to do.

When they reached the family room, he stopped and peered around the doorway. The room was empty.

Or at least it seemed to be.

The double doors that led to the east corridor were shut. That was good. If they'd been open, the gunmen on that side of the house would have heard them. Cal was counting on those closed doors to act as a buffer. And a warning. Because when the pair opened them to search the room, Cal would hear it and would be able to shoot at least one of them.

"Check the furniture," Cal told her. "Make sure we have this room to ourselves."

She moved around him while he tried to keep watch in all directions. But Jenna had barely taken a step when there was a sound.

Cal braced himself for someone to bash through the doors. Or for one or more of the gunmen to appear in the corridor. But the sound hadn't come from those places.

It'd come from above.

He glanced up and then heard something else. Hurried footsteps. He spotted a lone gunman as he rounded the corner of the east corridor. Cal turned to take him out.

"Check the ceiling," Cal told Jenna as he fired at the man. But the man ducked into a room, evading the shot.

Cal made his own check of the ceiling then. Just a glance. The next sound was even louder. Maybe someone moving around in the attic.

He didn't have to wait long for an answer.

Two things happened simultaneously. The gunman who'd just ducked into the room across the hall darted out again. And there was a crash from above. Cal hadn't noticed the concealed attic door on the ceiling. It'd blended in with the decorative white tin tiles. But he noticed it now.

THE ATTIC DOOR flew back, and shots rang out from above them.

Cal shouted for her to get down, but Jenna was already diving behind an oversize leather sofa. From the moment she saw that attic door open, she knew what was about to come.

An ambush.

At least one of the gunmen had accessed the attic, and now she and Cal were under attack.

She fired at the shooter in the attic and missed. He ducked back out of sight. She couldn't see even his shadow amid the pitch-darkness of the attic.

But shots continued to rain down through the ceiling. That alone would have sent her adrenaline out of control, but then she thought of Sophie.

Oh, God.

Was the ceiling in the gun room bulletproof?

She couldn't remember her father saying for certain, but she had to pray that it was. She hoped there was no attic access in there. But just in case, they needed to take care of this situation so they could make sure that Sophie and Meggie were all right.

Cal fired, causing her attention to snap his way. He wasn't aiming at the ceiling, but rather at someone in the east end of the hall. Mercy. They were under attack from two different sides.

Dividing her focus between Cal and the ceiling shooter, Jenna saw a bullet slice through Cal's shirt-sleeve. Bits of fabric fluttered through the air.

"Get down," she yelled, knowing it was too late and that he wouldn't listen.

Cal leaned out even farther past the cover of the doorway and sent a barrage of gunfire at the shooter in the hall. If Cal was hurt, he showed no signs of it, and there wasn't any blood on his shirt. He was in control and doing what was necessary.

Jenna knew she had to do the same.

She took a deep breath, aimed her gun at the ceiling and fired. She kept firing until the magazine was empty, and then she reloaded.

There was no sign of life. No sounds coming from above. She kept her gun ready, snatched the phone from the end table and pressed the intercom function.

"They might come through the attic," she shouted into the phone. She hoped the warning wouldn't give away Sophie's location.

Jenna tossed the phone aside and aimed two more shots into the ceiling. On the other side of the room, Cal continued to return fire.

The gunman continued to shoot at him.

Bullets were literally flying everywhere, eating their way through the walls and furniture. The glass-top coffee table shattered, sending the shards spewing through the room.

Cal cursed. And for one horrifying moment, Jenna thought he might have been hit.

Then the bullets stopped.

Jenna peered over at Cal—he wasn't hurt, thank God—and he motioned for her to get up. Since he no longer had his attention fastened to the corridor, that meant another gunman must be dead.

But there was still at least one in the attic.

Except with the silenced guns, she no longer heard any movement there. Had the person backtracked?

Or worse—had he managed to get into the gun room?

"Meggie, are you okay?" Cal shouted in the direction of the phone. He was trying to use the intercom to communicate.

While Cal kept watch of their surroundings, Jenna

scurried closer to the phone that she'd tossed aside on the floor. She, too, kept her gun ready, but she put her ear closer to the receiver.

And she held her breath, waiting. Praying. Her daughter had to be all right.

"I hear something," Meggie said. "Someone's moving in the attic above us."

Oh, God. Even if that ceiling was bulletproof, it didn't mean a person couldn't figure out a way to get through it. If that happened, Meggie and Sophie would be trapped.

Jenna put her hand over the phone receiver so that her voice wouldn't carry throughout the house. "Someone's trying to get into the gun room through the attic," she relayed to Cal.

He cursed again and reloaded. The empty magazine clattered onto the hardwood floor amid the glass, drywall and splinters. He motioned for her to get up, and Jenna knew where they were going.

To the gun room.

It was a risk. They could be leading the other shooter directly to Sophie, but judging from Meggie's comments, he was already there.

"Take the phone off intercom," Cal mouthed. "Tell Meggie we're coming, but I don't want her to unlock the door until we get there."

That meant for those seconds, she and Cal would be out in the open hall. In the line of fire. But that was better than the alternative of putting her daughter at further risk.

Still keeping low, Jenna hurried back to the phone cradle and pushed the button to disconnect the intercom. She dialed in the number that would reach the line in the gun room. Thankfully, Meggie picked up on the first ring.

"Cal and I are on the way," she relayed. "Don't unlock the door until you're sure it's us."

"What's going on, Jenna?" Meggie demanded. "Where are Cody and Jordan?"

Jenna feared the worst about Jordan. They hadn't heard a peep from the man since the gun battle. Jordan must be hurt or worse.

Jenna heard a slight click on the line, and knew what it meant. Someone had picked up another extension and was listening in.

"I can't talk now," Jenna said to Meggie, hoping the woman wasn't as close to panic as she sounded. "Just stay put...in the pantry. We'll be there soon."

She hung up and snared Cal's gaze. "Someone picked up one of the other phones."

Cal nodded.

Jenna hoped the lie would buy them some time so they could get inside the gun room. She got up so she could join Cal at the doorway.

"We do this back to back again. And hurry," he whispered. "It won't take the gunman long to figure out that they're not in the pantry."

Jenna raced toward him and got into position. She would cover the left end of the corridor. He'd cover the right just in case the gunman was still in place. They had at least thirty feet of open space between them and the gun room.

However, before either of them could move, something crashed behind them. They turned, but somehow got in each other's way.

And that mistake was a costly one.

Because the ski-mask-wearing man who broke through the doors on the other side of the family room started shooting at them.

CHAPTER SIXTEEN

CAL SHOVED JENNA out of the doorway and into the corridor. She'd have bruises from the fall, maybe even a broken bone, but her injuries would be far worse if he didn't get her out of there.

He dove out as well, somehow dodging the spray of bullets that the gunman was sending right at them. He barely managed to hang on to his guns.

This wasn't good. Either the guy in the attic had gotten to them ridiculously quickly, or there were more men in the house than they knew.

Cal didn't dwell on that, though. With his gun ready in his right hand, he caught Jenna with his left and dragged her to her feet. He got them moving, not a second too soon. Another round of shots fired, all aimed at them. Because he had no choice, Cal pushed Jenna into the first room they reached.

It was a guest room. Empty, he determined from his cursory glance of the darkened area. Thankfully, there was a heavy armoire against the wall between the family room and this room. That meant there was a little cushion between them and the shooter.

Cal positioned Jenna behind him and got ready to fire. "Other than where we're standing, is there any another way to access this room?" he whispered.

She groaned softly, and the sound had a raw and ragged edge to it. "Yes."

Hell. He was afraid she would say that. "Where?"

"There's a small corridor off the family room," she explained, also in a whisper. "It leads to that door over there."

Cal risked glancing across the room. He figured it was too much to hope that it would be locked or, better yet, blocked in some way. But maybe that didn't matter— this gunman had a penchant for knocking down doors.

He peered around the door edge, saw the shooter and pulled back just as another shot went flying past him.

Well, at least they knew the shooter's location: inside the family room. "Make sure that door over there is locked," he instructed. "And drag something in front of it."

He'd keep the shooter occupied so that he didn't backtrack and go after them. Of course, that wouldn't do much to neutralize the one in the attic.

"Jenna?" someone called out.

It was Meggie. It took Cal a moment to realize her voice had come over the central intercom. Anyone in the house could hear her. Hopefully, they hadn't already pinpointed her location.

Cal glanced at Jenna, to warn her not to answer.

"Someone's trying to get in here," Meggie said.

Sophie was crying. She sounded scared. She probably was. It broke Cal's heart to know he couldn't get to her and soothe her.

God knew what this was doing to Jenna. The sound of her baby's tears had to be agony. This was a nightmare that would stay with her.

Cal wanted to check on her, but he needed to see if anyone was in front of that gun room door. It was a risk. But it was one he had to take.

He took a deep breath and tried to keep his wrist loose so he could shift his gun in either direction. He leaned out slightly, angling his eyes in the direction of the gun room. No one was there, which probably meant someone was still trying to get through the attic. He didn't have time to dwell on that, though.

A bullet sliced across Cal's forearm. His shooting arm. Fire and pain spiked through him, but he choked it back and took cover.

But for only a split second.

With the sound of Sophie's cries echoing in the corridor and his head, Cal came right back out with both guns ready, and started shooting. He didn't stop until he heard the sound he'd been listening for.

The sound of someone dying.

Still, he didn't take any chances. While keeping watch all around them, he eased out of the room and walked closer until he could see the fallen gunman on the floor. His aim had hit its mark.

The guy was dead all right. The bullet in his head had seen to that. His eyes were fixed in a lifeless, blank stare at the ceiling.

Cal glanced up and listened, wanting to hear the position of the fifth and hopefully final gunman. He heard something. But the sound hadn't come from the attic. It'd come from the guest room, where he'd left Jenna to block the door.

Hell.

He sprinted toward her, aimed his gun and prayed that the only thing he'd see was her trying to block that other door leading from the family room.

But that door was wide open.

Jenna was there, amid the shadows. Her face said it all. Something horrible had happened.

It took Cal a moment to pick through the shadows. Someone was standing behind Jenna.

And whoever it was had a gun pointed at her head.

JENNA REFUSED TO PANIC.

Her precious baby was crying for her. And Jenna wanted nothing more than to make sure that Sophie was okay. But she couldn't move, thanks to the ski-mask-wearing monster who'd come through the door off the family room.

It'd only taken the split-second distraction of Sophie's crying and the shots Cal had fired. Jenna had been listening to make sure he was okay. And because of that, she hadn't been watching the door. The gunman had literally walked through it and grabbed her. The gun had been put to her head before she'd even had time to react.

Now that mistake might get them both killed.

Cal stopped in the doorway, and Jenna watched him assess the situation. Either this person was going to kill them both, or he'd try to force them to give him access to the gun room.

That wasn't going to happen. Which meant they might die right here, right now.

"I'm sorry," Jenna said to Cal.

He didn't answer. He kept volleying his attention between her and the corridor, looking for the guy who'd been in the attic. Of course, that gunman could be the very person who now had a semiautomatic jammed to her head.

"I'm in here!" the guy behind Jenna suddenly yelled

out. He ripped off his ski mask and shoved it into his jacket pocket. "Get down here now!"

Except it wasn't a man.

It was Helena Carr.

Jenna hadn't known whom to expect on the other end of that gun. Holden, Hollywood, Gwen and Helena had all been possibilities. All had motives, though they hadn't seemed clear. But obviously Helena's motive was powerful enough to make her want to kill.

"I'm stating the obvious here," she said, "but if either of you makes any sudden moves, I'll kill you where you stand."

"You're planning to do that anyway," Cal tossed back at her.

"Not yet. You're going to give me that screaming baby, and then you'll die very quick, painless deaths."

Oh, God. It was true. She wanted Sophie. Thankfully, her little girl's sobs were getting softer. Jenna could hear Meggie trying to soothe her, and it appeared to be working.

"Why are you doing this?" Jenna demanded.

"Lots of reasons." That was the only answer Helena gave before she started maneuvering Jenna toward the door where Cal was standing.

"Put down your guns," Helena ordered. "All of them."

Cal dropped the one from his right hand. He studied Helena's expression as she came closer. He must have seen something he didn't like because he dropped the other one, too.

Jenna's heart dropped to the floor with those weapons.

Cal wouldn't have any trouble defeating Helena if it came down to hand-to-hand combat, but Helena wasn't going to let it get to that point. She would use Jenna as a human shield to get into that gun room. Worse, she had a henchman nearby. After all, Helena had called out to someone.

With Jenna at gunpoint and Cal unarmed, this could turn ugly fast. It was a long shot, but she had to try to reason with Helena.

"Why do you want my baby?" Jenna asked. She hated the tremble in her voice. Hated that she didn't feel as in charge and powerful as Helena. She desperately wanted the power to save Sophie.

"I don't *want* your baby." Helena shoved her even closer to Cal. "But I need to tie up some loose ends."

So this was about Paul's estate. He'd left Helena some diabolical instructions as to what to do to her in the event of his death.

"I didn't do anything to hurt Paul," Jenna pleaded. "There's no reason for you to seek revenge for him."

"I'm not doing this for Paul."

Jenna heard footsteps behind her.

Helena's associate pulled off his ski mask and crammed it into his pocket. He was a bulky-shouldered man with edgy eyes. A hired gun, waiting to do whatever Helena told him to do.

"What?" Cal questioned Helena. "You don't have the stomach to kill us yourself?"

Jenna couldn't see the woman's expression, but from the soft sound that Helena made, she probably smiled. "I've killed as many men as you have—including Paul when I learned he was sleeping with both Gwen Mitchell and Jenna. The man had the morals of an alley cat."

"He slept with me to get his hands on my business,"

Jenna pointed out. "And Gwen slept with him to get a story. There was no affection on his part."

"That doesn't excuse it. I'm the one who set up your meeting with Paul. I'm the one who suggested he marry you so he could inherit your estate. Sleeping with you and getting you pregnant was never part of the bargain. He was supposed to marry you, drug you and then lock you away until the time was right to eliminate you completely."

"So why kill us? Why take Sophie?" Cal demanded.

Jenna could have sworn the woman's smile widened. "Oh, I don't want to take her. With my brother out of the way, I can inherit Paul's entire estate. Once any other heirs have been eliminated."

Helena's threat pounded in Jenna's head. She wasn't going to kidnap Sophie. She was going to kill her.

That wasn't going to happen. Rage roared through her. This selfish witch wasn't going to lay one hand on her child.

"Kill Agent Rico," Helena ordered the gunman.

Jenna heard herself yell. It sounded feral, and she felt more animal than human in that moment. She didn't care about the gun to her head. She didn't care about anything other than protecting Sophie and Cal.

She rammed her elbow into Helena's stomach and turned so she could grab the woman's wrist. Jenna dug her fingernails into Helena's flesh and held on.

A bullet tore past her.

Not aimed at her, she realized. The shot had come from the gunman, and it'd been aimed at Cal.

Jenna couldn't see if Cal was all right. Helena might have had a pampered upbringing, but she fought like a wildcat, clawing and scratching at Jenna. It didn't matter. Jenna didn't feel any pain. She only felt rage, and she used it to fuel her fight all while praying that Cal had managed to survive that shot.

The gunman re-aimed.

"It's me," someone shouted. Jordan. He was alive.

That only gave Jenna more strength. She latched on to Helena with both hands and shoved the woman right at her accomplice. But the gunman got off another shot.

It seemed as if everything froze.

The bullet echoed. It was so loud that it stabbed through her head and blurred her vision. But Jenna didn't need clear vision to see the startled look on Helena's face.

The woman dropped her gun and pressed her hand to her chest. When she drew it back, her palm was soaked with her own blood. Her hired gun had accidentally shot her.

Helena smiled again as if amused at the irony. But the smile quickly faded, and she sank in a limp heap next to her gun.

Jenna forced her attention away from the woman. But she didn't have time to stop the gunman from taking aim at Cal again.

Another shot slammed past her, so close that she could have sworn she felt the heat from the bullet. A second later, she heard the deadly thud of someone falling to the floor.

The echo in her head was already unbearable and this blast only added to it. That, and the realization that Cal could be hurt.

Or dead.

She felt tears burn her eyes and was afraid to look, terrified of what she might see.

But Cal was there, his expression mirroring hers.

"I'm alive," Jenna assured him.

So was he.

He raced to her and pulled her into his arms.

CHAPTER SEVENTEEN

CAL TRIED NOT to wince as the medic put in the first stitch on his right arm.

He'd refused a painkiller. Not because he was alpha or enjoyed the stinging pain. He just wanted to speed up the process. It seemed to be taking forever. He had other things to do that didn't involve stitching a minor gunshot wound.

"Hurry," he told the bald-headed medic again.

The medic snorted and mumbled something that Cal didn't care to make out. Instead, he listened for the sound of Jenna's voice. The last he saw of her, Kowalski was leading her out of the family room so he could question her.

Cal wasn't sure Jenna was ready for that. He certainly wasn't. Cal needed to see her, to make sure she wasn't on the verge of a meltdown. But Kowalski had ordered him to get stitches first. Cal had figured that would take five minutes, tops, but it'd taken longer than that just for the medic to get set up.

He heard footsteps and spotted Jordan in the doorway. The man looked like hell. There was a cut on his jaw that would need stitches, another on his head and he probably had a concussion.

Still, Jordan was alive, and an hour ago, Cal hadn't thought that was possible.

A fall had literally saved him. Jordan had explained that he'd climbed onto the gatehouse roof to stop the attack, but one of the gunmen had shot him. A minor scrape, like Cal's. But the impact of the shot had caused Jordan to fall off the roof, and he'd lain on the ground unconscious through most of the attack.

It was a different story for Jordan's assistant. Cody had been shot in the chest and was on his way in an ambulance to the hospital.

Of course, Cody was lucky just to be alive. Their attackers had obviously thought they'd killed him or else they would have put another bullet in him.

"All the gunmen are dead and accounted for," Jordan relayed.

"What about Jenna?" Cal wanted to know.

"Still talking to Kowalski in the kitchen." Jordan looked down the hall. "But you're about to get a visitor."

Cal winced. He was going crazy here. But he changed his mind when Jordan stepped aside so that Meggie could enter. She had Sophie in her arms.

"Hurry," Cal repeated to the medic.

"I'm done," the guy snapped. He motioned for Jordan to have a seat.

Cal gladly gave up his place so he could go to Sophie. The little girl automatically reached for him, and even though he had blood splattered on his shirt, he took her and pulled her close to him. Like always, Sophie had a magical effect on him. He didn't relax exactly, but he felt some of the stress melt away.

"You've seen Jenna?" he asked Meggie.

The woman shook her head. "She's still with your boss."

Enough of that. She shouldn't have to go through an

interrogation alone. Cal shifted Sophie in his arms and started for the kitchen.

"Your boss has been getting all kinds of phone calls," Meggie said, trailing along behind him. "I heard him say that the guy who works for Jordan is going to be all right."

Good. That was a start. But God knows what Jenna was going through.

Cal got to the kitchen and saw Jenna seated at the table. Kowalski was across from her, talking on the phone. Jenna had her face buried in her hands.

"Jenna?" Cal called out.

Her head snapped up, and he saw her face. No tears. Just a lot of weariness.

"You're okay," Jenna said, hurrying to him.

She gathered both Sophie and him into her arms. Her breath broke, and tears came then. Cal just held on and tried to comfort her. However, the hug was cut short—Kowalski ended his call and stared at them. God knows what the man was thinking about this intimate family embrace.

And Cal didn't care.

"Holden Carr is dead," Kowalski announced.

Cal didn't let Jenna out of his arms, but he did turn slightly so he could face the director.

"Helena murdered him before she came here with her hired guns," Kowalski continued. "It appears from some notes we found in the Hummer that she eliminated her brother so he wouldn't be competition for Paul's estate."

"That's why she wanted Sophie out of the way," Cal mumbled, though he hated to even say it aloud. He had seen the terror in Jenna's eyes when she realized what Helena wanted to do. Cal had felt the same terror in his heart.

The director nodded. "Helena was going to set up Hollywood to take the blame."

"And what about Gwen Mitchell?" Jenna asked. "Did she have anything to do with this?"

"Doesn't look that way. She just wanted a story. Helena did everything else. She planted the tracking devices on your cars. Tried to run you off the road. Faked emails from Paul and sent Salazar after you. Helena wanted to get you and your daughter out of the way."

So it'd all been for money. No hand from the grave. No rogue agent. Just a woman who wanted to inherit two estates and not have to share it with anyone.

"With Helena dead, the threat to Sophie is over?" Jenna asked. Cal reached over and wiped a tear from her cheek.

"It's over. You and your daughter are safe." Kowalski tipped his head toward Cal's stitches. "How about you? Are you okay?"

"Yeah." Cal had already decided what to say, and he didn't even hesitate. "But I'm not going to stay away from Jenna and Sophie."

Kowalski made a noncommittal sound and reached into his jacket pocket. "That's the letter from the promotion committee. Read it and get back to me with your decision."

"I don't have to read it. I'm not going to stay away from them."

"Suit yourself." Kowalski strolled closer. "There's no reason for me to continue with that order. Ms. Laniere is no longer in your protective custody. What you two do now is none of my business."

It took Cal a moment to realize the director was backing down. There was no reason Cal couldn't see Jenna. Well, no legal reason, anyway. It was entirely possible that Jenna would want him gone just so she could have a normal life.

Cal couldn't give her normal.

But maybe he could give her something else.

Kowalski walked out, and Cal realized that Jenna, Sophie and he were alone. Meggie had left, too. Good. Cal had some things to say, and he needed a little privacy.

He was prepared to beg.

Cal looked at Sophie first. "I want to be your dad. What do you say to that?"

Sophie just grinned, cooed and batted at his face.

He nodded. "I'll take that as a yes." He kissed the little girl's cheek and turned to Jenna.

"Yes," she said before he could open his mouth.

"Yes?" he questioned.

"Yes, to whatever you're asking." But then her eyes widened. "Unless you're asking if you can leave. Then the answer to that is no."

This had potential.

"Wait," Jenna interrupted before he could get out what he wanted to say. "I've just put you in an awkward position, haven't I?" She glanced at the letter. "You'll want to leave if you didn't get the promotion."

"Will I?"

She nodded. "Because it'll be my fault that you lost it. You resent me. Maybe not now. But later. And when you look at me, you'll think of what I cost you."

Cal frowned. "In less than a minute, you've covered

a couple months, maybe even years, of our future. But for now, I'd like to go back to that yes."

"What about the letter?" she insisted. "Don't you want to know if you got the promotion?"

"Not especially."

But Jenna did. She snatched the letter from the table, opened it and unfolded it so that it was in his face. Cal scanned through it.

"I got the promotion," he let her know. Then he wadded up the letter and tossed it.

Jenna's mouth opened, and she looked at him as if he'd lost his mind. "Don't you want the promotion?"

"Sure. But it's on the back burner right now. I'm going to ask you something, and I want you to say yes again."

She glanced at the letter, at Sophie and then him. "All right," Jenna said hesitantly.

"Will you make love with me?"

Jenna blinked. "Now?"

Cal smiled, leaned down and kissed her gaping mouth. "Later. I'm just making sure the path is clear."

"Yes." Jenna sealed that deal with a kiss of her own.

"Will you move to San Antonio with me so I can take this promotion?"

"Yes." There was no hesitation. He got another kiss. A long, hot one.

Hmmm. Maybe he could talk Meggie into watching Sophie while they sneaked off to the bedroom. But Cal rethought that. He intended to make love to Jenna all right, but he wasn't looking for a quickie. He wanted to take the time to do it right. To savor her. To let her know just how important she was to him.

And that led him to his next question. "Will you marry me?"

Tears watered her eyes. "Yes."

Cal knew this was exactly what he wanted. Sophie and Jenna. A ready-made family that was his.

"Now it's your turn to answer some questions," Jenna said. "Are you sure about this?"

"Yes." He didn't even have to think about it.

"Why?"

Cal blinked. "Why?" he questioned.

"Yes. Why are you sure? Because I know why I am. I'm in love with you."

Oh. He got it now. Jenna wanted to hear the words, and Cal wasn't surprised at all that he very much wanted to say them.

He eased Jenna's hand away and kissed her. "I'm sure I love you both," Cal told them. "And I'm sure I want to be with you both forever."

Jenna smiled, nodded. "Good. Because I want forever with you, too."

It was perfect. All the yeses. The moment. The love that filled his heart. The looks on Jenna's and Sophie's faces. It wasn't exactly quiet and intimate with Sophie there, batting at them and cooing, but that only made it more memorable.

Because for the first time in his life, Cal had everything he wanted, right there in his arms.

* * * * *

We hope you enjoyed reading

Deception Lodge

by *New York Times* bestselling author

LISA JACKSON

and

Expecting Trouble

by *USA TODAY* bestselling author

DELORES FOSSEN

Both were originally Harlequin® series stories!

From passionate, suspenseful and dramatic
love stories to inspirational or historical,
Harlequin offers different lines to
satisfy every romance reader.

New books in each line are available every month.

SPECIAL EXCERPT FROM

HQN

*With her life in free fall, Hadley Dalton returns to
Lone Star Ridge, Texas, to check on her beloved
grandmother—and quickly discovers the woman's
embarked on a mysterious road trip. Hadley's best hope
of bringing her home is Sheriff Leyton Jameson, a man
she's been trying to get out of her head for decades.
Now, as they work to uncover clues to the
past, they struggle to resist the attraction that refuses
to be ignored...*

Read on for a sneak peek at
Wild Night in Texas,
the third book in the Lone Star Ridge series from
USA TODAY bestselling author Delores Fossen.

"I want you," she went on. "You know that already. You
can tell by the way I look at you."

He risked touching her by gently putting his fingers
under her chin and turning her head so they were facing
each other. Yeah, he could tell by the way she looked
at him that she wanted him. Could also tell that it was
causing a war inside her. Leyton wanted sex, but he
didn't want this to spin her into a bad place. That made
him a good guy. A very hard, very frustrated good guy.

The silence came again, but she didn't look away.
Hadley kept her eyes locked with his, and he waited—not
easily, though—for her to make the first move. Or rather

the second one. She'd made the first move by coming to this room.

"I can handle something casual," she added a moment later. "Something that won't mean more than just sex."

His erection thought that was a damn good idea, and had this been any other woman but Hadley, he would have already had his mouth on her. But Hadley was different. Fragile. And it would piss her off to know he thought of her that way.

"It can be casual," he said. "The first time anyway."

She pulled back her shoulders, frowned. "You're getting ahead of yourself. This could be a onetime shot, ace."

He nodded, skimming his finger over the bunched-up lines on her forehead. "But if it's not, if it's more than once, then you might have to accept there's more than just lust between us."

"It is just lust," she insisted.

As if to prove it, Hadley took hold of the back of his hair and dragged his mouth down to hers. That sure didn't soften his erection. The kiss was hard and rough, and more than a little desperate. The kiss of two people who were starved for each other.

Leyton felt the starvation. The need. Felt, too, that whatever she had in mind could take care of that need. For now. And for now was what he would settle for.

Don't miss
Wild Nights in Texas *by Delores Fossen,*
available October 2020 wherever
HQN Books and ebooks are sold.

HQNBooks.com

HARLEQUIN
INTRIGUE

SEEK THRILLS. SOLVE CRIMES. JUSTICE SERVED.

Save $1.00

on the purchase of

ANY Harlequin Intrigue book.

Available wherever books are sold, including most bookstores, supermarkets, drugstores and discount stores.

✂ -

Save $1.00

on the purchase of ANY Harlequin Intrigue book.

Coupon valid until December 31, 2020.
Redeemable at participating outlets in the US and Canada only.
Not redeemable at Barnes & Noble stores. Limit one coupon per customer.

52616772

5 65373 00076 2 (8100)0 12462

BACCOUP14687